AN ELEGANT THEORY

NOAH MILLIGAN

central
avenue
publishing

2016

APR - 2017

Published by Central Avenue Publishing, an imprint of Central Avenue Marketing Ltd.
www.centralavenuepublishing.com

Published in Canada
Printed in United States of America

1. FICTION/Literary   2. FICTION/Thrillers - Psychological

Library and Archives Canada Cataloguing in Publication

Milligan, Noah, author
       An elegant theory / Noah Milligan.

Issued in print and electronic formats.
ISBN 978-1-77168-099-8 (paperback).--ISBN 978-1-77168-100-1 (epub).--
ISBN 978-1-77168-101-8 (mobi)

       I. Title.

PS3613.I52E44 2016   813'.6   C2016-902755-4
                                                  C2016-902756-2

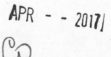

For Esmé

If we take in our hand any volume of divinity or metaphysics, let us ask, does it contain any abstract reasoning concerning quantity or number? No. Does it contain any experimental reasoning concerning matter of fact and existence? No. Commit it then to the flames: For it can contain nothing but sophistry and illusion.

—David Hume

THE ANCIENT GREEKS BELIEVED THAT IN THE beginning there was Chaos. Chaos birthed Earth, Earth produced Sky, and then Sky fathered children upon her. In Norse mythology, a chasm preceded mankind. It was called Ginnungagap, and it was bound by fire and ice. Fire and ice mixed and formed a giant named Ymir and a cow named Audhumbla, and we were then birthed from this cow. In the book of Genesis, there was darkness, and God created the heavens and the Earth in six days. All elegant theories when you think about it—simple, concise, linear. Before our world, disorder preceded creation, then creation begot something better. It's human nature to believe our existence must be an improvement on what came before. We are at the top of the food chain. We are capable of thought and art and language. We must then be the pinnacle of existence. Being a scientist, I have my reservations about this.

The advent of scientific inquiry spawned many more ideas, some of them good, some of them not. The Ptolemaic model bridged the gap between theology and science, confirming that Earth was not alone, though, it placated the church with its geocentric supposition. Copernicus first broached the idea that we weren't the center of the universe—controversial, yes, but elegant nevertheless. Then came Newtonian laws of physics, classical mechanics, Einstein's theory of relativity.

Many people believe they understand relativity, but they don't. Perhaps most misunderstood is time as a dimension. Despite common belief, time is not a constant, ticking away at regular, pre-determined intervals. It depends, among other things, on speed. Picture two parallel mirrors and a light pulse between them, bouncing off one mirror and then the other to mark the passage of time, much like a metronome. Tick tock. Tick tock. Tick tock. If the mirrors are stationary, the light pulse travels up and down ad infinitum. The distance remains constant; therefore, the speed of time is constant. If, however, the mirrors are in motion, the distance changes. It becomes longer. Time passes slower. The faster the mirrors travel, the slower time moves. It's why astronauts who might travel to distant galaxies would age slower than the rest of us.

Perhaps strangest of all is quantum probability theory. Understanding it requires a high degree of technical knowledge, a non-classical probability calculus depending upon a non-classical propositional logic. Most people can grasp the faintest idea of it with a simple experiment, the same experiment I begin each semester with: the double-slit light.

The last semester I taught it, Quantum Physics 1 was overenrolled. Students filled every seat, every stair between rows, even the narrow walkway between the highest row and the exits. Most weren't even enrolled in the class and only showed to get a glimpse of the Nobel Laureate, Dr. Allen Brinkman. Dr. Brinkman was eccentric like many scientists, but he was happier than all the ones I knew. He wore cardigans even in summer and dark-rimmed glasses too large for his face. He smiled incessantly. He carried fingernail clippers with him at all times. He, on numerous occasions, would miss important meetings or lectures, so certain he had more to gain by talking with a stranger at a coffeehouse or in line at the grocery store checkout. And I admired him greatly. As a teenager, I'd followed his career with great verve, much like my peers worshipped the Michael Jordans and Ken Griffeys of the world. I carried around his scholarly articles long before I understood them. He had, at the age of twenty-four, his first year at Cambridge, outlined a cosmological timeline down to hundredths of a second after the Big Bang, mapping billions of years of the universe's existence. In my mind, he came closest to omnipotence.

We both stood at the front of the packed lecture hall, Dr. Brinkman and I, and readied the experiment. It didn't need much: a reflector plate, a barrier with two slits, and a light source.

Light has always posed problems for thinkers, philosophers, and scientists. A vexing phenomenon, the ancient Greeks such as Euclid and Ptolemy thought light to be a ray, somewhat like a laser, that travelled from the eye to the observed object, an apple for instance, or a horse. Not a bad argument, but again, it highlights the human tendency to overestimate our importance in the world. Eight hundred years later the controversy was settled. Abu Ali al-Hasan Ibn al-Haytham argued that if you look at the sun for a long time you will burn your eyes; this is only possible if the light travels from the sun to our eyes, not vice versa. Later, in 1672, another controversy erupted over the nature of light. Newton argued it consisted of particles. Hooke and Huygens argued that it was a wave. Thomas Young proved them all wrong in 1801 with the double-slit light experiment.

I explained this history to my students who stared at me with eyes like oysters. They did not come here to listen to me lecture. They only wished to hear Dr. Brinkman, and this petrified me. Public speaking had always been a weakness of mine. Each time I stood in front of a group, my body proportions felt all wrong, my hands too big, my head too small. My tongue swelled. The inside of my palms crawled. Now, in addition to this, I had become, and was aware I had become, negligible in my audience's eyes. I was merely the opening act to the Nobel Laureate, the band who played before the Rolling Stones while everyone stood in line for the toilet.

To top this all off, I was being judged by Dr. Brinkman. While my graduation hinged on my successful dissertation defense, teaching had always been one of Dr. Brinkman's passions, one of those rare academicians who didn't sacrifice his students for his research. He always said he could judge a professor by the tone of his voice. Mine wavered more with each syllable I uttered, and the audience reflected this. Their faces sagged and their shoulders drooped as if my inane drivelling caused the gravitational force to strengthen, each word uttered pulling them closer to the center of the earth. I imagined their mass coagulating until they formed a singularity, puncturing the space-time continuum and turning all of MIT, all of Cambridge, the entire eastern seaboard even, into a black hole.

"It was a revolutionary experiment. It still is, I mean. It hasn't lost its importance. I think you might be surprised anyway what it shows us about our universe. Well, maybe not surprised actually. Some of you might have already learned this in your high school classes. So this will actually be old hat for you—" I waited for Dr. Brinkman to come to my rescue as he'd been apt to do in previous semesters, but he declined that morning. For nearly half an hour, he'd stood off to the side, a smile on his face, his smallish chin upturned, eyes aglow. I couldn't tell if he enjoyed watching me squirm or was trying to show support with a friendly face. Either way, it didn't help—the students continued to sag with each awkward silence, my "ummms" echoing through the lecture hall like a sports announcer addressing an empty stadium. I had taught many classes before. I did have experience. Yet the first day of class never became easier.

"Perhaps I'll just show you."

I turned on the light source. The barrier's two slits remained closed, so the light did not reach the reflector plate on the other side.

"Since the light is blocked by the barrier and does not travel to the reflector plate," I said, feeling more comfortable as I demonstrated the experiment, as I delved into the science and not the lecturing, "what can we determine about the nature of light?"

No one responded. This was common amongst undergraduates. They were content being a part of the pack, a quark amongst billions of quarks. Over the years, they'd all even started to look alike to me. I wouldn't even learn their names. Apart from there being too many of them to make this possible, I didn't even try. Instead, I distinguished them by some outward physical attribute: the color of hair, type of dress, an unfortunate birthmark. Some professors had three or four Meghans in their class. I would have nine blonds, four big noses, and seven cap-wearers. I knew this to be dehumanizing to my students, and, if not unethical, simply wrong. I did it anyway, though. Not to be condescending, but more as a means of self-preservation. If I pictured them as people rather than individual sponges there only to soak up as much knowledge as they could, the pressure became unbearable—I would've never been able to summon the courage to stand in front of them day in and day out, to maintain the authority and expertise I feared I pretended to have.

I opened one slit.

As expected, a single line of light illuminated the reflector plate. I closed that slit and then opened the other.

"What does this tell us about the nature of light?" Again, no response.

I opened both slits at the same time. The students, for the first time, snapped to attention. It really is a remarkable sight, one that had floored me when I first witnessed it as an undergraduate. Back then I wasn't much different than the students I later taught. I sat in the back of the class. I never spoke out or offered to answer a question. I took notes diligently, yet I never let my classmates know how hard I studied. When my professor had opened both slits, it was nothing like I'd been expecting. Instead of two slits of light appearing on the reflector plate, an interference pattern emerged, resembling a barcode, with intermittent sections of illumination and darkness. It seemed more like magic than a natural phenomenon, an illusion conducted on unsuspecting ignoramuses, so that I sat stunned and speechless like a man who had just witnessed the Statue of Liberty disappear. From that moment on, I no longer tried to blend into my peers, camouflaged as a normal student amongst many. I became obsessed. I wanted to be the best. I wanted, more than anything, to be the first to completely understand the very nature of the universe.

"What does this tell us about the nature of light?" I again asked.

Again, no answer.

"Have you seen anything like this before?"

No answer.

"In the ocean maybe?"

Nothing.

They didn't understand. But I couldn't blame them for this. When I'd first witnessed this phenomenon, I'd been amazed, but I hadn't understood. It took many years for me to grasp the possibilities. What we observe in the double-slit light experiment is called a probability wave. In essence, we're not viewing actual light travelling from the light bulb through the slits to the reflector plate, only the probability that we'll find light there. The brighter the reflection, the more probable we'll find an individual photon. Darker, the less probable.

At first I had accepted this as a plain fact, a probability wave. It made sense. I could do the math associated with it. I could regurgitate it on a test. I could impress my father with it at home. But I always knew I was missing something. And then, at my first year of graduate school, it hit me: the nature of probability in quantum realms does not bend to certainties. There will never be a one hundred percent chance that an event will happen. Nor, for any given location is there a zero percent chance that light can be found there. It may be miniscule, approaching a billionth of one percent, but it will never reach zero. An individual photon must literally travel through every conceivable path from the light source to end up on the reflector plate. It travelled from the rear of the auditorium and back to land on our reflector plate. It zigzagged up Blonde #2's nostrils, out her ear, and then landed on the reflector plate. It zoomed from the light source to Alpha Centauri and landed back here, on Earth, on our reflector plate. In quantum mechanics, we cannot pinpoint exactly where a particular photon will be in one given instance, only the probability of it being in that spot. The strange reality is that all these possibilities *actually* occur.

I oftentimes daydream I can see all these possibilities playing out, the smallest changes causing ripple effects that alter the future, what's called the Butterfly Effect. Yet, they don't feel like daydreams. They feel so real, the scene unfolding before me so vividly, my consciousness so lucid. It's as if I am an astral projection, an invisible voyeur able to witness all of our alternate universes. Sometimes I'm not even there. I'll see my mother after she'd left home and moved to California. I'll see myself as a child with my father and his girlfriend right after Mom left. I'll see myself in the future with my dead wife and son, us middle-aged, he a teenager. It's a strange feeling these sightings. When they happen I lose all sensation of the present, and when I come back to, I have no memory of the lost time.

My students that day in class, however, did not surmise the possibilities of the double-slit light experiment. They'd been impressed, but they didn't understand. None could answer my question about the nature of light, not even scratching the faintest of surfaces by noting light's duality. Before I could point this out to them, though, the class ended, and each of them trampled up one by one to shake Dr. Brinkman's hand and introduce themselves, hoping beyond hope he would remember their names and take them under his wing and forgetting completely my lecture and what I had failed to teach them about the fundamental nature of reality—it is so much stranger than we ever would've thought.

Ж

A storm system rumbled through southwest Oklahoma, the result of a Rocky Mountain cold front colliding with warm Gulf of Mexico trade winds. This mixture had accumulated over the panhandle of Texas, grown in mass, and then spun out of the jet stream with such force that any sane person hid underground, grasping a handheld radio, waiting to hear that all was clear.

Coulter, his father, and his father's intern, Dianne Feinstein, a graduate student at the University of Oklahoma, approached the storm system from the southeast, well out of harm's way. This was the first time Coulter had tagged along storm-chasing with his father. "A birthday present," he'd said. "A chance for you to prove how much you've grown."

To prepare, Coulter had studied all that he could about storms. He read about the water cycle, how heat evaporated water from the ground so that it turned to vapor. The vapor would then rise into the atmosphere, and as it cooled, it would turn back into water. The molecules would collide, causing electrons to charge—the positive would rise to the top of the system, the negative to the bottom. Air ionization would cause a conductor, and the electrical current would flow to the ground, creating lightning.

Despite this understanding, he harbored a very specific fear: that he would be struck by lightning and instantly burst into flames.

His father, however, showed no such fear. In fact, Coulter had never seen him afraid or worried or crying. Not that he was stoic by any means or relentless under pressure; he just had this calmness about him, that if Coulter ever felt afraid, he could look at his father and know that everything would be all right. Because of this, Coulter would get into arguments with his classmates, debating whose father was the bravest and strongest and always right. My dad is a molecular biologist, they would say. Mine is a firefighter. Mine is a lawyer and puts bad guys away. Well, Coulter would say, mine chases tornadoes. Beat that.

His father checked the equipment, adjusted the position and angle of the Doppler satellite. Dianne scanned the GPS for state highways and old dirt roads. There was a mounted anemometer and a sling psychrometer and a handheld HAM radio broadcasting NOAA weather updates. Dianne grabbed an instrument to read atmospheric pressure, and his dad's hand was already outstretched to take it from her, his eyes still locked on the road.

"We're going to have to punch it if we're going to stay out in front of this thing," Dianne said. "There's not too many roads from here to the city that get us very close."

Coulter's father gassed the Bronco, lurching them forward. They barreled over dirt roads, the Bronco bouncing over mounds of clay and gravel. Rocks clamored against the undercarriage. The storm cloud billowed upward toward the stratosphere shaped like an anvil, resembling a volcanic eruption or a bomb explosion, sort of. An atomic bomb would send millions of pounds of sand and dirt into the air, and the heat would pulverize it into trinitite. Everything would constantly be in motion. Smoke would swell and debris would burst into flame and ash would flutter to the ground like snow. This storm, however, looked frozen. With the exception of bulbous bursts of lightning, it appeared to simply hover. In reality, the floating was a mirage. The molecules making up the cloud were lighter than air, and the cloud lay on top of the atmosphere because it had less mass, like oil on water. But the illusion was sublime nevertheless. It made Coulter's heart sticky and pound faster in his chest.

As they got closer, it began to rain. Droplets collected on the windows and streaked sideways from the wind. The sunrays shone at a weird angle. The storm was west of them, and the sun beat down from the east. Being caught in the middle of sunlight and storm added to Coulter's illusion. Everything seemed so surreal: the way his father held the steering wheel loosely as they careened down curvy and potholed roads, how Dianne was able to perform multiple tasks at once, navigating the GPS and refreshing the Doppler radar and contacting NOAA for any updates.

His father pointed out the window. "There," he said, and that was all. It was a funnel cloud, looming low and spinning. The sky burned a mixture of green Coulter had never seen before: algae and seaweed and mint. Dianne snapped pictures on a digital camera, and his father circled toward the southwest of the funnel. Rain fell harder, and the funnel became harder to see. Lightning flashed, the winds howled, and stalks of corn bent near the root like worshippers on their knees.

"You've got to get closer," Dianne said. "It's rain-wrapped."

She called into the station, giving coordinates, speed, and direction. Hail battered the truck. It sounded like gunshots. It scared Coulter. He tried to not let it, but it did. They were getting too close.

"Closer," Dianne said. She leaned forward and placed her palms on the dash. "Get us closer!"

The Bronco veered in the wind. His father turned against it, accelerating, but the strong wind kept pushing them sideways, the wheels grazing the Indian grass on the side of the road. Coulter was afraid they would lose control and careen into the pasture. They'd be injured, and there would be nothing he could do. The tornado would touch down and shift direction and come right for them. He'd be helpless. They all would be.

The funnel snaked its way out of the storm, the cone reaching for the earth, the earth somehow reaching up to the cloud. The dirt and the wind met in the middle, and the base grew in size and in strength.

"It's on the ground," Dianne said into the CB. "Repeat. We got one. F3. Maybe an F2. Heading north-northeast at about thirty-five miles per hour."

"Get the camera!" Coulter's father yelled. "Get it. Get It. GET IT!" Coulter's father grasped Dianne's knee. It was the first time Coulter had ever seen his father touch another woman besides his mother. Well, he'd hugged Grandma before, but that didn't count. This was different. This was something intimate, like a shared, lucid dream.

Coulter had to cover his ears as hail pounded the car, and his father slammed on the brakes. The tornado twisted in front of them, a giant snake spinning up into the sky above. Coulter leaned his head against the window, palms glued to the glass, and tilted his head up to see where tornado and cloud met. It was like peering into the destructive nature of God. It was transcendent. It was the most glorious thing Coulter had ever witnessed.

The tornado loomed not but a hundred yards from them; it then turned and headed north. As it receded, the rains quieted and so did the hail. Dianne opened the door and stepped outside. Before she walked toward the tornado, though, she turned back.

"You coming?" she asked Coulter.

He nodded.

"Here, take this," she said as she handed him her camera. "And take my picture, too, will ya?"

When Coulter snapped it, he'd never felt so close to anyone before.

"HELLO? HEY!" SARA WAVED HER HANDS IN front of my face, snapped her fingers. "Woohoo, Earth to Coulter! Anyone there?" she asked.

"Yes, sorry. What?"

"I've been asking you which brand of diapers we should register for for like five minutes, but you've just been conked out. You feeling all right?"

I felt fine—head clear, vision crisp, body energetic—but I couldn't remember how I'd gotten to the store. We'd talked that morning about registering for the baby shower, and then I had a few hours of free time to grade tests and work at the lab. Afterwards, I went back home to our apartment in the Dot, and then that was it. Leaving home and the bus ride had been a blur. The half-mile walk from the nearest stop to the store had been lost. I couldn't remember entering Babies R Us or standing here in the diaper aisle, holding a scanner in my hand like a checkout clerk. When I tried to find snapshots of these memories, there was nothing, like I'd blacked out. This had been happening more and more lately. My mind would be wandering—I'd be thinking about my research or the coming baby or I'd be planning my afternoon at the lab—and then I'd start daydreaming about winning the Nobel or storm-chasing with my dad. By the time I came to, I'd look up at the clock and notice six hours had passed.

"I don't know," I said. "I think so."

"Good, great, grand! Diapers then. Which ones?" She held out two packages. Both pictured pudgy babies, smiling up at some anonymous figure behind the camera. They both promoted their relative absorbency, the softness of their fabric, the less regularity of diaper rash, claiming that they were "mother approved." They were even priced identically, $24.99 for a package of thirty-five.

"I don't really see the difference in them."

"Don't do that. Don't just say it's my choice. I need you to make *some* decisions. I picked out the nursery color, I picked out the bassinet, I picked out the baby monitor, I picked out—"

"You're right. I know. I'm sorry. I'm just distracted right now, that's all."

"I don't want to hear about your big research paper."

"Dissertation."

"Whatever. It's your professor who is throwing this party, so you need to make some decisions."

"I know."

"Fine. Then do it. Which diapers?"

There were dozens of brands to choose from: Huggies, Luvs, Playskool, Nature Babycare, Pampers, Seventh Generation, and on and on and on. Then these were broken up into types: Overnites and Extra Protection and Free & Clear and Ultra Leakguards. The possible combinations increased exponentially. A statistician wouldn't have been able to make sense of it.

"I really don't have a clue."

She tapped her foot against the linoleum. "We need to do some product testing," she said.

"I'm sorry?"

"Product testing," she said. "You know—see which one works the best."

"How're we going to do that?"

Sara glanced around like she was about to steal something. No employees stood nearby, stocking shelves or assisting other customers. A few other pregnant women and mothers bolted to and fro like electrons in an excited state. They picked up what they needed and moved on. None were stationary like us. I'd expected mothers to seem lethargic and weighed down, but they weren't. They all had the telltale signs of exhaustion—purple and paunchy eyes, frizzy and unkempt hair—yet their legs moved at an incredible rate. Either they had consumed enough caffeine to run on fumes or their bodies were just conditioned to function without energy, like a zombie.

"Keep a lookout," Sara said.

"Huh?"

She motioned for me to do something, flailing her hand so it bounced on her wrist, but I had no idea what she meant. Before I could ask, though, she ripped open a Huggies package and took out a diaper.

"What are you doing?" I asked.

"Product testing. I told you."

From her purse she grabbed a bottle of water and poured it onto the floor.

"Hey! Hey? Are you trying to kill somebody? There are pregnant women everywhere!"

"No shit, Captain Obvious. I'm one of them."

"Then you should know better."

"Just keep a lookout, will you? And quit bitching. You sound like my dad."

She bent down, or tried to. Even though she'd only just reached her third trimester, Sara's downward mobility was impeded. She grunted and inched her way to the floor, knees and hips popping. Once there, she swiped the water puddle with the diaper and studied it.

"Not bad," she said. "Pretty damn absorbent, actually." She held the diaper out toward me. "Want to see?"

She was right; it was absorbent. Impressively so. While I was still a little worried about the repercussions should someone discover us, my interest was piqued—this was something I could relate to, an experiment of sorts.

"Let's try Pampers next," I said. "Might as well get the expensive stuff when other people are paying, right?"

"See!" Sara said. "I knew you would like this if you just gave it a chance."

"Yeah, yeah, yeah," I said, smiling. "Just move out of the way, you're going to hurt yourself."

I bent down and wiped up the rest of the water. Pampers was absorbent, too. If only I had a way to compare the volume of water in each diaper, I could make an informed decision.

"Can I help you?" A middle-aged lady in a blue vest approached us. She had a scar around her jaw like she'd been badly burned, and her name tag said, *Debbie: Assistant Manager / Serious About Service*.

"Yes, thank you," I said. "Do you by chance have some kind of instrument, sort of like a hygrometer say, but for testing diapers instead of the air?"

"Excuse me?"

"I'm trying to determine the difference in absorbency between Pampers and Huggies. An hygrometer tests humidity."

"Uh-huh," she said as she eyed me.

"It doesn't have to be so much like a hygrometer, actually. Even a scale and a measuring cup would work. Do you have something like that handy?"

Sara burst out laughing, hunched over, arms wrapped around her belly.

"You're going to have to pay for those. You know that, right?" Debbie said.

"Yes. Of course. Yes," I said even though the thought hadn't occurred to me.

"You could've killed somebody. Somebody could've slipped and gone straight into labor. What would you have done then?" She paused for us to answer, but neither Sara nor I offered one. Sara stopped laughing, straightened up like a child being scolded by a teacher. Debbie grabbed a radio from her apron and pressed the button. "We need a cleanup in aisle seven. Repeat—we need a cleanup in aisle seven." Her voice echoed over the intercom system, mangled by static. It reminded me of storm-chasing with my father as a child, the news reports coming in over his handheld. When done, she returned her radio to her apron and then pointed at us. "You two, come with me."

Debbie herded us like cattle and veered us toward the cash wrap, the tattered diaper bag in hand. Sara and I walked down the aisle, the object of sideways glances and sneers. *Who were these people? Who would do such a thing?* I ignored them, but Sara, of course, wouldn't stand for such public humiliation. "Run!" she yelled, and she took off, laughing again as she hobbled past Debbie the Assistant Manager. Not knowing what else to do, I followed her out of the store, past confused mothers, shielding their children from the lunatics brushing past them. I half-expected someone to tackle us, a young store clerk maybe, eager to impress his boss, or at least an announcement over the intercom about suspected shoplifters, the command to call the police, but no one tried to stop us—two packages of diapers must not have been worth the chase—and we continued to sprint away until we had made our escape down the street and around the corner and could no longer see the megastore.

"You okay?" I asked.

Sara was hunched over, grasping her belly, and sucked in deep breaths through pursed lips. Instead of answering, she held up a finger. "Yes," she finally said. "Just got these sharp pains in my sides."

I went to her and placed my outstretched hands close to her hips, spotting her. "Do you need to go to the doctor?"

"No, no," she said. "I'm just out of shape."

"This isn't the time to be a hero, Sara."

"I'm not being a hero. I'm just out of breath. That's all."

"Are you sure?"

"Yes, Coulter. Jesus."

"I just want to make sure."

I looked back at the store, but no one appeared to have followed us. Sirens didn't blare in the distance, the Doppler effect causing them to get louder. We were safe, it seemed. "I still have the scanner," I said as I held it up. My hands shook from sprinting; I was the one out of shape. "Do you think they'll put out a warrant for our arrest?"

"Oh God, who cares? That was great!" Sara stood, coughed, and then wiped the back of her mouth with her sleeve. "I needed that," she said. "Really bad."

"Maybe I should take it back," I said. "If we apologize and just pay for the diapers—"

"Don't be stupid." She wrapped her arm around mine and pulled me toward to the bus stop.

"But we registered with them. They have our names. They have our address. They got my work number even."

"They're not going to do anything. It's like a fifty-dollar machine and a few packs of diapers. Not enough to send out the SWAT team."

"It's not worth the risk, Sara." I counted on my fingers and said, "If I get arrested, I won't be able to pass a background check. No school will hire me. I won't be able to get a job. We'll be destitute. We'll be living in the same crappy apartment, and our kid's going to starve."

"Stop," she said as she grabbed my face and pulled me toward her. "Everything's going to be fine."

"What we did was illegal."

She kissed me, wrapped her arms around my neck, and said, "Listen to me. There's nothing to worry about. You're not going to get arrested, and we're not going to be destitute. One of these days, life is going to be easy. No more buses and small apartments in crappy neighborhoods and long nights at the lab. We'll be happy."

She kissed me again and rubbed my earlobe between her fingers, calming me. Before we'd married, Sara had never been this affectionate, always keeping her distance while out on dates, twisting her hand away from mine whenever I tried to grasp it. I always thought her lack of intimacy was the result of us not having that much in common— she loved do-it-yourself home-repair shows and reading book blurbs and trivia quiz bowls and N'Sync, and I'd ramble on incessantly about banal scientific matters and her eyes would glaze over and she'd twirl her straw in her Dr. Pepper. It wasn't until she got pregnant that she began to touch me in public, kiss me when others could see us, call me pet names like sweetie or honey or biscuit. She never explained the change. I liked to think it was because she could finally allow herself to be vulnerable around me, but I secretly feared it was because she finally accepted that ours was an attraction that grew out of proximity, both of us left with few options and a common dread of being alone.

"We'll have a big house and five kids and a tree fort out back," I said.

"That's right," she said. "You'll have summers off, and I'll be a day trader and go to ballet recitals and run for city council."

"I'll win the Nobel and retire, and we'll buy some land back in Oklahoma."

"Everything's going to be perfect," she said. "Trust me."

"Yes," I said, unconvinced. "Perfect."

❊

For as long as I can remember, I've found the notion of fate unpalatable, never understanding those who accept calamities because "things happen for a reason" or that they're all "part of God's plan," but I suppose the belief offers a level of comfort. It allows people to shirk responsibility for their actions, to find solace in their faith that a benevolent benefactor looks out for their best interests. It's like never growing out of childhood, always under the watchful eye of your mother.

Instead, I've always looked to science for answers. Fate does not exist in physics or biology or chemistry. Evolution is the result of billions of years of chance, coincidence, and sheer trial and error. Mistakes lead to extinction, success to progeny. Chemical reactions create heat and cold and water and the conditions amicable to the birth of life. The laws of physics govern the motion of the physical bodies throughout the universe, predictive in nature, sure, but not deterministic. There is cause and effect, but science does not presume motive or premeditation. I find comfort in that. It's how I make sense out of an otherwise senseless world.

Take Heisenberg's Uncertainty Principle, for instance, which solves the problem of particle-wave duality, the problem I'd introduced during the double-slit light experiment. Simply put, certain quantities in nature, such as position, energy, and time are, on the subatomic level, unknown except by probabilities. If we know where particle A is at, we have no idea where it's going. If we have an idea of how fast it's moving, we have no idea where it is. A strange conundrum that seemed to plague more than the subatomic—I often can't understand where I'm at in life, or if I do, where I'm going, or why.

But there is some evidence to the contrary. One interpretation bends toward a version of fatalism. When we observe a single constituent, the probability wave collapses, and the particle only inhabits a singular location in space and time. It's as if our very observation affects the properties of these quantum elements, leaving them in their most probable location, where we happen to be looking. Since everything in the universe, including us, consists of these quantum elements, logic follows that we inhabit the most probable location. Everything that has led us there, every decision we have made, the electrical neurons and synapses that fired that brought us to work or school or prison is merely the most probable path that could've been taken. It's an interpretation I've long rejected, but I can't help but acknowledge its intrinsic logic. When I first stood before my dissertation committee, I couldn't help but wonder if all the choices I'd made leading up to standing there, in front of the very people who would decide my academic fate, and theirs as well, if all these choices, the fields we had decided to pursue, the institutions at which we studied, the spouses we'd married, the name of our first born, even the innocuous acts like brushing before flossing or vice versa, added up to the successful defense of my dissertation. It was enough to make me nauseated, standing there, trying not to puke.

Composing my committee was Dr. Brinkman, of course, acting as chair, accompanied by Dr. Cardoza and Dr. Barbarick. Cardoza was a distrusting type, infamous amongst academic circles as an anal-retentive peer reviewer, holding up years of research for weeks or months as she nitpicked her way through colleagues' findings before they could be published. I'd selected her to keep me honest in my research, knowing fully well I wouldn't be able to make unsubstantiated assumptions during my modeling. Barbarick, on the other hand, was a young professor, tenure track without the tenure, and fresh out of his fellowship at Stanford. His research focused on quantum electrodynamics, a field closely interrelated with my own, and his insights could, I hoped anyway, provide a breakthrough if I happened to get stuck.

We met in the auditorium in which I taught, the place eerily empty compared to class time. The lights were dimmed so that I could make my presentation on the projector screen. The three committee members sat in the front row. I couldn't see their faces, only the glow of their penlights.

I began my first slide. It pictured a Calabi-Yau manifold.

I explained to them that it's a theoretical shape studied in algebraic geometry, theoretical physics, and lately superstring theory. It's always been proposed that the universe is constructed from subatomic particles. It appears to be the most logical solution. In a vacuum, matter will compress into a sphere through the force of gravity. Think of planets and stars and such. But anomalies exist. Take, for instance, Newton's famous inverse square law. It postulates that as we get closer to a miniscule particle, gravity will reach infinity, an impossibility.

Slide Two:

String Theory solves this problem. Because the string is a finite looped space, the anomalies are solved. Gravity no longer approaches infinity because it's dictated by the length of the string. It's remarkable, really. Simple in its design, it posits that rather than particles, the smallest constituents of the universe are in fact tiny, vibrating strings. Picture a rubber band, plucked so that it oscillates like a violin string. It's the energy exerted through the oscillation that determines its nature. Light has its own frequency. Electrons. Bosons. So on and so forth. This idea has solved what had puzzled scientists for years—it predicted with great accuracy both the motion of the very tiny and the very large.

More problems arose, of course.

The most problematic of which is that string theory is not compatible with a four-dimensional universe. Divergences beyond Newton's law emerged, and the only way to eliminate them appeared to be a universe with eleven dimensions. This at first appeared to kill the theory. It's common knowledge that the universe consists of only four dimensions, three spatial and one time. All observations known to mankind have seemed to support this doctrine. But the math kept bending to this multidimensional hypothesis, that the universe consists of invisible dimensions, ten spatial and one temporal.

Slide Three:

The theory of relativity once revolutionized how we thought of the universe by introducing the curvature of space-time. Instead of space and time being two distinct characteristics of the universe, they are intertwined irrevocably into a singular fabric. One cannot exist without the other. Think of space-time as a sheet pulled taut, and the sun as a ball placed in the center of the sheet. The ball will warp the fabric, creating a dimple around it, and a marble, representing Earth, if set in motion will not travel in a straight line but instead follow the curvature caused by the sun's mass.

The theory of relativity solved the problem of gravity and motion for the very large, an ingenious breakthrough, yet still lacking—the equations for the very large did not translate to the very small. There appeared to be two distinct laws of the universe, which couldn't be. There should be one law that governs the laws of motion for every physical body, regardless of size. String theory solves this problem. The universe is warped and curled into miniscule Calabi-Yau manifolds, each the same primary shape and size, and they act like a flute, shaping how air flows through its chamber in order to execute a singular note.

My audience scribbled away in the darkness, their lights illuminating dim halos around their faces. Their hurried scratching echoed through the oversized auditorium.

"What I propose to prove, then, is the actual shape of the universe. The curls and warps that form the notes that constitute our universe."

I ended my slideshow and clicked on the overhead lights. I had to squint to adjust to the light. My committee members each did the same; their heads tilted downward, at once trying to keep my gaze and averting it, like they were torn between two equally desirable propositions.

"It appears you have chosen a very ambitious topic," Dr. Brinkman began. "How do you propose you'll accomplish this? Nobody's even come close to solving this problem. What will be different for you?"

I had anticipated this question. In fact, I had counted on it.

"Their approach has been flawed," I said. "They calculated the innumerable possibilities that could arise. The trillions upon trillions of possible Calabi-Yau shapes. I'll instead reverse engineer the universe."

"Reverse engineer the *universe?*" asked Dr. Cardoza.

"Yes," I stood stationary, regarding my hands. "The strength of gravity and the weak force and the speed of light and everything else. The reason why they have the properties they have are because they have no other choice; the strings that constitute everything in the universe must vibrate in certain frequencies because our universe has a particular shape. I simply need to calculate the shape that provides these frequencies."

"You're joking, right?" Cardoza asked. She had taken off her glasses and curled the earpiece around her finger. They must've been titanium frames—when she released, they sprung back into a straight line.

"No," I replied.

"That is the dumbest thing I've ever heard," she said.

"I don't know," Dr. Barbarick chimed in. "It might be worthwhile to take a look. How far have you gotten?"

That was the problem. Calabi-Yau manifolds were complexly shaped: minute, curved, warped, angled, almost to an infinite degree. The amount of calculations needed to provide all of the universe's defining characteristics would test even the most advanced supercomputers.

"I've built a model," I said. "It produces random Calabi-Yau manifolds and then runs matrices through it, testing Boh's radius, the strength of gravity, et cetera."

"So you are relying upon luck to prove your hypothesis?" Dr. Cardoza asked.

"I can refine the model. Each incorrect answer eliminates possibilities."

"You will die before you eliminate enough. Your children will die. Your grandchildren. At this rate of discovery, the sun will have exploded." Dr. Cardoza snapped her notebook closed. "This has been a complete waste of time."

"You haven't any work to show us today, have you?" Dr. Brinkman asked.

"No, sir."

"That," he said as he and the others stood, "is a problem." He excused Dr. Cardoza and Dr. Barbarick, mentioning that we'd convene again sometime next month. "May I have a word, Coulter?"

"Of course, sir."

Dr. Brinkman approached and clasped his hand on my shoulder. He smelled of chalk dust and sunflower seeds, the latter a habit he couldn't kick. He kept a package on him at all times, spitting the empty shells into a Styrofoam cup. If you caught him smiling, you oftentimes could see dark remnants of his snack stuck between his teeth.

"Have you any other ideas for your dissertation?" he asked.

"I'd like to reserve time at the lab. If I could utilize the department's mainframe, I think I could—"

"What I'm saying is that we're not expecting you to win the Nobel, Coulter. There's plenty of time for you to dream big. But later. Now is the time to just get your degree."

"I'm sorry, sir?"

"Maybe you should consider focusing on a hypothesis that is more testable. Like the double-slit light experiment. You seem to be fond of that. What new insights can you provide on the behavior of light?"

"But, sir—"

He cut me a glare above the rim of his glasses. It was the look a father would give a misbehaving child, one who swore he hadn't broken the lamp despite it being shattered at his feet.

"It will be difficult for you to be awarded your PhD with an incomplete dissertation," he said. "Impossible, in fact."

In the world of theoretical physics, warnings do not come theatrically. Faculty and researchers do not shout over one another or upend PCs, tossing them about in a panicked frenzy. It is a quiet life, usually, subdued and laced with insinuations and metaphors. Rivals do not sabotage experiments, but rather publish articles listing "questionable experimental designs" and "indeterminate findings." The impact is more crushing. It eats at you psychologically. You begin to doubt yourself. You begin to think that you're not worthy. Not of the degree or the goals you aspire to. You feel betrayed and lied to. You feel like a fraud. And it only becomes worse because you keep trying—you've invested too much of your life to stop now.

"I understand, sir."

Dr. Brinkman pulled a bag of sunflower seeds from his pocket, palmed a handful, and chucked them into his mouth. "I hope you do," he said. "I really do."

※

The Stockholm City Hall was covered in purple and gold, banners hanging from the balcony and stage, flowers lining the aisles. Men donned black tuxedos and tightly wound bowties. The smell of several perfumes clashed with one another, ginger and jasmine and sugar. Elaborate crystal chandeliers lit the auditorium in a hushed glow, and diamond necklaces and gold watches glittered like a refraction experiment. It was almost too much to take in, like a fireworks display gone horribly wrong, each rocket ignited and lighting up the sky all at once.

Never one for public speaking, Coulter dreaded having to give his address. Hundreds attended, all expecting greatness. He was, after all, a Nobel Laureate. What he would say would be part of the public record for eternity. It would be published and reprinted and distributed across the globe. Critics and colleagues would read it, analyze every word, turn his musings on their head, denounce him or ridicule him or revere him. And now, moments before he was to begin his acceptance speech, he couldn't help but think that he should've gone to urinate before the ceremony had begun.

Sweden's King Carl XVI Gustaf waited for him up on stage, prize in hand. He was much taller and statelier than Coulter, who worried he would look like a dwarf next to the royal. It was an irrational fear. He knew it. He told himself it was irrational. Yet he couldn't but help remember Dr. Brinkman's advice after his post-doctoral fellowship at Harvard had ended, "Better looking people are sixty percent more likely to be hired than unattractive people. *Sixty percent.* It's been proven." Other stats occurred to him—In ninety-five percent of presidential elections, the taller candidate has won; eighty percent of memorable communication is perceived through how the material is presented, not what is said; an uneducated person is three times more likely to be convicted of homicide than an educated one—all these stats rushed through his head and made him feel so miniscule he feared he had shrunk to an atomic level and that the attendees would not be able to see him.

For the fifteenth time, he popped his knuckles, applied Chapstick, repeated silently his address, thanking Dr. Brinkman and MIT and Harvard and his wife and son and all those who had helped him and his research throughout the years. Gustaf approached the lectern to introduce Coulter, paused, and smiled to the audience. He appeared so comfortable up there. At home, radiant, as though he couldn't quite be himself unless being adored by his loving people. Coulter envied this to the point he had thoughts of hurting the King. He had to stop himself from grabbing him, placing his thumb on the soft spot of the neck, just below the Adam's apple, and pressing down until he could feel the insides go pop. He tried to brush these violent thoughts aside, but they were ever-present, like the way a wound will make your whole body itch just before it gets infected.

"Tonight," the King began, "we honor not so much a man but the remarkable achievements of mankind. Isaac Newton once said, 'If I have seen further, it is by standing on the shoulders of giants.' This is true of

Dr. Zahn, who we honor tonight, but it is also true of all of us, in all fields. Whether it is in literature, in medicine, or in physics, to further mankind's achievements, we must first understand what has come before us in order to advance the canon. While we only honor a single recipient, we hope by honoring him that we honor the incremental steps along the way that led to such an extraordinary discovery, the multi-verse.

"According to his research, an infinite number of alternate realities exist, and one out there is much like the one we are experiencing at this very moment. Although in that one, perhaps he is the King, and I am the newly-crowned Laureate."

The King winked, and the audience laughed. At this point Coulter couldn't sit still, the urge to pee making him fidget in his seat.

"Our recipient for the Nobel Prize in Physics is Dr. Coulter Zahn, renowned string-theorist, for his work on the disappearance of gravity in areas of space-time smaller than the Planck Length. Like Einstein's theory of relativity, it has vastly changed our understanding of the universe. We now know, although much differently than the generations before us had imagined, that we are not alone. This is frightening in some ways, lessening what we believed to be our prominence and our importance in what we call the universe. But it is also comforting. There is another self out there, somewhere, who represents the noblest of us, even when we, in this universe, can't see it.

"Without further ado, Dr. Coulter Zahn."

The King smiled and gestured toward Coulter to take the stage. He stood and buttoned his jacket and breathed. He tried not to think about it, this pressure building in his bladder. Instead, he thought back to his days when he'd taken biology. How much can the human bladder hold? Fourteen ounces? Could it burst? Would it cause an infection? Would his kidneys be damaged? Could he die from it?

He approached the stage. It felt good to start moving; the rhythmic cycle of his legs alleviated the urge a bit. Not much, but enough for him to make it up the few steps to the stage. The King greeted him, hand outstretched, and Coulter hoped, he hoped beyond hope, that the King wouldn't squeeze his hand too hard and make him stay in that position for too long—it would just be too much to bear. The King's hand was large and overpowering, a contractor's hand, a man's hand, yet he did not exert the force it was capable of. His handshake was gentle and subdued. Coulter was grateful for the gentle King. The King gestured toward the galley, and both he and Coulter posed for pictures. "Congratulations," the King said. "I have no earthly idea what you have proven, but I'm sure it's great." He winked and pointed toward the lectern. So many gestures, Coulter thought, just movements of his hand, like he could rule his country without uttering a word, only motioning for what he desired, and watching on pleasantly as his wish was obeyed.

Coulter stood at the lectern and reached for his notes in his breast pocket. He pulled them out and unfolded the pages and flattened them out on the lectern, but when he went to speak, he found he couldn't. It wasn't that his mouth wouldn't move or that it was just dry or that he needed to unclog pockets of phlegm from his throat—he literally could not speak. Every time he opened his mouth, his brain misfired, the electrical impulses needed to control his vocal folds unable to travel from his cerebral cortex to the nerve endings necessary to talk, the communication lines somehow severed.

Just speak, he pleaded with himself. Speak! Say something, you idiot!

Unsure what to do, Coulter looked up from the lectern and faced the audience. They all glared back up at him, their eyes expectant and glowing. To stall time, he reapplied Chapstick, flipped through the pages of his address, but soon the attendees began to get impatient. They whispered amongst themselves and fidgeted in their seats, the hinges of the chairs squeaking underneath their weight. They were turning on him— he could tell by their animated hand gestures—like their king, they motioned up toward him accusingly, like he was making a fool of them on purpose. How dare he? they thought. How dare he come to our country and fool us like this. Some jumped to their feet, and they were shouting something to their compatriots, but their words were jumbled, their demands incoherent, and others rose to their feet—they were going to rush the stage! But before they could, Coulter felt the wiring in his brain reconnect, that familiar buzz in his throat indicating that he was ready, he could speak, so he opened his mouth to do just that, to calm the crowd, the angry mob about to storm the stage, but before a sound could escape, he felt a warm sensation trickle down the inside of his thighs.

WHILE I WAS TYPICALLY THE WORRIER, THE one who was paranoid, the one who panicked, Sara, on the other hand, had always been calm, no matter if we were simply sitting at home, me studying, she watching reality TV, or if we were in an emergency, a car accident say, or caught in a tornado during a spring thunderstorm. As if by instinct, she would know exactly what to do. Get out of the car, she would say. Find a ditch. Stick your head down and your ass in the air—it's the safest place to be struck by lightning. When it came to our unborn son, however, she expected our roles to reverse.

"What if they find something wrong?" she would ask. "What would we do? I don't even know if I can take care of a *healthy* baby for Christ's sake."

"Nothing will be wrong. Trust me."

"He could be autistic or have Down syndrome or born with one eye or with two heads."

"The odds of anything like that happening are remote. Damn near impossible."

"I thought you said nothing is impossible. That double-slit light thingy you told me about, remember?"

"I'm just saying—"

"It could be a millionth of one percent you said, but nothing is impossible."

"You're missing the point, Sara. Just because it's possible doesn't mean it's going to happen."

"Okay fine," she'd say. "Then stop telling me shit like that. You're freaking me out."

Despite my best efforts, I knew my reassurances sounded hollow and suspect. Inside, I too felt my chest cavity swelling under the pressure, fearing I would, at best, be an inadequate father and, at worst, an absentee parent like my mother had been. Doctor visits amplified this fear, a grim reminder that the inevitable was imminent, endless poopy diapers and sleepless nights and the constant need for attention, that little child forever reaching, clawing, grabbing at you, and this trip was no different. Despite our cramped quarters—I touched shoulders with a lady who smelled of ginger and who smacked her gum—we each endeavored to maintain our personal space. We avoided eye contact. We perused gossip and pregnancy magazines that had been released years ago. We cleaned our fingernails with a ballpoint pen. I had taken a sociology course as an undergrad. In it we were taught that humans were social creatures, longing for interaction and community. I didn't find it to be a very scientific field of study. This belief, for instance, seemed to stem from our *wish* to be social, or perhaps our tendency to believe that everyone likes us. Upon objective observation anyone could see that this was false—we endeavored to isolate ourselves any chance we could, lest someone realize just how petrified we actually were.

"Am I as big as her?" Sara asked as another patient entered the waiting area. She waddled as she approached the receptionist desk, her face strained in obvious discomfort.

"No," I said. "Not even close."

"You sure?" she asked, glancing down at herself, then back up to the new arrival.

"Positive. You really haven't gained that much weight. You probably could gain a little more, actually."

"I just don't feel sexy," she said. "I mean, I know I'm pregnant. But my stretch marks—they look like Freddy Kreuger gutted me with those knife fingers. They'll never go away, you know."

"You've been rubbing that cocoa butter on it, right? You've been stretching and eating healthy and hydrating. They should be fine."

"You never have understood a woman's body. You think foreplay is like microwaving a bag of popcorn—you press one button, then wait four minutes before it's your turn."

"I think you might be overreacting."

"I think you might just be an asshole." She pulled out a tissue, blew her nose, then returned it to her purse. "Sorry," she said. "You know I don't mean it, right? It's just these fucking hormones."

I didn't answer. Sara didn't want an answer, only an audience.

"Oh God, I'm going to look like my mother," she said, coiling her hands around her face. "Are you still going to want to have sex with me after this?"

Sara was a beautiful girl—red hair the color of autumnal leaves and a complexion like powdered milk. When I touched her skin, it turned pink, like she was a fragile bird, yet her personality gave her an intimidating presence. I found this contrast startling and irresistible. Pregnant, she still seemed beautiful to me. Although I didn't see the radiance others claimed—she appeared tired, her eyes yellowed as if she suffered from a vitamin D deficiency—this didn't make her unsexy to me. Instead, it made her seem noble and courageous in a way, sacrificing herself for us, our family. Oddly, this sense of martyrdom turned me on, making me want to make love to her anywhere, anytime, in this very waiting room actually.

"Can we talk about this later?" I said instead.

"I'm just saying I'm fat, that's all. Jesus."

The nurse called Sara's name and led us to an examination room. Examination rooms always irked me. On the counter stood macabre replications of the skeletal and digestive systems. Soap and hand sanitizer were abundant, near the door, hanging above the sink, near the biohazard waste bin, as if advertising the place was a repository of disease. The paper adorning the examination table proved that they did not want you, the sick and infectious, to make contact with any of their belongings. I felt like something to be studied and poked and prodded and measured, and when I left, I always suffered an unshakeable feeling of shame.

This one, however, was more comforting than most, with pictures of babies smiling back at us, happy families cuddled up in crocheted blankets and animal hats. All of them had cute little dimples and shiny gums, caught in the act of cooing or yawning, reaching out their tiny fingers toward the camera. Though most would fawn over such pictures, exclaiming how adorable they were, to me they seemed more like propaganda—they were hiding all the rest that came with parenthood: the worry, the crying, the frustration, that agonizing tug that everything might not be okay.

The nurse led Sara to the scale to measure her height, her weight, and then her belly. After scribbling the results down on her clipboard, the nurse strapped on a sphygmomanometer to measure Sara's blood pressure and pumped the little bulb, her face scrunched into a pucker as she did so. I tried to discern information as she read the measuring unit, but she didn't divulge any, remaining stone-faced like a poker player. She wrote down the results on her chart, grabbed a thermometer, and stuck it in Sara's ear. It beeped; she again wrote down the results and said, "The doctor will be with you shortly."

After she left, Sara said, "A friendly one, isn't she?"

"She's probably had a long day."

"Hasn't everyone?"

"Well, yes. Sure. I'm just saying you shouldn't be so hard on her."

"Oh, so I'm the bad guy?"

"That's not what I'm saying." I kissed the top of her head. "She might not always be like this."

Sara sighed. "Yeah, yeah, yeah. I need to be more understanding. Empathetic. Whatever." She picked at her sweatpants, pulling off little balls of lint. All of our clothes were covered in them, remnants left behind by the communal dryers in our apartment building. "I just think I should get a pass sometimes, since I have a bowling ball growing inside of me and all."

I walked over to the baby pictures to take a closer look. Some of them were adorable—there was no denying that—but some were pretty ugly. Their heads seemed misshapen, squished together, insulated with excess fat. Ears seemed perched too high atop their heads or an eye looked to be lazy. I wondered if it would be different if they were my children. Would I be blind to their idiosyncrasies and their unattractive qualities? Would I ignore them? Would I delude myself that my child is absolutely perfect?

I had no idea.

"Do you want to take pictures like this?" I asked, pointing at the wall.

"Yeah," Sara said. "Why not?"

"I don't know. It just seems a bit pompous, don't you think? Hey, look at me. Look at my kid. Look how awesome we are."

"It's not like that at all. There's nothing wrong with being proud of your family."

"It just seems like we're showing off. I mean—having a baby is a pretty common thing."

"You're missing the point."

"Maybe we could just send them to family. Not people we hardly know."

"I'm hungry," Sara said. "Would you want to go to Steak N Shake after this?"

Dr. Remington knocked and entered. A kind lady, she appeared overworked and weary. Purple bags held up her eyes like dams. "How're things?" she asked. Her complexion had yellowed to the color of an infected sore. Her hair had thinned and grayed, probably the product of too much stress. All in all, she looked sickly, not a good sign for a doctor. "Good, I hope?"

"About as well as they could be," Sara said. "We haven't lost our minds yet."

Dr. Remington forced a chuckle and snapped on some latex gloves. They were covered in a white, chalky powder, which left remnants behind on whatever she touched. She smiled reassuringly, prepared her stethoscope, and listened to Sara's heartbeat. "I'm worried about your blood pressure," she said. "It's awfully high."

"Considering the circumstances," Sara said.

"No excuse," Dr. Remington said. "Stress is bad for the baby. Have you noticed irregular urinations?"

"Irregular?"

"Darker. Discolored."

"Not that I'm aware of. I don't normally study the toilet after I go, though."

"Any pain?"

"While peeing?"

"While urinating, yes."

"No."

The doctor grabbed an otoscope and examined Sara's ears. Sara rubbed her hands together like she suffered from terrible arthritis.

"Pain in your kidneys?" Dr. Remington asked.

"I didn't even know I could feel my kidneys."

"This isn't a joke, Sara."

"I'm not joking. I've never noticed my kidneys before."

"Lower back pain then."

"I'm pregnant. What do you think?"

"Have you had a hard time keeping down food or loss of appetite?"

"Option one yes. Option two absolutely not. I'd eat the ass end out of a rhino if I could get my hands on one."

"I get the feeling you aren't taking this seriously."

"Just tell us what is wrong!" I yelled.

Both the doctor and Sara blinked at me as if they needed to get a better view. I couldn't help it, though. This line of questioning felt like an interrogation, like we were guilty of something.

"Nothing is wrong," Dr. Remington said. "Your baby is perfectly healthy. If Sara's high blood pressure continues, though, she could simply suffer damage to her kidneys and the baby could be born prematurely."

"Simply?"

"It's just a possibility."

Sara placed her hand atop mine and patted to reassure me. "That's it?"

"Well," Dr. Remington said. "There's a remote possibility that you could develop preeclampsia."

"And what does that mean?" I asked.

"It could lead to seizures. Stillbirth. The mother's death."

"The mother's *death*?" Sara asked.

"Your death." The doctor readied the ultrasound machine and then plopped neon blue gel onto Sara's plump stomach. "But like I said, it's a very remote possibility. Odds are you're going to be fine. Just fine."

A picture appeared on the monitor. It was one of those three-dimensional images where Sara and I could make out the baby's features. This was the first time we'd seen our baby in such high definition. I could make out the little nose and ears and fingers and its clamped eyes.

"You still want the sex to be a surprise?" Dr. Remington asked.

Neither Sara nor I answered. We both stared at our child as if in disbelief. This tiny little thing would forever be in our care. There was no escaping that fact. It would come. It was inevitable. The sun will rise tomorrow, I will be hungry, taxes will be due, rent has to be paid, I will grow old, I will fall ill, I will die, and it will be born, and I couldn't help but think this is wrong, so wrong, all of it, her and me and the baby, every last bit of it.

∦

Coulter always thought a psychiatrist's office would be much larger. He'd pictured chaise lounges and plush leather and burnished gold buttons embedded into chair backs, countless volumes of psychiatry journals, textbooks, and degrees adorning the walls so as to impress him. They wouldn't. He'd attended those same universities, had earned the same degrees, the same accolades and awards and accomplishments, even had been the star pupil in the MIT physics department, thank you very much.

To his surprise, though, the office was quaint. There were pictures of the doctor's family, three children, two boys and one girl, all redheaded and freckled. Plain cotton curtains let in the morning sun. Everything was in its place. A briefcase fit into a slot between the desk and a bookshelf. A filing cabinet hid in the corner, a potted plant resting atop it like an aged cat. Coulter sat in one wing-backed chair, Dr. Hamlin in the other, an old, worn rug between them. Not an antique Persian but rather something you would find on sale at Wal-Mart, tucked away in the bargain bin.

"Why do you think your son acts in this way?" Dr. Hamlin asked.

He did look genuinely concerned; Coulter had to give him that. He was an academic type, studious and sincere. He wore a leather-elbowed coat and thick glasses. He smelled of soil and sandalwood and rubbed his facial hair with a thoughtful air. He used words like "id" and "ego" and "transference." He made allusions to Homer and Freud and Nietzsche and only drank diet Pepsi. He made sucking sounds when he was in deep thought, and he squinted his right eye before speaking. Perhaps Coulter could trust this one. He'd known and dealt with his type before.

"Who knows?" Coulter sighed. "I'd never—nor Sara for that matter—neither one of us has ever done anything like this. And it's like he can't help himself. We've spoken to him extensively, of course, counseled him—I mean, we are his parents for Christ's sake—but he just won't listen."

"There's been a lot of study out there, unconfirmed I admit, but there are indications that arson could be a fascination instinctive in nature, a genetic predisposition, passed down from when we evolved from Cro Magnon. *A priori* and such."

Dr. Hamlin had the smallest hands Coulter had ever seen. They unnerved him, like he may be dealing with a child masquerading as an adult.

"Then why aren't his mother and I like this?"

He shrugged. "Perhaps it skips generations."

"Or his grandparents, or my grandparents?"

"Perhaps it lays dormant for several generations."

"That's your professional opinion, then? Neanderthals made my son like this?"

"Cro Magnon, not Neanderthal. All I'm saying is that this is not your fault."

"Then whose is it?"

"Why does it have to be anyone's fault?"

"I'm a physicist, Doctor. I deal with cause and effect."

"Then you should know that some things aren't that black and white."

Every single psychiatrist (six already) had been quick to assert that Isaac's problem was not Coulter's fault. Nor Sara's. Not even Isaac's for that matter. This pissed Coulter off (*whose damn fault was it, then?*), and, up until this point, was a good indicator that Coulter would find another psychiatrist online tomorrow, or by a recommendation from a colleague, or hell, he might as well give up and try an alternative route, religion, or acupuncture, hypnosis even, anything to keep Isaac from burning down another house or business. Anything to keep him from going to jail.

Thank God he was only fourteen, not old enough to be tried as an adult.

At first Isaac's problem had arisen from a natural, and healthy, Coulter thought, fascination. Isaac would light matches, watching the flames until they burned down to his fingertips. He would conduct controlled burns in the backyard, raking the fall leaves into a large pile and setting them on fire. He would fill balloons with hydrogen gas and then burst it with the stroke of a lighter, the balloon erupting into a ball of flame. Even his bedroom reeked of sulfur; one time the stench had been so bad that one of Coulter's elderly colleagues was afraid that he was suffering a stroke. His behavior alarmed Sara, but Coulter thought that he was just being a dutiful, curious, and an inquisitive child. He'd daydreamed of Isaac having a career in science like himself, experimenting in combustion engines, producing the next rocket that would open up exploration to Mars and beyond. He'd even gone so far as to start a matchbook collection and bought Isaac toy rockets so they could fire them off in their backyard together, Isaac smiling as he lit the fuse and raced back to stand next to his father, the man's arm wrapped around the boy's slim shoulders.

But then two weeks ago, Coulter, Sara, and Isaac had gone to their favorite restaurant, an Irish gastropub with authentic corned beef and cabbage and fiddlers. Coulter had been on his fourth or fifth Guinness, and had, for the third or fourth time, made his way back to the restroom and was relieving himself when he'd heard someone strike a cigarette lighter in the stall next to him. He'd totally forgotten that Isaac had left the booth a few minutes before him, had been so engrossed in the music and food and drink that he hadn't remembered that his son had gone to the restroom, that his son had a fascination with fire, and all Coulter could think about was that a stranger was about to enjoy a surreptitious smoke, and he contemplated asking him if he might have a puff or two. He'd quit years before, but those several pints had reawakened that familiar, and welcome, tugging on his lung tissue. That's when he smelled the smoke. And it was not from a cigarette.

"Okay, sure, sometimes the cause isn't so easy to find, I admit," Coulter said. "But there is always a cause whether we can see it or not. Even if it's only theoretical, there is a cause."

"It sounds like you have a theory. Is that why you're here, Dr. Zahn? Do you want me to validate your theory?"

"I don't want validation, you asshole. I want to help my son."

Coulter saw the reflection of flames on the floor and ceiling. He'd drunk a lot of Guinness and was still pissing, the stream jetting out clear and diluted. There was a moment of sheer panic, that he was going to die with his dick flapping around, dribbling pee down the front of his chinos, that he nearly vomited on himself, too. To catch the puke, he covered his mouth with his hands, causing his pants to fall around his ankles, and Coulter turned to run, to escape the fire, but stumbled backward, still peeing this entire time, and landed hard on his back, pee shooting out like a fountain until his legs were soaked and Isaac fell backwards out of the stall, his arm on fire. Lying on his back, covered in his own urine, and his son on fire, Coulter couldn't help but be surprised at his reaction. Instead of concern, or fear, or even shame, he felt an uncontrollable and unwavering rage.

If the fire didn't kill Isaac, Coulter would.

"Perhaps we're focusing on the wrong thing here, Dr. Zahn," Dr. Hamlin said. "How did this event make *you* feel?"

"You've got to be fucking kidding me."

"I can assure you that I am not."

"I was the epitome of a proud father. What do you think? I was covered in piss. My son suffered second degree burns. He got taken to the hospital in handcuffs. He caused tens of thousands of dollars in damage. I was just peachy. Ecstatic even!"

"Have you always used sarcasm as a coping mechanism?"

Dr. Hamlin leaned back in his chair, delighted with himself, like he had, in just twenty minutes, figured out Coulter and his family. This was what had bothered Coulter most about every psychiatrist he had seen thus far. He wanted to vet them before they met Isaac, make sure they weren't some whackjob. But that was the thing. They were all whackjobs, as if this characteristic was a prerequisite of the profession, like unkempt beards and breath that smelled of pipe tobacco and mentholated breath mints.

"I'm sorry," Coulter said, suppressing the urge to smack this pompous bastard. "I just want to know if there is something I can do, a prescription, psychoanalyses, something, to fix him."

"You think your son is 'something' that needs to be 'fixed.'" He used finger quotes. He *actually* used finger quotes.

"You know what I mean."

Dr. Hamlin leaned forward and puckered his lips. "Tell me, Dr. Zahn. How demanding are you that Isaac performs well in science?"

"Science particularly?"

"School in general."

"Like any parent I hope he does well," Coulter said. "Why? Do you think his pyromania stems from me pressuring him to do well in school?"

"I don't think you're the cause. I think I've already mentioned that."

Coulter crossed his legs and felt a pinching on his left thigh. Reaching into his pocket, Coulter found a book of matches. "Sean Cummings," it said. He'd picked it up at lunch today to give to Isaac for his collection, despite the fact that both arms were bandaged from burns. He didn't even remember doing it on purpose. It was instinct, to give his child the materials needed to start a fire.

"I think it would be helpful if next session I sat down with the entire family," Dr. Hamlin said. Coulter twirled the book of matches between his fingertips, imagining he smelled that familiar sulfur wafting through the air. "And I'd especially like to speak to Isaac alone."

"Sure," Coulter said, even though he knew he'd never see Dr. Hamlin again, or any other psychiatrist for that matter. "Same time next week?"

X

Depression is a fluid continuum, hard to pinpoint or articulate. There's shame. Guilt. Fear. Self-loathing. All swimming around without sufficient cause. That's obvious. But to say one person is something, in this instance depressed, and one person is not, seems to indicate a dividing line, a threshold that one must cross. If you are on one side of the line, you are emotionally stable. If you are on the other, you are disturbed. You need help. You will not be okay on your own. How do I quantify that? By how many times I thought per day about death? It seemed about as good an indicator as any.

I was a lot at that time, thinking about death. It wasn't that I was suicidal; it was more a fascination, like seeing a new device for the first time, an iPad say, or Google Glass, and wondering exactly how it worked. At the lab, I fantasized about dipping my face into liquid nitrogen. It would flash freeze, and my brain wouldn't be able to transmit electrical impulses to regulate my breathing or my cardiovascular system. Within seconds both would stop, and I would die. I would lose my balance, whether I was sitting or standing, and I would topple over. When I hit the ground, my head would shatter into frozen shards of flesh and tissue. I also considered placing the proton laser on a timer, something short, perhaps five seconds or so, just enough time for me to stand in front but not enough for me to lose my courage. The beam wouldn't shoot a hole in my chest like in a sci-fi movie. There would be burns, of course, but nothing as catastrophic as that. Instead, my body cavity would act as a furnace, and my organs would heat until they boiled. The smell would be horrid, and it would only be a few moments until I was discovered.

At home, the technical details of how I would kill myself became more difficult. First, Sara was there. As she got later into her pregnancy, she went out less, to markets or simply to walk about town. Not being employed, she had few commitments. She would shop for groceries. She would prepare for the baby, buying onesies and little plastic tabs to keep the cabinets from opening all the way. I would have to be more discreet at home. I wouldn't simply be able to take the toaster into the bathroom, plug it in, and jump into the shower. There would be questions, interference. I would have to answer for what I would do. Secondly, I didn't have the tools I had at work. More could go wrong. There would be more of a mess to clean up. I would have to slit my wrists in the bathtub or overdose on sleeping pills. I would leave behind puddles of blood and excrement and vomit. Worse yet, I could be found before I died, resuscitated and forever unable to apologize for my actions, Sara's and my relationship marred thereafter by mistrust.

Of course, beyond thinking about my death, there were other manifestations of my depression: I picked at unhealed pimples, turning them into gnarled knots of scar tissue; I washed my hands so frequently they remained pink and cracked from exposure; I talked to no one; I suffered from insomnia. For that I tried Ambien and warm milk, antihistamine and hydrocodone. I tried eating a greasy meal before bed and working out. I watched television. I read. I tried to lie still and clear my mind of all thought, but nothing worked. After a while, I gave up on forcing myself to go to sleep. Instead, I would work until I collapsed from exhaustion, sitting at the dining room table, my head resting upon my laptop's keyboard. I would awake to a start, only having been asleep a few hours, with Sara scrambling some eggs, not even acknowledging the fact that I hadn't slept in the same bed with her for several weeks.

"Morning," she would say. "You're late for work."

This was how I found myself at the lab at 4:00 am, my head resting atop the mainframe computer's keyboard. The monitors had gone dark hours ago. I rose up and stretched, trying to alleviate the dull ache lodged in my shoulders and neck. I tasted copper, licked my teeth, and noticed a little blood. I must have bit my lip, I thought. How strange.

Everyone else had gone home hours ago. Only security guards roamed campus now, idling along the streets in their sedans, a tattered copy of Dickens and day-old donuts in the seat next to them. But that would change soon. Lab techs and graduate students would start clamoring in around 5:00, sleepy-eyed and smelling of coffee. I had class at 8:00 and again at 11:00, then office hours in the afternoon, so the only opportunity I would have to work on my dissertation would be in the next few hours—no point in going home now.

The computer itself was housed below ground, dozens of towered servers aligned in neat rows inside a refrigerated room. Upstairs in the lab, six monitors and a keyboard provided access. Students and faculty used it to solve Einstein's field equations or to model hypothetical particle collisions. I was using it to compute matrices of Calabi-Yau manifolds and to project string frequencies to determine if they produced certain universal characteristics such as the force of gravity and Planck's constant. It gave simple "yes" or "no" answers to a small subset of variables, determining whether or not that manifold had the required shape to allow the frequency in question to exist. The model then narrowed down the various manifolds that satisfied the requirement and then moved on to another subset and another and another until no manifolds remained in the original, random configuration. Once I reached zero manifolds in the possibility queue, I randomly generated another matrix of manifolds and repeated the process.

I tapped the Return key. Numbers filtered down the matrices, cascading like soapy water down a shower curtain. In experimentation, the scientist is supposed to be an objective observer. He may design the experiment, account for controls and sound methodology, but then he should withdraw. Granted, this wasn't an experiment, only research modeling, but the idea is the same: the scientist should not in any way determine the outcome. When faced with such an astounding possibility of failure, however, this becomes difficult. If the needle in a haystack metaphor could be used, the needle would be the size of a single cell of a human eyelash and the haystack would be the size of the Andromeda galaxy, a flawed methodology to say the least that would take me over 400,000,000 years to stumble upon the correct answer. It was also time consuming and boring and, in the end, worthless. After two hours of modeling, not one manifold made it past the first subset of universal variables. For my dissertation to be passable, I surmised, it would have to at least pass 118 subsets.

After logging out of the mainframe, I packed up my things and headed down to the radiation lab to take a shower in the decontamination unit. A creepy place, it was located in the basement and had no windows. The shower unit had glass walls and stainless steel floors. Every time I came down here, I imagined being surrounded by a group of epidemiologists, decked out in nitrile rubber hazmat suits. They would be decontaminating me, then readying me for isolation and my impending death from some slowly incubating virus.

The water, despite being only one temperature, tepid, felt good. It washed the grease off my face and relaxed my tense muscles. It rinsed the blood from my mouth and helped me regain some faculty of my senses. I wasn't quite awake, but I was getting there, still in that moment caught between dream and reality, the world streaming in a fluid manner like I was walking across the bottom of a pool. Still lingering, though, was the remnants of my dream, the effect it had on my nervous system as it convinced my brain that it was actually occurring. In my dream, I had been held hostage by a group of domestic militants, known for their savagery. They were torturing me, not for any information, not to gain some strategic advantage over their enemies, but just for fun. I was tied up, bound to a wooden chair at the edge of the North Canadian River outside Oklahoma City. The water ran shallow and was stained red from clay. It tasted gritty and coppery, thick with limestone sediment. I knew this because they kept dipping my head back into the water. I fought each time they did so, thinking that if I could just wriggle hard enough, I could break free and run to safety. I never could, though. I was just on an endless loop: they would dip me underwater, I would fight for my life, and just before I was to lose consciousness, they would bring me back up for a few, short gasps of air.

Finished with my shower, I got dressed and headed upstairs to my office. It was a small room, tucked between the men's washroom and a janitor's closet. It always smelled of urinal cakes and Pine Sol. I booted up my computer and logged my results from the night before. I poured through the data, each manifold that had been created by the model, and pinpointed the universal characteristic that had not been met, gravity or the electromagnetic force, whatever it had been, and attempted to determine why it had gone wrong, then I would eliminate that possibility from the modeling code. It was a painstaking process that went slowly and had a high propensity for error, but I knew no other way in which to proceed.

I continued on in this way for hours, perusing my data sets, waiting for my early class to start, when Holly, the physics department administrator, burst into my office. I was startled at first for I didn't realize how much time had passed. The clock on my computer monitor showed 8:30. I was late for class. Three and a half hours had gone by, but it seemed no longer than five minutes. It was a strange phenomenon of sorts, losing so much time. It wasn't that I had blacked out or had one of my vivid daydreams, but time didn't seem to contain the same properties as it usually did, instead streaming much faster, as if my velocity through space had slowed to a perpetual stop.

"I'm sorry to interrupt you, sir," Holly said.

"I know. I'm heading that way," I said, meaning class.

"You do? Oh. I was told no one has been able to get in touch with you."

"Who's been trying to reach me?"

"Dr. Brinkman. Your wife."

"My wife?"

"Yes. She's in the hospital."

Immediately I checked my phone. I had turned it off the night before so as not to be disturbed while working, and in the interim I'd received twenty-four voicemail messages, six of which were from Sara and the rest from a number I didn't recognize. Dozens of scenarios popped into my head—my wife had gone into labor prematurely, killing both she and the baby. Or only Sara had died, the baby in ICU, isolated in an incubator and barely clinging to life. An intruder had beaten Sara and raped her. She had been in a terrible bus accident. She had contracted HIV during a botched blood transfusion. She had tried to kill herself and was awaiting a psych evaluation.

"Sir?"

"Yes?"

"Do you need a ride?"

"Yes," I said. "Please."

Holly didn't know anything, only that Sara had been admitted. She didn't know her condition or the cause of her illness or injury. She didn't know if she was alive or dead or all alone, drugged up and confused—she only could respond with a scared, dumb look and say, "I don't know, I don't, I'm sorry." I couldn't get in touch with anyone either. I called Dr. Brinkman and Sara, both of whom didn't answer. I phoned the hospital, but I remained on hold, the low hum of a saxophone ringing in my ear. When we reached the visitor's parking lot, I hung up the phone and sprinted into the hospital.

I found myself in a large foyer. There was seating over to the right, the kind found in airports, two rows of chairs bolted to a center foundation, and an information kiosk directly ahead of me. Two young women worked there. The first clacked at a keyboard. She had her mouth open, her head perched forward like an ostrich as she studied the screen. The other was on the telephone telling someone that she didn't care if she lived with the patient, "only blood-relatives and spouses can visit—it's the law," and smacking her lips every time she pronounced a "P." When I approached, the one clacking on the keyboard stopped and turned toward me.

"My wife," I said. "She was admitted here last night. Sara Zahn."

She clicked the information into the computer, then clicked her tongue. I couldn't help but think it was a derisive cluck, as if she saw on her computer screen that I was the deadbeat husband who no one could reach all night.

"Here she is. Room 376." She pointed toward the elevator. "Third floor and to the right. Can't miss it."

Despite her assurance to the contrary, I still managed to get lost. The hallways were frequent and confusing, the signs indicating the direction of the rooms had faded to an off-white sheen. The nurses and doctors were too busy to help. It wasn't until an orderly escorted me to her room did I finally find Sara, sitting up in bed, eating scrambled eggs. Oxygen tubes had been inserted into her nostrils, and an IV stuck into her arm.

"About time you made it," she said between bites.

She chewed with her mouth open and refused to look at me, her head angled in exasperation.

"I'm sorry," I said. "I am so sorry." I went to her and tried to take her hand, but she snapped it away.

"I'm trying to eat here."

"I got here as soon as I could."

"Eight hours late. Not too bad, I suppose."

"You look good. I thought—I thought you might have—I don't know what I thought. But you look good. You look like you're fine."

She glared at me, then returned her attention to her eggs, stabbing the fluffy scrambles with the fork's plastic tines. "Trying to get out of here already?" she asked. "Are you late getting back to the lab?"

"That's not what I meant."

"Then what did you mean?"

"I meant to ask what is wrong."

She nodded toward the foot of the bed. "Chart's down there," she said.

Preeclampsia, extremely high blood pressure, dehydration, exactly what Dr. Remington had warned us about. They had her on a saline drip and hydralazine.

"I thought I was dying, Coulter."

"I'm sorry."

"Sorry really isn't good enough." She jabbed the fork into a biscuit, the handle sticking out and oscillating back and forth. "In fact, apologizing like that is kind of a bastard move. Cowardly at best."

"I understand. I do. Let me explain—"

"Really?" she asked. "You're going to delve right into your defense without even asking me what happened? How I'm doing? If anything is wrong with our baby?"

"I—"

"Please just go. I can't look at you right now." I remained sitting. She rimmed her applesauce cup with the plastic spoon, getting the bits that had dried into a film along the edges, and plunked it into her mouth. "I'm starving," she said. "All we had to eat at the apartment were olives, and I couldn't keep them down."

"What happened?" I asked.

She sighed and set down the cup onto the tray. Nearly empty, it tipped over, and the spoon fell to the floor and skittered across the linoleum. I went to pick it up, but Sara stopped me by raising her hand.

"It started out like heartburn," she said. "I took some Tums, but it kept getting worse. It got so bad I couldn't swallow. I was nauseated. I dry heaved for a while. Then I threw up. It felt like a hole was burning in my throat, and I was getting scared that something was wrong. That's when I called the first time, but it went straight to voicemail. When you didn't answer, I decided to get in the tub, thinking the hot water might relax me, but that didn't work either. Soon my chest constricted, and I was having a hard time breathing. My muscles began to spasm. I thought I was having a seizure. I called again. Again you didn't answer. I started to hyperventilate. Then I really started to be afraid because I knew I didn't have anyone else to call. I have no friends here. I have no colleagues. No family. If you wouldn't come, no one would. I would be completely alone."

"I was at the lab. I was working on my dissertation. I turned my phone off so I wouldn't be disturbed. I forgot about—"

"I panicked and tried to get out of the tub, but I slipped and fell back into the water." She pulled up her hair and leaned forward so I could see her back. A bruise covered her neck where she had hit the porcelain tub.

"I'm not trying to use my dissertation as an excuse. I'm not. What I did last night was inexcusable. But you have to understand. I'm under a lot of pressure right now."

"I've been alone since we've been here. The last three and a half years, alone. I'm turning into one of those sad, desolate women who stay home and have babies and cook and clean and have no voice. I am turning into something I hate, Coulter. Don't you see that?"

"If I don't get this done, I won't graduate. I'll have wasted ten years of my life."

"I feel worthless right now. I feel subhuman."

"This isn't permanent. I will figure this out. I will graduate. We will move. I will find a job closer to home."

"I want to go back to work."

"I will defend in March, and the semester will end in May. Then we can move. We just have to hold on until then."

"I can't wait that long."

I paused, wondering if I heard her correctly.

"I'm going to start finding work now."

"Now?"

"Yes."

"But you're pregnant."

"So? It's illegal to discriminate against pregnant women."

"You have severely high blood pressure. Preeclampsia. Hypertension. Starting a new job is stressful. *Searching* for a job is stressful. We have to do what is best for the baby."

"What's best for *me* is best for the baby."

"That's unfair."

"He's a part of me. He's growing inside of me. My health, both physically and mentally, indeed does affect him, Coulter. You can't deny that."

Sara pushed the food tray away from her. It was connected to the bed and swiveled outward and to the side. With more room to move, she cinched up to an upright position, using only her arms to pull herself up, like she was paralyzed from the waist down.

"I can't allow you to do this," I said.

"Allow?"

"That's the wrong word."

"*Allow?*"

"That's not what I meant. I just mean that you need to relax right now. After the birth, then you can look for work again."

"I don't need your permission, Coulter. I'm a person, too."

"You're focusing on the wrong thing here, Sara."

"I don't think I am."

Preeclampsia coupled with hypertension could cause cerebral hemorrhaging, killing her and the baby both. I'd read more about it when Dr. Remington first told us about the possibility of Sara developing it, and since then I'd been dreaming that I could see Sara's brain, the little electrical synapses fluttering from the cerebral cortex down the nervous system, keeping her bodily functions working, keeping the baby alive, and then an artery would erupt, like a volcano might, a stream of blood that would flow down the rippled curvature of her brain's tissue, flooding the nerves until all the little electrical currents flickered out. I would awake in a panic, and I wouldn't be able to get back to sleep until I checked her breathing, making sure she was still alive.

Not that I hadn't thought about what life would be like if Sara weren't around, if I wasn't about to be a father, if they both abruptly died. I supposed these little fantasies are normal to some degree—each of us dreams about the proverbial greener grass. What if I could devote my life full-time to my research? What if I mapped out the shape of the universe? What would I be capable of then?

"You think this is what is best then?" I asked.

"Yes," she said. "I do."

A knock sounded on the door, and Dr. Remington walked in, smiling. She appeared as tired as always. Her sneakers squeaked as she walked toward us, her soles sliding against the linoleum as if she was too exhausted to even pick up her feet. Glasses drooped down onto her nose, and her eyelid twitched like she was running on an inordinate amount of caffeine. She took in deep breaths, her nostrils flaring out each time she inhaled. I'd read somewhere that deep breaths curtail yawning, as yawns are caused by lack of oxygen to the brain. Perhaps, I thought, that could be useful for me, too.

"How're you feeling?" Dr. Remington asked. She sat on a swivel stool and rolled it over to the side of Sara's bed, using her legs as propellers.

"Better," Sara said. "Calmer."

"That's good. You gave your little one quite a shock last night."

"Is he okay?" I asked.

"The baby?" Dr. Remington asked.

I nodded.

"Yes," she said. "He'll be fine. His heart rate was way above normal. Oxygen flow was disrupted." She took out her stethoscope and placed it against Sara's chest. "But he'll be just fine."

"Good," I said. "That's good."

"You'll need to rest for a while," Dr. Remington said to Sara. "I want you to keep all physical activity to a minimum."

"Are you putting me on bed rest?"

"No. Not bed rest *per se*, but you should limit your activities. No heavy lifting, plenty of fluids, walk slowly, eat healthy, and, most importantly, ample sleep. You should be sleeping ten to twelve hours a night at this point. No walking up and down stairs. No extraneous exercise. No standing for prolonged periods of time. No deep cleaning. No activities making you bend over repeatedly. No long walks— "

"No shellfish. No jumping on trampolines. Microwaves. Standing too long. Heat. Cold. Breathing. Salt. Nothing is good for the baby. I can't do *anything*."

"Sara, I'm being serious. I'm worried about you. You'll need to take it easy for the remainder of your pregnancy. No stressful activities. Nothing strenuous. Physically or mentally."

"Does that mean she shouldn't work?" I asked.

"You're working?" Dr. Remington asked Sara.

"No," Sara said. "It was just something I was considering." Sara glared at me, her cheeks sucked in and her lips puckered. "Nothing is set in stone."

"I highly recommend that you do not begin a new job at this time."

"It was only a thought," Sara said.

"Promise me you won't," Dr. Remington said. "I'm serious, Sara. In your condition, any more stress-induced behavior could severely distress the baby. Alongside the preeclampsia, he could come prematurely. There could be brain traumas. Lack of oxygen. Severe birth defects. You *have* to take it easy."

"I will. I promise. It was just a stupid idea anyway." Sara pulled the blanket up to her chin like a child afraid of a monster underneath her bed. "Could you turn the heater up, please? It's freezing in here."

"I'll talk to the staff." Dr. Remington handed me a clipboard. "Here are her discharge papers. You take good care of her. Okay, Coulter?"

"I will," I said. "I promise."

SARA REFUSED TO OBEY THE DOCTOR. A DAY after being released from the hospital, she was cleaning the apartment, shopping for new clothes for job interviews, revamping her resume, combing the classifieds for any openings in commercial banking. Before the subprime mortgage crisis, she'd worked as a risk analyst for a small community bank, and when the FDIC shuttered its doors, Sara was out of a job. At first, it hadn't seemed to bother her to be unemployed. She was still the same crass Sara, declaring this time in her life to be an opportunity, not an obstacle. She took painting and literature courses. She volunteered at the food bank. She took up gardening. But then I got accepted into MIT, and we moved to Boston. Here, she lost her enthusiasm, not having the energy to finish a painting or a book, and with no place to continue her garden, she stayed inside mostly, calling banks around the city for any openings. Mired in the worst economy since the Great Depression, though, she wasn't able to find work, and weeks turned to months turned to years, and she eventually gave up. When we'd gotten pregnant, I hoped she would throw herself into the pregnancy, excited to become a mother, but she withdrew even more, I later realized from a fear she'd turn into her mother, a stay-at-home mom whose opinions always came second behind her husband's.

It was after a trip to Staples to buy Sara a day planner that we found my dad sitting on the steps of our apartment, a large box sitting at his feet. This was unlike him, to show up without warning. Usually we planned a visit weeks in advance. We would schedule itineraries, buy tickets for Red Sox games, tour the Boston massacre site, the Boston Tea Party site, go on a gastropub scavenger hunt in search of the best corned beef and cabbage, a tour of the Sam Adams Brewery, or just sit at home and watch marathons of weather disasters on the National Geographic channel. Something, I knew, had to be wrong.

I worried how long he'd sat there. Dot inhabitants didn't enjoy the presence of strangers, especially loitering strangers, ones with cowboy boots and darting eyes and who smell like they don't belong. It's not that the Dot has a trouble with outsiders, really. It's more of a trust issue. If they hadn't known you since you were in diapers, then you were to be avoided. Dorchester wasn't a bad spot. Like any urban neighborhood, there were abandoned houses, windows boarded up and tagged with graffiti. Empty lots rough with grated gravel and concrete pockmarked the area. But the houses that were still occupied had been taken care of. Patio rails were freshly painted. American flags waved in the breeze. Gardens were well manicured, vines of potato plants wrapping around slatted fences. Those who remained took pride in that fact. And I couldn't blame them for that. Sometimes just standing can be an achievement.

Dad looked good, though, un-harassed at least. He had a dark tan, a consequence of spending most his summer days in the field, chasing thunderstorms across the plains like an old hunter stalking bison. His hair receded to the shape of a horseshoe, but it hadn't grayed; instead, it appeared to have been tinted blond, the sun having destroyed any remaining melanin. Despite spending most of his time behind the wheel of his '86 Bronco, he kept in good shape. His forearms had always struck me as something Herculean, chiseled to that of a Greco-Roman style wrestler. I'd look at my own, thin and pale and with wrists a child could wrap her fingers around, and wonder why I hadn't inherited his physical features. Why did I have to look so much like my mother?

He smiled and waved a large paw as we arrived in front of our building.

"What're you doing here?" I asked.

"What? No hello? No, 'hey, Dad, how's it going?'"

"It's just odd. Is there something wrong?"

"Not at all!" he said. "It's just been too long, that's all. I wanted to surprise you. Thought it would be good to see each other."

We hugged. He smelled like the inside of public transportation, the stale air of an airplane cabin, the gas station air fresheners that hung from the rearview mirror in every Boston cab.

"It is," I said. "It's good to see you."

He turned toward Sara. "And you, my dear, how are you?" he asked, beaming and approaching for a hug. "Come here." He pulled away and held her hands. "How is my grandbaby doing?"

"Good," Sara said.

"Well, we did have a little scare the other day," I said.

"What?" Dad asked. "What happened? Is everything okay?" He held his hands out like a spotter.

"Nothing," Sara said, shooting me a look. "I'm fine."

"And the baby?"

"The baby's okay, Dad," I said. "It's Sara."

"What happened? Are you okay?"

I told him about her preeclampsia and hypertension. "And now she's looking for work."

"For work?" He looked at her, dumbfounded. "Seriously?"

"There's nothing to worry about," Sara said. "I have everything under control."

Dad didn't interrogate her further, though I could tell he was concerned, frightened even. He'd wanted grandchildren ever since Sara and I had started getting serious, bringing up the topic anytime we got together. He'd ask what names we were considering, whether or not we'd stay close so he could spoil them, and we'd have to remind him that we'd only been dating for six months, that it was a bit awkward that he was bringing it up. "I'm just excited," he would say. "I can't wait to be a grandpa." Later, after we moved in together, he'd slip the question in between innocuous things. "How're the studies going? You pregnant? Plan on going to grad school?" Once we got engaged, we made a deal with him, every time he mentioned children we would add another year he had to wait. Before we'd gotten pregnant, it had reached 187 years.

"I got you something," he said. He pointed to the box at his side. It was a crib. "I hope you like it. It was a bitch hauling this thing around in a cab."

Sara ran her finger down the picture on the box. It was a plain crib, white wood, cylindrical rails, no ornamentation of any kind. Even on the picture it looked flimsy. "It's great," Sara said.

I borrowed a dolly from the building's super, and Dad and I lugged the crib up the stairs and unloaded it into the nursery. The instructions to assemble consisted of twenty-eight single-spaced pages filled with tiny diagrams. I'd seen software code that made more sense to me. The box consisted of fourteen wood rods, four pieces of railing, thirty-eight small screws, fourteen large screws, fifty-six washers, a Phillips head, a flat head, and an offset screwdriver, nineteen nails, seventeen plastic rods, and dozens of more pieces I had no discernible idea what they were. Dad and I struggled to make sense of the mess, and we didn't make any progress.

The nursery was the only bedroom that had a window. It didn't have any curtains yet—another item we needed or Sara would make—and across the alleyway we could see a large Irishman washing his face at his kitchen sink. We'd lived here for years and so had he and we still didn't know each other's names. We'd acknowledge each other every once in a while if I happened to see him on his stoop with a slight nod of the head and eyes that we dared not let linger for too long. But that was it.

He'd been here all his life and we hadn't and that's all we needed to know about each other.

Next door we could hear the hushed, stern voices of a man and woman fighting. The walls were paper-thin here, and despite their best intentions to keep their kids from hearing their argument, they failed— she wanted him to get help, see somebody, anybody, his drinking needed to stop. He didn't see why—he took care of them, didn't he?

"I think we need to start with number three," Dad said. "It just doesn't make any sense to start putting these rails together without first putting in the rods."

"We should probably just stick with the directions, Dad."

Sara supervised our work from a rocking chair in the corner. A sly smile spread across her lips like she knew how this would turn out.

"But how are we going to latch the rods in place once the rails are already attached?" Dad asked. "The rods are longer than the opening."

I'd heard horror stories about in-laws from colleagues in the physics department. A few of my fellow candidates were married, and they spoke of their in-laws like they plotted to dissolve their marriages. Their mother-in-laws practiced spiteful things to say at dinner, "You still haven't graduated from school? For such a smart man, you'd think you would've devoted your life to something that did the world some *good* for Christ's sake. Medicine or law or hell even dentistry. At the very least brought home some money." Their father-in-laws bought them hammers and electrical drills for Christmas, knowing fully well they'd only serve as a constant reminder their daughter did not marry a man's man. I felt blessed in this regard. Sara got along with my dad quite well, and her parents had accepted me, and at times even pretended to be interested in my research.

Dad jammed each rod into the top railing one by one, twisting until they fit. Although I should've been thankful for the help, I couldn't help but feel slighted. This was, after all, *my* home, *my* son's crib, *my* job as husband and father. But it had always been this way—my father doing the work as I stepped aside. Changing the oil in my first car, putting together microscopes given to me at Christmas, anything at all, my father would do the heavy lifting, and I'd stand idly by, disparaging the fact that his actions made me seem like an entitled, spoiled brat.

"Why are you here, Dad?" I asked again.

Dad was having problems with the corner rod. The grooves weren't catching, and each time he swiveled, the rod inserted crookedly. I could tell he was getting frustrated with it, a tirade boiling underneath his calm façade, and that familiar childish anxiety I'd felt growing up returned right behind that soft spot in the neck—he'd get angry, and it was all my fault.

The couple next door continued their fight: "What do you think bought all them shoes in your closet, huh? Monopoly money?"

"I just figured I should tell you this in person rather than over the phone," Dad said. He put down the rod and rail, the former sticking out of the latter at an odd angle, like a piece of hay stuck in a maple tree after a tornado. "I heard from your mother. She'd like to see you."

At first I thought I'd heard him wrong. There was just no way that those words could've come out of my father's mouth. I hadn't seen my mother, or heard from her, in fifteen years. My last memory of her I couldn't even conclude authoritatively had even happened. The memory begins with me in my room. I'm getting dressed for school. I'm anxious as I get dressed, but I'm not entirely sure what about. Maybe I had an exam that day, in English perhaps. That had always been my worst subject. I'm interrupted by a knock at the door. It's Mom. She's nursing a mug of coffee and is fully dressed. This is unusual. Usually a late sleeper, she would be clad in only a robe when she kissed me goodbye as I headed down the street for the bus.

"Hey, bugger," she says. "Whatcha doing?"

I don't say anything to her. I'm mad at her. Again, I'm not sure why.

She slumps into my room. I can tell by the way her shoulders drag and how she sips on her coffee, letting her lips linger on the hot liquid as if punishing herself, that she feels guilty about something. This has troubled me for years, not knowing. What did she do to feel so badly?

"You got a second?" she asks.

"I have to go to school."

She would've been only about thirty-seven in this memory, yet she seems much older. I'm not sure if that is the case or if I'm only remembering her from the skewed perception of an eleven-year-old boy. She walks slowly and with stilted movements, like her joints needed grease to work properly. Her hair is pulled back into a ponytail, but not tightly, so errant loose strands stick out. She has deep crow's feet and bloodshot eyes and purple half-moons for cheeks. It looks like she hasn't slept and has been crying.

"I think we deserve a day off," she says. "What do you think? Instead of school, how about the Omniplex?"

I fall for this every time. The Omniplex is the biggest museum in Oklahoma City and my favorite place in the entire world. We spend hours there. I, of course, am drawn to the science exhibits. I climb over a life-size replica of the Lunar Module used in Apollo 11. I shake hands with a Buzz Aldrin mannequin. I name off the constellations in the planetarium.

"Orion. Andromeda. Cygnus. Ursa Major. Auriga. Caelum. Gemini. Antlia. Apus. Cerberus. Custos Messium."

Only Mom and I are there. The museum is mostly deserted being a weekday morning. No field trips must've been scheduled on that day.

"You are so smart," Mom says. "I'm just so proud of you."

"Did you know the Big Bang happened 12.5 billion years ago?" I ask.

"I didn't. Tell me more."

I tell her about the singularity. How everything in our universe from the carbon and water that makes up the majority of us to the methane on Jupiter's moons to the farthest molecule of hydrogen millions of light years from Earth all had been condensed into a mass so minute that it would've been imperceptible to the most advanced microscopes ever invented. I tell her that around 12.5 billion years ago—which really is a long, long time when you think about it—this singularity expanded, and although a lot of people think it was this huge explosion, like a big nuclear bomb or something, it wasn't, not at all; first of all, sound waves had nothing to travel through, so a loud bang was impossible, so it just sort of inflated, like a balloon kind of, to millions of light years across in a matter of seconds, and the whole thing is still expanding today. The Hubble Telescope taught us that. It shows that everything is moving away from us.

"So one day, a long time from now, we'll look up and nothing will be there?" Mom asks.

"Well, maybe," I say. "Maybe in a long, long, long time from now. Maybe."

She pauses and sits down in the middle of the floor, her legs criss-crossed like a child. It makes me feel strange to see her like this. It makes her seem vulnerable, and I'm overcome with the urge to run to her and hug her until she feels better. But I don't. I stay right where I am.

"That's the saddest thing I've ever heard," Mom says.

A loud bang shook the wall between our apartment and the fighting couple's. All of us—Dad, me, and Sara—flinched and looked at each other, asking with our eyes if we should do something to intervene. Call the cops. Go see if everyone was okay. Barricade ourselves in our apart-ment. It sounded like a blunt object had been thrown into the wall. But there wasn't any shattering afterward like it was a lamp or vase. There was just a thud and then nothing. Just silence.

My dad and I both inched closer to the wall and stuck our ears against it. I couldn't hear a thing. Not the muffled cries of someone who was hurt or frightened. Not a television transmitting static in the background. Not the small children who I knew lived there, wondering what had happened. It was the first time I had heard silence coming from their apartment. I'd never imagined the lack of sound could be so scary. But it was. It was downright horrifying.

X

The Temple—or what was called a temple but was actually a ranch— was much larger than she'd anticipated. Nestled into the hills in the middle of over 300 acres, she couldn't see the end of it. As far as she was concerned, there wasn't an end. There were just the endless rolling knolls covered in thick Bermuda grass and Black Walnuts and perennials and Tanoaks. Everything seemed brighter and crisper, like the sun devoted more of its energy here than back home. It made California hotter, too. But the sun felt good against her shoulders. Oklahoma had been hot, sure, but it was a different kind of hot in California. Drier, surprisingly, since the ocean was so close, and less sweltering. Natalie felt freer, without inhibition, like she could move.

She was mending clothing alongside two Senior Ladies of the Unification Church—she had to, among other things, burn her clothing when she'd arrived a few months back so as to throw off the bonds of the material world. It had never occurred to her that she could've appreciated such a task. In her previous life, she would have been judgmental of such domestic work, ashamed at having to fight feelings of condescension towards women who stayed home and did laundry and scrubbed floors and popped Tylenol from back pain caused by hours bending over to put potpies in and take cookies out of the oven. An attorney for Eller & Detrich, one of the largest firms in Oklahoma, she had specialized in mergers and acquisitions, toiling day in and day out with leveraged buyouts and settlement packages, important things that affected a lot of people. Her therapist had said it's what led to her depression, an inflated sense of ego that she could no longer fulfill. She also enjoyed the simplicity of sitting in the shade, sipping hand-squeezed lemonade, and not feeling like she needed to argue anything, or to say anything, to discipline her son, to devote herself to a marriage she no longer believed in. She could fully dedicate her time to herself, her newfound family, and her burgeoning faith in God.

From the gates, Natalie saw a yellow school bus appear, the new family members arriving. Natalie remembered when she'd first arrived, how frightened she was, how skeptical that the Unification Family could help her. She'd tried therapists, psychiatrists, medication, Xanax and Zoloft and Pristiq, meditation, even tantric sex, with her husband and others, but none of this offered any comfort, any solace that she could be healthy, be loved, and be a part of something bigger than herself. Before, being an agnostic, she wouldn't have had attributed this longing to a higher power, but now she knew that God could be the only love and belonging that could fill her completely. No penis or Xanax could ever replace the feeling of God's love.

The new members were all kids in their teens or twenties, wild-eyed and hesitant. From the houses and barns and the Temple, the members flocked to the newest arrivals, embracing them in hugs and telling them that they loved them, unconditionally, and that nothing they could ever do would change that. Their eyes softened, and they felt that first, gleaming embrace of God envelop them like a favorite blanket. They were safe now. And they knew it. Natalie could see it in their eyes.

With new arrivals, the Leader always held a service. The Temple was located in the very center of the ranch. It was domed and made from white stucco. No ornamentation decorated its façade, no stained glass windows or painted murals, no cast iron crosses or carvings of saints, only unadorned, brilliant white walls. Inside, simple pews lined bare wood floors. The stage had a podium. There was no organ or place for a choir, none of what the Leader called distractions to true faith. Worshipping was not a moment of jubilation and an exercise in fun; instead, it was a moment of self-reflection and penance. A sacrament to God, it should not be diluted by song or frivolity. It remained pure that way, and Natalie felt comforted by this. She had something in which she could, unabashedly, trust.

The entire family gathered for the event, and each senior member paired off with the new arrivals. For the first three weeks, the new arrivals would only be able to interact with a senior member, dubbed their mentor. They would be completely immersed in their new culture from waking to rest. They would sleep on a cot at the foot of their mentor's bed. They would bathe in their mentor's tub. They would wear their mentor's clothes. They would eat their mentor's food. They would work alongside their mentor. They would worship with their mentor. They would study with their mentor. They could not, for any reason, leave their mentor's side. They could not speak with the other new members. They could not listen to the radio or watch television. They could not, in any way, have contact with the outside world.

During Natalie's apprenticeship, as it was called, she had trouble at first. She couldn't sleep, racked with regret and shame. She couldn't stop thinking of Coulter, his freckled face, as his father told him that his mother would not be returning, that she was sick, and that it would be better this way. It would be better for all of them. She had cravings for the outside world, too. For the simple things, like a hot fudge sundae or a bowl of popcorn. A cashmere blanket and a cheesy 1980s romantic comedy. The way her leather seats used to make that staccato sound as she pulled herself into the driver seat of her luxury sedan. She'd heard about narcotic addicts going through withdrawals when trying to wean themselves off of, say, heroin, but she never thought the mundane could evoke such cravings. Slowly, though, these material and familial matters ebbed away. They were merely residue left behind by a greasy hand, able to be wiped away with the mildest of cleaning agents.

Once everyone had been seated, the Leader entered through a side door and walked up to the podium. When Natalie had first met the Leader, she'd been surprised. Of course, every member spoke reverentially about him, nearly elevating him to a deity himself, though he disputed the claim, saying he was no more than a conduit, if even that, but he didn't have an overwhelming presence. He didn't command attention. In fact, unless you were purposely made aware of him, he would most likely go unnoticed. He was an average looking man, middle-aged, perhaps 5' 7" or 5' 8", with an average build, not fat, not scrawny, not particularly handsome. He had brown eyes and brown hair. He didn't have any scars or tattoos or birthmarks. The only thing that really stood out about him was his face—it was the most symmetrical face Natalie had ever seen. Most people have slight, but oftentimes noticeable, asymmetries. A nostril will be wider than the other. An earlobe will droop further. One eye will be wider. But not the Leader. Natalie swore that if she drew a line down the middle of his face, each side would be the mirror image of the other. To be sure, this was impossible, but Natalie couldn't help but wonder.

When he took the stage, he smiled at his audience and began to speak in a nasal voice. "I'd like to be the first to welcome you to our home. I know it must have taken much courage to leave behind everything you've known in order to come here, and this courage does not go unnoticed. This is no ordinary kind of courage. You didn't save a child from oncoming traffic or jump into a pool to save someone from drowning. You didn't cover a grenade to save your compatriots or subdue an attacker assaulting an elderly woman. While these acts are indeed heroic and deserving of our adoration, these acts are, for the most part, instinctual. Many of us, perhaps even a majority, have this instinct hardwired into our genetic makeup. Fight or flight. Since the dawn of mankind, we've had this instinct. It's programmed into us by evolution and design.

No, what you've done is much more impressive. Your actions are a different kind of courage, requiring forethought, premeditation, planning, and execution. This type of courage is altogether more uncommon. It makes you special. It makes you unique. Don't ever forget that. You are, on a fundamental level, one of a kind."

The first time Natalie had heard this sermon, she couldn't bring herself to believe it. She wanted to. She wanted to be special, to have courage, to be brave when faced with tribulations. Being a lawyer, though, she'd always entrenched herself in fact. It was a fact she had left her husband. It was a fact she had tried to kill herself. It was a fact she'd abandoned her child. Her life consisted of the letter of the law, and that was it. What she failed to consider, however, was the nuance. The greater welfare. The right thing to do. She couldn't care for her child. She couldn't love her husband. They could not make her happy. What she did then was the most courageous. To slip out in the dead of night. To not say goodbye. To never return. That was the courageous thing to do.

We scheduled to meet at the Old North Church because I didn't want her in my home. To do so would seem to forgive her, which I couldn't for obvious reasons, so we decided that all of us, Sara and me and Dad and her, should meet at a tourist attraction like we were doing a ransom drop. It aggrandized the whole thing for me, which seemed to alleviate some of the conflicting emotions I had about the whole scenario. First, I wanted to make her feel guilty for what she'd done, to shame her publicly, to shout out at the top of my lungs for everyone in the church to stop what they're doing and point and hiss at this woman who abandoned her child. But, on the other hand, I also wanted to study her. I wanted to recruit two or three psych PhDs and design elaborate experiments to see if she'd save a drowning child as she walked by a swimming pool or if she would just keep on walking, pretending not to notice. I hated myself for both these impulses, the first seeming to be the effect of crass emotionalism, the second the detached neurosis of a mad scientist, but I couldn't help either. They were impulse. Instinct. Devoid of premeditation.

"Are you sure you're up to it?" Sara asked before we walked in.

"Of course," I said. "Yes."

"We don't have to do this if you don't want to," she said. She played with my hair, running her fingernails down my scalp. It was comforting, but it annoyed me. I was not a child any more. "We can go home and call the whole thing off."

"No," I said. "We're already here."

Even though we'd lived in Boston for years, this was the first time we'd visited Old North. A few members of the congregation spotted the pews, their heads bent in prayer, hands clasped in front of them, but the church was mostly empty, the tourist season having ended a couple months prior. During the summer months, it would be full not with worshipers but history buffs, snapping photographs with high-resolution lenses in order to catch a bit of the American Revolution flavor, daydreaming about when Paul Revere had warned the patriots the British were marching toward Concord. Of course, this bit of history wasn't all that factual, elevated to mythic lore by Henry Wadsworth Longfellow. Not that anyone cares all that much. Sometimes, I've come to learn, the legend is much more compelling than the truth.

"Coulter?"

I turned to find my mother, Natalie, standing to the side of the aisle. I knew her right away. She looked the same as she did in my memories, like she'd been stuck in a time capsule, not marred by the undertakings that are everyday life. She did look a bit differently, of course. Her skin wasn't so taut. Discernible wrinkles framed her eyes, and her hair seemed a bit thinner, although it still had the same blond sheen I remembered. It was her demeanor, though, that hadn't changed, that cockiness lodged in how she stood, her shoulders perched with kinetic energy like she might lunge at you if you so much as flinched. As a child, I had erroneously believed that all mothers were hardwired this way, but later I learned that it was more a defensive posture, the result of being a lawyer when it was still a boy's club, she always having to prove herself and fight twice as hard as her male colleagues.

"How are you?" she asked. She attempted to smile, but she seemed incapable of mustering one, instead her expression challenging, lips puckered, chin upturned.

"Good," I said. "And you?"

"Good," she said. "Nervous. Thought you might bring a gun or something. Shoot me down." She chuckled nervously.

When I didn't answer, an awkward silence followed. It was as if the electromagnetic force had strengthened around us. Being of the same blood, we had the same charges, creating an overwhelming repelling force. Sara stood to the side, her fingers interlocked underneath her belly. She peered at her feet and dragged her left toe along the floor like she was drawing a line in sand. Dad, I could tell, wanted to intervene, to serve as a buffer between the two of us. He kept sucking in his teeth like a toothless man eating oatmeal. Natalie popped her knuckles, the cracks echoing against the centuries-old brick, and I stood there feeling like I should do something, anything, shake her hand or tell her off or backhand her. She had occupied my daily thoughts for years: where she was, what she was doing, who she was with. As a kid I'd made up fantasies, that she'd been whisked away by the C.I.A. to work as a spy or that she was an astronaut colonizing Mars in some top secret NASA mission. As a teenager I yearned to ask her questions about her life, her habits, her hobbies and passions and pet peeves. Later, as an adult, my thoughts were of how I'd ignore her if I ever saw her on the street, act like she was nobody, even after she confronted me, said hi, begged for my forgiveness, and all I would say is, 'Sorry, lady, you're a stranger to me.' But all I could say was, "It's nice to see you again."

"It's good to see you, too," she said. "And this must be Sara. Marcus told me about you."

"Hi," Sara said. "It's nice to meet you."

Natalie—I couldn't bring myself to call her "Mom"—took in a deep breath and smacked her hips like she didn't really know what to do next. "You look good," she said to me.

"Thanks," I said.

"Marcus tells me you're working on your PhD."

"Yes," I said, seemingly unable to utter more than one-word answers.

"I always knew you would do well. You were such a smart child. Loved science especially."

"Yes," I said.

She motioned toward a pew. "May we sit?"

"We'll look around," Sara said as she looped her arm around my father's and pulled him away. "Just call if you need us."

Natalie and I sat in a pew, both of us staring straight ahead. She wore long sleeves, just a cotton T-shirt, cheap, weathered, and worn. Just beyond the hem of the sleeve I could make out the ends of scars. I imagined that they ran up her entire forearms and biceps, crisscrossed like a tic-tac-toe board, the flesh raised and rough and slightly discolored, like a healing sunburn just before it peels and reveals the pale skin underneath.

"It was very difficult to come here," Natalie said. She averted her eyes to the pew in front of us. Carved into the wood was a heart, the initials "J. L. + L. B." in the center. "Your father actually wasn't the one who told me about you getting a PhD," she said. "I don't know why I lied. I have a problem with that."

"Then how did you know?"

"An old teacher of yours. Mr. Dolph. I went looking for you last year, and he told me where you were."

Mr. Dolph had been my A. P. physics teacher in high school. A bit eccentric, he used to play pranks on his students, bringing in a fake arm once and "sawing" it off during an experiment on force and leverage.

"I'm working on it. The lying, I mean. When you've been lying for so long like I have, though, it becomes difficult to stop. My counselor calls it an addiction. Like to nicotine or caffeine. Chronic shoplifters and hoarders have a variation of it."

"I see," I said.

"I'm sure you have a lot of questions," Natalie said. "I'll answer them. If you want, of course."

"Why now?" I asked. "Why did you go looking for me?"

She shrugged. "Curiosity, I guess. To see what kind of person you've become. I wish I had a better answer. I wish I could say that I'm racked with guilt and that I want to atone for what I did to you. But I'm not sure that's it. Guilt's something I've longed stopped feeling, surprisingly."

I nodded, impressed with her honesty. "Where are you staying?"

"You mean, where do I live?"

I shook my head. "While here."

"The YWCA. They have a shelter there." She was embarrassed to admit this, I could tell by the way she stared that she had to force herself not to look away. "It's actually nicer than I expected. The mattresses are new. Newish anyway."

I fought the urge to offer my couch. Sara would be against the idea. She hadn't supported the meet at all, saying that a woman who abandoned her child gave up all rights afterward in one fell swoop, irrevocably and forever, like matter that crosses a black hole's event horizon, a threshold that once you've crossed, it's impossible to return. Not that I disagreed with her. It wasn't that I yearned for a mother/son relationship—that notion had long dissipated. There wasn't a familial connection anymore, and what remained seemed novel to me. She wasn't a stranger. She had been there for more than a third of my life, but she was, in many respects, unknown to me. I wanted to get to know her, not as a friend or a son or even an acquaintance, but the way a doctor gets to know a patient, understanding how they work, how they tick, why exactly she does what she does.

"Did you think about me?" I asked. "When you left, I mean."

"Every day," she said. "At first I couldn't stop thinking about you. Everything would bring back memories. The phases of the moon for instance. You used to keep a journal of them, remember?" I nodded although I had forgotten that. "I thought of you in the mornings, right when I awoke, half-expecting you to come in and wake me up. Every morning you would lie next to the bed and tell me that you were ready to eat if I was ready to make it. I used to find that so funny." She chuckled to herself and shook her head. "It became easier after a while, though. You don't expect that. At first, I could hardly look at myself. I felt like a failure. You are my child for Christ's sake. And I just left. What kind of mother does that? I was ashamed, and I loathed myself. I tried to tell myself that it was for the best. That I was unfit. That you would be better off without me. And although I doubted my ability to look after you, the words just sounded hollow. Even in my own head I knew I had made a mistake."

"Then why didn't you come back? Why'd you leave in the first place?"

She purged her story like a woman in a confessional: she began at my eleventh birthday party of which I remembered little, although, she admitted, she could've started many years before. The party had been held at our house in our backyard. Being spring, my parents rented out a plethora of playthings, bouncy castles and a miniature carousel and clowns and magicians, the envy of any prepubescent child. All the neighborhood kids and my classmates were there. There was punch and cake and chips balanced with healthy snacks like broccoli florets and carrot spears that we ended up having to throw out. The kids gobbled up all the junk and ran around on a collective sugar binge.

With the children, of course, came their parents, all young and happy and overjoyed to chase after their children. They played tag and hide-and-go-seek and carried their children on their shoulders like they were trophies. They kissed their sons on their shiny balloon cheeks and ruffled their hair and stuffed their hand in their spouse's back pocket. There were winks and stolen kisses underneath our willows and wiped icing from each other's lips all the while smiling and laughing and poorly impersonating famous actors. They just seemed so exuberantly happy. *How could this be?* she thought. How could they be so joyful? She never had been. Looking back, she couldn't remember ever feeling close to that kind of happiness. If she was honest with herself, she more often than not experienced a reproachful and sublime loathing. She hated herself. She did. There was no way around it. She hated herself. She hated her unfaithful husband. She hated her child and his friends and their parents because they could not spark in her what she so envied, just to be like everyone else here at this party. Normal. Happy. Loved.

But this, she knew, would be impossible. Her doctor called it a chemical imbalance in her brain. An abundance of cortisol and noradrenaline. A shortage of serotonin. Mixed up wiring with her neurotransmitters. They tried to correct this with drugs—Prozac and Xanax and Pristiq and Abilify and Adapin and Effexor and Etrafon and Sarafem and Oleptro and Serzone. Nothing worked. At the end of each day, she wanted to crawl into the bathtub and take a cheese grater to her wrist and see how deep she could get before she flinched. Like the old Tootsie Pop commercial and that stupid owl, how many slices would it take before she hit bone?

She put on fronts, sure. She made love to her husband if not every week at least every month. She tried to enjoy it. Usually, though, she would end up rolling over exhausted without the energy to even fake it. She drove her son to Boy Scouts and soccer practice and helped him design science fair projects. Her professional life was going well, having incarcerated some of the biggest methamphetamine dealers in Oklahoma City the month before and was looking at a promotion. But she brimmed with guilt and self-loathing that had no discernible cause. She'd find herself daydreaming about how she would kill herself. None comprised of those romantic fantasies of a mourning husband and hundreds of guests at her memorial service pining for one more opportunity to tell her they loved her. These daydreams were much more technical and schematic, like an architect's blueprints. Federal law demanded a seven-day wait in order to purchase a gun—too long to maintain the courage to pull the trigger. Hanging presented problems, too. Where would she tie the rope? The banister? Where could she learn to tie a noose? What if her neck didn't snap and she had to dangle there choking to death? How painful would that be? Carbon monoxide poisoning, on the other hand, might work. It would be painless. She'd fall asleep first, her last conscious moments nothing more than a fleeting dream.

That night after the party she had her chance. I was asleep, exhausted from my birthday party. My father had gone to work unexpectedly as a storm cell ripped through the southern tip of the metro. When she stepped outside, she could hear the thunder rumbling moments after the lightning flash. It was quite fitting in a way, she thought, how those charged electrons spread like finger bones and then sparked to darkness once all the energy had been consumed—her own life was a minutia of overwhelming intensity that drove her to this point in her life, to wink out in a moment, leaving no trace behind that she ever existed with the exception of those that happened to have seen it, and only then in memories that would become dimmer with each second that passed by.

She sat in her car, a charming little thing Marcus had bought her after she'd successfully argued for life for those meth dealers. It was a comfortable place as any to die. The leather seats had warmers so that she wouldn't get cold during the winter. All her music had been placed in the twenty-five-disc CD player. That way she could listen to Vivaldi or Bowie or even Prince if she wanted to. She chose not to play anything, though. Her death shouldn't have a soundtrack.

She turned the key and hoped the reverberation of the engine wouldn't wake me. When I didn't immediately come down, she figured it hadn't. Spring storms must've conditioned me to sleep through anything. The smell surprised her. Of course she had smelled exhaust fumes before, the hint of gasoline and motor oil, but never in such a cramped space so that the plumes had nowhere to go.

It took longer than she'd expected. For several minutes she sat there. She tried to close her eyes and go to sleep. She leaned the chair back so that she could lie down, but the driver side didn't recline as far as the passenger. She got out and changed seats. She grabbed the blanket she kept in the trunk for emergencies and wrapped herself up. She started to feel lightheaded and then nauseated. Her vision blurred, and she could see stars. She felt high, like back in college when she'd used to smoke pot. Her mind began to wander. Should she have written a note? The thought hadn't even occurred to her to do so until now. What could she say, really? That she was sorry? She was a little bit, she supposed. It wasn't fair to Marcus or to Coulter. They would have to deal with the mess she made. With the body. A funeral. Mourning her death. They would have to find some new balance in their lives, reorganize, and put on a brave face to the world when they didn't quite understand what had happened. She had seemed happy, hadn't she? What else could she have wanted? She had a successful career, a loving husband, a bright if a little introverted child. They wouldn't be able to make sense of it. For that then, she needed to leave a note, if only to provide some sort of clarity.

She left the car running when she went inside and got a notepad and pen from the junk drawer in the kitchen. She sat at the bar and wondered how to begin. Do suicide notes have salutations? Dear Marcus? Dear Marcus and Coulter? Just their names maybe? Or should she just delve right into the body? And where exactly should she start? Like writing a brief she started to make bullet points—the loathing, the chemical imbalances, the way she hated herself and her family. She scratched that last part out. Or should she keep it?

"Mom?" I stood at the bottom of the stairs rubbing the sleep from my eyes. "Can I get a glass of water?"

She put the pen down and tore up her scribbled notes, dumping them in the trash on her way to the kitchen. "Of course, honey," she said. "Ice or no ice?"

It was three weeks later when she left. At first she had every intention of returning, once she got some help. But as each day passed it became harder to do so. The rest, she said, doesn't really matter.

"No," I said. "It does. I want to know."

She obliged, telling stories about where she'd been, what she'd done, and what she had seen. "There's an epidemic in this country," she said. "Depression, mania, schizophrenia, antisocial disorder. Worst of all, our healthcare system doesn't have the resources to provide what's necessary. I mean, it's better than it was sixty years ago, don't get me wrong, but doctors have patients in the hundreds, when they should only have about thirty or thirty-five tops. The overflow, the deemed incurable, is institutionalized, heavily medicated so that they're just waste-producers. Wipe their asses, change their diaper, and they're good to go. It's sad. It really is."

"It sounds terrible," I said. "Sort of like *One Flew Over the Cuckoo's Nest*."

"I'm not saying there's a Nurse Ratchett abusing people by any means," she said. "The nurses and doctors, they care. They do. They're just overworked, and, as a consequence, people aren't getting the help they need."

"But you did?" I asked. "You're all better?"

"No, honey. No. No. It's not like a cold. It's sort of like drug addiction. I struggle every day. Every day I can smile is a good day."

"But here you are."

"Yes," Natalie said. "Here I am."

She was quiet for some time. She glanced around the church like how I imagined a discoverer might, Columbus or Magellan, finding herself in a distant and never-before-seen land. Her mission was to observe the natives in their natural habitat, analyze their habits, their motives, their desires and flaws and idiosyncrasies, their culture, then report back to the King.

"How long were you institutionalized?" I asked.

"I hate that word," Natalie said. "'Institutionalized.' It sounds like I was a prisoner of some sort."

"I'm sorry," I said.

"It's okay," Natalie said. "I received inpatient treatment for three years."

"Three years?"

"I'm sorry," she said. "That was a lie. It was six months. Discharged to a halfway house for a few more months until I could find a job, a place of my own." She took a tube of Chapstick out of her purse, applied it liberally. "Not all times were bad. For a few years there, I lived with a man in Boulder. His name was Gary. He owned a gourmet sandwich shop in the Pearl Street Mall. Great sandwiches. Place smelled of sauerkraut and pickles all the time. He collected rare books. We woke up at dawn and baked fresh bread. It was really great for a while. Idealized. Clichéd. What every woman wants, what years of romantic comedies will do to you. We started talking about marriage. About kids."

"What happened?" I asked.

"I entertained the idea for a while. We went ring shopping. We put in an offer or two on a house. I got scared. I left."

"Didn't you love him?" I asked.

"No. I did." She smiled, turned a little red from embarrassment, and glanced at the door like she expected either this man or the husband she'd left to be standing there. "It was more complicated than that, though."

"Maybe we shouldn't talk about this right now," I said. "Maybe it's best if we don't get too personal—"

"No," Natalie raised her hand, cutting me off, "it's okay. I want to answer your questions." She returned the Chapstick to her purse, searched for something else hidden near the bottom but pulled out nothing. "He had a daughter, about your age. She was a nice girl, named Jessica, about sixteen when I knew her. She had a wild streak in her, though. She often snuck out of the house and went partying with older boys, students at the college there. Sometimes we'd be called at all hours of the night, a girlfriend of hers would tell us that we needed to come pick her up, that she was passed out and naked and she was afraid what might happen to her. We tried everything—grounding her, taking her to counseling, AA meetings, even one of those scared-straight things where we took her to a local prison and the inmates yelled at her and showed her what life was like behind bars. None of it worked, though. We found pot and pills and liquor in her room. She wound up getting pregnant, knocked up by a sophomore at the university."

"Let me guess," I said. "Her behavior got worse about the time you showed up."

Natalie nodded.

"And you blamed yourself."

She nodded again. "I felt like I was ruining their lives."

A young couple entered the church. Both were dressed in what I assumed to be their Sunday best, he in pressed wool slacks, and she in a dress and pea coat. They weren't new garments, but they were well taken care of. Natalie and I watched as they made their way down the aisle. Near the pulpit, they kneeled and crossed themselves, their heads bowed before the crucified Christ. As they began to pray, I turned toward Natalie who watched the young couple, a look of disdain etched into her expression. She felt superior to them. She felt contempt. As if their faith was an affront to reason and common sense. As if she knew something that they, or I for that matter, didn't.

"I'd really like it if you stayed with us," I said.

Natalie turned to me and blinked in surprise. It didn't last long, though. She turned back to the couple, and her expression returned to one of superiority.

"I would like that," she said. "Thank you."

Sara and he were having a good night. They were at Fenway Park, despite Sara being only a few weeks out from her due date, watching the Red Sox play the Yankees. It was an important game, although Coulter didn't know why. He'd never really followed baseball, but he could surmise that since it was late fall, and baseball was played outside, that this was an important game. That, and the crowd seemed riled up, waving Styrofoamed hands in the air and screaming beer-induced obscenities at Derek Jeter. Thirty thousand fans were standing and dancing in the aisles, waving little white towels emblazoned with the Red Sox logo above their heads or pointing to the sky with those inordinately large foam hands which indicated that their team and no one else's was number one. Normally Coulter couldn't care less about sports—and neither did Sara as far as he knew—but tonight he found himself a part of the mob. The collusive environment enthralled him. He imagined being a single hydrogen nucleus inside the sun powering it alongside billions of others just like him through nuclear fusion. The energy that radiated from this place was that powerful. Besides that, though, the tickets were free, a gift from Dr. Brinkman.

Dr. Brinkman and his wife were there with them. They had been gone for a while now, though, leaving just after the first inning to pay a visit to the gift shop. It was now the bottom of the fourth, and Coulter was starting to get worried. Dr. Brinkman had been distant the entire first inning, leaning forward in his seat, chomping on sunflower seeds, the remnants of salted shells sticking to the corners of his mouth, ignoring Coulter's attempts to spark some sort of conversation toward his research. In fact, Dr. Brinkman hadn't said a word to Coulter all night, from when they'd picked Coulter and Sara up from their apartment to when Mrs. Brinkman suggested that she and the doctor go shopping. It was odd; now that Coulter thought about it, *really* thought about it, he couldn't remember Dr. Brinkman making a noise all night. By this he meant not just language or communication, but even a slight moan from enjoying his hotdog or the clogged coughs of clearing his throat or even a heavy sigh when he realized a large man blocked his view of home plate. It was like he'd been muted. This, of course, couldn't be true. Could it? Coulter had to be misremembering. Or hallucinating. He started to worry. No. Calm down. He couldn't be hallucinating. Dr. Brinkman had just been quiet, that's all. Sure. No big deal. Long day. He could empathize.

Coulter breathed. He tried to forget that his hosts had been gone for nearly an hour. He tried to enjoy the game. He tried to forget the stale smell of beer and relish that wafted over him and focus on the white ball zooming across the diamond, the smack of the leather as it collided with Dustin Pedroia's glove, the metal spikes digging into the moist infield. He'd never realized how scientific a game baseball was. Hitting a pitch was an awesome mathematical calculation. The scoreboard showed the previous pitch had blazed by at a whopping ninety-eight miles-per-hour. That only allowed the hitter a fraction of a second, somewhere along the lines of 300-500 milliseconds to calculate, unconsciously, the directional vectors, spin, angle, and velocity and then unload his swing so that a small cylindrical bat, roughly 2 5/8 inches in diameter, would collide with said baseball. It was miraculous, really, a testament to the boggling powers of human capability.

Big Papi, David Ortiz, a name even Coulter knew, stood at the plate, swinging his hips in rhythm in order to establish his timing. His entire body was in motion, a harbinger of kinetic energy. The pitcher released the ball. It looped almost vertically from his fingertips to Ortiz's waistline on the inside corner of the plate. Ortiz swung and connected, and as the ball rocketed through the air toward the right-center-field gap, Coulter pictured calculations spurring from the baseball itself, continually changing in mid-flight, a sort-of mindless sensory hallucination.

"Jesus!" he exclaimed, "Did you see that!?" And his wife, seemingly bored and uncomfortable in the small, plastic seats, said, "Yep, sure did," without the slightest trace of enthusiasm.

He tried blinking his eyes, but the numbers and equations still floated there, tracing the ball wherever it went. He rubbed his eyes, shook his head, and the formulas blurred to the point he convinced himself that they had just been a figment of his imagination, but then gridlines reappeared, diagrams, and graphed predictions of how the ball would fly along certain vectors. Coulter began to get worried. Was this healthy? Was he going crazy? First Dr. Brinkman not making any noise, not even the slight sound of his breath, and now this? He hadn't been sleeping much lately. The baby was getting closer, only a few weeks away now, his dissertation was going nowhere, the math just felt right, but he could not, for the life of him, find the evidence, the proof, that little smoking gun he could point to and say Here! I've done it! I have proven the ultimate theory of everything!

Adrian Gonzalez came up to the plate, the big, left-handed power-hitter for the Red Sox. He dug his spikes into the dirt and readied for the pitch, his body spring-loaded to deliver as much mass and velocity he could muster. The pitch came, and the same grids and measurements emerged from thin-air. Coulter leaned forward in his seat studying them as Gonzalez swung and connected, and the ball rocketed foul down the first baseline, right for Coulter and Sara. The people around them squirmed, some bracing for impact, others readied their gloves, some simply ducked, but Coulter stood mesmerized and watched the ball travel a nearly level path from home plate to just behind the dugout where they sat until the ball struck his wife's pregnant belly.

BACK AT HOME, SARA AND I ARGUED. "ARGUED" actually isn't the right word—it seems to denote some sort of debate, two opposing sides on equal footing. We, on the other hand, fought. We were not trying to persuade the other of the merits of our position. No, what we wanted was to induce shame and guilt and pain. When we fought, Sara's anger escalated quickly and the tenor of her voice would become sharp and she often threw things: TV remotes and books and knick knacks given to us by her mother, bits of plastic shattering when it struck wall or tile. I would poke holes in her argument, try to make her feel more stupid than me, confuse her until she became so frustrated that she relented, spent the rest of the night flipping through bad sitcoms and not saying another word. She always said I never fought fairly. I maintained that we'd never established ground rules in the first place.

"What the hell do you mean she's staying with us?" Sara asked. We were in our bedroom, the door shut. We were both aware, however, that our conversation was audible in the living room where my mother was sitting, her unpacked bag at her feet. "You didn't think it appropriate to ask me if your mother—who abandoned you as a child—could live with us?"

"She's not living with us," I said. "She's just staying for a little while."

"How long exactly is a little while?"

"I don't know. Until the baby is born maybe."

"No. No. Absolutely not. That woman will not be around our baby." Sara waved her arms like a football referee calling a no-catch after a bobbled ball.

"She's *my* mother. Will you please let *me* handle this?" It was the first time I'd called her "mother" since I'd been a child, and the words felt wrong in my mouth, like soured milk.

"That's pretty loose terminology there with 'mother,' don't you think?"

"I'm not getting into a semantic argument with you. She gave birth to me. I share her DNA. Yes, she is my mother."

"That's like saying an organ donor is a recipient's first cousin."

"With the exception the organ donor didn't carry the recipient around in her womb for nine months."

"And they didn't abandon them when the recipient needed them the most, now did they?"

"You really know nothing about it."

"That's because you never share anything with me, Coulter! I know really nothing about you before we started dating! It's like you popped into existence when I finally said that I would go out with you."

"That's just irrational. Everybody has a past."

"Then what is yours? Can you tell me that?"

"You're avoiding the central argument here."

"I'm not! The point is that she'll do the same thing to our son as she did to you. He'll get to know her and love her and depend on her, and then she'll disappear again."

I couldn't rule out that possibility. She very well could spend years getting to know our son, attending birthday parties and playing G. I. Joe and concocting little inside jokes, secrets only they knew and never would tell, and then, without warning, she could vanish, leaving our son bewildered like I'd been, with an aching void of what once was there, what he thought to be someone who loved him. We would probably lie to him at first, Sara and I, much like my father had to me. Grandma went on vacation, we'd say. She's travelling Europe, seeing the Leaning Tower of Pisa and the Mona Lisa and drinking sweet wine. He'll buy it. He'll still make her Christmas presents and send her emails and pray for her before falling asleep. But the lies will turn less convincing as more time passes. We'll try to contact her, but her phone will have been disconnected—no one would have been paying the bill. To at least introduce some closure, we'll lie some more and say she'd died. We already had a funeral, we'll say when he asks. We just thought it would be better if you didn't attend. You'll understand when you get older.

"I'm worried about you," Sara continued. "You haven't been the same lately. You're out all hours of the night. You don't come home. Even when I needed you, when I was in trouble and in the hospital, you—"

"I'm *working*. I am doing that for us. You know that!"

Interrupting her made her angrier. She twisted strands of hair around her finger and pulled them out by the roots, a nervous habit she'd had for as long as I'd known her. When particularly stressed, a bald spot would grow around her right temple. She'd try to hide it by wearing wool hats or styling her hair differently, but she couldn't keep her guard up all the time—eventually I'd find out, and I'd point it out as inconspicuously as possible, like it was no big deal, and she'd say that everything was fine, just fine.

"There's been a change in you, Coulter. And don't say you haven't noticed. Ever since the semester started you've been distant and argumentative and defensive."

"Maybe I'm just tired of you telling me how it's going to be."

"See. Right there. You don't *see* that?"

"All I know is that you're wrong. Can you admit that? For once in your life can you admit that you don't know everything?"

"Me? Out of the two of us, you're saying I'm the know-it-all? Mr. I-am-God's-greatest-gift-to-the-world-of-science? I can't talk to you right now. I can't."

Sara grimaced and grabbed her stomach and buckled over. I instinctually went to her, not knowing how to help, but before I could reach her, she raised a hand to stop me.

"Is it where you got hit?" I asked.

"What?" she asked through clenched teeth.

"Where you were hit. At the game."

"What game?" She stood, breathing through her mouth. Her face was flushed, and sweat formed in beads around her hairline.

"What do you mean what game? The baseball game. Red Sox? When we went with Dr. Brinkman. The foul ball?"

"What are you talking about? We've never been to a baseball game with Dr. Brinkman."

I paused, trying to think back. We had gone to a baseball game, hadn't we? Or was it just a false memory, a daydream I'd confused as reality? The details had been so *real*. I could taste the salt from the peanuts I'd eaten. I could feel the chair's metal arms digging into my side. I could hear organ music blaring over speakers much younger than rickety Fenway Park. I could feel my heart rate quicken and my endorphins flow when I'd realized Dr. Brinkman had turned mute. The light from the rafters brightened and my pupils dilated as calculations materialized out of nowhere. Dreams have this surrealistic quality. The world seems fluid. Emotions are dulled. Time has no meaning. But these, whatever they were, were different. They seemed as real as the red-bricked steeple of Old North Church we'd just left, its white pews and colonnades and clear windows letting in dismal, gray light. I could smell the dirty laundry in our bedroom the same way I could smell the moist dirt of the infield at Fenway. I could still tell the difference between reality and fantasy. I could. I now knew that standing there with Sara arguing was real and that daydream about Fenway Park had not been, that it had been an invention of my subconscious. Yet, I couldn't help but wonder if I'd feel the same exact way in a daydream as I did then, convincing myself in that world that this, looking at my frightened wife, arguing about my mother staying with us, was indeed the fantasy and that, that horrifying place where everything seemed as it did here but with qualities impossible in nature, was in fact reality.

Maybe she was right. Maybe I was changing. Maybe I did need help.

"Will you please go see someone? A doctor. A therapist. A psychic. I don't care." Sara said. "You're really starting to scare me."

"I'm fine."

"You're not. You're not fine. You are the exact opposite of fine."

"I got confused. I dreamt about a game last night. I'm tired. I haven't been sleeping well."

"All the more reason to get some help. Maybe they could prescribe something to help you sleep. Perhaps they can give you some perspective."

"*This* will help me, Sara," I said, pointing toward the living room where Natalie sat. "My mother staying. Getting to know her. Can't you see that? Maybe that's what's missing—closure. Knowing why she left and what she did and why she came back now. Maybe that is what I need. Not some pill."

Sara turned toward the door as if she could see through it, Natalie sitting on the couch, listening to us argue. It was like Sara was measuring Natalie up, deciding whether or not she could win this fight.

"Okay," she said, her expression softening, not out of sympathy or understanding, but out of defeat. She knew she'd lost. "She can stay."

Despite winning, I wasn't relieved. I was scared. I was scared I was starting to lose touch with reality. The more I thought about that night at Fenway, the less it seemed like a dream. There were no physical manifestations, of course. I didn't have a souvenir, an overpriced baseball bought at the gift shop or a plastic helmet that served as an ice cream bowl. I hadn't bought a t-shirt or found a crumpled ticket stub tucked away in my pocket. I didn't suffer a hangover from drinking too many flat beers. I didn't have heartburn after eating a polish dog soaked in mustard and sauerkraut. Nevertheless, I couldn't stop thinking about it. The lights and the crowd and the smack of a bat connecting with a fastball, the clouds of dust as Carlos Beltran slid into second base. It was just as real to me as Natalie returning, Sara's swollen belly, my failing dissertation and the impending embarrassment of being kicked out of the program. With that understanding, the fact that I had a hard time convincing myself it hadn't happened despite the overwhelming evidence to the contrary, I knew Sara to be right—I did need to speak with someone.

Getting an appointment, however, was more difficult than I'd anticipated. The school offered counseling programs free of charge, but attached with using those services came this stigma. It was supposed to be confidential, but people talked. Staff talked. Janitors talked. The counselors. Soon, faculty, your dissertation committee, the other PhD candidates, they'd look at you with suspicion, doubtful you could cut the rigors of theoretical physics. Though academic, cutting edge scholarship was by its very nature cutthroat. Published articles were difficult to come by, breakthroughs even scarcer, and grant dollars on the endangered species list. Any sign of weakness could derail a career before it even started with rumors spread about mental instability, depression, hallucinations even. You'd be labeled a charlatan before you'd even had the chance to prove yourself.

So I called around. I called private psychiatrists throughout Boston. Most had waiting lists, were not taking on any more patients, or solidly booked for months to come. I supposed Natalie had been right; we were facing an epidemic in this country. The ones that did have openings were way out of my price range, quoting hourly rates in excess of $200. Insurance wouldn't cover it—not that I would've claimed it anyway, too afraid to start a paper trail.

Without any other options, I decided to ask Dr. Brinkman. I trusted him, and he would, I believed anyway, keep it discreet. He expressed concern when I asked, asking if I was sure I wanted to do this, but when I said yes, I was certain, he recommended Dr. White, the chair of the Department of Brain and Cognitive Sciences at MIT, and she agreed to see me right away as a favor to Dr. Brinkman.

I met her in her office on campus, tucked away in Kendall Square. Framed degrees lined her walls like family portraits: Oxford, Johns Hopkins, Stanford, University of Chicago, PhDs in psychology and neurobiology. Artwork adorned her bookshelves, small expressionist paintings of human subjects, a certain portion of their bodies distorted, akin to some Van Gogh inspiration. One man's right hand ballooned to impossible proportions, another woman's head so small it seemed a speck above an otherwise normal human body, hard angles not found on any person who ever lived.

Dr. White herself appeared out of proportion. Her head seemed too small for her body, her ears large and a bit pointy. Her arms were gangly and her legs thin, so much so it amazed me they could withhold her body weight. She seemed elfish in a way. But, despite that, she had a warm presence to her, a smile that was genuine and welcoming. As soon as I walked into her office, I felt better, relaxed, as though all the anxiety and pressure of my dissertation and the baby and my mother had drained from my body.

She had me sit in a chair facing her. A tape recorder sat on a stool between us, but it wasn't recording. She had no other documents out. Not records from the physics department. She didn't have a computer of any sort. A filing cabinet wasn't stored away in the corner. I found this to be odd. I figured she must have the best memory in the world.

"Where do we begin?" I asked.

"Let's begin with why you're here." Her voice had a throaty, soothing quality, the way a raspy country singer can swoon a ballad.

Under normal circumstances, I would've probably lied. I kept myself guarded. It was a learned trait, not intrinsic, but more of a survival instinct, a type of occupational Darwinism.

"We're protected here, right?" I asked. "Doctor-patient confidentiality and all that."

"For the most part, yes."

"The most part?"

"If you plan on killing someone, yourself included, I would have to report that."

"But beyond that?"

"Our little secret." She winked. I trusted this woman, although I'd only just met her. She put me at ease so that I felt I could disclose anything to her. Besides my wife, I'd never felt that way toward anyone.

"I've been having these dreams lately." She leaned forward and clicked on the tape recorder. "But I'm awake."

"Daydreams."

"Not exactly." I explained them to her in great detail. I told her of dreams I had where I was alone, of me urinating my pants when accepting the Nobel, how I could feel the warmth flow down my inner thighs and how I could smell ammonia. I told her of chasing a tornado with my father and how that might've actually happened, I wasn't sure, and that it was the first time I was ever conscious of becoming aroused. I told her of seeing my mother at a religious commune in California hugging newly-arrived members mere months after she'd abandoned me. I explained to her that they were vivid hallucinations. I would lose blocks of time, black out from reality, and wake up on the floor unable to catch my breath, how I could still taste the salt from my peanuts eaten at an imagined baseball game even though I became fully aware of my return to reality. I explained to her, with as much aplomb as I could muster, that my mother had recently returned, how fragile a state of mind she appeared to be in, and how I was now deathly afraid of winding up like her, an unfit human being, scared of everything around me. I was afraid

I'd lose my mind and abandon my wife and child.

I confessed all this like a tire hemorrhaging air pressure. In one big, satisfying rush, I told her things I'd never told anyone, things I was barely conscious of myself, and as I spoke, Dr. White hardly moved. But she was attentive. The way she held her mouth slightly ajar, I got the feeling of overwhelming empathy, as if she could experience my fear through some sort of cosmic osmosis. She had a motherly way about her, gentle and caring, though I noticed no pictures of family, only her paintings of people that did not resemble people, just a mash of human characteristics, an eye here, an eyebrow there, a foot turned to an impossible angle.

"Recently," I continued. "I've been confusing them with my actual memories. It takes a while for me to register if a memory occurred or if it was one of these hallucinations. I'm never entirely sure, though."

Dr. White nodded knowingly, like this was nothing to be alarmed at. "I would like for you to do something for me." She reached into a drawer in her desk and pulled out a stack of paper and a pencil. "Draw a picture of your family. Don't worry about your artistic prowess. This isn't a contest. But I do ask you not to draw stick figures and that you draw the entire body, not just a portion."

I wondered who I should include, what she meant by "family." My immediate family? My wife? My unborn son? Father? Cousins? Grandparents? She filled in the time I spent thumping the eraser against the paper with small talk. She asked me about the University of Oklahoma, if I missed it there—she had visited once on a speaking tour and thought Norman was a lovely town. I loved the way she said "lovely," like how hot caramel slides down melting ice cream. She asked if I was married, and I answered in the affirmative, and she told me about her three husbands, all dead now, one murdered, another heart attack, and the third in a car accident, strange she didn't have pictures, but no children, though. How about you, she asked, and I told her about Sara and I expecting, and she congratulated me, again warmly, with the utmost sincerity.

"Let me see your picture," she said.

I'd drawn a picture of my family, not even recollecting that I'd made a decision on who to draw or even putting pencil to paper. There were three of us, Sara, me, and the baby. We weren't holding him. He was on the ground, swaddled and off to the side. Sara and I looked forward, but had no faces.

"Have you ever driven someplace," Dr. White said, "perhaps someplace that you're used to going to, home maybe, or work, and minutes will go by on your commute, but you have no memory of actually driving. You'll all of a sudden find yourself in front of your house or your office, but you don't remember if you had to stop at a red light or if you saw the mailman delivering letters or if you had to swerve around a familiar neighbor taking an early morning walk? Your mind was elsewhere. You were thinking of your day ahead, meetings you had scheduled, problems that needed to be addressed, something you had said to your wife before you left that morning, rushing to get that last drop of coffee in before you walked out the door."

"I suppose," I said. "I'm sure that happens."

"Would you say that you were unconscious then?"

"Well, no. I couldn't have been unconscious."

"Or you would've driven off the road, right?"

"Sure. Yeah. I guess."

"But no matter how hard you tried you couldn't remember it."

"So you're saying that maybe I don't lose touch with reality during these hallucinations?"

"Maybe," she said. She took my picture from me, stared at it for a good long while, nodded, and then put it down on her desk. "Have you heard of heterophenomenology, Mr. Zahn?"

"Heterophenomenology?"

"Yes."

"I haven't."

"It's a scientific, objective approach to the human consciousness. As a heterophenomenologist, I do not take any opinion other than what you tell me is fact, as you perceive it. If you tell me something happened, then it happened. Though, I don't try to understand what is causing you to believe what you say. You could have experienced it, yes. But you could also be controlled by a computer program, say, that spits out a stream of thousands of digits of binary code. Or you could be a zombie, dead inside, yet somehow speaking, or maybe controlled by Descartes's demons, a poltergeist masking as a soul."

"You're not serious."

"I am, Mr. Zahn."

She crossed her legs. Varicose veins crisscrossed her ankles, and her skin was so pale I thought I could see the blood flow through her capillaries. The stream appeared to float in blobs much like a lava lamp would, and I blinked several times thinking that I was about to black out again and slip into one of my hallucinations or maybe her slow, raspy voice was somehow hypnotizing me.

"So you think I'm a zombie?"

"I didn't say that. My point is that I can't make a judgment about your condition as something wrong or unhealthy or as an illness."

"I see."

"What do you think is causing your condition?"

"Stress probably. Sleep deprivation. Maybe genetics. A brain tumor."

"All possibilities, I suppose." She grabbed another piece of paper. "I would like for you to draw another picture for me. Your home."

This time she didn't feel the need for chitchat, instead letting me focus on my drawing. I drew a street view of our apartment complex, and once complete, she took it from me and dropped it atop her desk without taking the time to look at it.

"I'd like to run an experiment," she said. "Would you be okay with that?"

"What kind of experiment?"

"A simple cognitive exercise."

"Can you be more specific?"

"A light experiment. Color. I want you to tell me what you see."

"Sure."

She readied a projector and aimed it at a white, bare wall. She dimmed the lights and clicked on the machine. A humming noise followed by a clicking filled the silence.

"Ready?" she asked.

"Yes."

A red circle illuminated against the wall. At first it was static, but then it moved rapidly to the right and as it did it turned into a green color.

"What did you see?"

I told her.

"Are you sure?"

"Yes."

"At first it was red, but then it moved fluidly to the right and somewhere in the middle it turned green?"

"Yes.".

She smiled. Again her smile was warm, and it made me feel comfortable. My muscles relaxed, and I could feel the apprehension draining from my body, the knots in my shoulders and neck dissolving. She had a powerful quality about her, like her presence could be used as an anesthesia.

"What if I told you that is not what actually occurred?" she said. "The tape is one red circle followed by a green circle three inches to the right. Two distinct pictures separated by 500 milliseconds."

"I would believe you."

"But you saw the circle move between a space where there actually wasn't a circle."

"Yes."

"Does it not startle you that your consciousness somehow filled in a circle where there was no circle, it not only traversing time and space but also the color spectrum when in fact it didn't?"

"I would say it's fascinating."

"This phenomenon is well-documented. It's one of the reasons why films seem fluid. The color-phi."

"I'm sorry?"

"That's what the phenomenon is called." She paused a moment as if allowing me to digest what she'd just revealed. "Do you not see the implications of such a phenomenon?"

"I'm sorry. I don't."

"It means that our consciousness is fundamentally flawed," she said. "Two scenarios are possible. In one, there is a Stalinesque rewriting of our consciousness. We perceive the one green light and then a distinct red light shifted to the right; however, a master editor revises this conscious experience with what you have just reported to me, the one circle moving fluidly and changing color, with the first conscious experience completely erased from your memory. Or," she lifted her finger in the air as if making a very important point, "an Orwellian editor is somehow editing the information that streams in from your eyeballs before it can reach the master control center in the brain where consciousness occurs."

What she said made sense, and I could tell by the way she melted into her chair, a pleased smile spread across her elfish face, that she could see the idea register in me. I was intrigued. The implications of such revisionism could, in some sense anyway, unravel the mystery of my hallucinations. My consciousness could be being rewritten by my very brain, some sort of Stalinesque mechanism being activated for some reason, perhaps in a defensive posture, repressing harmful memories and replacing them with lurid trappings of my subconscious.

"How do we stop this revision from occurring?" I asked.

Noah Milligan

"You can't," she said. "It's an intrinsic part of human consciousness that has evolved over millions of years."

She reached back into her desk and pulled out a rectangular cardboard pack. It was purple, with large, flowing script. Systique, it said. 150 mg. A larger name was printed underneath, a long string of consonants practically illegible to me.

"What's that?" I asked.

"A sample of a medication I would like you to try."

"These will help?"

"It depends on what you mean by 'help.'"

"Will they slow down these revisions?"

"No."

"No?"

"I want to propose something," she said. She opened the pack. Inside were seven bubbles filled with rectangular pink pills. "Something that is a bit, well, experimental. As a scientist I would think you might be a little more open to the suggestion than some of my other patients."

There seemed to be two voices competing for my attention inside my head. One was telling me to beware, while the other completely trusted Dr. White. She picked lint off her black pants as she spoke, her warm and peering eyes still locked on me, unblinking, but her fingers picked away, like a chimpanzee looking for lice in the coat of his brother. Her gaze made me trust her. Her eyes were deep and brown and rich, like freshly brewed coffee, and just as comforting. But her ability to perform such detailed tasks at the same time while not devoting her full attention unnerved me, like she might have ulterior intentions just below the surface, ones that she didn't even know that she was constructing, but still they were there, implacable and unavoidable.

"What does it do?" I asked, pointing at the pills.

"They will accelerate what you call your hallucinations. Make them more intense."

"Why would you want to do that? I came here for help."

"I believe this will help. Think about it, Mr. Zahn. Your subconscious is revising your memories for a reason. We could take a traditional treatment course, numb your senses, disable some of the chemical secretions in the brain, slow down the electrical circuitry so that you don't feel a thing. That would stop these revisionist histories replacing your own, but at what cost? You wouldn't be able to function. You wouldn't be able to finish your dissertation. You wouldn't be the same husband to your wife or the same father to your son. You wouldn't be yourself. This way we might sooner discover why your mind is behaving in this manner, and either correct the error that is occurring or—"

"Or?"

"Exploit it."

"This is crazy."

"What you're experiencing might very well be an evolutionary step in cognizance."

"Or I could be suffering from severe problems."

"All I am asking is that you think about it."

She stood and glanced at her watch. Our time was up. She hadn't stood since I'd arrived. She was even shorter than I'd anticipated, only coming up to about my armpits.

"You have a good day, Mr. Zahn."

As she showed me to the door, she pushed the packet of pills into my hand.

𝓧

Marcus felt dirty. He wanted to take a shower and scrub the first two layers of skin off. He wanted to burn his clothes. He wanted to sandpaper his bones. He wanted to do anything he could to get Dianne's smell off of him, whatever that took, if it meant scraping it off with a paring knife, burning it with a blowtorch, even tearing it off with his fingernails, but, most of all, he wanted to grab Coulter and hug him and make sure that Natalie hadn't already found out and taken his son away from him.

Not that it excused his infidelity, but he and Natalie hadn't touched each other intimately for some time now—six, eight, nine months maybe. And when they had, it'd seemed so cold. Their lovemaking was a chore like washing the dishes or trimming the hedges. Natalie wouldn't look at him, instead opting to lie on her side while he scooted in behind her. She didn't move. She clasped her hands underneath her chin and didn't blink as if she was daydreaming. Was she trying to picture herself someplace else? With another man? Was she scanning the grocery list by memory or checking off the bills that were due? Should that bother him? After fifteen years of marriage? Was that justification enough to cheat on his wife? He knew it wasn't. But that hadn't stopped him.

The thing that bothered him most, though, more than the infidelity itself, was that he knew he would not fire Dianne, and he would, if the opportunity arose, do it again and again and again. He would go out of his way to initiate it, in fact. He would, now that he had touched her, that soft flesh, the way her sweat tasted strangely of grapefruit, buy sleazy motel rooms at hourly rates, meet her at her apartment, risk a sexual tryst at work, in the editing room post broadcast. He'd try to tell himself not to, remind himself of all that he could lose. His son. How would he be able to live if he couldn't see his son every day? But he was weak. The first opportunity that presented itself, he would fall deeply into Dianne.

His house appeared quiet, which was good. Natalie and Coulter must be asleep. The storm he was chasing had left the metro hours ago. Usually Natalie didn't watch the news and simply waited for Marcus to call. "Take cover," he'd say. "It's bearing down on you right now." Coulter would probably be asleep in his parents' bed, cuddled up next to his mother. Despite being highly intelligent for his age, he still harbored an irrational fear of thunder and lightning. Marcus could see in his face that he still believed monsters lived in his closet and came out on Halloween and stormy nights to eat children. Natalie would have a file open on her lap, a brief she needed to finish in the morning or notes for an opening statement or a piece of evidence. She brought work into bed every night now. She claimed she was simply busy and overworked and trying to get that promotion. Marcus didn't quite believe her, though. Her ambition was part of it, sure, but he couldn't help but feel that she intentionally filled every moment of her waking life so she wouldn't have to face him anymore.

He was right; Coulter was asleep in his parents' bed, curled around a body pillow that was almost as big as he was. He had his thumb stuck in his mouth. Damn near twelve and still sucking his thumb. It was a habit he and Natalie had been trying to get Coulter to break, but he wouldn't stop. They just didn't understand it. Their doctor had said it was a comforting reaction to external, unpleasant stimuli, but they had no idea what could be causing it. He and Natalie never fought, not where they screamed and cried and threw things anyway, and never where Coulter could hear them. He never complained of being bullied at school, although Marcus had the suspicion that he might be. He didn't come home with bruises or in tears from names he'd been called. But he was such a gangly kid, prone to get lost in a book rather than playing video games or talking on the phone with a friend. He was the type of kid Marcus would have bullied when he was in school.

But where was Natalie? Her side of the bed seemed untouched. Worried, Marcus walked downstairs. The throw blanket she kept in the living room was neatly folded atop the arm of the couch. The television was mute, the remote control stored neatly away in a glass container on the coffee table. The kitchen was empty—she wasn't making a late night sandwich or enjoying a glass of wine before going off to bed. Nothing seemed to be out of place. The office was quiet, the computer monitor dark. It was like she'd disappeared, left her child sleeping unattended.

That wasn't like her.

There, on the foyer table, was a ring, reflecting the scant light filtering in through the window. Had that been there this morning when he'd left for work? Natalie had left before he had, and she wasn't one to just leave jewelry lying around. It was her wedding band. In fifteen years of marriage, he'd never known her to take it off. She had even worn it while scuba diving last year on their trip to the Cayman Islands when the instructor had warned the pressure would make her finger feel as though it were being clamped to the bone. He picked it up and twirled it between his fingers. The metal felt cool.

Marcus was scared. She hadn't answered when he called earlier. The phone went straight to voicemail.

That's when Marcus heard a low rumbling, like a car engine. Confused, he walked slowly to the garage where he found Natalie, killing herself by carbon monoxide poisoning. He could hardly breathe. The fumes filled his lungs, and he couldn't find any traces of oxygen. He pushed the button to open the door and rushed to his wife's side. There was a pulse; she was still alive, thank God. He grabbed her underneath her arms and dragged her out onto the driveway where she wheezed for air. She didn't wake right away, though, her eyelids fluttering, her breaths escaping in short wheezy gasps, and Marcus let her lay. He didn't call an ambulance or a doctor or ask the neighbors for help; instead, he waited until she woke up on her own. When she came to, he didn't say a word, just went back into the house and shut the door behind him.

The next time Marcus lay with Dianne was the next morning. Surprisingly, he didn't feel any guilt at all.

DR. BRINKMAN AND I HEADED TOWARD THE MIT Sailing Pavilion to take his skiff out for a spin. Unseasonably warm for September, undergraduates assembled in Killian Court. They enjoyed lunch and spread out their study materials over quilts. A few boys sporting backward hats and gym shorts threw around a Frisbee, trying to impress girls reciting Sylvia Plath underneath an oak tree. They all seemed so relaxed, carefree even. They were months away from the stresses of final exams. They didn't have nervous tension built up in their shoulder blades, making it impossible to turn their necks. They were joyous. They frolicked and laughed and showed off. They were, undeniably, happy.

I couldn't help but feel a strong contrast to their sentiments, as if I represented some sort of polarized dichotomy, an opposite charge to bring balance to the ecosystem. Dr. Brinkman had scheduled our meeting to discuss my research progress. The problem was that I hadn't made any progress. The model was built, sure, but I had not stumbled upon any findings. Not one manifold had been able to satisfy a single subset of matrix parameters, not to mention the needed 118 to be remotely passable. I felt like a fraud. I had no idea what I was doing, or what I was going to do. Dr. Brinkman hadn't broached the subject as of yet, though, commenting instead on the Red Sox's run in the playoffs. They were playing inter-divisional foe, the Tampa Bay Rays, for a spot in the AL playoffs. Going into the last game of the series, they had identical records, the winner almost guaranteed a date with the dreaded Yankees come October. They played that night at Fenway, and Dr. Brinkman had tickets.

"You and Sara should join us," he said. "We have two extra, and I'd much rather hang out with you than Dr. Cardoza." He made a face like he'd just bitten into a sour pickle. "Eeeeck."

"That sounds like fun." It really didn't. It'd be humid at the game, crowded, loud, and Sara would still be pregnant, aching from being squashed into a tiny plastic chair and having only eaten a greasy hotdog doused in relish and sauerkraut. She'd complain because the insides of her thighs would be drenched in sweat, and I'd feel guilty for not staying home and attempting to alter my approach to my research. Not to mention the lucid daydream I'd experienced—that borderline hallucination still haunted me, and I couldn't summon the courage to take the pills prescribed to me by Dr. White. I did not, for the life of me, wish to expedite more of those nightmares. "I'll have to see if Sara is up for it, though."

"Oh, I'm sure she will be. It'll be good for you both," Dr. Brinkman said. "The late summer night. The joyous feeling of camaraderie. Josh Beckett throwing hundred mile-per-hour heat."

"I'm afraid I wouldn't be too much fun. I don't even know who that is."

"You have to be kidding me. How long have you lived in Boston?"

"I've just never been a fan of baseball."

"Don't tell me you're a soccer guy."

"I've never really been interested in sports in general."

"You've always been a science geek, huh?"

He had this pejorative tone that made me feel like I was in high school again. It wasn't that I'd been an unpopular kid or disliked or an outcast. I had friends. Some played sports, the proverbial jocks, I supposed. Greg Adams, a neighbor kid who I'd tag along with to keg parties, wrestled and had even won state his junior year. Granted, I did tutor him and got him academically eligible so he could qualify to attend Oklahoma State. When we'd hung out, I always felt like I had to impress him somehow, so I overcompensated. I oftentimes lied to make myself seem cooler, weaving tales of exploits with girls and small-scale larceny. I'd boast and brag and hope they never found out the truth. I thought I'd gotten over this phase of yearning to be accepted, but here I was again, desperate for Dr. Brinkman to like me, not to respect me, not to find merit in my work, but to find me *cool*.

"I did storm chase with my dad, remember?"

"Yeah, of course. But that's still science-related. Or maybe science-adjacent. Whatever. Did you act or write poetry?"

"No."

"Hike in the woods?"

"No."

"Blow things up with firecrackers?"

"No."

"Get in fights just for the hell of it?"

"No."

"Manage your father's investment portfolio? Anything."

"No. None of those."

"God, you have lived a very boring life, Coulter. Today, we're going to live a little. *Carpe diem* and such. What do you say?"

"I do have a lot of work to do."

"This will help with work. Trust me."

The Sailing Pavilion wasn't very impressive, a small little shack with a dock and a few sailboats harbored there. Despite the new coat of white paint, it still seemed duller than its surroundings, its wooden frame sad in comparison to the majestic architecture of campus, a scorned little brother, separated from the campus by the bustle of Memorial Drive.

Dr. Brinkman's boat, aptly named "Black Hole," was a tiny thing, a Sunfish, Dr. Brinkman said, that barely had enough room to fit two. I didn't see any life preservers either. It wasn't that I could not swim; I'd prided myself on being a strong swimmer in my youth, but that had been years ago, and the Charles stretched wide and far and deep. Then again, my fear didn't so much stem from me falling in and drowning. I probably could still manage myself in the water. Instead, I feared I might jump in, relax my body, and drift toward the bottom. Perhaps I'd even count to see how long it took me to fall asleep. I'd heard drowning, after the initial panic of course, was one of the most comfortable ways to die. I'd pass out from lack of oxygen, then fall into the most relaxing REM sleep I'd ever had.

"Let me guess," Dr. Brinkman said. "You've never been sailing before."

I admitted I had not.

"That's okay," he said. "You just sit back and relax."

We pushed out onto the river. A brisk wind came from the northwest; it would be turning cold soon. I hated the winters in Boston. They transformed the landscape into a dreary gray, the ground covered with snow so that when the wind blew it looked like salt mines. My sinuses bled, and everything tasted of copper. I hadn't brought a jacket and soon I was tense and achy. Dr. Brinkman did all the work, manning the sails and the steering. Not that I would've known what to do, but I couldn't help but feel like a child.

The water chopped against the sides of the boat, and we lurched forward, tilted at an angle so that I had to hold onto the rail.

"How was your meeting with Dr. White?" he asked. "Did it help?"

"It did," I lied, not wanting to admit it had not, that I was still suffering from lucid daydreams and that she, in her professional opinion, thought it best to expedite them, not to make them go away.

"Good," he said. "It's good to get some help every once in a while. Stabilize your focus."

I nodded.

"Not that it's any of my business, but why did you need to see her? No trouble at home, I hope."

"No, no. Nothing like that."

"Good," he said. "Family is what is important. And with the baby on the way..." he trailed off. "Work then?"

"No," I said. "It's nothing serious. Just needed perspective. That's all."

He nodded, tied a rope into a knot around the mast. "I understand completely. Been there myself, actually." He stepped down from the mast and grabbed the wheel of the craft, steered us toward the middle of the river. "How is your work coming?" Dr. Brinkman yelled over the wind, finally broaching the subject we had convened to discuss in the first place. "Well, I hope."

"It is. Yes." I lied again.

"You have pages for me then?"

"I'm tweaking it."

"Tweaking it?"

"The model isn't quite right. My parameters are boundless. I have too many possibilities to reject."

"What?" he yelled over the wind.

"I need to narrow my focus."

"Meaning, you have nothing."

"I'm not worried. A few more edits, and it'll be in your hands."

Dr. Brinkman turned the wheel, and the ship veered right so that we were now parallel with the riverbanks. I sat so that I looked at him in the rear of the ship, part of his face blocked by the flapping sail, the water and city in the distance seemingly travelling away from me. If it wasn't for our velocity pushing against my back, it would appear the world was moving and I was sitting still, an odd phenomenon when you think about it: the relativity of perception.

"Have you thought any more about changing your dissertation?" he asked.

I didn't respond.

"You should really look into the duality of light and Heisenberg's Uncertainty Principle. You have a great grasp of the concepts, and I think you could elucidate new insights into complementarity pairs. Perhaps we could know more about future trajectories, speed, et cetera than our current understanding instructs."

"It's a possibility."

"I can tell by your tone you're not going to."

"I have thought about it."

"But you're not going to change."

"No. Probably not."

"I think you're making a grave mistake, Coulter. Your dissertation, while ambitious, insightful even, is impossible."

"Nothing is impossible."

"Improbable then. As the chair of your dissertation committee, I must advise you change the focus of your research."

"I wouldn't have time. Not if I wanted to graduate on time."

"You wouldn't graduate at all without a completed dissertation."

Ominous clouds moved away from us in the northeast, large cumulonimbus, the color of recently poured blacktop, sporadically brightened with lightning. As a child I had been deathly afraid of lightning, holing up underneath several blankets, a weak plastic flashlight my only company. Dad would be gone, chasing the storms with Dianne, and Mom would be God-knows-where. With each crack, I watched the lightning illuminate the dark sky, feel the reverb of the explosion up my spine. I always expected the initial explosion to continue, to strike our house, and for me to burn to death. To alleviate my fears, Dad had explained to me how lightning worked, the water cycle, how heat evaporated water from the ground so that it turned to vapor, how the vapor rose into the atmosphere, and how, as it cooled, it turned back into water. These molecules would collide, causing electrons to charge; the positive would rise to the top of the system, the negative to the bottom. Air ionization would cause a conductor, and the electrical current would flow to the ground in the form of lightning. Despite the explanation, I was still afraid. It didn't matter the cause, the results were always the same. I was convinced I would, at some point in time, burst into flames.

"We should probably be heading back to the dock!" I yelled over the wind.

"You just have to relax. Quit putting so much pressure on yourself, and the answers will come. You'll find what you're looking for."

Dr. Brinkman thought I was still discussing my dissertation. "No! The storm. The mast will be a lightning rod."

The lightning intensified. It was one of those rare moments where sunshine still beat down on us from the west and above, yet I could feel sprinkles from the storm off in the distance. An odd feeling accompanies such moments, torn between the rapture of a warm, fall day and the fear of an oncoming storm. The slightest move can alter your fate. A slip of the hand and the warm embrace of the sun envelops you, too much force on the jig and your sail will catch the winds and you'll succumb to tumultuous forces of nature. You're acutely aware of how little control you have at such times, that the slightest derailment could cause you to be lost forever.

"The storm's miles away, Coulter. We're fine. Settle down." He smiled and adjusted the Red Sox cap on his head, pulling it tighter around his forehead. "Come."

"I'm sorry?"

"Come over here." He waved me over like he wanted to introduce me to a colleague. "Take the wheel."

"I can't."

"Sure you can. Come."

"I'd really rather not."

"Nothing bad will happen, Coulter. I promise."

Despite my misgivings, I took the wheel. Through the plastic and metal casing, I could feel the motion of the river underneath my fingertips. It was remarkable, even though it was the product of simple physics. Each action accompanied by an equal and opposite reaction. Wind acted upon the water. The water upon the hull. The hull upon the rudder. The rudder to the wheel. The wheel to my hand. However, despite that, there wasn't much control. To test its function, I turned counterclockwise. The sails pivoted, but the angle and direction of the vessel lagged behind. Eventually it turned, but my control appeared to be limited. This distressed me a great deal. I could feel my chest tighten as my blood vessels and arteries constricted. It wasn't so much I feared a collision—the river was wide and the other boats sparse—but it appeared the boat was more at the whim of the elements than my direction. An unexpected Atlantic jet stream shift could alter the wind, and the storm could be pushed ashore, sneaking up on us before we could safely return to the boathouse.

"Relax, Coulter," Dr. Brinkman said. "Pull on that rope there. Tighten the jig."

"Here?"

"Yes. It'll help you keep the boat more stable."

I let loose the rope in order to tighten it, but when I did, my grip slipped, and the rope pulled out of my hand. The sail dropped but snagged about halfway around the mast. It flapped violently in the wind and ballooned out to the right of us, turning the boat cross the current and waves. Dr. Brinkman jumped from his seat, but the deck was wet and his footing unsecure. He hit his head on the mast and fell overboard before I could reach out and grab him.

There's a prevailing misconception that panic speeds events up. This is erroneous. Time appears to slow down in such circumstances. At least for me. The waves lapped the boat less frequently. The sail beat with less force. Gravity didn't pull down the water from Dr. Brinkman's splash at 9.8 m/s². It was like I had the time to analyze every conceivable course of action.

Dr. Brinkman didn't surface right away. The water where he fell in bubbled white from his splash. I remember thinking I should jump in and save him. I was a strong swimmer. I'd used to go noodling with my dad at Bluestem Lake. I could fight a twenty-pound catfish in his element and yank him out of the water with my bare hand. Because of its swimming power, it was like pulling a man out of the water. Harder actually. The Charles here was clear and clean, and Dr. Brinkman wouldn't be fighting me.

But then I reconsidered. If I didn't save him, his death would buy me time. He would die and I'd be traumatized and I'd be granted an extension on my dissertation. A new chair would have to be found. There would be understanding and sympathy and an exception made in my case. I wouldn't amount to a failure and have to drop out of the program. I'd be able to make the breakthrough I needed to land a job and provide for my wife and my son and we would be happy.

I counted to ten, to twenty, to thirty. He didn't surface. The bubbles from his splash soon dissipated, and the water went calm. He must have been holding his breath for otherwise some bubbles would remain, or, if he was deep enough, they would burst before they could reach the surface, the pressure becoming too much to bear. I looked around to see if any other boat had witnessed Dr. Brinkman going overboard, but none were in vicinity. There was a powerboat speeding away off in the distance, but it was much closer to shore, its engine a mere buzz drowned out by the water splashing against the hull. There would be no witnesses. I could come up with any story I wanted, that I had jumped in and tried to save him, that I dived and dived and dived, nearly drowning myself, but I couldn't find him. No one would be the wiser.

But then he surfaced. He broke through the water and gasped for air, and I threw him a life preserver. Blood gushed from a gash in his forehead, and he flailed his arms around in panic. I bent down and reached out to grab his hand. He swam over, pulled himself back onto the skiff, and collapsed in the floor. Wheezing, he looked up at me and said, "Thank you. Thank you, Coulter. You saved my life."

X

He had everything he needed—he had double and triple checked, his laptop, the flash drive with his calculations, his dissertation, the four-hundred page manuscript he had slaved over for the past five years, all his research—he was ready to defend; he would after today be Dr. Coulter Zahn, and finally his real work could begin when Sara, dear sweet Sara, approached him with a look on her face like she was about to puke. "I think my water broke," she said.

"Are you sure?"

"No, I'm not sure."

Sara had her hands underneath her stomach. The inside of her thighs were wet. He thought he could smell ammonia.

"Maybe you just peed yourself."

"Will you shut up?"

"Well, how are you supposed to know?"

She leaned against the dresser like she'd just run a marathon. Sweat drenched her brow. Her flesh had turned pale and thin looking. If he looked close enough, he thought he could see the blood course through her veins around her temples.

"Google it," she ordered.

"Are you serious?"

"Just fucking do it!"

Coulter searched for "how do you know if your water broke?" In 0.20 seconds he got 6,430,000 returns. He clicked on the first one. "Amniotic fluid surrounds your baby during pregnancy," it said. "Towards the end of pregnancy, the amount of collagen decreases in the chorion, the outer layer of the bag of water. Collagen is a fibrous connective tissue. It can be found in cartilage, ligaments, and tendons." All facts, pointless, stupid facts that told him absolutely nothing.

"Did you feel something pop?" he asked, finally getting to information that provided some hints.

"I don't know."

"You don't know?"

"I don't know! I don't! Fuck. I'm freaking out here."

Dr. Brinkman would be waiting for him right now along with the rest of his dissertation committee. He was supposed to be there in twenty minutes. Twenty. Minutes.

"It says to lie down. Wait for like five minutes or so and then stand up again. If your water broke, more fluid should leak from your vagina."

"Okay, okay."

Sara lay down, her head propped up by two pillows. Her hair splayed about her like she floated in water, the strands drenched at the root to accentuate the effect.

"I can't believe this is happening," she said. "Oh my God, what are we going to do?"

"What does the fluid smell like?"

"I mean, I knew it was coming and everything, but fuck, it's here. It's here. We're having a baby!"

"Did you see it? What color was it? It should be clear more than likely. But it could also be yellow, pinkish, brown, or even green. That's not very helpful."

"How can you be so calm?"

"Maybe we should call your doctor."

"Okay. Hand me my phone."

Coulter did, and she called by pressing one button, her doctor on speed dial. Her breaths were short and quick, and spittle jumped from her open mouth when she exhaled. She looked scared, like she had for the past five or six months now. Of course, Coulter was scared, too—having a baby was an intrinsically terrifying experience regardless if the pregnancy was planned or not—but he hadn't worn it on his expression like a disfigured Halloween mask. This had become a point of contention for them over the months.

"Aren't you worried?" she would ask. He'd be bent over a book, penciling in a diagram on a piece of graph paper, his fingers flying over calculator buttons all at once. She'd be across the kitchen table from him, clipping coupons and organizing them into an accordion folder.

"Of course I am," he'd say, his pencil still scribbling with such force that pieces of graphite flaked onto the page. Each time he wiped them away, they would discolor the paper like smeared soot.

"You don't show it."

"Everyone shows anxiety differently," he'd try to tell her.

She'd make a popping noise with her mouth and look slightly above Coulter's head. She didn't believe him. That much was obvious.

"I don't feel like you're in this with me. I mean, I know it's different for us. He is growing inside of *me* after all." Whenever she felt it necessary to point out this little tidbit, he could feel agitation crawl over his skin and he had to fight the urge to wonder what it would be like to slap her across the face. Not hard, just a little tap to let her know that he didn't appreciate it. "Everything I've read says that you won't really feel like a father until he's here and you can hold that little love in your arms, but I thought you would be more involved than *this*."

"I'm involved. I am."

She cradled her stomach as if it was a breadbasket. It was about as large as one and as soft, nothing like the firmness of pre-pregnancy. Not that Coulter wasn't attracted to his wife any longer—that wasn't it, not really anyway. It just felt inappropriate to touch her in that way now—

she was somebody's mother.

A motherfucker.

He would be a motherfucker, and that thought, for whatever reason, troubled him. He couldn't get it out of his head. While they made love, he'd try to think of other women, attractive women, actresses and pop-stars, even girls from those dirty movies he'd watched as a kid.

"I'm not saying like going to the doctor or anything. I know you're there. But you're not emotionally there. You know what I mean?"

Each time she'd get into this line of questioning, Coulter would attempt to persuade her otherwise, but even to himself his persistent refutations sounded thin, like an exhausted parent too tired to use reverse psychology on his child anymore. Eventually he'd just drop it, shrug, and return to his work.

That, unfortunately, was not an option this time—as soon as Sara stood up, amniotic fluid ran down the inside of her thighs.

"Oh fuck," Sara said. "Oh Jesus shit fuck Christ."

Coulter, to his surprise, went straight mechanical, moving at a steady and quick pace to the closet, grabbed the bag they'd previously packed for this occasion, and looped his arm around Sara's.

"Can you walk?" he asked.

She nodded. She was scared, but at least she was responsive.

"Okay," he said. "Follow me."

The delivery room was larger than Coulter had anticipated. It resembled a hotel suite, not some cold and sterile operating room. A large television hung from the ceiling. The bed appeared comfortable, the mattress thick, the pillows plush, though it was clad in simple white sheets the texture of sandpaper. Floor-to-ceiling closets framed the bedside. They were pre-fabricated and assembled on the spot like a fixture bought at Ikea, but they were nice, roomy, and easily stored their overnight bag along with both their oversized coats. A couch was pushed up against the far wall underneath a large window that overlooked downtown's skyline. Low-hanging clouds blocked out the sun, enveloping the city in a hushed glow.

Sara was still freaking out, sitting straight up and already doing the breathing exercises she had learned at Lamaze class although they weren't necessary yet. Hee—hee...hooo. Hee—hee...hooo. A slight, reverberating moan could be heard coming from her throat, like she was about to growl or maybe bark. Every few minutes she doubled over, clenched her stomach, and ground her teeth so that Coulter could hear the molars sawing down enamel. He wished he could do something for her. Massage her shoulders or get her a wet rag or inject her with morphine, but his excitement and anxiety and absolute, positive, prodigious terror kept him cemented to the linoleum floor with exclamations of Oh My God Oh My God Oh my fucking God on a recurring loop silently shrieking at him inside his skull. He'd never been much of a Cartesian theatre proponent, instead deferring to a more material reductionist view of consciousness, but yet he didn't feel as though he had control of this voice. Some other being did.

Sara wanted the epidural NOW. Not that he could blame her, but what in the hell could he do about it? There were just these two nurses here, chitchatting away about stupid reality television for Christ's sake, who the Bachelorette, that slutty Becky, was going to end up marrying— not Rick, for the love of God, they didn't want Rick. "The doctor will let us know when she would like for you to have it." The doctor wasn't even in the hospital. They had been communicating by cell phone, and who knew how long it would take before she could reach the delivery room. A Pitocin drip had been hooked into Sara's arm that caused her to scream uncontrollably every couple minutes and inch along toward that finish line of pushing a human being out of her. It was like the two of them were in completely separate realities from the nurses—he in a panic, unsure of what to do or say, and Sara, doubled over in pain and about to give birth, and then there were these two women, discussing the goings on of reality television as if the outcome were the most pressing matter of their lives. It seemed unfathomable to Coulter. Unconscionable, really. So much so, in fact, he couldn't help but wonder to himself: Did they even exist?

"OOOoooohhhh my Godddddd!" Sara screamed. "I think I'm dying."

"Just breathe," Coulter said. "We'll get through this together."

"I just wish Bobby knew what that slut said to Rick," the fat nurse said to the tall one. "I mean, if you're two-timing someone, you should give the one you're stringing along the benefit of the doubt, you know what I'm saying?"

"Unh-huh. I do. Just ain't right."

"When did the doctor say that she would be here?" Coulter asked.

The nurses continued to ignore him, jabbering along in that southern drawl that didn't fit. Where were they from, Oklahoma? How many Oklahoma transplants could be in one Boston hospital room at one time? It seemed like one of those riddles that were constructed to be unanswerable—like the one that questions the evolutionary timeline of chickens.

The egg came first, Coulter answered nobody, not the chicken. The egg was an evolutionary by-product created deep in the sea long before birds set foot upon the earth.

"She'll be here when she'll be here, honey. Don't you worry. We do this *all* the time."

They continued their prep work, which consisted of readying a cart for the doctor. There was betadine and forceps and latex gloves and an orthoscope and stethoscope. They stocked baby powder and antiseptic ointments and needles and IV bags of antibiotics and painkillers. They could've supplied a small nation-state with medical supplies with all the items they had. And all of it had its own little place, its own little compartment, planned and organized, well-prepared, and this should have calmed Coulter, but it didn't. It didn't at all. Why would they need so much stuff?

"All right, sweetie," the short, fat nurse said. She had the face of a pug, canine cheeks and bicuspids that gave Coulter the impression she would bite him if he said the wrong thing. "We're going to go ahead and get started now. You just lean on back and don't worry your pretty little head off, *k*?"

They readied Sara. She lay back in the bed and propped her feet up on the stirrups and instructed Coulter to pull back on her knees when it was time to push. It wasn't time just yet but would be soon. Coulter stayed near Sara's torso so as not to wander too far south where he could see her dilated vagina. Not that he wasn't curious. He was. Watching a human being born, nonetheless his son, was a fascinating event, a miraculous feat of evolutionary biology that had always astounded him. We could grow people. Just amazing. But he was timid, too, afraid that he wouldn't be able to look at his wife, who he loved dearly, the same afterward. Would he still find her attractive? Would he still be able to make love to her? And there was that smell. It was a mixture of pesticide-treated soil and sautéed onions.

Sara continued her breathing, and the pug-faced nurse crouched down like a catcher and peered inside his wife.

"Everything's looking hunky dory," she said. "I can see the head. Hairy little thing. You must've had some nasty heartburn, little lady."

"I want the epidural!" Sara said. "I want it now!"

"Oh, it's too late now. We done missed our window."

"You. Give. It. To. Me. *Now!*"

"Brace yourself, sweetie." The pug-faced nurse winked. She actually winked. "We're in for one hell of a bumpy ride."

Dr. Remington finally arrived with hands upturned in the air, looking like a woman who had eaten too much. Her eyelids drooped, her shoulders slumped, and her belly protruded. She looked like she could use a nap. She sat on a stool between Sara's legs and slapped on some latex gloves. This was all routine to her. She'd done this billions of times before. In fact, she seemed more concerned with digesting her large meal than she was with delivering the baby. She belched slightly, her mouth filling with air before expelling it in a small whoosh. She twisted her torso, as if helping the food down her intestinal tract. Her nonchalance didn't comfort Coulter at all. Instead, it scared the ever-living hell out of him. It was, after all, when practitioners got complacent that dreadful mistakes were made.

"Betadine," she said in a sleepy voice.

She lathered up his wife's inner thighs and vagina. Curiosity got the better of Coulter, and he looked. It wasn't an aesthetically pleasing sight by any means, but the sight captured a beauty Coulter had never experienced. Within him came an outpouring of feeling, not so much an abstraction, an emotional idea such as love or empathy or happiness, but a physical reaction to the sight he was seeing—the birth of his son, Isaac. Neurons fired more intensely. His heart rate increased. His blood pressure escalated. His breathing quickened. He became attuned to his anatomy like he'd never been before. All the pain he had from clenching his muscles ebbed away. He felt numb on the outside, yet everything was magnified on the inside. It was an amazing effect, really, one that he never wanted to end.

"When I say to," Dr. Remington said, "I want you to push. Understand?"

Sara nodded. She had the expression of a woman just told that her arms and legs needed to be amputated to stave off an infection that would, if not cut out, dissolve her heart and lungs into a black and vile sludge. Despite the worst imaginable pain known and experienced by mankind, she was determined to see it through. It was the bravest thing Coulter had ever witnessed, or, he was convinced, that he ever would. He'd never know that type of bravery. If faced with similar circumstances, he would, he was sure, opt for death.

The baby's head crowned. Dr. Remington rubbed her index and middle finger along the bottom side of the birthing canal. "Push," she said. "Now. Push."

He pulled back on her left thigh as Sara strained to push out their child. Its head slid up and out of the canal, the coned skull just past the threshold, but then Sara tired out and gave into the pain and relaxed, and the head seeped back inside of her. A thick, phlegmy fluid soaked the child and the inside of the mother and the inside of her thighs. It coated everything, and it smelled of mold and exposed human tissue. The child's thick, tangled hair matted against its pate, like the fibers of a brush soaked by paint. Coulter was afraid it couldn't breathe, that they would have a stillborn baby. Why wasn't it crying yet? Why wasn't it moving? An anxiousness gripped his chest and constricted his respiratory system. It became tight and shrunk to a child's size. He would, if this lasted much longer, suffocate. He was absolutely sure of it.

"Keep going," Dr. Remington said. "You're almost there. Keep pushing."

But then, without warning, their child slid out of her and into the waiting arms of the doctor. It didn't cry right away, and Coulter stopped breathing. It was purple. Wasn't it purple? The doctor lightly smacked the baby's butt, but still it didn't scream. Sara had fallen back into the bed, too tired to lean forward any longer, but she reached for her child. She wanted to hold her baby.

"What's wrong?" Sara asked. "Why don't I hear him?"

"Come on," Dr. Remington said. "Come on, little one."

Coulter waited for it, a sound. Anything. A cry bursting from weak lungs. The tiniest little whine, an asthmatic wheeze, pilfering through clenched lips. And then it came: a shrill, cackled scream, reverberating like the Doppler effect. He was here, his son, his baby boy, and there was nothing he could do about it now.

I'M NOT USUALLY ONE FOR EMOTIONAL OUT-
bursts. It's not that I find them crass, nor do I look down upon them
with derision. If anything, I see my lack of emotion as a flaw. Emotions
have evolved over millennia to serve particular functions. Fear can be
used as a motivator to flee a predator. Sadness can assuage a grief-stricken
individual. Happiness increases serotonin and triggers the pleasure cen-
ters in the brain. My lack of feeling has resulted in a numbness towards
life, carved by short bursts of sublimity. Psychiatrists refer to this as re-
pression and compensation. For example, a victim might repress abuse
from a perpetrator for years, even forgetting the memory, replacing the
lashes from a belt or the unwanted sexual touch with happier and fabricated lies, and then, much later, an event will trigger these unhappy
memories, sending the victim into a hysterical bout of anger and self-
loathing and lowered inhibitions. I didn't realize this was happening to
me until I met my neighbor for the first time. But my outburst wasn't
immediate or short-lived. It was something I carried with me for a little
while before acting out.

Her name was Becky, and she'd been married for fifteen years, all
of it spent in the apartment next door to us. She had a black eye, but it
wasn't her first. I could tell by the sunglasses she wore despite the over-
cast weather and the practiced way she tilted her head when she looked
at you, so that at first glance you weren't sure whether or not the bruise

was just a shadow.

The four of us—my mother, father, Sara, and I—had been returning home from dinner when we came upon her digging through her purse. She couldn't find her keys.

"I'm such an idiot sometimes," she said. "I swear to Christ my ass would fall off my hips if I swung 'em hard enough. Good thing Taylor never takes me dancing."

We offered her water and crackers as we didn't have anything else to give, and I called a locksmith who told me he would "get there when he got there." I refrained from pointing out his unproductive tautology.

She had an odd mix of personality, Becky did. She had the abrasiveness of a tomboy, a girl with older brothers, a girl who would rather build a fort and play with old tires than with a Barbie. Dirt lined her fingernails, and she wore men's denim jeans. She didn't filter her language, spurting out curse words that would make any Gloucester fisherman blush. But she had her reservations, too. She covered her mouth as she chewed, and she kept her knees touching and her shoulders hunched as if trying to take up the smallest amount of space as possible.

Taylor was her husband and, presumably, the cause of the black eye. We'd often heard them fighting next door, arguing about money or how to discipline Gavin, their seven-year-old, but we'd never heard anything turn violent, with the exception of the other night. The thud we'd heard had apparently been her head being struck by something solid. A lamp base maybe. Or perhaps just a hard, closed fist.

"Oh, I know what you mean," Sara said. "Before, I thought this whole 'pregnancy brain' I was told about was a bunch of crap, but it's true. I'll walk into a room without the slightest idea why. I'll run a bath and then forget about it and flood the bathroom. It's like this little guy is eating half my brain."

"You don't recover. Believe me," Becky said. "When I was pregnant with Gavin, I tell you, I was as bad as one of them kids that rode the short bus to school. Still am, evidently."

"There's a hormonal reason for that," I said. "Pregnancy has a negative impact on the neurons in the parts of the brain responsible for spatial memory, particularly the hippocampus."

They all just blinked at me.

"Don't mind him," Sara said, discarding my input with a flick of her wrist. "He just talks to hear the sound of his own voice."

Becky laughed and snorted. "Taylor is the same exact way. Though he'd never use such big words. Anything over five letters gives him fits."

"I never had that problem," my mother said. "Loss of memory or anything like that. Pregnancy was a breeze with Coulter. He rarely kicked. I didn't gain that much weight. No morning sickness. I ate a lot of Hot Tamales, though. Heartburn got a little bad sometimes."

"Oh, I get the weirdest cravings," Sara said. "I mix together peanut butter and chocolate chip cookie dough ice cream and diced cucumbers. It's like going to heaven."

"That's not so strange," my mother said.

"Not at all," Becky said. "I used to douse pancakes with buffalo wing sauce."

Dad made a face like he felt nauseated. My mother and Sara chuckled.

"That actually doesn't sound all that bad," Mom said. "Coulter and I, we used to have breakfast for dinner at least once a week. Eggs Benedict or French toast or biscuits and gravy. It was always our little tradition. Not that we mixed together wing sauce and pancakes, though."

"I remember that," Dad said. "You wouldn't let me cook the eggs in the bacon grease."

"It's just so unhealthy that way," Mom said. "A heart attack waiting to happen."

It was odd hearing my mother reminisce about us together. She had this nostalgic tone to her voice, a slow and repetitive cadence that gave her the air of a storyteller spinning a fairy tale, which surprised me. She was the one who had left. She was the one who had said that it became easier to cope without me over time. She was the one who effectively ended any semblance of a normal relationship. It made me jealous in a way I hadn't felt before. Despite the fact she'd abandoned me as a child, she could remember fondly those memories that came before her desertion without the slightest hint of shame or guilt. I couldn't do that. I couldn't remember those happy times. It was like I'd erased those memories, or she had fabricated them, a form of manipulation maybe, to make me let her back into my life, or possibly a result of her mental illness, a lie born of her intrinsic neurosis.

"You just have the one child?" my mother asked Becky.

"Two actually. Gavin and Kyler. Gavin's seven, and Kyler's three."

"They are wondrous, aren't they?" Mom beamed, her cheeks flushed like an alcoholic's. "Does your husband hit them like he hits you?"

"Jesus, Natalie," Dad said. He covered his face in embarrassment.

"Excuse me?" Becky asked.

"Does he strike the kids?"

"I'm so sorry, Becky," Sara said. "She doesn't know what she's saying."

"I'm only trying to help," my mother said. "You should go to the police. Even if he isn't hitting the kids."

Becky stood. She assumed an aggressive posture, hunched forward with her finger outstretched like a mother scolding a child. "You, lady. You—you've got no idea what you're talking about."

"I truly do not mean to offend," my mother continued. "I lived through a family life of dysfunction myself, mostly of my own doing."

"I don't have to take this," Becky said as she moved toward the door.

Sara struggled to her feet and followed Becky, apologizing as she did so, but Becky didn't stop, slamming the door as she left. The reverberations rattled the collection of family pictures on the wall, and we all jumped despite anticipating the slam. Sara followed after her into the hallway, and my mother looked befuddled, like she couldn't believe someone could be offended by such a question. This bewildered me even more, her incredulity. She spoke of wanting to make amends, with me, with my father, but she couldn't even filter her own consciousness. It was like she had no control over her actions. I simply couldn't understand it. Was her amends simply a fleeting impulse, not governed by rational, deep desire? Would she, once she grew bored, leave me once again?

I had to admit it seemed likely.

"You really know how to ruin a perfectly nice conversation, don't you, Natalie?" Dad asked once Sara and Becky had left.

"I'm sorry. Denial doesn't help anyone, though. My therapist says you must confront your problems if you ever hope to heal."

"No one gives a damn about your therapist, Natalie," Dad continued. "Apparently he isn't worth a damn. You're still bat-shit crazy."

"This is some of the dysfunction I was referring to earlier."

I couldn't help but feel like a child again, hearing my parents argue. Strangely, I didn't have any memories of them fighting, though surely they did. People fight. Especially people living in proximity. Human nature always trumps good intentions.

"Dad, listen. It's not a big deal. Maybe she needed to hear that. Maybe it'll do some good."

"All I'm saying is that she is a stranger. It's not our place to interfere." He pointed to my mother. "It's definitely not *her* place."

"Please don't turn this into something it's not, Marcus. This has nothing to do with what I did to you and Coulter years ago."

Dad didn't say anything. He crossed his legs and averted his gaze, biting his tongue. My father had never been a confrontational type, instead opting to turn the other cheek, allow whatever crime had been committed against him to go unpunished.

I couldn't help but feel angry myself, at my mother for her nostalgic, perhaps untrue stories, her unfiltered intrusion into a stranger's life; at my father for allowing my mother to eat away at him, his inability to stand up for himself, or others for that matter; even at my wife for reasons I couldn't really articulate. But it was there, like a heat burning underneath my ribcage. I could feel my blood pressure heighten, my pulse thumping in my wrists, in my neck.

But then it came to me. I hated her for running after Becky, for sympathizing with her. It was irrational, I knew, but her act seemed to communicate that beyond sympathy, there was empathy, too, like she was a battered and abused wife, that I, like Becky's husband, was guilty of some abysmal crime. It was like she was accusing *me* of something.

After a few moments, Sara returned, accompanied by Becky. She appeared much calmer, even obsequious. She had the look of a pizza delivery girl, waiting for a tip that wouldn't come.

"I'm sorry," she said. "I feel embarrassed."

An awkward silence ensued. I seethed. Dad seethed. Mom sat there vindicated. And Sara stroked Becky's back, like a mother comforting a child. The whole moment was akin to an infection. We could all feel the hard lump festering, the tender skin throbbing with a deep contusion. It wasn't an ordinary clogged pore or an under-turned hair. It was staph instigated by an arachnid bite. Mashing it wouldn't help. Hydrogen peroxide wouldn't help. All of us would have to wait for it to come to a head, and then slice it away with a scalpel in one satisfying cut.

X

When Coulter first smelled smoke, he thought Sara may be burning a candle, or lighting a fire, or maybe a bit of spaghetti sauce fell onto a lit stove-top burner. It was an odd occurrence, smelling smoke, but common enough that at first he didn't panic. He was in his study reading a lecture Richard Feynman had given years before about the conflict between religion and science, noting how cowardly such a brave man had sounded, how so insincerely diplomatic, when the smoke alarm sounded.

When he and Sara had first been dating, she asked him what he would take with him if the house were on fire. She answered first, listing family photographs and her grandmother's cookbooks, beloved heirlooms and keepsakes mostly. But Coulter always thought this to be shortsighted. New memories could be created. The pictures remembered fondly with nostalgia. It would actually grant them a sort of mythos that may even be more valuable than the things themselves. He wouldn't grab his work or his books either. His work was always backed up on servers at the university, each day saved and stored so nothing would be lost. The books could all be bought at discount prices online. The thing was, he never had an answer for Sara. He would, if the opportunity ever arose, simply walk out of the building, empty handed.

He rose from his desk and out of instinct hovered his hand above the doorknob. Hot. The flames were not far outside the door. In fact, he could feel the heat emanating from the crack under the door and hear the crackle of the wood splintering from the extreme heat. Smoke began to billow in from the vents and from underneath the door. He'd have to go out the window. It was a few feet away, and he could see his expansive yard, a willow tree whose branches swayed in the breeze like a child's tire swing just abandoned from play. He could see the creek that separated his property from his neighbor's to the south. There was a sandbox out there that he had built for Isaac when he'd been small. He hadn't played in it in years, of course, now in high school and hardly ever home. He'd rather go out with his friends doing who knows what. Smoke weed. Break into the abandoned hospital west of town. Huff paint. Conduct experiments on alternative rocket fuels. Orgies. Coulter had no idea because his son wouldn't talk to him. It had all happened so quickly, this distance. When he'd been younger, Isaac used to climb all over his father like a jungle gym. Now, when Isaac was home, Coulter noticed a change in his tone, one of annoyance and exasperation, the way his mother sounded sometimes when Coulter hadn't done some chore he'd promised he'd do. When Isaac's friends came over, he'd scurry them upstairs and lock the door before Coulter would be allowed to introduce himself. He avoided Coulter's smiles and waves when they were in public, at a school function say, when Coulter spotted him from across the room. Perhaps it was a gradual change, this transformation from dependent child to independent teenager, but that's not how it seemed to Coulter. Just yesterday Isaac had poured over Coulter with love, and today he couldn't stand to be around his father, as if embarrassment was a natural side-effect of being in his presence. Coulter pretended this didn't bother him and suffered silently, but this was a façade. Isaac's shame at being his son was the hardest thing he'd ever had to endure.

Coulter could hardly see through the smoke. Thick and dark and full of ash, it clung to his lung tissue, making it difficult to breathe. He got down on the floor and crawled over to the window. He pushed the window open and pulled himself to safety. Turning back, the roof had collapsed just west of his office, and flames burst forth as it engulfed his family's home. Everything would be lost. Family portraits vacationing in Yellowstone and faded pencil marks on the wall where they'd measured Isaac's height growing up. His publications, framed in shadow boxes in his office. His diplomas. Sara's wedding dress. The armoire given to her by her mother. All gone. That didn't really bother him, though. He was just glad his family wasn't home. They were safe. That was what was important.

Sirens sounded from the street, and Coulter walked up the hill toward the front of his home in order to greet the firemen. There were two trucks out front, about eleven firemen in all, dressed in full gear, large yellow coats and black helmets. Their boots clamored along the pavement as they dragged their hose within firing range. Before Coulter could let one know that no one was inside, they unleashed a jettison of water that had so much force Coulter was amazed the burning home didn't collapse underneath the pressure. Coulter, exhausted, sat on the road and watched the firemen extinguish the blaze. It was an awesome sight, these men working in tandem. It wasn't long before they had the fire under control.

A crowd had gathered as the firemen worked. Coulter scanned their entertained faces. Dozens of onlookers watched the show. There were so many of them that they blended together, their faces dissolving into featureless slates of flesh. However, across the street, just where the tree line started and backed into about forty acres of woods, Coulter thought he saw his son, standing alone, holding a gas can.

X

The airport wasn't busy. Cabs didn't jockey for position in the unload drive. Passengers didn't push to hail one before their hands froze. Bag handlers didn't compete for tips. The first snow of the year fell, the ground not cold enough for the flakes to accumulate, instead melting as soon as they hit pavement. No wind blew. It was uneventful. It was peaceful.

My father was going back to Oklahoma, having to return to work. Although spring is his busy season, an unexpected winter mix was heading toward Oklahoma City. They wouldn't get more than a few inches more than likely, a mixture of freezing rain and snow. It would turn to slush and clog the roadways for a few days. But the city would come to a standstill. Commerce would halt. Traffic would be zero. The citizens would curl up by a fire and watch Christmas movies even though it wasn't even Thanksgiving yet. It made me a little nostalgic in a way. When I'd been young, I conducted experiments, studying the effect of cold on our neighbor's dog's shaven paws or testing the density of water as it approached zero degrees Celsius from below freezing and above it. Sometimes my father helped. Other times he didn't. Mom reviewed the paper I prepared afterwards, correcting grammar and punctuation and logical fallacies. Then we would all get together and celebrate a job well done. We'd rent a movie or go out to eat at The Garage, a little burger joint where we could get buffalo patties and loaded cheese fries.

It had been strange seeing my father and mother interact these past few days. When I'd been a child, they had been aloof and distant and cold toward each other. The last memories I had of them together tended to be short and marked by one-word sentences. Yes. No. Later. Bye. But lately they had talked. They had fought. They had screamed at each other and acknowledged that the other one existed. I should've been happy about this, but I wasn't. Growing up, my father and I had always enjoyed this us-versus-them mentality. It was just us against the world, a united front. But now that wasn't the case. We all had our own side. There was the three of us—disparate, distinct, and unyielding.

"Will you be coming back?" I asked him. "When the baby comes, I mean." We were standing on the curb, just outside the ticket counters and the line for security. It was long, but not long enough to cause worry. Every few seconds the line would bumble forward a step or two, followed by the drag of bags along the hard floor. It almost seemed synchronized in a way, like a choreographed stage number casted with dreary automatons.

"Of course," Dad said. "I'm not going to miss the birth of my granddaughter. You just better give me a heads up if she comes early."

"It's a he."

"You never know." He winked. "Sometimes those nurses can be wrong."

That seemed unlikely, but I didn't feel like arguing.

"Mom seems to be happy."

"She has a grandbaby on the way. She's seeing you again. She's happy. I don't know how long it'll last. I never could tell with her. One minute she was ecstatic, the next I was hiding scissors from her lest she cut herself."

"She cut herself?"

Dad stuck his tongue in his cheek as if questioning how he should answer. "I was always afraid she'd hurt herself. It became unbearable at times. Especially near the end."

He unzipped a compartment in his bag and pulled out his itinerary. He scanned it, and felt his pockets for his belongings: wallet, keys, cell phone. He did all these things without thinking, I knew, a nervous impulse. Despite chasing tornadoes for a living, the man was scared of flying. Funny, sometimes, what makes people afraid.

"Was she happy with me?" I asked. "When I was born, I mean."

"Was she excited?"

I nodded.

"Well, yeah. Of course, yeah."

"You don't sound so sure."

"It's different. We were first-time parents. We were broke. We were scared. I'm sure you can attest to that."

A traffic cop blew a whistle at my cab and waved it forward.

"In or out, bub," the cabbie said. "I'm blocking traffic here."

"Just a second." I turned back to Dad. "So she loved me?"

He sighed, his breaths white puffs, and laid a heavy palm on my shoulder. In an instance, I felt twelve again. "Of course she did, Coulter. I know it's hard to imagine given what she did. But she did. I'm sure of it. She just didn't know how to show it. She didn't know how to take care of herself, let alone you."

It was hard to believe that she'd ever been happy, though I hardly remembered her being around. I remembered her being depressed. My last memory of her she'd been passed out and poisoned from carbon monoxide, slumped over the steering wheel to her luxury sedan. Then again, according to Mom, that had never actually happened. She'd said I'd found her inside the house, writing a suicide note. Odd, though, I could still make out that moment, my mother unconscious, my confusion, the smell of car exhaust. Not knowing which was true, my memory or my mother's, made the whole act surreal somehow, as if the two contradictory accounts marred the validity of the whole act. This prompted so many more questions. Did we have fun with each other? Was I a difficult child? Distant? Loving? What did she enjoy doing? Did she read scholarly evolutionary biology articles for the hell of it? Did she not learn to swim until her early twenties? When she'd left, my father and I never really spoke of her. Dad would out of the blue tell me she liked her sundaes with extra pecans and a dash of salt or that she liked to let the air out of her tires so she had a viable excuse to go late into work. I wanted to ask her if that was true, if that's how she actually remembered things. I really wanted to know because the more I thought about it, the more I realized I knew absolutely nothing about her, and the things I thought I knew I now questioned.

Of course, I did remember some things. I remembered that day at the museum, the last we had ever spent together. I remembered her taking me to school in the mornings. As a game she'd sometimes not stop but instead coast along the parking lot of the elementary school and allow me to jump from my seat to the amazement of my peers, and the trepidation of my schoolteachers. She smoked cigars sometimes, after a party, or to celebrate something I didn't understand from work. She'd loved risk, going spelunking and skydiving and bungee jumping. She was also prone to terrible sadness and locking herself up in her room for days. When she would emerge, her nose and lips would be raw and the color of dried, burnt salmon.

But were these memories even true? Were they fantasies I'd imagined to fill the void she had caused? Not knowing for sure made it even worse, like my mind had been damaged somehow, or I was deluded, insane even. Like some of our estrangement was actually my fault. I could ask her, of course, an admitted liar who from one second to the next changed moods and stories like an adjunct changed universities. It maddened me more and more, and it seemed I wouldn't get any details out of my father. He'd kept them hidden for this long; he wouldn't start admitting anything honestly now.

"Either get in or find another cab," yelled the cabbie. "I ain't fucking around here."

"I better go," Dad said.

"Sure. Sure."

We hugged farewell. "Give her a chance," Dad said. "I know it's not right or fair. Just try. Okay?"

"Okay, Dad."

"Promise?"

I nodded. "Of course."

SARA ASKED ME TO GO WITH HER TO THE IN-
terview just in case she had another one of her attacks and had to go
back to the hospital. I thought she was just scared, though. Scared to put
herself out there. Scared to be rejected. Scared she might actually get the
position. The job was at Blue Hills Bank in its credit risk department.
We waited in the foyer, furnished with rich, deep brown club chairs, in-
tricate Persian rugs, and faux-golden plated coffee tables. On the walls
hung generic paintings: landscapes, a British hunting party, a ship lost
in a stormy sea. It was one of those places that made me feel uncomfortable—I knew I didn't belong, and so did everyone else, casting judgment
behind stony gazes.

Sara sat next to me, chewing her hair. Her leg bounced like a woman
needing to pee, which she'd already done, twice since we'd arrived thirty
minutes earlier. The peeing, of course, had more to do with her pregnancy than nerves. She'd gotten much larger since my mother had arrived a couple weeks before. The amount she showed seemed to follow
an exponential function, growing at an accelerating rate with each passing week. At first, her belly had protruded like a low hanging summer
squash, but then it rose like baking bread, turning rounder and taut. She
now couldn't walk without waddling, having to cradle her belly in her
arms. For the interview, she wore a silk, grey blouse and a pantsuit, both
of which were much too small for her now, so that they resembled a tarp

pulled over too large of an area.

"I wonder what's taking so long," she said. "This can't be a good sign."

I didn't respond because she didn't want an answer, only to vent her anxieties.

"I think I'm going to be sick," she said as she rocked back and forth. She did look paler than normal, ghostly even.

"Really?"

She nodded.

I looked around for some sort of container for her to vomit in, a trashcan, even a potted plant, but could find nothing. There was a receptionist's desk, empty for the past half hour, but I questioned the appropriateness of getting behind there. Would they mistake me for a bank robber?

Sara gagged.

I didn't have a choice—the vomit was coming. Behind the desk there was a trashcan, already full with Starbucks cups and a sandwich wrapper and mounds of tissue. There would be no room. Without thinking, I dumped the trash onto the floor and rushed the container over to Sara. She grabbed it, hovered her head over the opening, and puked. She breathed deeply and erratically, one curt, staccato inhale followed by a breeze of an exhale. A bit of drool clung to her bottom lip, drooping down to the trashcan liner.

"You okay?" I asked.

She put up a finger, indicating I needed to stop talking, and then wiped her lip with her sleeve. "I think I'm okay," she said.

"You sure?"

"It's been getting worse lately, the morning sickness. I thought it was supposed to get better as time went on."

"Can I get you anything? Water?"

"No. No. I'm good." She spit into the trashcan. "It'll pass in a bit."

"You've been getting sick lately?"

She nodded. "Every morning. Comes out like fluid and phlegm. Then I have heartburn the rest of the day."

"I had no idea."

She shrugged, stuck out her bottom lip, as if unsurprised I had no idea about her morning sickness, and placed the trashcan on the ground. Her spit clung to the trash liner in a coagulated, white pool.

"Are you sure you're able to do this?"

"I'm pregnant. I feel sick sometimes. It's not a big deal."

"I just don't want you to overdo it. You heard what Dr. Remington said. You need to take it easy."

"We've talked about this."

"I know," I said. "You need this, and I understand. I do. It's just—"

"Not another word, Coulter. Back me up. Support me. I support you in your work. I don't complain when you don't come home until 11:00. I don't complain when you're out the door by 4:00. I don't complain that when I do see you, you won't talk to me. You're in your own little world. I need *my* world. Don't you understand that?"

"You're right. I'm sorry," I said, although I didn't mean it. It wasn't my fault that she didn't have a world. She was a banker in a time not well positioned for bankers, the greatest economic recession since the Great Depression. How could I possibly control world economic shifts? How could I affect the hiring situation in greater Boston? How could I grant her professional fulfillment when she obviously couldn't do it herself?

"Don't be sorry, Coulter." She pulled out a pocket mirror and checked her hair, her lips, making sure no bits of puke remained at the corner of her mouth. "I don't need you to be sorry. I need you to just get out of my way."

Just then, the receptionist returned. She smiled a superficial smile, a thin grin without revealing any teeth, and headed back to her desk. Once behind, she stopped and looked down, spotting the trash I'd left on the floor. There was a moment there that lasted only a few seconds, a wave of rage, where she wanted to scream and kick and bite. I could tell by the way her shoulders hunched up around her ears, the way her nostrils flared, and the way every muscle appeared to tense to the point of tearing. But then she tempered her anger. It came as quickly as the anger did, released in one hushed respire.

"Mrs. Musso will see you now," she said to Sara, who left without even a look to me for support.

As soon as Sara went back for her interview, the receptionist shot me dirty looks. She glared at me, then down at the floor, over to the trashcan, then back to me.

"I'm really sorry about the mess," I said. "My wife is pregnant."

She glared at me, the trash on the floor, the trashcan, then me.

"She suffers from morning sickness," I said.

Me, the trashcan, the floor, me.

"Would you like for me to clean that up for you?" I asked.

"No," she said. "No. *I* got it."

When she picked up the trashcan, she snatched it, hyperbolically slinging her arm up and to the side, the entire time staring at me, before returning to her desk to clean up the mess I had made. Once finished, she opened the door to the men's restroom and left the trashcan inside. The smell of vomit, however, lingered.

She was a young girl, the receptionist, with her hair pulled into a tight bun. When she typed, she struck the keys with such force that it sounded like popcorn popping. When she answered the phone, she spoke quickly and curtly, the words firing out of her mouth in rapid succession: Thank-you-for-calling-blue-hills-bank-my-name-is-amy-how-may-i-help-you. She shuffled papers and repeatedly clacked the button on her pen. She drank Mountain Dew between practiced movements, keyboard to inbox to soda to filing cabinet. She was in constant motion, frictionless and in a vacuum.

"Do you like working here?" I asked.

"Excuse me?"

"Here. Do you like working here?"

She shrugged as if I had just asked a stupid question. "Of course."

"What about it?"

She shrugged again, stopped what she was doing and faced me. She puckered her lips and cast her gaze up and to the right, as if in deep thought. "I don't know. I haven't given it much thought to be honest."

"You work a lot?"

She sputtered in derision. "Sixty hours a week sometimes. Fifty at least."

"And what do you do?"

"Administrative assistant to Mrs. Musso."

"I see."

"I know. Unimpressive title, right?"

"You like your boss?"

"She's demanding, but she's good. She's appreciative. Makes you feel important, even if you're not."

I nodded.

"You the husband?" she asked.

"Yes."

"When are you guys due?"

"Two months."

"And she's looking for a job now?" she asked. "*Now?*"

I nodded.

"Huh," she said. "Seems a bit crazy to me." She popped a piece of gum into her mouth. "No offense." She held out the pack of gum toward me. "Want one?"

I approached her and took the piece of gum, spearmint. It tasted cool, and the familiar tinge provided a semblance of comfort.

"I think it's a bit crazy, too," I said. "Who's going to hire her, then give her maternity leave?"

"But you're here."

"Somebody has to hold the puke can."

She laughed a high-pitched cackle then covered her mouth. "Touché. What's your name?"

She held out her hand, and I took it. "Coulter," I said. "Yours?"

"Amy."

"Nice to meet you, Amy."

"And you, Coulter."

She smacked her gum and smiled. She had the whitest teeth I had ever seen. "How long have you been married?"

"Four years," I said. "It'll be five next spring."

"That's sweet," she said. "First kid?"

"Yes."

"Excited?"

I hesitated, unsure really how to answer. "Anxious," I said. "Excited, nervous, happy, worried, terrified."

She laughed, and so did I even though I wasn't joking. At the beginning of the pregnancy, it didn't much bother me, the prospect of being a father, but ever since my mother had returned, I didn't feel one emotion, but many, swirling together to concoct an ulcer-producing cocktail. Sometimes, I burst with joy. I would be helping Sara decorate the nursery with stuffed baby blue elephants and a mobile dangling the periodic table of the elements, and I couldn't help but smile until my cheeks ached. Other times, though, I would feel nauseated from the pressure, the doubt that I could ever be a good father to my son, like my father had been with me. I felt inadequate and incapable, that I would, once he was here, count down the moment until I could flee like my mother had.

"Oh, I bet," she said. "I'd be freaking out!"

"Sometimes it's hard to breathe. I feel like I have asthma, like somebody has grabbed me and put me in a bear hug, and I have to breathe into a paper bag to catch my breath."

"But I bet it's great, too," she said. "You get to play with all those toys again, Legos and racecars and water guns, and watch him mold into a little you."

"Panic attacks, my doctor said. They come out of nowhere. I'll be at work lecturing, and all of a sudden, my vision will narrow like I'm looking through a pinhole."

"You get to watch him play tee-ball and cheer the first time he hits a home run. Get it on video and then embarrass him when he gets older, showing it to his girlfriends."

"There's just this little bit of light, and it's so bright, like getting your eyes dilated at the optometrist's office. It's so bright I actually hear ringing in my ears. A high-pitched whine."

"You get to teach him how to drive and give him advice about girls. It's the greatest thing in the world."

"After a while, I think I'm going to die. My throat constricts, and it feels like my chest is caving in. It's been so bad that I'm brought to my knees."

Just then, the door leading to Mrs. Musso's office burst open. Out came Sara, fuming. Her fists were balled up, her mouth locked in a straight line. She walked with purpose, her plastic soles clacking against the tiled floor.

Behind her, the door clicked shut.

"She didn't even give me a chance," she said. We were riding the bus, bumping along Memorial Drive on our way back to the Dot. It was crowded. Sara sat on a chair facing the middle aisle, two large men on either side of her. I stood holding a pole to keep my balance. The place smelled like all public transportation in Boston, a mixture of cleaning agents and motor oil faintly masking the aroma of urine and various other human secretions. "As soon as she saw my stomach, the interview was over."

"I'm really sorry," I said. "Maybe the next one will go better."

"You should have seen the look on her face. She was appalled. *Appalled!* Like I was some gross monster."

"I'm sure that wasn't her intention."

"You weren't there, Coulter. You didn't see her face. Her scrunched, little, smug face. I've never been so humiliated in my life."

"It's tough out there. You haven't worked in a while. It'll get easier once you get some more practice."

"She wouldn't even look me in the eyes. If she wasn't staring at my fat stomach, she was checking her email or her watch or her phone. I don't think she even heard a word I said."

"Probably for the best. Would you want to work for someone like that?"

"Maybe this was a stupid idea."

I didn't say anything.

Sara peered up at me, her gaze cold, and then back down. "You are supposed to say it's not."

The two large men began to take notice of our conversation. One had a shaved head while the other had a ponytail. Both were well over six feet tall. The bald man resembled a cue ball, shiny and rock solid—a speeding dump truck couldn't have knocked him over. The man with the ponytail was rounder, shaped like a light bulb, and sweaty, his perspiration soaking his shirt. They stared at me as if I was a threat to Sara, their chivalrous sides instinctually kicking in.

"You're not going to say anything, are you?" Sara asked.

"You know how I feel," I said. "I don't believe I need to explain myself anymore."

"I'm unhappy, Coulter."

"I know. You feel lonely. You feel unfulfilled. You need something to do. But the health of our son is at stake."

"No," she said. "You don't know." She covered her swollen belly with her arms, as if protecting herself. "I'm unhappy with you, Coulter. I'm unhappy with us."

"What are you saying?"

"I want to go back to Oklahoma. I *am* going back to Oklahoma."

"You're leaving me?"

"Yes," she said. "No. I don't know. It's not that easy."

"But you're going to Oklahoma?"

"To stay with my parents."

I felt as though the floor had dropped out from underneath me.

The bald man and the one with the ponytail became ardently intrigued now. They leaned forward in their seats. The bald man had his hands balled up in fists, planted on his thighs, and ponytail-guy held his together as if in prayer.

"You can't," I said.

"I know this is hard," she said.

"I'm almost finished with school," I said. "We had a plan. We discussed it together. We formulated it. We executed. And now that we're nearly done, you're going to leave me?"

"We've been unhappy for a long time, Coulter. You can't deny that."

"We knew it was going to be tough. You knew what you were getting into."

Baldy fidgeted in his seat, sat straight up.

"Things change, Coulter. I didn't mean for them to."

"Stay. Think about it for a little while. Don't do anything rash."

"Please, Coulter. Stop."

"Listen to me. We can—"

Ponytail perked up. "The lady wants to stop discussing it, bub."

"This doesn't concern you," I said.

"Coulter, please. Let's just stop the bus and get out," Sara said.

"When you fight in public," Ponytail said, "it becomes the public's problem." He stood up, followed by Baldy.

"I don't want any problems," I said.

"Why don't you leave this nice lady alone, then?" Baldy said. He poked me in my chest. Fight-or-flight instincts have been hardwired into the human genetic code by millions of years of evolution, and at that moment, mine jumpstarted. The bus, however, offered no room to escape, no room to fight, only room to stand still and wait what was coming to me: an inevitable Southie jab to my jaw. I inched as far backward as I could, until an elderly gentleman's knees poked into the back of my thighs. Turning around, he looked afraid, as if it was him who was about to be pummeled.

Before Baldy could lay a finger on me, however, his knees buckled, and he fell on top of me. "Ow! Fuck! Motherfucker!" he said.

Slipping out from underneath him, I saw Sara, leg outstretched from having kicked Baldy in the back of his legs. Stunned, Ponytail stared at his buddy who struggled to regain his footing. As he watched, Sara punched him in the groin, crumpling the much larger man into a ball. Before the men could retaliate, Sara leapt to her feet and pulled the emergency stop cord. The bus screeched to a halt, and she held out her hand toward me.

"Let's get out of here."

Once we exited, Sara struggled to sit on the curb between two parallel-parked cars. I tried to help her down, but she slapped my hand out of the way. The bus petered off into the distance, dark fumes puffing out of its exhaust pipe. Through the window, I could see both Baldy and Ponytail staring at us before again taking their seats, I hoped embarrassed for having had gotten beaten up by a pregnant woman.

"You can't deny that we're unhappy, Coulter," Sara said. "This job thing. I don't know. I want a job, that's true, but it's not all about the job. I feel like I've lost myself. I don't feel like I have an identity anymore."

"And this is my fault?" I asked.

"Partly," she said. "And partly mine."

"But mostly it's me."

"Don't turn this into something it's not. This is about me, not you."

"Don't insult my intelligence," I said. "Don't give me that teenage breakup bullshit. *It's not you; it's me.* How can it not be about me?" I asked. "You are abandoning *me.* I'm the one you are leaving."

"Oh, I see," she said. "Here comes the Mommy issues. She left you. I am leaving you. So now we're the same. Is that it? Me and your mother, the two bitches who abandoned you when you needed them the most."

She rolled her eyes at me, and I felt like I was going to explode. I'd never been so angry with her before. Of course, there were times when I'd get annoyed with her, when she placed her dirty plate next to the couch, for instance, refusing to clean it until her television show was over, some stupid reality show about quasi-celebrities only famous for making a sex tape, or her inability to see anything through to the end, cooking classes she abandoned after the first night, a novel left unread, the nursery she'd promised to paint. She was always delaying her responsibilities, rarely—if ever—seeing a long-term project through to completion. I'd always found her lazy in that regard, and it ate away at me. But this was wholly different. This was blinding, headache inducing rage. I wanted to scream at her. I wanted to grab her by the shoulders and shake her. I wanted to inflict physical pain.

But I didn't.

I took ten deep breaths.

I calmed myself.

"When will you be leaving?" I asked.

"I don't know," she said. "Soon."

"Soon?"

"I'll still go tonight to the baby shower if that's what you're asking," she said. "Keep up appearances and all that."

"Tomorrow then."

"Yes," she said. "Tomorrow."

In 1935, in response to the Copenhagen interpretation of quantum mechanics, Erwin Schrodinger postulated a thought experiment. A cat is locked up in a steel chamber, along with a tiny bit of radioactive substance. There's an equal chance that an atom could decay and an equal chance that it would remain stable. If one of the atoms decays, the cat dies, but if it doesn't, then the cat still lives. If the cat isn't visible to an observer, the mathematical formula representing the experiment would express this by having in it the living and dead cat mixed or smeared out in equal parts.

He, of course, formulated this thought experiment derisively, calling this view of the universe ridiculous. A cat cannot be both alive and dead. It was intuitively absurd. Although I see his point, I can't help but side with the mathematics. The math says, until an observer views the body of the cat, the viewer himself interacting with the environment on a subatomic level, the cat is for all intents and purposes both alive and dead. It is the observation which causes the probability wave to collapse and reality to manifest. Or, in other words, without a body, there is no crime.

The Brinkmans' house was a quaint brownstone not far from campus. It was full of dark wood and warm tones and aged copper. Mrs. Brinkman had placed mirrors in almost every room to give the illusion the place was larger than it actually was. For the baby shower, tables laden with hors d'oeuvres were set up in the dining room. They served white wine, and Dr. Brinkman promised me a private glass of port later in the evening. A toast to the soon-to-be father, he said. Might even light up a cigar if the wife allows it.

Sara was overdressed for the occasion. We'd fought about it before we left. She'd tried on everything in her closet, dresses and necklaces and pantsuits, stuff that didn't even fit anymore. I tried to tell her that we weren't going to see people who cared about style and garments, but she wouldn't have it.

"It's a cocktail party," she said.

"It's a baby shower. Not a cocktail party."

"Why is it at 6:00 then? Why is there going to be booze there? Why are they serving salmon?"

"They just want to do something nice for us. That's all. You can wear jeans. Sweatpants even. You don't have to wear that black dress."

"I think she looks beautiful," my mother chimed in. We didn't even know she was at the door.

"Mom, please."

"Can we have some privacy?" Sara asked.

"I'm just trying to help."

"You're always just trying to help. Funny since you never accomplish that," Sara said.

"Please," I said. "I don't want to fight."

"I thought you might want a feminine opinion on the matter," my mother said.

"I don't want your opinion. In fact, I don't even want you in this house," Sara said.

"Can we please just talk about this later?" I asked.

"No," Sara said as she patted her hair into place. "It's fine. I'm leaving tomorrow anyways."

My mother retreated, and Sara stormed out of the apartment.

At the party, we stayed mostly to ourselves, eating cheese in the corner, Sara's eyes drifting over to a chilled bottle of wine. I could tell she longed for a taste. She'd told me that right after the birth of our child she wanted nothing more than a drink. She didn't even care what it was—tequila, beer, white wine, pure ethyl alcohol, it didn't matter. She just wanted to get drunk. Exacerbating her desire, Sara didn't know any of my colleagues, having only met Dr. Brinkman a few times. We never went out with any of the other PhD candidates. We didn't double date or go get drinks at The Muddy Charles. Department parties went unattended. Banquets and award ceremonies skipped. All at the behest of Sara who felt marginalized by my peers. It was an irrational fear, I tried to tell her, but she wouldn't listen, instead concocting conspiracy stories that they all talked badly about her behind her back, calling her stupid and a buffoon. I told her no one uses the word "buffoon" anymore.

"I swear to God if you leave me alone at this party, I'll kill you," she said. "And this isn't an empty threat. I'll seriously cut your throat while you sleep."

"Stop. Please. Someone might hear you."

"Oh, so now you're embarrassed of me?"

Every once in a while a fellow candidate or a professor stopped by to offer their congratulations. They would say nice things about me, calling me brilliant, and how she should be so proud of me, and they'd complement her, say that she looked just radiant. Beaming, actually. A glow only a soon-to-be mother could have. Sara waved away the compliments with a flip of the wrist, and they'd ask to feel her belly, and she'd pinch my back, a sign that she was ready for this conversation to be over. We'd make some excuse. More wine. More cheese. More crackers. Have to pee. Soon, I was drunk, and running out of excuses.

By the time we were to open gifts, everything had blurred. The events seemed to unfold in fast forward. Dr. Brinkman's wife, Helen, had us sit in the middle of the room. It was cramped. Fifteen faculty members plus their spouses or dates plus just as many candidates all crammed in shoulder-to-shoulder. I felt beared down upon. Interrogated. Accused of something.

After the Babies R Us incident, we never ended up registering, so we received duplicate gifts. Diapers and pacifiers and bibs and diapers and pacifiers and a stuffed duck and diapers and bottles and a pillow with a giraffe stitched into it. "My favorite animal when I was a kid," the giver said. "Wonderful," Sara said. "Thank you so much." She set it to the side with the rest. There was just so much of it. Piles and piles of stuff. There were rattlers and noise makers and a mobile of stars that would hang above the crib. Night lights and a baby monitor and more bottles and more diapers. An endless stack. All of it made me realize how much I would miss this, Sara and me and the baby. She was going to take him away from me the next day, and I'd wind up like my mother, estranged and absent and depressed. At first I'd pine for him, my mind constantly turning to what he was doing, thinking, if he was good, ornery, or quiet like me. But then it would become easier. Days would pass before thinking of him, and then, without even realizing it, I'd forget a birthday, Christmas, his age even. I would, after awhile, not even be a father at all.

I felt this pain so acutely that I began to concoct a plan to persuade Sara to stay with me. Since that afternoon, we hadn't discussed the matter further, the subject dropped, like we had a fight over the correct way to bake a meatloaf, momentarily intense followed by the slow realization that it wasn't, in the end, all that important. But now a surge of anger and fear and anxiety swept me up. I made plans to immediately drop out of the PhD program. I'd teach high school physics. We'd move back to Oklahoma, on her parents' street if she wanted. Anything. Just as long as she wouldn't leave me.

Resolute in my new plan, I turned to Sara, smiled, and went to grab her hand. Before I could do so, however, she reached for the next gift, held it up to her ear, and shook it.

After presents, we sat down to dinner. I gulped down more wine. We ate smoked salmon. Sara sat next to me and pushed her food around with a fork. The host gave a speech. Dr. Brinkman stood and had us all raise our glasses. I couldn't hear what he was saying. His words mashed together like his tongue was swollen and scraped against his teeth. There was something about the miracle of life. Yes, he said. I used the word "miracle." Sara pinched me under the table. Everyone smiled and nodded and Mrs. Brinkman winked at us. But none of it made any sense to me. I could see his mouth moving, but he wouldn't stay still. He panned across my line of vision left to right, left to right. I had drunk too much.

Dinner ended, and Dr. Brinkman grabbed my elbow. "Let's go to my study," he said.

Sara scowled.

"I'll have him back in no time."

His study was a mess. Books lay open everywhere. Passages were highlighted, and illegible notes were scribbled in the margins. Loose papers strewn everywhere. A microscope leaned against the armrest of a plush lounge chair. A banker's lamp gave the room a hushed glow.

Dr. Brinkman opened a humidor and produced two cigars. He smelled one and smiled and handed me the other. "From Cuba," he said. "Don't tell anybody." He poured two glasses of port from a bottle that seemed to have materialized out of nowhere. The glasses were bulbous and difficult to hold.

"You're a lucky man," he said. "Sara is beautiful."

"Thank you, sir."

"Please. We've known each other for years now, Coulter. Call me Allen."

He moved the microscope and sat down in his chair. He swirled the brown liquid in his glass and took a sip. I did the same. It tasted like maple and burned all the way down.

"You're going to make a great father," he said. "I envy you that. I always wished I had the opportunity. It's been one of the greatest regrets of my life."

"You decided not to?"

"No. We tried. Helen and I tried for years. We tried fertility treatments. I got tested. She got tested. We tried everything. I'm not much of one for fatalism, but maybe it just wasn't meant to be."

"You eventually gave up?"

"I wouldn't put it that way," he said. "We just stopped trying." He snipped the end of his cigar and passed me the cutter. "I suppose it worked out in the end. I might not've accomplished what I have if I did."

"You think being a father would've held you back?"

"No. No. Not at all. That's not what I meant. I just think I would've found joy in other things. Better things maybe. Physics can't love you back."

"It's just chemical reactions in the brain," I said. "Love. It's akin to eating large amounts of chocolate."

"Don't minimalize the perception, though, Coulter. It's the experience of those chemical reactions that make them important. Without that conscious interpretation and the feelings that they emit, life wouldn't be worth living. Otherwise it would all be meaningless. Including your work."

We lit our cigars. It tasted terrible, like wood smoke and ash.

"How is your work coming along, Coulter? We haven't spoken in a while about it."

"Good, sir."

"Any findings yet?"

"Not yet."

"Have you given any more thought to changing your dissertation? There's still time. You can still graduate on time."

I didn't answer. I was too drunk to answer. He was right; my work would go nowhere. It wasn't even work anymore. It was simply hitting the enter key over and over again. The computer would produce a new Calabi-Yau manifold, and it would be entered into the parameters, and they would fail. I would hit enter again, and again it would fail. Enter. Failure. Enter. Failure. Enter. Failure. That was what my work had boiled down to, passivity. But yet I kept showing up every day, hitting enter. It was the very definition of insanity: repeating actions but expecting different results.

"You don't look well, Coulter. Are you feeling okay?"

"Yes, sir."

"You just haven't been yourself lately."

I didn't answer.

"Don't worry so much. It'll come to you. Like Archimedes and the displacement of water. You know the story, right?"

"Yes, sir." I knew the story—it had been canonized by science teachers from grade school to secondary. King Heron II had commissioned a goldsmith to create him a crown from gold but thought the guy had robbed him and made it with silver instead. Archimedes agonized and agonized over the problem, but he could not figure out a way to determine between silver and gold. This vexed him for weeks. He became depressed. He started talking to himself. He had thoughts of suicide. He was letting down his King. It was too much for him to bear. His wife told him to relax and drew him a bath. And then it hit him. Volume displacement. And he ran naked to the king with the good news.

"Get more sleep. Spend time with your wife. Enjoy this time with your son. There will always be time for science. Maybe you could come back next year and finish your dissertation. Whatever you decide to do, I'll support you."

The rest of the baby shower went by in snapshots. Dr. Brinkman poured another glass of port, and I dropped my cigar, burning a small hole in his carpet. We joined the others. Sara pulled a blanket over her shoulders. She glared at me and sat alone, which irritated me more than I could articulate. She wanted me to feel sorry for her, but I didn't. She could manage by herself for a short amount of time. Dr. Cardoza scoffed derisively at someone else's research. Mrs. Brinkman brewed me some coffee. There were more finger foods and promises to return to pick up the presents. And soon we left, having to borrow money from Dr. Brinkman for a cab as I was too drunk and Sara too pregnant to walk to the bus stop.

The cab smelled of potpourri and patchouli, a nauseous mixture masking a more nauseous mixture of vomit and sperm. Cabs in Boston were the communal wastebasket of tourists and unruly Red Sox fans.

"You said you wouldn't leave me alone in there," Sara said. "You promised."

"I know. I'm sorry."

"No, Coulter. Sorry doesn't cut it. You're always saying you're sorry but things aren't changing. They're getting worse. You said you would cut down your hours in the lab. You haven't. You said your mother would only be staying a few days. She hasn't left. You said you'd make it to every doctor's appointment. You haven't been to the last three. My blood pressure still isn't getting any better, Coulter. I have preeclampsia, but you haven't even asked me how I am. I mean who in the hell does that? I'm pregnant. This is supposed to be about me!"

"I'm sorry."

"Quit saying you're sorry."

"I'm sorry."

"Shut up!"

The cabbie glanced at us in the rear view mirror, though there wasn't a hint of worry in his expression, only annoyance. He'd seen much worse than this.

"I hate it here," Sara continued. "I don't have any friends. My family's thousands of miles away. I don't go anywhere. I don't do anything. I get up. I eat. I stay home. I watch soap operas. I go to the market for bread. I go to the doctor. I come back. I watch more television. I drink cough syrup even though I shouldn't, but goddamnit I just need something that will help me sleep at night. And all you can say is you're sorry. Well, Coulter, fuck you. That's what I think."

"I know," I said. "I'm sorry."

"Stop fucking apologizing, Coulter. It makes you sound pathetic."

The ride was short, and we paid the cabbie. Our building was dark even though it wasn't even 9:00 yet. People must've been out enjoying their Friday nights. Tires squealed in the distance. An engine backfired. Teenage laughter echoed against the brick and pavement. Our apartment was even quiet, my mother already having gone to sleep on the couch.

"Things don't have to be like this," I said.

"Shut up!"

"I'll quit school, we can go back to Oklahoma together, and we—"

"And then you would blame me. You'd always see me as what kept you from fulfilling your dreams."

"I'll find a job closer to home and—"

She punched me. She swung and connected squarely with my jaw. Pain shot up around my ear and in my temple. We were in the bathroom, and she lunged for me. It was all just a reaction. An accident. Everything seemed to move in slow motion. She lunged and I grabbed her by the arm, and I threw her into the shower. It was just instinct. I swear. But she wasn't big, even pregnant she wasn't, and she flew headfirst into the tile. She didn't even get her arms up in time to brace for impact.

The sound that it made terrified me. It was a loud thud, like a tractor tire falling onto dry, cracked earth. There were no reverberations. No reverb at all. Just loud and absolute.

She didn't move. She didn't twitch or moan or cry for help. A part of the tile had cracked where her skull had hit, and a smear of blood caked the grout. She lay face down, her legs sticking up out of the tub. It was an odd thing to see, such an unnatural position. Her dress was hiked up, and I could see the top of her pantyhose and her underwear. Both arms were somewhat under her so that I couldn't see if her fingers twitched, and her back didn't appear to rise and fall in rhythm with her breathing.

I went to her. I kneeled and was saying I was sorry and to please get up I am so sorry. But she didn't. She wouldn't. Blood gushed from a laceration in her forehead. The porcelain soap dish had shattered, and a large shard stuck into her neck, in her carotid artery. Blood gushed like milk pouring from a newly opened carton and pooled an inch thick at the bottom of the tub. I placed my hand over the wound, trying to stop the bleeding, but it just kept coming. I grabbed a towel, and in seconds it was soaked crimson and dripping. I checked for a pulse, but there was just too much blood around her neck. I tried her wrist, but couldn't find anything. I picked her up. I cradled her in my arms, and all I could say was I'm sorry. I am so, so sorry. I didn't mean it. I didn't. You have to believe me.

My mother came in and found us. She kneeled next to me and pulled me away and shook Sara. She shook her and yelled for her to wake up, but Sara didn't. She picked Sara up and dropped her. She slapped her face, her pleas becoming more desperate, cracked, and broken. Eventually, she gave up, and she pulled me to her. She held me against her chest, and she stroked my hair while I cried and pleaded to go back. I want to go back in time, I told her, please God I just want to take it back I want her back I want my Sara back, and my mother held me close, and I felt so warm against her. I felt warm and I felt safe and I never wanted to leave there. I thought if only I could stay next to her forever, everything would be okay.

Ж

Coulter's father ran much faster than he did. It took two or three strides just to equal one of his dad's. But he wanted to win. With everything he had, he wanted to win this race more than anything he'd ever wanted in his whole, entire life.

God, it felt good to run. To hear his and his father's feet clomp against the grass. The way the breeze rustled the pine needles against each other like softly brushing Brillo pads. Somehow he felt freer out here, not locked up in a classroom or confined to his room, reading *Scientific American*, as his parents pretended not to fight downstairs. They'd change their tones to mask their irritation with one another, their seething anger, into a soft, nearly benevolent cadence. Passive aggressive, it was called. Even Coulter knew that.

He fell! His father fell! Coulter couldn't believe it. Right before the river it looked like he tripped over a log or something, but Coulter didn't stop to see if his father was okay, he just kept pumping his knees, the excitement billowing inside of him like heated helium gas.

Coulter made it to the ledge first! He turned around, and there was his father, ambling up to him with a big, wide grin spread across his face. He looked like the Joker from the Batman cartoons his mother made him watch when he'd rather be outside trying to figure out what on earth was causing those mirages that made the road look like a river. He knew it had something to do with the heat and how the photons moved through the atmosphere, but how exactly this happened, he had no idea. And it made him think, this mirage, just how unreliable are his senses? What other illusions was he convinced of?

"Finally beat your old man, huh?"

Coulter beamed.

"All right now, let's see if you can beat me at something else." His father waded into the river so that the murky water soaked the hem of his swimming trunks. "You coming or what?"

Coulter hesitated. He could swim, barely. Well, he'd learned to doggy paddle and float on his back. But that was at the pool at the YMCA and he could see the bottom and make sure monsters that could eat him did not swim and live there. He knew his fear constituted a stupid, childish impulse, but he was a child, and prone to irrational fears. What if a shark sprang up and bit him? A freshwater shark. Something that had never been discovered before?

It could happen.

"C'mon now. It's all right. I got you."

His father smiled reassuringly. This did not alleviate Coulter's worries. He understood that it should, that his father only had the best intentions for him and would keep him safe, but inside his chest pumped a distrust of his father, mostly bred from his irrational side, but altogether existent and palpable; he could not shake it.

And there was the difference. The stretching miles of polar character traits of he and his father. His father, a storm chaser, lived for adrenaline and adventure. He'd gone bungee jumping and skydiving during their last vacation in Mexico, off the resort, where it was "just a tad bit more of a b-hole pincher," his dad had said. Coulter, on the other hand, strayed away from anything dangerous, or that involved heights, or could, if even of the slightest possibility, cause injury. He still used those dull, plastic scissors kindergarteners use in art class when conducting his physics experiment.

His father waded out further into the river so that the water stood to his waist, all the while coaxing Coulter to join him, but Coulter wouldn't budge. He could feel embarrassment growing as another family swimming on the other side of the river watched him, and shame built up inside him like a thin layer of burning gasoline. The two exuberant boys, both tanned and golden compared to Coulter's pale and papery skin, chuckled. Their laughter could have been at anything, but Coulter imagined they shared a private joke at his expense, mocking the pale and cowardly boy at the other side of the river.

Coulter dipped his toe into the water. Nothing. See? No reason to be afraid. He tiptoed out further, careful not to step on any rocks or fish or, he couldn't quite suppress the idea, a shark or stingray or the Loch Ness monster.

"What are you afraid of?" his father asked, the cacophony of the other boy's laughter echoing against the limestone banks. "Quit being such a wimp." His father was now using his stern voice, the one he used when Coulter did not do what his father had asked, the words biting and pointed.

"I'm not a wimp," Coulter whined.

"Then what's taking you so long?"

"I don't know. I can't see anything."

"You don't need to see anything. What are you, a chicken?" This was the first time Coulter had ever heard his father accuse him of something like that. "You are, aren't you? Just a big chicken like your mother."

Coulter didn't answer. He didn't know how. The short answer was yes, but he refused to admit this to his dad. To himself, sure, but not to his father who wasn't afraid of anything.

"Are you going to let those kids taunt you like that?" his father asked.

"I don't know."

"You don't know? You don't know? What does that mean, you don't know?"

"I don't know…I don't know." Coulter felt like he was on the verge of tears. "I'm sorry."

Coulter's father didn't wait for him any longer. He tromped over to Coulter, picked him up, and carried him into deeper waters, all the while Coulter screaming that he wanted to go back, the boys on the other side of the river too frightened themselves to laugh or taunt any longer, instead moving back up to the bank next to their mother who shielded them with her saggy arms.

Coulter's father plopped Coulter into the water. At first he panicked. He tensed up so that cramps like static electricity jolted his muscles. But, after a few seconds, the water cooled his body despite being the temperature of a warm bath. He could touch the sandy bottom, and he could feel his heart rate return to normal.

"See?" his dad said. "Nothing to be afraid of."

Coulter tested it out, and sure enough, there wasn't anything to be afraid of. They dipped and swam and Coulter doggy-paddled so that his little feet and chin bobbed around the surface. They splashed each other and laughed. They were having a good time. A great time in fact. The best time Coulter'd ever had with his father.

"I want to show you something," Coulter's father said. "Over here."

He swam to the nearest bank and motioned for Coulter to follow him, which, now unafraid of the river, he did. Coulter's father put his finger to his lips for him to be quiet and then submerged.

He was gone for a long time. Too long. Thousands of nightmares came to Coulter at once. He'd been sucked up into an underworld of sorts, a limbo for the drowned. An octopus had eaten him. He'd been swallowed whole by quicksand. But then he reemerged, just as quickly as he disappeared, but this time with a two-foot long catfish on his arm. Seriously, the creepy thing looked like it had swallowed his hand. But his father, instead of appearing petrified, was overjoyed, beaming as if he'd just tracked and trailed the largest tornado in recorded history.

"Now that's how you do it," he said.

The family from the other side of the river applauded. They actually clapped and whistled and yelled "bravo" to the man who had, just minutes before, scared the living daylights out of them when he'd carried Coulter into the water.

Coulter couldn't help but be impressed. The fish's wet scales glistened under the July sun like Petri dish jelly.

"Now it's your turn, son." Coulter's father released the fish, and Coulter saw it swim away, a V trailing behind its wagging tail.

"Do what?"

"Noodle."

"What's that?"

"What do you mean? I just showed…how could you—never mind. It's what I just did."

"Pull a fish out from underwater?"

"Exactly!"

"But how do I do that?"

"It's easy. Right underwater there," he pointed to where he just emerged next to the bank, "there's a hole. Stick your arm down in there as deep as you can, and when you feel a fish bite down, pull him up!"

"Are you out of your mind?"

Coulter's father showed a funny face, a mixture of perturbation and shock; this was the first time Coulter had ever questioned his father.

"Some would say so, I guess."

"There's no way I'm going to do that."

Coulter's father bent down to Coulter's level. "C'mon, son. For me?"

"No."

"Think of it as a character-building moment. A moment to not be like your mom."

"But I like Mom."

"I like Mom, too. Don't get me wrong. I'm just saying that she—well, she hasn't ever experienced life. And she's got a stranglehold on you. I mean, you're ten years old for Christ's sake, and you can't even swim."

"I can swim."

"You can't."

"Can too."

The boys on the other side of the river, feeling the threat over with, began to laugh again, this time Coulter sure that he was the butt of their jokes.

"They're laughing at you."

"I can hear them."

"Don't you want to show them you're not afraid?"

"I'd rather not drown."

"I'm right here."

"But you won't be able to see me."

"Look—"

"Are you going to get a divorce?"

"Just stay on topic, please."

"So, yes?"

Coulter's father showed him his hand, dunked it underwater, and then began to move his arm. Coulter could see the murky water ripple.

"See? I'll be able to tell if you are struggling by the movement of the water. Cause and effect, right?"

Coulter weighed this new evidence. Would his dad be able to distinguish panicked movement from regular movement? Would he imagine Coulter to be overreacting? Leave him down there for a "character-building moment" until he drowned or, worse yet, was horribly maimed by a monstrous catfish and doomed to live with a stump for an arm for the rest of his life, scarred with psychological trauma that prohibits even the mildest form of scientific inquiry, ultimately stunting his professional and social existence even before it began!

But, then again, those boys were laughing.

"You promise you'll save me?"

"Cross my heart and hope to die."

"Why would you hope to die?"

"It's a saying. An expression."

"Well, I've never heard it before."

"Are you going or what?"

Coulter didn't answer his father. Instead, he plugged his nose and submerged. The water tasted like mud and sulfur, but it wasn't as bad as he imagined, not nearly as frightening despite the fact he couldn't see, mostly because he was enthralled by the sound. His father's voice, the playful murmur of the boys across the river, their mother shouting at them to quit dunking each other, waved to him like muffled wings fluttering. It so entranced him that he almost forgot why he'd gone underwater in the first place. Like a summer mirage on a heated highway, Coulter became awed by how sound waves were manipulated by the substance in which it travelled, and it led him to wonder, exactly how is sound transformed by air, by a vacuum, by his very eardrums? Was what he heard anything like the source's actual sound? Ever? Has he been wrong about everything?

He found the hole his father told him about and stuck his arm in. At first, he couldn't feel anything, only the water and grainy sediment. He started to feel shortness of breath, his lungs constrict, and the sudden urge to breathe. But he held it. He did not want to disappoint his father, reemerge empty handed. He swept his arm back and forth, water, water, water, but there, just for a moment, he felt something squishy, warm, alive. He had to find it again. He had to! But he couldn't hold his breath anymore. In one quick burst, air erupted from his lungs and seeped out into the water, and as the bubbles tickled his nostrils, a catfish clamped down on his arm and dragged him further downstream.

MY FIRST INSTINCT WAS TO CALL THE POLICE, to turn myself in. It was, after all, the right thing to do. Admit what I'd done. Accept the punishment. I didn't have anything to keep me from doing this, really. No attachments. Sara was gone. The baby gone. My research going nowhere.

"No," Mom said. "No, no, no. We can't go to the police." She was standing over the body, shaking her head. There was still Sara's blood on her, on her hands and on her clothes, dried on her cheek.

"We have to. Don't we? We have to call somebody."

"Think about it, son. Think it through. Think about what will happen if you do."

I'd go to prison. I'd end up living with career criminals, drug dealers and murderers and rapists. I'd be labeled a baby killer. I'd be a pariah amongst pariahs. I'd be sought out, harassed, beaten, maybe even killed. It was inevitable. The long-suffering consequence of a moment's poor decision.

And I couldn't bring myself to do it.

I justified my decision at the time as an effect of being in shock. I couldn't think straight. The simplest thoughts eluded me. I forgot what day it was or what we'd done. My head still swam from the wine and port and nicotine, and I couldn't make my own decisions. It was easier just to do what Mom said to do.

Clean the body. Dispose of the body. "I don't want to lose you again, son," she said. And I obeyed. That way, I didn't have to think about what I was doing. It became an exercise, a chore I was compelled to complete.

The wound in Sara's neck had stopped bleeding after a while. Her heart had stopped, and the blood drained down toward her feet so that they looked purple, the rest of her body white and translucent. It didn't take long for rigor mortis to set in. Her limbs were stiff, and her muscles popped when we tried to move her. Her hair had been matted with blood. I washed it with a new lavender shampoo she'd recently bought. She hadn't even used it yet. It was expensive, a little treat she wanted to wait to open until the cheap stuff was all gone. I brushed her cuticles and washed her body and clipped her nails. I hurried because I couldn't really look at her. It was too hard. Her body didn't respond to my touch. Her flesh wasn't warm. Her eyes didn't peer back at me, instead rolling back into her head. Her flesh felt cold and hard, and her unresponsiveness made her cadaver seem more like a shell than my wife. I'd never given much credence to the idea of a soul, but something was undeniably missing. Her humanity had been sucked from her body, leaving behind nothing more than meat and bone and ligament. That's not to say it was like biology class, dissecting a frog—it wasn't so cold, so transactional. There remained a sense of an endless loss, of grief, and of guilt.

Mom wanted to throw the body in the Charles. She said it would be easier that way. No one would be the wiser. We would file a missing persons report in a couple days. We'd tell people she was unhappy. She wanted to move back home. I'd have to call her parents. I'd have to talk to her mother and father, ask them if they'd seen her when I knew they had not. I would have to lie and keep on lying until she was forgotten enough for people to stop asking questions. "It'll be better this way, honey," Mom said. "You'll see."

Again, I obeyed because I didn't know what else to do.

The body, however, was too heavy and too burdensome to travel all the way to the Charles, several miles to the east. We didn't have a car, and there was no way we could take a cab. This limited our options. We sat in the living room discussing, Sara's body beginning to decompose in the bathtub.

"I hate to say this, baby," Mom said. "But we may need to make her smaller."

"What are you saying?"

"You know." She paused, made a sawing motion with her hand. "Make her easier to carry."

"Are you insane?" I asked.

"We could get something handheld. Something that doesn't make a lot of noise."

"Out of the question."

"Okay," she said. She bit her thumb and crossed her legs. She wore gym shorts to sleep in, nondescript maroon mesh, exposing her legs. Varicose veins crisscrossed her calves like tubes of blueberry syrup.

"You have a better idea?" she asked.

We ended up stuffing her body into the empty box that had housed our son's crib. We had to bend her knees and cross her arms for her to fit, duct taping the lid shut as best we could. Her body contorted the box, bulging here and there, the lid distorted and the cardboard bending, but it was the best we could do under the circumstances. Together, we scooted the box onto the dolly I still hadn't returned to the super.

"This is a bad idea," Mom said.

To our left was a full-length mirror, and she was right: this was a bad idea—we looked like we were disposing a dead body.

"Do you have any others?"

She blinked at me. She had none.

"Okay," I said. "On three."

We walked out of the apartment. The hallway was clear, and so were the stairs. I walked backwards toward the elevator, pulling the dolly while

Mom pushed the button for the ground level. The elevator was empty, and through a low-quality speaker, a smooth jazz song played, the horns muffled under static. It reminded me of my father's CB radio he'd used when storm chasing, garbled voices singing out warnings of approaching storms. My mother tapped her foot along with the beat, her head bobbing like we were about to go out shopping or see a movie instead of dispose of her dead daughter-in-law. This didn't anger me as I thought it should. Instead, I found her reaction intriguing, her ability to dismiss the gravity of the situation around her, finding small joys in a terrible, generic song. I wondered if this represented her ingrained disposition or if it was rather the result of years of medication to treat her various mental illnesses. Regardless, it made me think of the pills Dr. White had prescribed me, if they would grant me serenity despite even the most tragic of circumstances. The thought, I had to admit, sounded appealing.

The foyer was empty, the front desk abandoned since we'd moved in years before. No one gathered their mail from the in-wall boxes. During the day, kids would sometimes play just outside the door, bouncing those red rubber balls from elementary school gym class, or just sit at the foot of the stairs, have a conversation out of earshot from their eavesdropping parents, but near midnight, the street was fortunately quiet. Every few minutes or so, a car would rumble past, its windows tinted, the passengers shrouded in darkness. But they didn't even slow down when they passed.

A few blocks away, we tried to dispose of her in a dumpster on the outskirts of the Dot, but she was too heavy. I was on one end and Mom on the other, but we couldn't lift her past our waists. We stood there arguing about what to do. Mom wanted to just leave her there on the ground, to run away, start some place new, Quebec or Rio, hell, catch a flight to Amsterdam, but I told her we couldn't. "People would come looking," I told her. "We'd always be on the run."

"Then what are we going to do?"

I looked around us. It was dark, and with every second that ticked by, I became more paranoid that we would be caught, but no one stopped us or asked us what we were doing. No one cared. There were no witnesses.

Eventually, I found a discarded wooden crate and some lumber leaning against the side of a building. I selected a 2x4 that seemed sturdy, that hadn't been warped by the elements or weakened by wood rot. There were bags of trash next to the dumpster, the purveyor of the neighboring noodle shop too lazy or too busy to throw them into the dumpster. I tore them away, looking for something I could use. Mostly, it was just food trash. Uneaten plates of ramen and pad thai, paper plates and napkins, the stench debilitating and overwhelming. I had to fight back dry heaves, and I tried not to breathe altogether. Eventually, I found something I could use: a long extension cord, the prongs broken off.

"A fulcrum and lever," I said.

"What?"

"A fulcrum and lever. And a pulley. Look." I placed a small, wooden crate a few feet from the dumpster and the 2x4 on top of it. Together we scooted the box onto the end of the 2x4 nearest the dumpster. I then tied my belt around the box and the extension cord onto my belt.

"When I say, I need you to stand and jump on the other end," I said, pointing to the empty side of the 2x4. I then climbed into the dumpster, holding the other end of my makeshift rope.

"Now," I said.

Mom started to jump, and I pulled, but it was still difficult. I could feel the box becoming lighter, it lifting into the air, and I struggled and grunted and pulled.

"Push!" I yelled. "Push the box."

It got lighter still, my mother on the other side of the dumpster wall pushing the box from below. Eventually, we got it over the lip, and the box came crashing into the dumpster. It landed on my hand, and I felt a pop in my wrist. It hurt, but I couldn't bring myself to look. I just pulled my hand out from underneath, my extremities throbbing from the pain, and climbed out without looking back.

X

The next morning, I went to the lab as scheduled. When I walked in, I expected someone to confront me. I expected them to be able to read my crime on my face, by how I said hello or how I sat at the mainframe computer. They'd know something was wrong because they'd still be able to smell the booze even though I'd taken three showers. They'd see I hadn't slept and just know. Murderer, they would say. How could you do such a thing? How could you murder your beautiful wife who you loved dearly and who loved you and who was carrying your child? Your *child*, Coulter? *Your* child. How could you? And I would say I don't know. I did love her. I do love her still. It was an accident. I swear it was.

But they didn't, of course. They smiled and gave slight nods of their head. They told me they enjoyed the baby shower, asked if we had gotten home safely, Sara's and my plans for the weekend. No one noticed anything was wrong. It made me think that life would be much easier if we wore signs around our necks. They would tell our secrets and what we're unable or too embarrassed or too ashamed to say out loud. Dr. Cardoza's would say that she was harsh on other people's work because she hasn't been able to live up to what she considers her potential. Dr. Brinkman's would say he feared he had peaked twenty years before or that he regretted never having children. Our neighbor Becky's could say that she wanted to leave her husband but was too afraid to do so. Maybe people would be more apt to help then. They wouldn't turn the other cheek when they thought someone was in trouble and chalk up their decision not to help as the right thing, minding their own business. I wanted to tell someone what I had done. I was desperate to tell someone. But I didn't know how or who I should tell. How could I explain my actions? How could I explain that I'd disposed of the body because I didn't know what else to do? I should've gone to the police right away. But I was scared and drunk and it was easier to be told what to do. It was easier not to make my own decisions. That doesn't excuse what I did. It wasn't an excuse. It was just the truth. Simple, unalienable fact.

I made a plan. I would leave here. I would pick up my mother. I would lie to her. I would say we're going to get something to eat. I would tell her we were going to see a movie or that I wanted to introduce her to someone, Dr. Brinkman maybe. It didn't matter. She would believe me. She would be gullible and would come when I asked. We would get on a bus, I would take her to the police station, and I would tell the truth.

I sat at the mainframe, hitting enter and watching the numbers cascade down the monitor as different Calabi-Yau manifolds ran through the universal characteristic matrices. Enter. Fail. Enter. Fail. It became hypnotizing in a way. The monotony of the enterprise let my mind wander and let me seem inconsequential and unimportant. What I did didn't matter; therefore, I could stay like this forever, in perpetual motion. Unless something came and stopped me, caused some friction, I would sit here. It could be in an hour or two, if another student had reserved the mainframe. It could be later when the janitor came to clean and mop the floors. It might be hunger or the urge to use the restroom. Eventually, I knew something would deter me. But for now I was content with postponing my confession for as long as I could. I would sit here until I couldn't any longer. Then I would go to the cops. I would confess and lead them to the body and let the system decide what punishment befitted my crime.

Enter.

Fail.

Enter.

Fail.

The lab was busy as usual. Finals were approaching, and students busied themselves with projects, experiments, and papers that needed wrapping up. They corroborated over calculations estimating the distance to a perceived black hole. They hunched over microscopes and argued over equations scribbled onto a chalkboard, and I couldn't help but think of ways to kill myself. I wouldn't want to make it a public spectacle, so I couldn't do it there in the lab. I could walk out to the Charles and wade into the deep part of the river. But it was so cold. It would be difficult to make it a few steps without confronting the overwhelming desire to turn around and warm up. There were proton lasers here in the lab. I could borrow one. No one would really say anything. I could take it down into my office, turn it on, and stick my face in front of it. I wondered if it would hurt or if the wound would be cauterized and if the nerve endings would be burnt away so that I wouldn't feel a thing.

Enter.

Fail.

Enter.

Fail.

But that wouldn't be fair. Not to Sara. Not to Isaac. Not to my mother and father and Sara's parents. They deserved the truth. They deserved to know what happened and what I had done. They deserved to see justice, or some semblance of it anyway, tight handcuffs clasped to my wrists as I am led away to prison. At least there will be closure. At least they could collect her remains and take them home and have some place to visit when they get lonely and sad. At first they would go all the time. They would go twice a week. Thursdays at lunch because it had been too long. Sundays after church because they would drive right by her grave anyway. Then it would fall to once a week. Then bi-weekly. They would stop going to church. They would withdraw and silently blame each other. They should've known I was no good for their little girl. And the other one should've done something about it.

Enter.

Fail.

Enter.

Fail.

Soon they'd start to resent each other. They'd secretly hate each other. Both would be too afraid to say anything aloud, though, or take any action. Gary, Sara's father, would bury himself in his hobbies. He would restore old WWII coding machines, T-89s and the Enigma, if he could find one. He'd collect classic car carburetors, and they would ionize and collect dust in his garage. He'd write un-publishable editorials to the *Oklahoman* supporting unheard of and minor legislation. Marissa, Sara's mom, would drink. She'd drink Bud Light and get into arguments with bartenders over what constituted a domestic beer during happy hours. She would try to tell them that Anheuser-Busch was bought by Belgians and that Miller and Coors were bought by South Africans and try to get a discount on Sam Adams because, "When the hell did Massachusetts secede from the Union?" She'd never win, though.

Enter.

Fail.

Enter.

Fail.

They'd separate eventually and file for divorce. They might end up alone or they might meet someone new. A divorcee like themselves. Or maybe a widower. Someone else who was alone and grieving and willing to say okay to someone new because it was better than being alone.

Dad would be destroyed. He'd probably blame himself and his relationship with my mother as the cause of this tragedy. For years he would analyze his own failed marriage and produce countless scenarios, wondering if he would have done something just a little bit differently, made one single different decision, would things have turned out better? The way they should've been. If he had gotten Mom help sooner, went to couples therapy weekly, twice a week, every single day, hadn't had that fling with that grad student, she wouldn't have been depressed and she wouldn't have tried to kill herself and he wouldn't have asked her to leave. They would've been happy and I would've been happy and there would be no way that I would've killed my wife. There'd be no way I could be capable of something so terrible.

Enter.

Fail.

Enter.

Fail.

Mom would disappear again, if she hadn't already. She'd move someplace new this time, Salt Lake City or maybe even out of the country. Vancouver. Chile. Someplace safe and conservative and where she could get a job at a pet store taking care of fish and puppies. She might even fall in love with one of them, a little min-pin that hobbles around on three legs even though the fourth is just fine. She'll call him Albatross for no particular reason at all and one night, when she has been promoted to night manager and is closing the store, she'll take little Albatross home and feed him little chopped up pieces of hot dog. She'll potty train him and take him on walks and cuddle with him on the couch when they watch reality TV and The Weather Channel. She'll buy him little sweaters because they're just too darn cute and because she can't say no. It'll feel good to be responsible for something again. The pills will help her forget about me and my father and what could've been and she'll be happy with a little dog.

Enter.

Fail.

Enter.

Fail.

Dr. Brinkman will question why he hadn't seen what I was capable of before. During the interview process prior to accepting me into the program. During all our research together as he enlightened me about the origins of the universe, his quiet belief that big bangs are a common phenomenon, that we are but one of many of these bubble universes in a quilted and layered multiverse, and that one day ours would simply run out of energy and soon pop, destroying everything. Or when he explained that because the multiverse is infinite everything is doomed to repeat itself, but we'll also have a second opportunity to make a different decision, even if it takes a billion millennia. We'd have the opportunity to right our mistakes. He'll wonder if he had maybe played a small part in the tragedy. He'll second-guess his decision to steer me in a new direction in my dissertation, warning that if I continued on with my current research that I might not be recommended for a doctorate. He will regret putting so much pressure on me. Later, when it comes to other students, he'll become more lenient. The students will become less stellar. They will achieve less, and the institution will become second-tier, taking a backseat to Stanford and CalTech. Dr. Brinkman will be pushed out with Dr. Cardoza taking over. Brinkman won't mind this so much. He'll retire and spend more time with his wife and they will travel overseas, in the Mediterranean and through Switzerland all the while thinking how nice it would've been to have children of their own.

Enter.

Fail.

Enter.

Success.

I will go to jail. I will go to the police station and be arrested and arraigned and appointed a public defender. She'll be right out of law school and living in a studio apartment above a consignment shop. It might even be close to my place. She will not have any sympathy for me. She will not offer any forgiveness because I will take responsibility for my actions. In fact, she will hate me. She will loathe me and secretly hope that I go to prison for the rest of my life and she will hate the fact that she has to defend me. She will question why she hadn't listened to her mother and joined the Peace Corps like she'd wanted or gone to Juilliard to pursue her music or become a cobbler like her father, whatever the case may be. But she will be professional, and she will give me sound advice. I'll reject most of it because I couldn't fathom not being punished as much as I should be punished. I'll start to think of myself as a martyr and be ashamed that I think this. I won't tell anyone that, of course.

Because I plead guilty, the judge will move sentencing in a month's time to expedite the process and save taxpayers some money. I'll stay in county during the interim. I'll eat Go-gurt and instant mashed potatoes and reflect on what I had done and what could've been. There won't be much else to think about. I'll make an attempt to become adjusted to my new life. I'll tell myself there is some value in its predictability and its structure. Awake by 7:00 a.m. and breakfast by 7:15 after head count. After that, I'll be taken to work. I'll make license plates and road signs. Armed guards will take me to clean up trash by the highway. After work I'll be given an hour free time before dinner. Being county and not a prison, there won't be as many amenities. There won't be a basketball court or workout equipment. There won't be cable television and a library to check out books. I'll write letters to family members and legislators and my lawyer. Most will go without a response. Lights out by 7:15.

My sentencing will be agreed upon by both the state and by the judge. I'll be convicted of second-degree murder, the desecration of human remains, tampering with evidence, and the illegal disposal of a body. All felonies. I'll be sentenced to fifty years with the possibility for parole in twenty-seven. At some point in time, I'll be released, and I'll have the possibility for another life. I'll move somewhere in the Midwest. Kansas or Nebraska or maybe Iowa. I'll get a job as a janitor or barista or stocking shelves at a municipal library. I might even make some friends. I might have a chance to find joy again.

Enter.

Success.

Enter.

Success.

I will grow old and work until I die. A few friends will show up to my funeral, and they will say nice things about me because they wouldn't know any better. Soon, they will die, and memories of me along with them.

Success.

Success.

Success.

Ж

A manifold had passed a matrix, then two, then three, then four. With each matrix it passed, I could feel my blood pressure increase, the slow secretion of endorphins, the neurotransmitters in my brain firing joy through my nerve endings. In total, it passed 745 matrices, enough to quantitatively confirm the veracity of the model's findings. I had succeeded where Susskind and Kaku and Feynman and Einstein had failed. I had, beyond a reasonable doubt, discovered the actual shape of the universe.

For years, I had dreamt about this moment. I'd imagined it would be akin to a religious experience. There'd be an epiphany, like Archimedes with water displacement, and I'd be overcome with joy and exuberance and streak through campus shouting at the top of my lungs that I had done it, I had done it, I had finally done it. Others would stare at me strangely, students and faculty casting worried glances, wondering if they should intervene or call security before I hurt someone, but I wouldn't care. It would feel like my blood vessels might burst through my skin. I'd somehow become aware on a cellular level, new proteins created and synapses strengthened to encode this moment into my genetics, right down into my RNA, so that I could at anytime revisit the pride and ecstasy of my discovery again and again and again, reliving it always in some perpetual euphoric induced hallucination, but it wasn't like that.

There was joy, of course. But there was also worry. There was anxiety. There was this burning in the pit of my stomach, and my muscles cramped up. I was overtaken by a sense of responsibility and burden. I was beholden by it. I now owed a duty to myself, to MIT, to Dr. Brinkman, and the entire scientific community. This very well could change the world in a very practical, and good, way. Quantum computing, the storage of energy, air and space travel, almost every industry imaginable could be impacted by such a discovery. Understanding the true shape of the universe could very well change the world, and I was the only one who knew the answer.

To be clear, this did not change how I felt about Sara. The desire to confess my crime was still present, and I still felt inclined to turn myself in, to plead guilty, to go to jail, to be punished. But I also had an obligation to share my findings with the scientific community—they were quite possibly the greatest discoveries since Einstein had published his theory of relativity. To not publish, to not share this with the scientific community, would be almost as great of a crime as I'd already committed, and I thought maybe, just maybe, it would dip the scales somewhat in my favor. Not condone what I'd done to my family, but maybe right my wrong in the slightest way possible. I knew it to be crazy, but I thought it anyway. I clung to it, in fact.

So I made a new plan. First publish, then confession. In the end, timing hardly mattered—the consequences would be the same. In order to accomplish this, though, I had to buy myself some time. When I left the lab, I didn't celebrate as I'd imagined. I simply downloaded my findings onto a flash drive, backed it up in my office, went home, and formulated a plan with my mother, a story we could tell.

After twenty-four hours had passed, I filed a missing persons report. The precinct in the Dot appeared much like those clichés in movies:

detectives crammed into a small bullpen, desks littered with paperwork and faded pictures of children, loose ties, and the smell of burnt coffee. It made my lies a little easier to tell. I could pretend I was an actor in a silly primetime procedural. I played the worried and frightened husband, and the detective would be non-committal and detached, having heard this same sob story day in, day out for his entire fourteen-year career. He'd say he empathized but that there wasn't much for him to do. Most times, he'd say, the missing just turned back up in a day or two. If they didn't, then they didn't want to be found. Simple as that. He just had too little resources to go out and look for every single one of them.

I'd never been much of a liar, though. Growing up, my father and teachers had easily seen through my fabrications. They weren't big lies by any means. They tended to be simple fibs. I like English class, I'd tell Dad, and I'm looking forward to writing my essay on *Tess of the d'Ubervilles*. I made a ton of friends and I think a girl named Kiley likes me. I climbed the rope all the way to the ceiling in gym class. I'd tell my teachers my mother travelled a lot for work. She was an attorney for the justice department and worked closely with the FBI, catching bank robbers and members of hate groups. That was why she didn't come to parent teacher conferences or the annual science fair. Of course, my father told them the truth, but they never corrected my lies. That wasn't their job. They were to teach me to read and write and do long division and then send me up another grade so I was someone else's problem.

The policeman who took my report wasn't much older than me, perhaps in his early thirties. I'd expected him to be exhausted, unshaven, his whiskers growing in like graphite, to be overworked and tired and smoke two packs a day and drink ten cups of coffee. He'd be overweight and smelling of deodorant and hand sanitizer. But he didn't. He seemed peppy. He seemed genuinely excited to be doing his job, like he enjoyed his work. His name was Detective Landsmen, and he had pictures of two small children on his desk, the boy's teeth gapped, the girl with ribbons in her hair. Neither one could've been older than five. They were smiling and holding hands and playing with dandelions and sunflowers. These were staged photographs, for sure. He and his wife had paid a professional photographer and they drove to a park and posed for pictures. They had to have. Nobody was this happy without preparation.

When we shook hands, his palms were a little greasy, like he'd just eaten a cheeseburger. He asked me to sit and offered me a drink. "Warm tea?" he asked. "Sometimes I feel warm tea helps me relax."

"No, thank you," I said.

"Are you sure? I know it's a cop station, but it's actually pretty good."

"I'm fine."

"Bagel?"

"I'm fine, thanks."

"Donut? Soda? Anything you want."

"Really," I said. "I'm fine."

"Okay," he said like he wasn't convinced, and sat down behind his desk. "Tell me what's going on."

I told him my story, the one my mother and I had come up with. It started right after the baby shower since that was the last time anyone had seen Sara. Parts of it contained truth. I told him we'd fought. We'd fought about the party. She accused me of purposely leaving her alone in there. We fought about my work, my hours spent at the lab. My absenteeism. My mother. She confessed her fear that she would be raising the baby alone, that even if I didn't leave that I wouldn't be present. All true. I told him we'd yelled at each other. She broke a lamp. She threw it at me but missed, and it shattered in the bathroom.

"In the bathroom?" he asked. "What was a lamp doing in the bathroom?"

"It wasn't before. It was in the bedroom. She threw it at me as I stood in the bathroom."

"I see."

She'd cried and cleaned up the mess, and I'd said some things I regretted. She didn't apologize and neither did I. I told her I thought she was holding me back. I blamed her for my failures as a scientist, that I might not be awarded my PhD. I told her that because of her I would end up a high school teacher, having to deal with sarcastic and stupid children all day. I blamed her for things that hadn't even happened yet and despite immediately regretting these things I still didn't apologize.

"You go to Harvard?"

"MIT."

"Good school."

"Yes."

Sara and I yelled at each other until we couldn't yell anymore. We'd run out of things to accuse one another of. We both began to realize how ridiculous we sounded. That's what I thought anyways. We still didn't apologize to each other, but it felt like we would in the morning. We just needed time to cool down; that was all. I went to bed but couldn't sleep. Sara stayed awake. I could hear the television on in the other room. It was tuned to infomercials mostly, she changing the channel every couple of minutes. Most of them had to do with weight loss. There would be one for a home gym, another for a miracle diet based on protein shakes. She must've filled her water glass six or seven times.

"How long did she watch television?"

"An hour. Maybe longer."

Then she stuck her head through the door. "I'm taking a walk," she said. Usually, I would've argued with her. She was seven months pregnant, and it was past ten in a pretty rough neighborhood. But I was mad and tired and I didn't. I didn't even raise my head or close my eyes. I couldn't tell if she looked angry still or if she had the look of resignation. Her voice had been monotone. "I'm taking a walk." It was like she was telling me she'd bought a new toothbrush. She didn't have any sort of feelings toward the idea. It was just "I'm taking a walk."

"And you haven't seen her since?"

"No."

"Phone call? Email? Text Message? Facebook update?"

"Nothing."

"Has anything like this ever happened before? You two fight, she disappears for a couple days, goes to her sister's place or something?"

"No. Never."

We'd fought in the past, of course. We fought about moving out here away from her friends and family. We fought about the baby. She'd broached the subject of having one first. I hesitated. But it wasn't because I didn't want children. I had the suspicion she was trying to fill a void in her life. She was lonely in Massachusetts and our landlord wouldn't allow dogs. She said she hated me for saying something like that. But she didn't leave.

"Have you spoken with any of her family members? Parents? Sister?"

"I came to you first. They don't know. Only my mother."

He smiled a practiced, warm smile. "I see," he said. "That might be smart. The sooner we get started the better chance we have finding the missing person. And I want to assure you that we will do all that we can to help find your wife."

"Thank you."

"So what do you think happened?"

"I'm sorry?"

"Do you think she left you? Do you think maybe something bad has happened to her? Do you think she might've hurt herself?"

"I think she's just scared. I scared her. We're about to be parents, and I, well, I haven't lived up to my part of the bargain."

"I see." He scribbled a few notes down onto a yellow legal pad. I couldn't see what they said, the words illegible, upside down. "Did she have any enemies?"

"No. She was abrupt with people. Profane at times. But no enemies.

People loved her."

"So no one, in your opinion, would want to hurt her?"

"Of course not. Do you think something bad has happened?"

"I have to ask these questions. I have no opinion right now. It's too early to tell anything."

"I understand."

"You should call your in-laws. More than likely, if she's scared, she's tried contacting them. They'll probably know where she is. She might already be in their living room. You never know."

"I will. I'll let you know what they say."

"In the meantime, it would help if we could get access to cell phone records. Financial records. That sort of thing. If she uses her debit card, we'll be able to see which way she's heading."

"Of course."

"And I'd like to speak with your mother. Natalie, is it?"

"Yes," I said. "Sure. I'll have her call, when she's available."

"She's too busy to make a statement?"

"No, no. That's not it." I thought about telling him about her mental illness, her institutionalization, her abandonment, her history of suicide attempts, but I decided against it—it might arouse too much suspicion. "She just hasn't been feeling well. That's why she's been staying with us."

He smiled, warmly, like he completely understood, and we shook hands, and he told me he would be in touch. It was odd, but I felt better after speaking with him. He had a comforting presence, much like Dr. White, the psychiatrist Dr. Brinkman had recommended to me. He had reassured me. He made me feel like he would find Sara and everything would turn out okay. This was irrational, of course. I knew everything would not be okay, but it was nice to think it might, even if it was for a short amount of time. I thanked him and said I looked forward to his call.

Telling Sara's parents wouldn't be easy. I thought about when Sara and I had told them we'd be moving to Boston. We'd gone out to dinner that night at a comedy club, The Looney Bin, in downtown Oklahoma City. The comedian was a young guy, overweight, and covered in acne scars. A portion of his routine involved heckling his audience, pointing out their flaws and idiosyncrasies, one of those guilty pleasures people enjoy, laughing at others' insecurities. One of his victims had been my father-in-law, Gary. Not a man's man by any stretch of the imagination, he was thin and pale and reticent, much like myself actually. The focus of the comedian's onslaught that night was Gary's red hair. Ginger was what he called Gary. Hey, Ginger, he said, I've always wondered, does the carpet always match the drapes? Huh, Fire Crotch? Gary'd chuckled like a good sport, but I could tell he was hurt by the comic's jokes.

Later that night, when he and his wife dropped Sara and I off at our apartment, close to the university, he'd asked to speak to me privately. We sat outside as Sara and her mother went inside to have a nightcap. It was a dark night. The clouds hung so low they reflected the orange glow of the city.

"You know, I'm going to hear it from my wife now," he said as we stood on the patio, overlooking the street. College kids roamed about, talking loudly as they strolled to the next party on their agenda. Bass beats could be heard a few apartments down. Laughter from up above. "She's going to be grilling me to move to Boston."

"I hope you don't think we're trying to run away or anything like that."

"God, how can you live so close to campus?" he said, pointing to the drunken kids, bumbling down the street. "Is it always like this?"

"Not always. Weekends."

He peered out over the railing and then up, trying to locate the party upstairs. When he did, a beer spilled from a few floors up and nearly drenched him, cascading down only a few feet away. Gary pulled his head back. "No. Not running away *per se*. MIT is a great school. No one could blame you for that. But Boston? It's so far from home. I guess I'm just being selfish."

"There'll be breaks in the school year. We'll be able to fly back. You can come visit anytime you want."

"You guys don't party with these kids, do you?" He pointed at the passersby. They carried cases of beer under their arms or paper bags filled with plastic gallons of vodka. They were already drunk, zigzagging from sidewalk to lawn to street, and about to get drunker. That's when bad things started to happen. Fights out in the street. A stolen car. A window busted in by a brick. "They look like they're twelve for Christ's sake. Doesn't anyone say anything to them?"

"It's college," I said. "I think most of the time people just look the other way."

He nodded, swatted at a fly buzzing around his head. "Just promise me you'll be good to her. Promise me you won't let her get lonely. Just promise me that, okay?"

"Of course," I told him. "I would never do anything like that. I love Sara. With all my heart. She is the most important thing in my life. She is my life. She is."

"Yes, I know," he said. "But you have to understand—she is mine, too."

I called as soon as I got home from the police station. Gary answered on the third ring but didn't say hello right away. I could hear Marissa in the background finishing up a story about a coworker who was getting a personal loan to get fake boobs. "Divorce does the craziest things to people." After he said hello, I told him the lie about Sara, and all he said was, "I'm on my way."

"No, Gary. You should stay there. More than likely that's where she's heading."

"She would've called us first. She would've told us she was coming, and we would know where she is. No. Something's wrong, Coulter. I just know it is."

"We don't know anything yet."

"We know that this isn't like her. She wouldn't disappear like this."

"I just don't want her to wind up there, and you be here. That's all."

"We're coming, Coulter. We'll see you later today."

My mother had given me a pep talk before they arrived. She told me to buck up, to put on a brave and hopeful face. We can't arouse any suspicions. She even picked out what I would wear, a baby blue sweater and chinos that needed to be ironed. "They're going to ask you questions," she said. "And you need to keep things simple. Tell them the same story you told the cop. Don't add any detail, don't take anything out. Word-for-word if you can." The next few days will be the most important, she said. If you tell a consistent story, and they can't find the body, then there will be no crime. Soon everyone will forget, and it'll be like she never even existed at all. Then everything can return back to normal.

She could tell I was wavering. I felt guilty and ashamed. I wanted to hurt myself as punishment. I wanted to break the mirror and cut myself with the shattered shards. It was just too tempting. Take a bath and throw in the toaster. Jump from the window. It was only three stories. I probably wouldn't die, though, just break my legs. My mother continued to coax me by appealing to my vanity. You are going to be a great man, Coulter. You have done what no one else could. You have achieved more than Newton and Einstein. You are too important to lose.

When Gary and Marissa arrived, they looked disheveled, frightened. They were scared, and they fought back tears and said they didn't understand. They didn't look as they did when we'd visited Oklahoma and told them we were pregnant. Then they'd been excited and upbeat. Marissa appeared to float as she walked, her feet barely grazing the ground. She served iced tea and tiny tuna sandwiches and beamed in a way only a soon-to-be grandmother can. She made plans to come to Boston more often to see us, at least once a month, any longer and she would just flat out die. Gary gloated. He offered up family names like party favors. Marshall after his great-uncle. Sara pointed out he'd never even met the man. James after his father. Sara pointed out she never even knew the man. Hal after his brother. Sara pointed out he was a drunk. "We're thinking Isaac," I said. "After Newton."

"Oh," said Marissa. "That's nice."

Gary's shirt, a Hawaiian floral print, was tucked in but not very well. It billowed around his right side, stretched taut on his left. Over the belly, the hem alongside the buttons had become twisted so that a small sliver of his skin showed. Marissa, on the other hand, attempted to keep up appearances. Her lips had been painted a bright peach color, her hair straightened with each strand in place, but she hadn't paid as much attention to detail as usual. Her purse, for instance, was the color of a funnel cloud, a mixture of mint and olive, yet her shoes were emerald blue, clashing with each other.

"How are you holding up, honey?" Marissa asked. She smiled warmly as if by instinct, an expression she used to defend against her worst anxieties. "Have you been eating?"

"Yes," I said. "I've been eating. How was your flight?"

"Good," she said. "Just fine."

Gary shook my hand with his usual limp grip. "Any word?" he asked. "Anything new?"

"Not yet," I said.

"Anything from the police? Any clues?"

"Not that I'm aware of."

"A credit card purchase? A text message? Nothing?"

"The detective said that sometimes no news is the best news."

"That doesn't make any sense," Gary said. "How could no news be good news?"

"It means that if something bad has happened, her death for instance, they usually know of that soon." My mother had slinked into the living room without any of us noticing. "A body turns up. A ransom note is sent. Someone confesses. Believe me," she said. "No news is the best news."

"Gary, Marissa. This is my mother."

Neither one of them said a word.

X

We sat at the dining room table making flyers. Have You Seen This Woman? $10,000 Reward. We used a picture taken at her parents' house in southwest Oklahoma, one I'd never seen before. In the picture, she had bangs and long, curly hair. She wore lots of make-up, purple eye shadow and deep, red lipstick. I hardly even recognized her, a stranger rather than my wife. Sara and I had never perused through old albums or reminisced through yearbooks. In fact, we hardly spoke of before we were married. It was like another life that no longer held relevance. She barely even looked like that girl in the picture anymore. Beyond the pregnancy, she now had straight hair that framed her face. She thought it made her look skinnier than her long, curly hair. Her cheeks had become rounder, fuller, her complexion paler. We didn't have any recent photos, though. We hadn't taken pregnancy pictures. It wasn't that we didn't want to. It was just that we never got around to it.

I told Marissa and Gary the story three times.

"Does she have a best friend here?" Marissa asked. "I remember her telling me about some girl she just met. Becky. Rebecca. Does that ring a bell?"

"She's our next-door neighbor."

"Have you asked her if she knows anything?"

"I haven't."

"Why not? She could know something."

"I doubt it."

"I'm just saying it might be worth a shot."

They were desperate to glean some type of motive or meaning behind her disappearance. Each time I told my story, they analyzed what I had said, what she had said, the accusations that we had thrown at each other. Was she truly unhappy? "She hadn't said anything to me," Gary said. "She always seemed to be laughing when we spoke on the phone. Just the same old Sara."

"We have our problems like any other couple," I said. "We fight. We argue. We make up."

"I don't want you to beat yourself up," Marissa said. "It's just a big misunderstanding. I'm sure of it."

"She's always had a bit of a hot head," Gary said. "She did run away once as a kid."

"She didn't get far, though," Marissa said. "Tried to buy a train ticket to Branson of all places. Turns out we knew the lady at the ticket window, an old friend from high school, and she called us to come pick Sara up. Grounded her for a month for that little stunt."

"She'll turn up," Gary said. "I'm sure of it."

"I don't know," I said. I didn't know why I said it. It just sort of slipped out. My mother glared at me from the other side of the table, scissors in hand. "This time is different."

"This isn't your fault," Gary said. "This isn't anyone's fault. It's just life. Fights happen."

"She's not coming home," I said. It just came out of me. It poured. All the grief and shame and guilt, I couldn't hold them back any longer. "I just got a bad feeling," I said. "She would've called you. She would've. She would've let you know where she was and that she was okay. It's just not like her to just disappear all of a sudden. Poof, and she's gone."

"Oh, sweetie," Marissa said. "Oh, honey." She hugged me and comforted me and told me everything would be okay. "She will come home," she said, "and the baby will be born and everything will turn out okay.

You just have to have faith."

Mom simply stared at me, concerned.

To distribute the flyers, we split up. Gary and Marissa took by the university, a safer part of town, easier to navigate, while my mother and I took the Dot, searching for a woman who wouldn't be found alive. It made the whole situation worse in a way. We placed the flyers on telephone poles and mailboxes. We placed them in store windows, barbershops and dollar stores and consignment shops. We tried handing them to people. Most threw them away in the nearest trashcan. Others feigned interest, nodded at the flyer without reading it, then stuffed it into a pocket. Some responded with heartfelt remorse and compassion, women mostly, older, who'd lost someone close to them. I could tell by how they seemed to shrivel when we asked them, "Have you seen this woman?" Their hearts broke. "Oh," they would say. "Oh, no. I hope she turns up."

I wasn't sure why Mom and I were even searching. To keep up appearances, I suppose. A man missing his pregnant wife would search for her. He would do everything he could to bring her back home. He'd travel to the other side of the world. He'd go after seedy individuals. He'd even hurt himself, cut off a limb if he had to, no anesthesia, nothing, just grit his teeth and take the pain. This made me feel less than human. I didn't possess the same normal responses others should have in my situation. I thought of Sara, yes, and the baby. I mourned for them. I grieved for them. I suffered with shame. But I also thought of myself, what would happen to my work, if I'd ever see my mother again, if I'd ever be let out of jail. These consequences scared me. To say they didn't would be a bald-faced lie.

Without prior planning, we avoided the street where we dumped Sara's body. We stopped at the corner, looked down the street, but kept on walking. Too risky, I suppose. We'd dumped the body less than forty-eight hours before; it could still be there, rotting. The smell could give it away. Though, the cold helped. It had been below freezing each of the past two nights. A light snow had fallen the night before, blanketing the street and sidewalk in a thin, white film. Without insulation, it would be like a freezer in the dumpster, slowing Sara's decomposition. The trash men would come by week's end, take her to the dump or an incinerator, I wasn't sure which. I hoped the latter. For her sake, I did. I didn't give much credence to burial rituals, the religious and spiritual implications, the solace in an afterlife, a chance for the survivors to experience closure, but a body rotting surrounded by refuse seemed beyond disrespectful. It was downright evil in fact.

At a deli we stopped for a cup of coffee and a croissant, a little breakfast to get us through the long day. It was a small place. There was a row of booths, old pictures framed above them, minor league sports stars and B-movie actors, and then the counter, little stools swiveling in front of it. There was an old Coca-Cola soda fountain, an ice cream machine, pies displayed. A short, Vietnamese man worked the counter. He cleaned dishes and stocked condiments. An older gentleman, he still had a spring in his step, like he enjoyed his work, took pride in it.

"Hello!" he said as we entered. "Hello! Hello! Hello!" He placed menus in front of us, smiling as he did so. His teeth had yellowed to a shade of spoiled corn, the result of perpetual coffee drinking and the prolonged absence from the dentist. I could smell his breath right away, a bit rank, stale, like an unwashed cup. "Can I get you something to drink? Coffee? Tea? Juice? I've got orange juice or cranberry juice or apple juice or grape juice. Any kind of juice you want." His English was irreproachable, even local-sounding. If I closed my eyes, I would've sworn him to be just another Irish boy, third generation American, having lived in the Dot his entire life. "I got milk, too. Or just water. Water's fine. Decaf. Whatever you need, I'll get for you."

He seemed wired, strung out on caffeine. His eyebrow twitched, and he constantly scratched his forearms. His hands shook as he handed us our drinks.

We nursed our cups of coffee and sat in silence. Despite being inside, I was still cold. The wind whistled outside as it swooped down the street, like we were in a tunnel.

The Vietnamese man brought my croissant. It was warm and soft and melted in my mouth. There was a hint of vanilla in it, brown sugar, and honey. He dropped off more napkins, refilled my coffee, and when he did, he accidentally spilled some on the flyers.

"So sorry," he said. "I am so sorry. Let me get a towel." He dabbed at them, though it really wasn't necessary; only a few were ruined. "You know Sara?" he asked. He pointed to the flyers.

"My wife," I said, surprised.

"Oh no. Did something happen? Is she okay?"

I told him that she was missing, had been for forty-eight hours.

"I wondered," he said. "She usually comes here every day. She eats pie and has a cup of tea. We talk about our homes. The ones we left behind. Oklahoma, right? She had cows and horses. She wore cowboy boots. I think maybe that's why she comes here. We're both homesick."

"She came here every day?"

"Sure. At least four or five days a week. She comes in about 10:00, sits where you are actually. She people-watched. She is quiet."

"Did she ever mention me?" I asked.

He thought a little bit, as if trying to remember, or maybe to formulate the right response. "I'm sure she did," he said. "We talked about so many things. You don't think anything bad happened to her, do you?"

"We don't know," I said, and we paid our tab. "We just don't know."

"Let me know if I can help at all," the man said as my mother and I left. We didn't turn back. "I'll pray for her."

We were at the corner of Ridgewood and Topliff, a residential part of the Dot, lined with brownstones and chain-link fences. Styrofoam cups and loose papers were pinned against the fence by the harsh wind. American flags draped from porches. There wasn't much foot traffic, just a lone man walking south down Ridgewood. He had a white oxford shirt on, a size or two too big, the sleeves rolled up as otherwise they would cover his hands. He walked slowly as if he didn't actually have a destination, only walked because he didn't know what else to do with himself. Somewhere I could hear music, classical, a single string instrument. It was faint at first, but grew louder slowly. It would start, play a few notes, then stop abruptly, like the musician was tuning the instrument.

Sara, apparently, had walked these streets everyday to and from the deli. I had no idea she used to frequent there, but, now that I thought about it, it made sense. She'd often complained how lonely she was in Boston. At the deli, she could sit for hours, drink tea, eat a piece of pie, strike up conversations with other patrons, the mailman, a couple cops, another soon-to-be mother. What troubled me, however, was that she never mentioned these trips. They were obviously important to her, to keep coming every single day, but she kept this part of her life hidden from me, like if it was exposed, my knowing would sully it somehow, taint her one escape from the drudgery that was our marriage.

"How're you holding up?" my mother asked.

"About as well as could be expected, I guess."

She nodded and scratched her chin with her thumb. Since the murder, she had changed her appearance; she wore more makeup, dark eye shadow, deep red lipstick. She became quieter, more distant, cold even. She would stand in front of the mirror for twenty minutes or thirty or forty, just looking, angling her face to the left, then to the right, then straight ahead. She wouldn't touch her hair or reapply her mascara, she simply studied herself, absorbing all her imperfections.

After a few more yards down the street, the musician began to play a song. Pristine music, a lone cello. It couldn't have been a recording. It was live, but I couldn't pinpoint where it was coming from. It was a very odd instrument for this neighborhood. I would've expected an electric guitar, a drum set, something a little more aggressive, visceral, not something so sweetly beautiful, so sad, or so sublime.

"I know there's nothing I can say to make this any better," Mom said. "And I know I'm not the one that should be offering you comfort. Not after what I've done to you."

"This isn't right. I should turn myself in."

She nodded again.

"I understand," she said. "I do. It seems like that is the right thing to do."

"It is."

"I know. But it was an accident, son."

"That doesn't matter."

"There wasn't any premeditation. There wasn't ill will. It's analogous to a car crash. The brakes malfunctioned on an otherwise perfectly capable car. It was going downhill. It had too much momentum. It blew through a stop sign and hit an unsuspecting driver. The driver of the car whose brakes went out would not be culpable."

"That's not the same thing, and you know that."

"Why? Tell me why. How is it different?"

"Because the driver didn't just drive off. He stayed and tried to help. He called the cops and told the truth."

"Tell me—what would change? Does telling the truth bring the dead back? No! Nothing changes. The driver still feels remorse. Regardless if the truth is told."

"It is not the same."

The cello music whined in the distance, sweetly, melodically. It was enchanting. I had to find it. I picked up my pace. I stuck flyers into the chain-linked fence. I handed one to the man in the Oxford shirt. He blinked at it as if he was illiterate. "Thank you," he said.

Mom walked faster, stayed stride by stride with me. "Do you think Sara would want you to go to jail? Do you think that is what she would want?"

The wind camouflaged the music's origins. For a moment it seemed to be coming from behind me, then ahead, then straight above. I looked up the street for open windows, a car idling, a window cracked and with an extraordinary sound system, though I didn't expect any car around here to have this type of quality. Few models do, higher-end, later models, luxury cars, cars not found in the Dot. I would've been less surprised to find a string orchestra at the corner, dressed in tuxedos and gowns, tuning for a performance.

"I don't," Mom continued. "I don't think that's what she would've wanted at all. Not after what you have accomplished, not with what you've shown with your work. Not now. She'd want you to become what you've always dreamed—the greatest scientist the world has ever known. She loved you, Coulter. She wouldn't dream of you throwing that away."

"Don't," I said. "Don't try to speak for her."

"I'm sorry," she said. She sounded desperate. "But I know I'm right. Punishment comes in many different forms. It doesn't have to be incarceration. You don't have to pay for this for the rest of your life."

"I'm aware of that."

"That doesn't mean you have to go to prison. I'm sure you're punishing yourself right now. If you're anything like me—" she cut herself off.

I continued down the street. The music became louder, slower, sadder. It seemed to be longing for something, a song of yearning. It seemed to be crying out for someone to please help, but no one did. I had to find it. It was like it was being played just for me.

"Please," she said. "Please. Just stop. Look at me, Coulter."

I didn't stop. I headed down the street, the music getting louder. I was getting close.

"I just can't lose you," she said. "Not now. Not after I just got you back."

It was right around me. I stopped, looked around, but couldn't find the source.

"Do you hear that?" I asked.

"I know it's not right. I do. I just can't stand to do the right thing."

And then I spotted it, the cello, through an upstairs window in a brownstone. A young girl played it. Her mother stood over her shoulder, looking at the sheet music. Her face appeared tense with consternation. The little girl looked anxious. Her fingers strained around the cello's neck. They quivered and flew over the fingerboard. But then came a false note, shrill compared to the silkiness of the rest. Her mother jolted, cringed. The daughter dropped the bow. This had happened before; I could tell by the way the young girl's face turned red, anticipatory. Her mother rebuked her. She pointed and censured, but the young girl didn't cry. She simply picked up her bow, her mother still chastising her, and continued to play where she left off.

AT DISTANCES LESS THAN THE PLANCK LENGTH, light behaves in peculiar ways, ways described in part by Heisenberg's Uncertainty Principle. Simply put, if we understand a photon's position, we do not know its velocity/momentum. If we know velocity/momentum, then we do not know its position. This property is called complementarity: as we know more about one, then we know less about the other. Because of this, we're only able to give the probability that we'll be able to show where a certain photon is located and where it plans to go. This creates an interesting conundrum. From a macro standpoint, we can only give the probability of where light is located, but as we look closer and closer and closer, we can pinpoint a particular photon, bending certainty toward one hundred percent. Therefore, for all intents and purposes, our witnessing that photon makes it more real. Our simple observance affects the certainty of a photon's position. How or why this happens, no one really knows for sure. But it answers that silly riddle, if a tree falls in the woods and no one is around to hear it, does it emit any sound? The answer is that maybe it doesn't. Maybe it's our presence that manifests reality.

When I think about motive in my case, I find analogies to complementarity pairs. It was a complex situation, and as one course of action made more sense, at that time hiding an accidental murder, disposing of the body, the reasons why I discarded another, turning myself in, accepting my punishment, made even less. I was capable of only one course of action, yet there seemed to be an infinite amount of alternatives. I could've fled to Argentina, started a new life as a janitor. There would be a language barrier, and no one would speak to me or offer companionship or judgment or hatred. I would be invisible. I would be marginalized. I would dissolve into the fabrics of people's everyday lives, like a clock might, bought at a flea market and forgotten on a shelf for years. I could've framed my mother. It had been her idea, premeditated. She had fought with Sara. She thought Sara threatened her chance at redemption with her estranged son. I hadn't even been there when it happened. People may have believed that story. My mother suffered from mental illness. She had been manic depressive and spent time in mental institutions. Her denials wouldn't be credible. Sara and I, as far as everyone in our lives were concerned, had a healthy relationship. All viable options. All of them discarded.

The further I got into my denial, the less likely any alternative seemed. After I had disposed of the body, other choices became less likely. After I'd filed the missing persons report, the chances of a confession diminished. After I'd called Sara's family and told them the news, the truth became a remote possibility. These acted as complementarity pairs: the more I lied, the less I was capable of telling the truth. So, without any lead in the case and at my mother's prompting, I tried to return to a semblance of normalcy. I returned to classes. I wrote about my discovery. I called the police station for any updates. There were none. I distributed flyers. I prepared my dissertation while the police and my family and Sara's family searched for my dead wife.

After a couple weeks without any clues to Sara's whereabouts, Marissa and Gary's hope had waned. Their theories of what had happened turned sparse. They no longer hypothesized that she had gotten a hotel room in town just to calm down after our fight. They continued to call home, hoping Sara might answer, but they no longer carried anticipation in their shoulders nor curled their fingers around the cord of our phone. They went to bed later and got up earlier. They'd get takeout once a day, but leftovers of salami sandwiches and clam chowder piled up in the fridge. It was disheartening to see, a family go through the five stages of grief. They started to believe she was dead. They didn't have to say anything. I could tell by the way their tongues seemed to stick to their teeth when they spoke of her. "She was our little girl," they would say, now in the past tense.

When I'd told Dr. Brinkman I'd be returning to the university, he'd argued against it. "This is the time for you to be with your family, Coulter. There's no need to rush things."

"I understand, sir. I'd like to return, though. Staying busy will be good for me."

"Why don't you take another week or two?"

"It wouldn't do any good."

"It might. Besides, we have everything covered here. Dr. Barbarick has been filling in on your classes. My research is going on fine. Of course, it's difficult to replace you, but family has to come first. You just take all the time you need."

After a while, he relented. It was, after all, my decision.

We were back in the lecture hall, Dr. Brinkman, Cardoza, Barbarick, and I. I hadn't told them anything about my discovery, and I had not been sending them updates, new pages, et cetera, and they hadn't asked for any. Perhaps they hoped I'd decided to change my dissertation after all, or that considering the circumstances of my missing wife, that I'd kept the scheduled meeting in order to tell them I intended to drop out. Whatever their expectations, they acted concerned and more attentive, less critically than before, and with more pity.

"We're ready whenever you are, Coulter," Dr. Brinkman said. "No rush."

I had to admit I was nervous. My mind kept wandering back to

Detective Landsmen and the search for Sara. It had been a month since I'd filed the missing person's report. While distributing flyers, I would walk by the dumpster we'd left Sara at. I had no idea how often waste management came to pick up the trash. I tried to smell to see if I could pick up wafts of a decomposing body. I smelled nothing. Just the normal stench of the Dot: the salty aroma of corned beef, the vent of freshly cleaned laundry out of the dryer, the sting of rubber and sweat. I'd scoured the news reports for the reporting of a body found. It never came. It appeared I would get away with it. As Detective Landsmen had said, "sometimes people don't want to be found."

"As you all know," I began, "my dissertation is focused on determining the shape of the universe in a unified string theory. Namely, I hoped to give the curvature, or Calabi-Yau manifold, that determines the innumerable, measurable characteristics of our universe. The strength of the four forces: gravity, electromagnetic, weak, and strong. The mass of an electron. The duality of light. So on and so forth.

"As noted in previous meetings, my methodology was imperfect. More a game of chance, really, a proverbial lottery, but without the right amount of numbers in order to play. I faced failure after failure. I had, it seemed, forgotten what it means to be a scientist. I was forcing the issue rather than deducing from observation. I had become a participant rather than remaining objective. My work was derivative of Greene and Kaku, with no new insights, but set out to discover what their math had deduced. You, of course, warned me of this, but, perhaps in arrogance, I didn't heed your warnings.

"But then," I continued, "I got lucky."

I clicked on the projector, revealing a computer model of my results. It showed the way a string oscillated within the curled-up dimensions of my Calabi-Yau manifold. The manifold worked like a flute. The strings that made up all the constituents of the universe were the musician's breath. Just as a musician would blow at different strengths to produce different octaves, the strings vibrated at different energies to produce various elements. Light vibrated at one frequency. Helium another. Magnesium still another. The curvature of the manifold acted as the flute itself, shaping the wind in order to create the notes. I produced for them Planck's constant and gravity and the weak force. I showed them the creation of water and iron. It all worked. All of it. Every last bit of it.

"Remarkable," Dr. Brinkman said. "Just remarkable." He stood and approached the projector, his glasses used as a pointer. "I've never seen anything like it."

"How did you do this?" Dr. Cardoza asked, a hint of incredulity laced in her undertones.

"Like I said, I got lucky. The model returned this manifold, and it worked."

"It's a miracle," Dr. Brinkman said. "Truly."

"How many tests have you put it through?" Dr. Barbarick asked.

"Thousands."

"Results?"

"Perfect."

"Perfect?" Cardoza asked.

"Not one skewed result. Precision to less than one-hundredth of one percent. I've never seen anything like it."

"It's like peering into the blueprint of the universe," Dr. Brinkman said. "Jesus, Coulter. Do you realize what you've done?"

"Sir?"

"Let's not get ahead of ourselves," Cardoza warned. "Nothing has been proven yet. And frankly, we don't have the resources to prove it. Right now it's just an unsubstantiated theory, albeit an elegant one." She stood and joined Dr. Brinkman and Dr. Barbarick. The projector behind them cast aglow their hands as they discussed the manifold, pointing there and then there, identifying little turns and quarks, counting the dimensions. It was like they were making emphatic shadow puppets. "It is quite impressive, though."

They wanted to see the model in action, with random variables thrown at it rather than my prescribed ones for my demonstration. I obliged. We went down to the lab and fired up the mainframe, and they threw at it everything they could think of. The mass of an electron. The duality of light. Photosynthesis. Nuclear fission. Why the hell not? It passed every test they threw at it. No matter the molecular and chemical complexities, the model proved to be successful regardless of the scenario. It was, undeniably, perfect.

"You have to publish this," Dr. Barbarick said. "As soon as possible. I could help you write it."

"We all could," Dr. Cardoza said. "Give you some credible backing. That sort of thing."

Dr. Brinkman said, "This is going to change the world."

They continued to hit enter. Success. Enter. Success. They recreated the artificial elements technetium and neptunium and livermorium and copernicium and bohrium. They acted like giddy children after finding a twenty-dollar bill, excited with what they would do with it, the largest amount of money they'd ever seen. They fantasized about all the things they could buy. Candy and gum and that action figure they didn't get for Christmas, and I got excited right next to them, reveling in the innumerable possibilities presented to us.

⋊

Things move quickly after such a discovery. First, you write. You write and you write and you write. You write for days. You don't sleep. You hardly eat. You stay at the office until three or four in the morning. You wake up at 7:00 a.m. and you revisit your model and you revise and revise and revise. You search for a humble tone, a skeptic's tone. You are not writing a treatise but rather reporting a phenomenon. Your boss will read it and his colleagues, and they will offer suggestions. You will discard them at first, then realize later some weren't completely crazy. You neglect your family. They will say it's okay, though. You've had a hard couple of weeks. You're doing something important. It's good to get your mind off of everything that's going on. No one blames you for that.

The search continued for Sara. By this time, it had become nearly a consensus that something bad had happened to her. Foul play, Detective Landsmen had called it. The Dot's a rough neighborhood, he'd said. "And the people here don't talk to the police. It's in their DNA." They have their own sort of justice. Not vigilantism, really. That's not what he'd called it. They marginalize the perpetrator. They ignore him. They make him and his family feel like they don't even exist anymore. On the surface, it doesn't seem all that bad. But this is a tight-knit community. Their identities are completely wrapped up in being a member of the Dot. Take that away, and the psychological impact can be devastating. Could even make someone go mad. And it makes the police's job difficult.

More hastily than normal, I sent out my paper to be published, listing Dr. Brinkman as co-author. A Nobel Laureate on the byline would help move the paper out of the slush pile and into the hands of an editor, but, he'd said, the credit would be all mine. It didn't take long to hear back. Every single journal I submitted to wanted to publish it: *Advances in Theoretical and Mathematical Physics, Classical and Quantum Gravity, Progress of Theoretical Physics, Annales de chimie et de physique, Acta Physica Polonica, Journal of Experimental and Theoretical Physics*. Editors personally called me to offer their congratulations. They wanted to do a profile, send out someone to interview me. They would personally come even. Just say the word.

Word got out. The paper was published. Fellow PhD candidates and faculty members treated me differently. They whispered when I entered a room and they agreed with everything I said and they offered to get me

tea or breakfast or anything I wanted really. Universities offered postdoc-
toral fellowships with generous stipends and benefits. At first, I enjoyed
all the attention. It felt good. How could it not? I was the next big thing,
and everyone wanted something from me. But they constantly demanded my attention. They offered their sincerest condolences about the loss
of my wife and child. It must be devastating, they said. She would be
so proud of you now; I am just so sure of it. It stung each time she was
mentioned. I grew bored with their attention. I became frustrated. I
only wanted privacy. I slept less. I ate less. I started to daydream more.
I lost larger and larger blocks of time. I saw Sara giving birth and Isaac
as a toddler, as a grown man. These dreams were getting more frequent
and more vivid. I relived the moment Sara had died, playing out various
scenarios that did not end with her death. I fantasized I had necrotizing
fasciitis. I could even smell the infection growing in my arm.

Worried, I made an appointment with Dr. White. She welcomed me
as she had last time, and right away I felt comforted by her. Since my last
visit, she'd painted more. Her art now nearly covered the entirety of her
walls, a mosaic of cubist representations, profiles of her patients, silhou-
ettes of deformed noses and irregular shaped eyes.

"They represent the fragmented psyche," she said.

"I'm sorry?"

"My paintings. There's a misconception among us that only the
mentally ill perceive the world in a fragmented and flawed way, but that's
not true. We all do. Our sensory perceptions are imperfect. Our experi-
ences are amalgamated misrepresentations that we take for granted. Take
this for example." She showed me a miniature carousel of sorts. Dancing
bronze figures, reminiscent of Kokepellis, circled the little statue, each in
a different though somewhat similar pose. One appeared to be clapping
its hands beside its head, another swinging his arms to the left, and another crouched with knees bent like a catcher. A light bulb was stationed
in the center. She turned off the overhead lights and switched on her

statue. The figures began to twirl, and the bulb flashed like a strobe. As it whizzed, it appeared the men were dancing. There were six of them, and they moved fluidly, up and down, up and down, repetitive but convincing. "It's off-putting in a way," Dr. White continued. "You're fully aware that they're stationary figures and that they're twirling and not dancing, but your mind interprets the images as such. You're aware of what reality truly is, but you're incapable of experiencing it that way. Instead, there is only illusion." She switched on the overhead lights again and turned off her machine. The figures slowed and stopped to their original stationary positions. "Have you been taking the medicine I gave you?"

"I haven't, no."

"But these daydreams are becoming more frequent anyway?"

"Yes."

"Interesting."

"I'd say agonizing."

"Of course."

"I need them to stop."

"'Need' is an interesting word choice."

"As opposed to what?"

"'Want' or 'wish' or 'desire' even. 'Need' seems to pinpoint a practical reason. You have a functional motive."

"I just want them to stop."

"I see." Dr. White took a seat and motioned for me to do the same. "When you have these daydreams, tell me, are you aware that you're daydreaming, or are you convinced that they're real?"

"I'm aware that they aren't real."

"Then you have the ability to stop them at any time?"

"Not really, no. It's weird. The reality of the daydream isn't something I question during. It's not like I'm convinced that that is reality. It's only after the daydream is over that I become conscious of the necessity to describe it as a daydream. During, the constitution of reality isn't a concern."

"Could you describe one for me? With as much detail as possible."

I told her about the one I was having most frequently. Two or three times per day it would happen. Sometimes the daydream seemed to last a few minutes at most. I only would get bits and pieces of it, like photographic stills, the audio running in the background uninterrupted. Other times it would feel like hours as I experienced every single second. In reality, hours did lapse. I would be in my office at 7:00 a.m., writing my dissertation, then I'd look up and it would be 3:00 in the afternoon, my cursor still blinking in the same spot it had that morning. The daydream occurs in the future. Sara and I are at home. I am only to be there a few minutes, though, as I'm collecting materials I need for class. The apartment is a mess, and I'm having difficulty locating my laptop, and I blame Sara for this although it's doubtful she moved it; she didn't touch my belongings unless she was absolutely sure I wouldn't get angry. Are you sure you haven't seen it? I ask her for the fourth or fifth time. I'm already running late. No, she replies. I told you. Last time I saw it was last night when you were working. To myself I say, but I didn't move it, though. I swear I didn't. I check under our bed and only find dirty undershirts and stray, single socks. It isn't on the dining room table, the last place I saw it, replaced by a half-eaten bowl of cereal. I search underneath the couch cushions and find crumbled Goldfish crackers. I even check the shower and only find a glob of wet hair clinging to the drain. Coulter! Sara yells from the other room. Coulter! In here! She finds me in the bathroom. I have my head stuck into the cabinet as I push aside deodorant sticks and shampoo bottles, knowing well enough my laptop isn't in there. It shouldn't be, anyway. I think my water broke, she says. I hit my head on the drainage pipe. What? I ask. I think my water broke. What do you mean you think? Did it or didn't it? I don't know, she says. I was looking for your computer and was standing in front of the television and I felt something warm trickle down my leg. Did you pee yourself? I asked. I don't know, she says. What did it smell like? I don't know. I don't know. I'm freaking out here. I lead her to the bed and have her lie down. I can't believe this is happening, she says. Everything is going to be okay, I tell her. Just lay here for a few minutes, and then stand up. If more liquid runs out, then your water broke. I'm not ready for this, she says. She looks scared. She keeps her knees in the air and has her hands crossed over her belly and she keeps licking her teeth. Every few minutes or so, she flinches. Contractions started. Stand up, I tell her. She does. Liquid soaks her pajama pants. Fuck me, she says. Jesus Fucking Christ. I grab her bag, and we head downstairs.

It doesn't take long for us to hail a cab. I'm not sure why. I didn't call one, and our street is not a busy thoroughfare, but one appears like magic. The drive to the hospital is quick and uneventful. Cars don't clog the streets, and those that do stroll around the neighborhood seem to get out of our way as if we have an invisible police escort. The nursing staff greets us and gets Sara in a wheelchair. She balloons her cheeks now and grimaces more often as her contractions become more frequent. I want an epidural, she says. Now. The nurse laughs. Let's get you into a room.

It's bigger than any hotel room or studio apartment I have ever been in. It has a full-sized couch and two closets and a washbasin and mini-fridge and a table and chairs and a recliner and Sara's hospital bed and a dresser with a large, flat-screen television. It literally is nicer than our apartment. The nurses appear to be identical twins. They are tall, nearly six feet, and have red hair and tons of freckles. They even seem to smile in sync as they get Sara into a patient's gown, into the bed, and set up an IV. Pitocin, the one nearest me says. This should speed up the labor time. What about the epidural? Sara asks. We have to get the doctor's permission, says the one farthest from me. We'll call her and let you know. She's not even here?

The nurses leave us alone in the room. I rub ice chips over her forehead and lips. Sara curses under her breath. It feels like my ass is ripping.

Just breathe, I tell her, and I mimic what we learned in Lamaze class. Hee hee hoo. I mimic what she should do with her mouth, lips wide, cheeks hurting from the stretch. Hee hee hoo. In and out, sweetie, I say. Just like me. Oh my GOD! She screams. She turns pale, then pink, then red, then pale again. She bites her lips so hard I'm afraid she'll bleed. It's coming, she says. I can't wait any longer. I look between her legs, and the baby's head is crowning. Wait, I say. Please just wait. I hit the button to call the nursing station but no one answers. It just rings like a telephone might, on and on and on. Oh My God! Sara screams. OH MY FUCK-ING GOD!

I open the door and peer down the hallway. It's empty. I listen. There isn't any sound. There isn't the clicking of a keyboard. There isn't a static-y voice spewing orders over the intercom. There aren't the squeaking wheels of an orderly's cart. The whole hospital has been abandoned. All I can hear is Sara screaming for someone to help her. This baby is killing me! She screams. Please someone just get it out of me. I walk down the hall. All the rooms are dark. The nurses' station has been shut down. The computer monitors are black. Papers are filed away. Doctors do not rush down the hallway, stethoscope in hand. There's no one there to help us.

Please, Coulter! Help! Help me! I'm dying!

And I run. I find the stairwell, and I run. I burst through the door, and I don't turn back. I'm too scared to turn back. I think if I turn back, then I'll surely die. I race down five flights of stairs, and I know I will never go back. I will never speak to Sara again. I will never see my son. Everything has gone silent at this point in the daydream. I can't even hear my shoes squeaking on the stairs. It's like I've gone deaf. Then I see the exit. It's one of those fire emergency doors, and it says that the alarm will ring if I push it open, but I don't care at this point, and I push it open anyway. Then everything goes black, and I feel this raging pain run down my neck and spine. That's when I come to.

Dr. White placed her thumb underneath her incisor and pushed and pulled as if checking to see if it was loose. "I see," she said. "And you feel bad for this imagined abandonment? Do you think you have commitment issues, perhaps these daydreams are defensive psychological mechanisms of escape?"

"I think it has more to do with her disappearance."

She removed her thumb from her mouth and dried it on her pants. "Your wife is missing?"

"I believe she is dead." I told her the same story I'd told the police, Sara's parents.

Dr. White remained quiet for several seconds, scrutinizing me. It was like she was studying to see if I was lying.

"Can you make them stop?" I asked.

"I don't want you to take this the wrong way," Dr. White said. "But I have to ask this. Did you do anything to hurt Sara?"

"I just need them to stop."

"Coulter. Answer me. I can help you. Did you do something? Did you do something you shouldn't have?"

"I told you what happened."

"She left you?"

"Yes."

"And she hasn't returned."

"Yes."

"And you believe she is dead?"

"Yes."

"Why?"

Because she was. Because I was tired of lying about it. "She would've called someone by now."

"Okay," she said. "I believe you." She lay her pen and notebook down and smiled a motherly smile. "Why don't we call that enough for today?"

I nodded and got up to leave. Before I made it through the door, however, I felt a feeble finger on my shoulder. She handed me a card with a phone number written in blue ink.

"My home number," she said. "Just in case."

>|<

I found my mother alone, sitting on the couch, her head tilted back, eyes glazed over. She must have doubled up on her pills again. Methprylon. A generic downer. She'd told me she took them because of her anxiety, that she'd tried pot before but didn't like it, made her dizzy and hurt her throat. This was the only thing that worked. "Makes me numb," she'd said. "Best feeling in the world."

She looked more than numb; she looked dead. I placed a mirror under her nose to see if she was still breathing. The glass clouded with fog and then faded away. Her pulse thrummed weakly. She'd be fine in about eight hours. Dehydrated, groggy, and suffering from a severe headache, but she'd be alive.

When I sat down next to her, she didn't move, save for the rhythmic bouncing caused by my sitting, an equal and opposite reaction. Once the bobbing stopped, she continued to stare up into the ceiling, without the slightest clue I was there. I wished Sara was there at that point. I missed her. I did. But it didn't really hit home until that moment. I wanted someone to talk to. I wanted someone to laugh with and complain about my day with. We'd used to do that before I started on my dissertation full time. I'd come home from work, and I would complain to her about the stupidity of my students, how a freshman would confuse the integral under the curve with a differential equation about rates of change of motion. A no-brainer, really. And she would laugh to humor me. She'd tell me a story about a woman who was spanking her child at the grocery store when another woman scolded her for punishing her child. "They ended up brawling right in the middle of the store. In front of the kid and everything. Funniest thing I've ever seen." Jeez. I would've said. "Didn't anyone try to stop them?"

"No," she said. "Everyone just let them get away with it."

Χ

He'd seen her around campus now a dozen or so times. He knew her name, Sara, though not her last. She drank iced coffees and sang eighties pop songs underneath her breath. He knew she had class at 8:00 am, intro to biology for non-majors, and again at 10:00, English Composition I, on Mondays, Wednesdays, and Fridays. Tuesdays and Thursdays she took college algebra and intro to political science. She abhorred taxes and the right-to-life movement. She would have something greasy for lunch, a cheeseburger, or a Reuben, always with French fries covered in brown gravy. She chewed fruit flavored gum and read fantasy novels and Homer and celebrity gossip magazines. She smelled of peanut butter and honey sandwiches. In the afternoon, she hung out with her friends, picnicking in the sunshine or playing Ultimate Frisbee. She drank out of the hose and wiped her nose with her wrist. Sometimes, when she thought others weren't looking, she scratched behind her right ear like a dog might. Coulter found this irresistible. It was like they shared a deep, intimate secret.

He watched her every chance he could. He skipped electricity and magnetism class in the mornings and special relativity in the afternoons. Instead of going to the lab, he would watch her play a pickup soccer game or watch her watch television. Her apartment she shared with a Vietnamese girl who never was home, so Sara had different boys over regularly. Since he didn't know their names, he gave them some. Dan was the tall, athletic boy. He ran track and used an inordinate amount of hair product. Craig appeared to be the artistic type and attempted to be dark and brooding with his horn-rimmed glasses. More so, he was timid, and

Sara always looked disappointed when he left. There was Hollowitz, the Jewish kid who made up hyperbolic stories about his and Sara's sex life, telling his friends about that "one time" in the library when she'd let him touch her breasts. Two or three times per week a guy would come over. Then he wouldn't be seen for a few weeks, recycled with new, anticipatory guys, anxious guys, guys who knew her reputation. For Coulter, these midnight hookups resembled a mangled car crash on the side of the road. It was difficult for him to watch, but he couldn't tear himself away.

Her mother sent her care packages of candy and socks and short story collections, anything longer, like a novel, and she would be afraid Sara would blow off her studies in lieu of a good book, Coulter imagined anyway. She read *Jesus' Son* and *Nine Stories* repeatedly. She ate jawbreakers and spit green when she couldn't finish them. She attended punk rock concerts alone and looked awkward and out of place, wall-flowered near the bar as the rest of the crowd head-banged to three-chord power riffs. Coulter did the same, trying to find the courage to introduce himself, but always he chickened out, afraid she might laugh at him, or maybe even worse, invite him to her room.

On a few occasions, he became afraid she noticed him watching her. One time, she attended a Delt frat party with some girlfriends. Usually, Coulter wouldn't follow her into places like this. They were too small, and he would stick out, a nerdy loner who came uninvited. There was just too much risk he would be caught. So he'd stay outside, around fifty meters or so down the street. He'd find some place to hide, behind a car or shrubbery, or he simply might walk the street, passing before the house every half hour or so, fearful she might leave without him. These times were the worst because he wouldn't be able to see her. He liked to think she gossiped with her friends and played innocent drinking games like quarters or pong, but instead he dreaded something more sinister was going on, a line of coke in the bathroom, whippits making her dizzy, half-conscious sex in a closet with a guy who didn't even know her name.

He knew this to be irrational, paranoid, creepy even, but he couldn't help himself. This time, he had to get in there to make sure she was okay.

It wasn't like Coulter'd expected. Kids sat on dingy couches, huddled in groups of two or three. Music blared a little too loud, drowning out the awkwardness. Boys stayed to one side of the room, girls the other. No one questioned Coulter why he was there. No one seemed to notice him. He slid past them, grabbed a beer, and wandered, searching for her. He checked the living room and kitchen, the garage and back patio. She wasn't in the bathroom or in one of the bedrooms. But then he heard her voice. It was clogged and shrill, dry from cigarette smoke and yelling. She was in the dining room, playing a card game with a few people. It was a simple game they called conundrum. One player held the cards, a dealer of sorts, as the others would guess the position of the next card relative to the last one or two in play, whether it would be higher, lower, outside, in between, red, black, or one of the suits. If you got three correct, you could pass your turn to the next player, and the person who got a guess wrong had to take an equal number of drinks as the cards on the table. A rudimentary understanding of statistics would allow someone to be good at the game, but Coulter's eidetic memory allowed him to never be wrong. He could even recite the order in which every card had been played. Jack of clubs, ace of hearts, two of diamonds, nine of spades, four of spades, three of clubs, queen of diamonds, king of spades, four of hearts, seven of clubs, seven of spades, seven of hearts, ace of spades, jack of hearts. They each got a kick out of the three sevens in a row. Coulter didn't understand their amazement. It was bound to happen sooner or later.

Coulter watched from the threshold of kitchen to dining room, not four or five feet away. He became transfixed by the game, the players' excited yips when someone had to drink, the losers' satisfied burps after taking their punishment, the way Sara chewed on her hair when faced with a tough decision, a six and a ten maybe, one a diamond, the other a club. He watched two rounds, then three. He watched four, then five. At first they didn't notice him, but then Sara looked up at him, then one of the boys, just glances, a bit uneasy, a bit skeptical.

"Would you like to play?" Sara asked, finally.

"I'm sorry?" Coulter asked.

Sara pointed to the stack of cards. "You can play if you want to."

"Oh no. No. I couldn't." He smiled, or tried to. To him, it felt more like baring his teeth.

"Okay," she said, her voice trailing off. "If you change your mind." She didn't finish her thought.

Embarrassed, he left quickly, hoping she didn't see where he went.

How could he be so *stupid*?

How could he get so close?

It wasn't like him to be this careless. Usually meticulous, he had escape routes pinpointed, excuses rehearsed, lies he could've dispensed. He'd replayed countless scenarios in his mind. Hi, he should've said with sign language. My name is Coulter. I am deaf. She would've been taken aback, and he could've had a chance to escape. Instead, he looked like a fool, a creep, a lunatic.

He tried to tell himself to go on home, to go to bed, that everything would be okay in the morning. She probably wouldn't even remember him. He would be a prop in an otherwise normal evening out with friends. Some drinks, some games, some laughs. A strange guy. But she might start putting things together. Maybe she recognized him. She couldn't quite put her finger on it, but she knew him.

He walked the campus. He toured the library, one of the few buildings still open at this time of night. He went to a diner, ordered a cheeseburger, and didn't touch it. He was only stalling, though. In the end he succumbed to the temptation, walked to her apartment, and perched underneath the frozen willow tree, and waited.

Sara arrived after about an hour, alone. She hurried to the front door, her hands shaking as she fumbled with her keys. When she finally got the door open and stumbled inside, she flipped on the light and her silhouette appeared behind her thin curtains. She put up her coat and then disappeared deeper into the apartment. Probably she was in the kitchen making a hot cup of tea or in the bathroom washing up before bed. Although he couldn't see that part of her home, he imagined she had a very set routine. He bet she washed her face with good soap, not that cheap stuff from Wal-Mart or even worse the Dollar Store, but imported stuff, the stuff that costs eleven bucks a bar. He imagined she flossed until her gums bled and brushed her hair exactly 125 times. She probably gargled with hydrogen peroxide just to be safe and exfoliated each night with a rough-textured sponge.

She returned a moment later and pulled her hair back into a ponytail. Her bedroom was at the northwest corner of the building, facing the street. Usually, she would sit on the edge of her bed, then do some stretching exercises. Every night she would do them, no matter how hard or how long her day had been. She would stand up and twist and grab her ankles and rotate her head. Her arms would outstretch and circle to alleviate the tension in her shoulders. The knots would dissolve, and acid would settle into her muscles. She would have a glass of water on the night stand to help with that. Next, she'd lotion her thighs, then her calves, and then her feet. He imagined she'd be more comfortable now, out of the clothes that seemed to strangle her. The dresses she wore were tight, and the heels of her shoes left blisters on her feet. By now she would be in some old track shorts from her high school days, maybe a T-shirt from a concert she'd attended with a boy who didn't work out. At last she would pull the blanket up to her chin and curl up like a child scared of the dark.

But not that night.

For the first time since Coulter had been watching her, she did not trouble herself with her routine. Instead, she clicked off her lamp, and her bedroom went dark.

Something was wrong. He could tell. Really wrong. She shouldn't be alone. He had to do something. More than anything he wished to slide in next to her. To hold her and run his fingers through her hair and tell her that everything would be okay. It didn't even matter if he believed it or not, just telling her would help. He tried to will himself not to go up to her window. It wasn't the right time. It wasn't. Soon he could. Outside of class he would talk to her again. He would ask her if she'd like to go to dinner. She'd say yes, and they'd go to Pazetti's where he'd learn she's a vegetarian, or trying to be, but every once in a while she couldn't help but cheat, and she would with him, she'd order the veal and feel guilty and want to call it an early night because of it, but he would talk her out of it, and they would end up having their first kiss outside the restaurant where everyone could see them.

He couldn't wait, though. He knew he couldn't. Before he realized what he was doing, he was walking across the street toward her bedroom window, careful not to make any noise. When he reached the sill, he noticed he could see through a slit of the curtain. Sara's bed was right underneath the window. Her back was to him, the blanket down by her ankles. She was sweating, and her clasped hands were clenched in between her knees. He wanted to reach in and towel her off and fan her with his hand and tell her that he was there for her. He would get a cool washcloth and dab at her shoulders and neck and chest. He would rub ice chips over her lips. Anything she wanted. It didn't matter. He would do anything for her. He would stand here for hours and never leave.

She flipped over. He dropped, but before he did he noticed her eyes were open. He panicked. She had to have seen him. She was going to call the police. He told himself to move, to stand and run, but he couldn't. He was frozen with his back pinned against the wall. He tried not to breathe. She'd be able to see his foggy breaths. A minute passed, and then two. He listened for sirens or the idling engine of a police cruiser, but neither came. His heart rate returned to normal. Slowly, he turned and raised his head over the sill. She was still lying in bed and staring out the window, her eyes locked on him. Strangely, she didn't move or blink or seem worried at all. Maybe she couldn't see past her reflection in the glass. Maybe she'd known that he'd been watching this entire time. Maybe she'd been waiting for him to knock on the door and ask to come in. He mouthed "hi" and waved and hoped she'd acknowledge him and smile. He hoped. He hoped. But she didn't. She only lay there. And then it hit him, and he couldn't help but curse his good fortune—she couldn't see him at all. She was sleeping with her eyes wide open.

CAUSE AND EFFECT IS A FUNNY THING. PEO-ple see evidence of it all the time. They kick a can, it scuttles down the road. They turn the wheel of their car, the car veers. They cut themselves, and they bleed. Many take it for granted, chalk life up to fate and destiny, their actions predisposed by a benevolent creator. Others take the opposite extreme, giving too much credence to the phenomenon, to the point the historical record collapses into a linear function. Lost are the appreciation for happenstance and dumb luck, the complexities of motive and accident, the systemic interplay between the natural and the synthetic, the conscious and the unconscious, the animate and the inanimate worlds. We over and underestimate our importance in the universe. We grieve over our mistakes too much. We too often do not make amends. We celebrate our victories with too much aplomb. We give credit where no credit is due. Human history is an endless web of interrelated mistakes and accidents.

I take solace in that fact. No matter what I could've done differently, I still would've made mistakes. Perhaps not as grave. Perhaps more so. The only certainty is that I would have erred. This does not excuse what I did, of course. But, on the other hand, the choices I made are only relevant for a short amount of time, to a few select people. Then they are as minuscule as the choices of a gnat, whether to continue to fly or to fall to the floor, giving up after only a few, short days.

I'd been back to work for three or four weeks, and my dissertation was finished and under review by committee. Sara's parents had gone back to Oklahoma. After three months, the search for Sara had gone cold. Calls from Detective Landsmen went from every day to every third to every week to not-at-all. Dad called regularly, though. He asked how I was holding up and how my mother was doing, and I told him fine, and he said "sure" like he didn't believe me. Mostly, though, I stayed in with Mom. We watched television and ate dry cereal and hardly spoke. It was lonely and depressing and thoughts of suicide returned. For hours I would fantasize about cutting my wrist, laying in the same tub my wife had died in, about buying some rope and hanging myself from the second story banister at work, about jumping from the Longfellow Bridge. I wanted to ask my mother for advice. How had she tried it before? Why did she fail? What suggestions would she give to go painlessly? Slowly? Agonizingly?

I didn't ask, though. Our conversations were short and often one-sided. She would ask me how my day went, and I would tell her about my classes, about lectures on Newton's Laws and the Standard Model. The news about both my missing wife and my work had spread throughout the department, even reaching the undergraduates, and I would tell my mother about these eighteen- and nineteen-year-old girls, looking up at me with pity, with longing, with soft eyes full of adolescent crushes. They wanted to take care of me, to comfort me, and it made me want to throw up. She would tell me about her day. Often she went sightseeing, back to Old North Church or to Boston Harbor. Sometimes she would apply for jobs at delis or at clothing stores, Gap or Abercrombie & Fitch. She never received a call back. We avoided any meaningful conversation, afraid, I supposed, that if we broached anything about what had happened, we would somehow make ourselves more culpable in the crime. Condone it, or justify it, or even acknowledge it had happened. It was easier to live like this, as if we didn't even speak each other's language.

We were basically strangers, and through our actions, we'd decided to remain that way.

We were in the living room when Dr. Brinkman knocked. The place was a mess, hadn't been picked up in weeks. At first, both my mother and I simply stared at the door as if we both believed that if we just stayed quiet, the person would eventually go away.

Another knock. "Coulter? Are you home?" Another knock. "Coulter?" There was desperation in his voice. I had been avoiding him lately. With my dissertation finished, I no longer spent several hours at the lab. I'd teach class, then go home. He'd called and emailed a few times, but I hadn't returned any of them. "I need to speak with you."

"Maybe you should answer," Mom whispered. She nudged my elbow. "He sounds like he's about to panic."

"He'll go away."

"He might call the cops. He might think you've done something to yourself."

"So what?"

"They've just been gone. You want them asking questions around here again?"

"Fine."

I opened the door. Dr. Brinkman did look concerned, apprehensive even, digging at his cuticles.

"There you are. You had me worried. You haven't returned my calls, my emails. Nothing. Not a word."

I apologized. "I've just wanted to be alone."

He smiled, took off his glasses, and cleaned them with his shirttail. "No. I'm sorry. I overreact sometimes. Of course you want to be alone." He grinned but didn't look relieved. After he put on his glasses, he glanced around the room. To his credit, he attempted to hide his disgust at the dishes caked in dried marinara, at the laundry strewn everywhere, the shirts over a chair's back, underwear lodged under the coffee table. It was the home of a person who simply didn't care anymore. That wasn't the case, however. Depression, at least for me, wasn't that I had given up. I hadn't, which exacerbated the problem. I wanted to go into work, to reach out to contemporaries for insights into my discovery, to try and formulate an experiment that would prove my theory to be correct. But I couldn't. I didn't have the energy, or the motivation, the willpower, whatever. I didn't shower. I didn't move. I simply lay, defeated, and longing.

"I'm sorry," Dr. Brinkman said to Mom. "I don't believe we've met."

"My mother," I said. She stood to take his hand in hers, but I put a hand on her shoulder, stopping her.

"Let me make tea," she said.

Mom disappeared into the kitchen, and Dr. Brinkman and I stood and stared at everything but each other: the ceiling and the floor and the coffee table and the television. A cartoon aired, an old *Looney Toons* episode. Wile E. Coyote chased the Roadrunner through the desert while driving a racecar, but he couldn't quite make the turn before the ledge of a butte. The car hovered there for a moment, Wile E. facing the audience with a knowing expression on his face: he would fall, he was sure of it—it was, after all, just a matter of time.

Mom returned with three cups of iced tea. Dr. Brinkman took his and sipped, flinched from the bitter taste.

"I've heard so much about you," my mother said. "Coulter looks up to you greatly."

Dr. Brinkman blushed, and we all three sat on the couch, the only place to sit, and crouched in shoulder to shoulder. Each of us faced forward, watching the cartoon.

"I should've called," Dr. Brinkman said. "I didn't know Coulter had company."

"During trying times, a mother is always needed," she said. She played with her hair, pulling it back into a ponytail. She was putting on a hyperbolic farce, it seemed, the worried and hovering mother, perhaps just to see how Dr. Brinkman would respond. It was like a game to her, to try and shock people into awkwardness. I didn't know if she did it on purpose or if it was rather some sort of ingrained instinct, having for so long been treated like she was crazy and a bad person she now simply acted in a way she thought other people expected.

"A truer statement has never been spoken," Dr. Brinkman said.

"Right?" she said. "I remember when he was little. He didn't always have the easiest childhood, being as smart as he is." She glowed, continuing her performance. "He used to come home with bruises all the time. Fights with the other boys. They picked on him incessantly. Just because he was different."

"Coulter never told me."

"Oh, he wouldn't. He never complained. But a mother always knows." She tapped the end of her nose. "Even if he doesn't say a word. A mother always knows."

"Intuition," Dr. Brinkman said.

"Just love," Mom said.

"Paranoia," I said. "Delusion."

"Of course," my mother continued. She took a sip of her tea and grimaced. "I wasn't always there. You see, I left when Coulter was about eleven."

"Oh," Dr. Brinkman said, uncomfortably. "I'm sure you had your reasons."

"I did. They weren't good ones, but I did have reasons. That's why he's not very good with loss. That's why he's holed himself up here. That's why he won't get himself off the couch. That's why he won't return your phone calls. It's my fault."

"It takes time," Dr. Brinkman said.

"Sure."

"Everyone grieves differently."

"I wouldn't know."

An awkward silence followed. Dr. Brinkman placed his tea on the coffee table, atop two-year old *National Geographic* magazines and Goldfish crumbs.

"Abandonment twice in his life now," Mom continued. "First it was me. Now his wife. I'm sure he'll never trust a woman again."

"Okay, Mom. That's enough."

"I'm sorry," she said. "I have a problem with not filtering what I say. I've been working on it."

"Honesty is a virtue," Dr. Brinkman said.

"Maybe," Mom said. "I just find it gets you into trouble."

"Well," he said, "I should be going. Coulter, would you join me in the hallway?" He smiled, rose, and took my mother's hand in his. "It was very nice to meet you."

Mom smiled without revealing her teeth, cocked her head at an odd angle, like she had an unbearable crick in her neck. "It wasn't," she said. "But I don't blame you for lying."

Dr. Brinkman bowed his head and walked away without saying a word, the first time I had ever seen the man speechless. Out in the hallway, he took off his glasses, cleaned them with a handkerchief, and said: "Coulter, I'm worried about you."

"Yes," I said. "I understand."

"Have you been to see Dr. White?"

"Twice. I have more meetings scheduled."

"And are you going to go?"

"I don't know."

"You should, Coulter. She can help you. She did me, when my wife and I were trying to have children, and we couldn't, she helped. I was angry then, and sad. Depressed even. I couldn't understand why it wasn't happening for us. Even though I don't believe in fate or karma or anything like that, I felt like a victim of divine judgment, like I had done something to be punished. She helped me find acceptance." He reached out and grabbed my forearm. It shocked me, literally, with static electric discharge. I flinched, and he let go. "Just think about it, okay? You should keep your appointments."

"I will. I promise."

"I know it will take some time."

"Yes."

"And you can take all the time you need. I'm not saying you need to stop grieving or anything."

"I appreciate your concern, Dr. Brinkman."

"Before I go—" He trailed off and smiled. He looked giddy, like a child might, told he'd finally get that bike he'd always wanted. "I have some exciting news. CERN called. They think they might be able to prove your theory."

"You're joking."

He shook his head. "No," he said. "They wish to speak with you."

The LHC stood for the Large Hadron Collider. It's the largest and highest-energy particle accelerator in the world, built by the European Organization for Nuclear Research. A 38,000-ton supercollider that runs twenty-seven kilometers in a circular tunnel one hundred meters below the Swiss/French border at Geneva, it is the engineering marvel of our generation, perhaps in all of human history. It accelerates thousands of protons at 99.99991% light speed from opposite ends of the tunnel so that they will collide and erupt into millions of miniscule particles.

"They think they can show mass disappearing," Dr. Brinkman explained. "Before the experiment, they will measure the strength of gravity, collide the particles, and then measure it once again. They hope to find a discrepancy from prior to the experiment: mass will have disappeared."

It was an elegant experiment, really; since gravity is directly related to mass, mass must have disappeared. Mass is a form of energy, as is seen in $E=mc^2$, and can neither be created nor destroyed according to the

Law of Conservation of Energy. Thus, it had to have gone somewhere. The question is then where. Where in the hell did it go? The answer, if string theory is correct, would be in higher dimensions, the fifth or sixth or even the eleventh, lost in the curvatures of my Calabi-Yau manifold. If the experiment worked, it would prove the theory of everything, the scientific framework that would bridge quantum mechanics and general relativity.

"Jesus," I said.

"Indeed."

"When should we know?"

"They want you to come."

"This is happening so quickly."

He sighed and laid a hand on my shoulder. "I know," he said. "But if they are correct, you'd be the frontrunner for the Nobel, Coulter. The Nobel Prize. No one else would even be close."

It was hard not to feel conflicted. Excitement and anxiety came naturally, like the rush of endorphins after a long jog. Everything I'd ever dreamt about, everything I had worked for was coming to fruition. The Nobel Prize. Nothing compared to that. Yet, it seemed ironic Dr. Brinkman had broached the subject of karma and fate. Where was the justice for me? I had murdered my wife, covered it up, yet it seemed I was being rewarded. But I suppose that was his point. Good people experienced terrible things. Terrible people experienced good things. There was no such thing as karma or fate. Only cause and effect. Luck and happenstance. Indiscriminate causality.

"When would we leave?"

"In about a month. We'd be gone for a few days at most. See the experiment. Come back. You can take time off work again. As long as you need."

"Okay."

"Okay?"

"I'll go."

He hugged me. "I'm glad," he said. "I'm glad."

✗

I applied for a passport, paid for expedited service. For work, I requested other PhD candidates to cover my classes. I wrote my students' final exams. I honed my dissertation, clarified, perfected. I stayed away from the press. A few larger, mainstream magazines had gotten whiff of the story, *The New Yorker*, *The Atlantic Monthly*, *The New York Times*. They understood something big could be discovered, but they only had a crude understanding of the implications. They were more interested in reporting that some young graduate student had claimed to have proven Einstein wrong than the truth, the discovery of a grand unified theory. The universe as a whole could be understood, explained, even artificially replicated. Einstein wasn't wrong. He just wasn't completely right.

I was at the grocery store perusing the produce aisle with Mom, getting her supplies for my week away in Switzerland. Since Dr. Brinkman had broken the news about CERN a couple weeks prior, we'd decided to make a concerted effort to get healthy. The idea focused upon diet and exercise. We believed if we ate better, green vegetables and fruit and broccoli, and if we exercised, going for a mile walk each day, we'd begin to feel better, both physically and mentally. Serotonin and endorphins would elucidate happiness, a sense of euphoria, and we'd be able to beat our depression, like it was some sort of obstacle to overcome, like learning a foreign language despite a speech impediment. We simply needed dedication and perseverance. So we'd implemented our plan. We walked, and we cooked healthy meals. While we ate, we talked about our plans for the future, where we'd move after I graduated. We both wanted out of Massachusetts, out of New England and its cold, biting winters. This limited the schools mostly to California. Top choices were Pasadena,

Stanford, La Jolla, or Berkeley. She'd go with me, though she'd get a place of her own, a small studio apartment close by. I'd try to get her a job at the university, perhaps at the library, restocking shelves, that sort of thing. We discussed getting a dog, a Weimaraner. I'd name him Isaac, and he'd stay with me, but we'd take care of him together, feed him, take him for walks. We were excited. Planning felt good, like we were beginning to move on, to be happy.

As we shopped, Mom told stories from her past, like one time when she and a friend, who she'd helped escape from institutionalization at a psychiatric hospital in San Bernardino, had gone to Yellowstone National Park.

"We were above one of those geysers," she said, "on this wooden swing bridge. Fog was everywhere. We couldn't see a thing. It's one of those surreal moments—we felt like we were trapped in this bubble, a cocoon. Maybe trapped isn't the right word." She picked up a grapefruit, squeezed it, then placed it back into the bin. "More like we were being comforted, kept safe. It was like being wrapped in a warm blanket and being held by someone you loved. We stayed up there for quite a while. We talked. We had snuck some rum up there and were sipping on that. We must've been up there for about an hour. Then we both got the urge to pee. Not having anyplace else to go, we just dropped our trousers right there, popped a squat, and let it fly. That's when the wind picked up. This whole time we thought we were alone, but it turns out we weren't. The bridge was packed with people, children even, some not even five or six feet from us, and there we were, pissing off the bridge!"

She laughed, and I laughed, and others glanced at us out of the corner of their eyes as if to glean what our secret was, deciphering why we were so happy when they were not.

"We slept in our cars and ate peanut butter crackers and travelled the country for six months. We saw the Grand Canyon, the National Mall, Miami Beach. I was truly happy then."

"Have you ever stayed in one place for a long time?" I asked.

"I like moving," she said. "I like adventures. Staying mobile. It keeps things interesting."

"I could see that," I said. "Starting anew. Something fresh."

"A clean break. The past is unchangeable. The future malleable."

"You can make of it what you will."

"Exactly," she said.

We decided to have salmon that night. At the butcher station there were all sorts of red meat, white meat, fish, seafood lined up under the glass. There were sirloins and filets and prime rib and chicken breasts and lamb chops and stuffed pork chops and lobster and scallops and shrimp. Being from Oklahoma, I'd devoured red meat. Steak and hamburgers were served three, maybe four times per week, always accompanied with potatoes and dinner rolls, heavy starches. They'd always made me feel lethargic and overstuffed. A meal was something I had to recover from, not fuel that energized me. We were changing that now, my mother and me, and it seemed to be working. I felt like I had more energy. I felt like I could accomplish more, achieve more, take on more projects. It was rejuvenating. I had never felt so good.

"Oh gosh," my mother said. "I almost completely forgot about this. Later in that same trip—I think we were in Detroit, passing through on our way to the Great Lakes—we stole a car."

"No."

"Really. A Jeep Wrangler. It was summer, and it didn't have the top on or the doors. We just hopped right in. Milly started it up, hotwired it, and we were off."

"What happened?"

"Nothing. We took it for a joyride for a while. We brought it back. No one was ever the wiser."

"You didn't get caught?"

"No one ever even knew it was missing."

My phone rang. It was Detective Landsmen. I didn't answer at first, instead showing the phone to Mom, his name highlighted on the screen. She squinted at it, then looked up to me, concerned. "Aren't you going to answer it?"

"Should I?"

"Of course," she said. "Answer it."

"Mr. Zahn," Detective Landsmen said, his voice an octave lower than normal. "I hope I'm not calling at a bad time."

"No. No. Not at all," I said. "What can I do for you?"

"We have new information," he said.

"'Yes?" My pulse quickened. My pupils narrowed.

"We think it would be best if you came into the station. Could you come by this afternoon?"

I looked to Mom who peered back at me quizzically.

"Of course," I said. "I'll be right there."

"What's going on?" Mom asked as soon as I hung up the phone.

"I don't know. He didn't say."

"Do you think they found her?" she whispered.

"I don't know."

"It was so long ago, though. There's no way she could still be in the dumpster. Don't you think? Don't you think someone would've picked her up by now?"

"Probably."

"But what do they do after they pick up the garbage? I thought it was incinerated. Isn't it incinerated?"

"I don't know, Mom. I don't. I don't know."

"What did he say?"

"Nothing. Just that he wants me to come by the station."

"And nothing else? He didn't give any clues as to what he has to say?"

"I told you. No. He didn't say anything. Just drop it, okay?"

"What are you going to do?" she asked.

"I'm going to go. What else can I do?"

"I think he knows," she said. "I think he knows what happened."

"Why?"

"He'd come to you otherwise. If they had more information but didn't know what you did, he wouldn't make you come to the station."

I didn't say anything. The couple in front of us grabbed their steaks, briefly glanced at us with a disconcerted look, and quickly walked away.

"I think we should leave town," she said.

"That would incriminate us."

"We're already incriminated."

The butcher pointed at us, asking what we wanted. "Salmon filets," I told him.

"How many?"

"Just two."

"Listen to me, Coulter. Now is our only chance. We have to leave tonight."

The butcher was a large man, stocky, with wide shoulders. He had the physique of a rugby player, not bulging with muscles, but solid, sturdy, with a low center of gravity. Though I knew he could hear our conversation, his expression didn't reveal as much. He kept to himself, cut the fish with precision and efficiency.

"I can't leave," I said. "I'm not going to run."

"Please, Coulter. Listen to me. I'm begging you."

"You can. You can leave if you want. But I'm not."

The butcher finished cutting the filets and began to descale them. His hands were gloved and bloody, the scales sticking to the white latex. He smelled of fish and meat and flesh, like copper and guts. Taken together, I began to feel nauseated.

"I'm not going to leave you," she said. "I promise you that. I'm not going to leave."

Once he slid his knife underneath the scales, he grabbed the edge of the flesh with his fingers and peeled it back, revealing the pink meat. It glistened underneath the fluorescent light. Marbling stretched from skin to meat, little white strands of fat.

"Are you okay?" Mom asked. "You're turning pale."

"I think I'm going to be sick."

The butcher looked up when I said this. He held the blade out to his side, little bits of salmon stuck to it. "Please don't," he said, but it was too late. I puked over the glass counter, the floor, him, splattering everywhere. "Get out," he said. He pointed his knife at me. "Get *out!*"

)(

Mom waited outside the police station when I went in to speak with Detective Landsmen. It looked much like it had before, a crowded bullpen full of gruff and loud cops. The heater blasted from ceiling vents, and I began to sweat immediately, my shirt turning damp and clinging to my skin. My mouth still tasted like vomit despite the peppermint gum I chewed. I felt like I had drunk too much coffee, jittery and anxious, my teeth grinding, my eyebrow twitching. I wouldn't be able to hide my nervousness; that much was clear. I just had to hope Landsmen mistook it for apprehension about what he had to tell me, not over what I had done.

He greeted me politely, shaking my hand firmly, not reacting to my sweaty palms. He smiled, revealing his luminous teeth. He offered me coffee or water or tea, asked me how I was holding up, like he was hosting me for lunch rather than meeting me at the police station to discuss my missing wife. This, however, did nothing to comfort me. Instead, it exacerbated my worry—good cops always get people to talk. After all, they're only there to help.

"I thought we could go someplace a little more private to talk," he said. He led me past the bullpen down a long hallway lined with win-

dowless rooms. His boots squeaked against the linoleum floor. They
were odd footwear for a detective. On television, they always wore suits.
White shirts, dark coats, plain ties. They slicked back their hair and had
mustaches and wore dark sunglasses. They were mysterious and reserved
and chewed on toothpicks. Landsmen, on the other hand, wore a down
vest, jeans, and hiking boots, like a man planning to go on a fishing
trip. He was clean-shaven, and his hair seemed devoid of product, waving whenever he walked underneath a ceiling vent. If I'd met him anyplace else, I wouldn't have pinned him as a missing-persons detective.
I would've guessed him to be a geologist maybe, a high school teacher,
perhaps even an athlete, but not a policeman.

He led me to one of the last rooms before the hallway ended. It was
an interrogation room, empty with the exception of a plain table, two
chairs, and a video camera fastened to the wall. We sat, the walls so close
we barely had enough room to push our chairs back.

"Are you sure you don't want something to drink?" he asked. "Something to snack on? We don't have much, but I could get you some crackers or a candy bar or something."

"No, thank you. I'm fine."

"We are recording this," he said as he caught me looking at the camera. "It's the law now. If we're alone with anyone, we have to show we
follow protocol, don't harass anyone, break any laws, yada, yada, yada.
Does it bother you?"

"No," I said, though it did.

"Good," he said. He smiled again. His teeth were the whitest of any
person's I had ever seen. It almost hurt to look at them. "There's no reason for it to. I only wanted to speak with you alone."

"About Sara."

"Yes."

"You have news?"

He nodded. "She has been found. I'm sorry to have to tell you this, but she is dead."

"Where?"

"I'm sorry?" He looked confused.

"Where was she found?"

"At the Rockland Landfill."

"What happened?"

"It's hard to say," he said. "But there appears to be foul play."

"Foul play?"

"Homicide."

"How do you know?"

"There're lacerations over her face and neck. Jugular wound. She appears to have bled to death. Head trauma. A large contusion on her forehead."

"She was murdered?"

"It appears so."

"Any leads?"

"Not yet," he said. "Though there are some peculiarities."

"Peculiarities?"

"There's no sign she fought back. Usually we'll find flesh underneath her fingernails, maybe in her teeth where she clawed or bit her assailant. Fingers and knuckles bruised from throwing punches. Forearms will have scrapes. And in the wound itself, we found bits of ceramic porcelain, an odd weapon for someone to have out on the street."

"Porcelain?"

"From dishware, a coffee cup, or maybe a soap tray. Home décor stuff. It looks like she was inside when she was attacked, and it seems like she knew her attacker."

"How do you know that?"

"Because she didn't fight back. She didn't try to defend herself, shield her face. She must've been surprised. The attack came from the front. It was a puncture wound, not a slice like an attacker would do from behind. She was stabbed, so she would've seen it coming." He shook his head, looked down at the table, smiled again, and leaned forward. It wasn't a smile of happiness or welcoming, but one of sympathy. I couldn't tell if it was an act, though, designed to manipulate me into trusting him, into seeing him as a confidante and not a detective. "I know this must be hard."

"I've suspected that this was how it would end."

"You did?"

"She would've contacted someone by now."

"Oh. Yes." He took a deep breath and let it out slowly. "Of course, we've mapped out all the trash routes that end up at that particular land-fill. It does cover Dorchester. So we believe she was murdered in your neighborhood."

"I see."

"We, of course, found this odd. When she first went missing, you said she didn't know many people in the area. You couldn't provide the name of a single friend or acquaintance she would've confided in locally. After your fight, I mean. You were quite adamant about this."

Sweat trickled down my back. My cotton shirt stuck to me, and my hair matted against my forehead. The humidity choked me. I could hardly breathe. My esophagus felt swollen, my tongue too large for my mouth.

"There is one man," I said. "When we went out searching for Sara, we found one man who knew Sara. A shop owner. Asian man. I believe he's Vietnamese."

He peered at me, taken aback by my answer. "Really?"

I nodded.

"What else do you know about him?"

"Not much. Nothing really."

"Name? Type of shop? Description."

"Deli. Café sort of place. He's short, maybe 5'5". Fifty maybe sixty years old. A bit of a gut. Thin everywhere else."

"Tattoos? Birthmarks? Piercings? Distinguishing marks at all?"

"Not that I can recall."

"How did he know Sara?"

I told him about her going there to eat pie, to people watch, to talk about home.

"And you didn't know of her relationship with this man?"

"Not at all."

"So you have no idea about motive? Romantic entanglement? A feud? An unpaid debt? Drugs?"

"She never mentioned him."

"So it would be unlikely she would confide in him after your fight?"

"I don't know. I don't know how close they were."

"So all you know is that she kept secrets from you? That you two fought, she left, she wound up dead?"

"I guess you could say that."

He smiled again. This time it was not a sympathetic smile, but one of pleasure. He was pleased with himself. "I think that is enough for now. You've gone through an awful lot."

"I can go?"

He nodded, stood, and held his hand out like an usher showing me to the exit. The walk to the front of the police station, he didn't say a word, just matched his steps with mine. It was like he was mirroring me, synchronizing our movements, mocking me. This, for some reason, disturbed me more than his questioning had.

When we made it to the door, he tapped me on the shoulder. "Mr. Zahn," he said. "If you wouldn't mind, please stick around town for a while. I'm sure we'll want to speak again soon."

As soon as they got home, he told his mother all about it. He expected her to worry and scold him and his father for allowing him to get so close to a tornado, putting him in harm's way, but she didn't. They were in the backyard, and he was helping her get ready for his birthday party later that afternoon. He expected her to get riled up, maybe even livid, but instead she simply smiled and said, "That's nice, Coulter."

That's nice, Coulter? He could've been killed!

He went on.

"It was an F3. The Bronco was getting pushed all over the road. It was the coolest thing ever!"

"That does sound exciting."

She was making party hats out of cardboard and finger paint. Sitting here now, Coulter regretted his decision for a carnival theme. After what he'd experienced that morning, it just seemed so childish. There was a bouncy castle and a petting zoo with goats and pigs and a pony ride and a piñata and an apple-bobbing station. He didn't even like carnivals. He'd been to one, about three years prior with his grandfather, and his opinion then had remained largely intact—they stunk, they were hot, and he didn't care to ever return. When he'd made the choice of a carnival theme, he did so considering what the other kids might like. They wouldn't have enjoyed an outer space themed party where they learned facts about the various constituents of the solar system, the number and names of Jupiter's satellites or Mercury's polarization, for instance. He already had the reputation for being a nerd, an over-achiever, a teacher's pet. He didn't want to exacerbate that with a science-themed birthday party. Best to appeal to their curiosities, their interests.

"Dad's car got messed up pretty bad," he continued. "There was hail the size of a grapefruit. The backdraft from the cell nearly tipped the car over."

"Good, sweetie." Mom was cutting triangles out of the cardstock with scissors, folding them into cones, and taping them together. She

Noah Milligan

wasn't even listening to him anymore, dazed into her own little world. Her cutting had a rhythm to it. She didn't scissor the pieces but instead sheared them, scraping the blade across the paper's edge. Each time she made a cut, it sounded like a wave receding over a sandy beach. Shear. Scrape. Shear. Scrape. Shear. Scrape. It was mesmerizing, and she had gotten lost in the monotony of her activity. She was doing this more and more lately. Coulter would come home and tell her about his day at school, what he'd learned, what he'd already known, who he had made friends with, and she'd look at him blankly and nod her head and tell him to go to his room as she folded laundry, each shirt given her complete attention. She wasn't mean or neglectful by any means—she still hugged him goodnight and made sure he was safe and warm and fed and clean—she just seemed distant, a bit cold.

"One actually crashed through the windshield. It killed Dianne on impact. Just crushed her skull. Look! I still have brain stains on my pants!"

Shear. Scrape. Shear. Scrape. Shear. Scrape.

"We buried her in a field. Not before some crows started picking at her, though. One ate her eyes."

Shear. Scrape. Shear. Scrape. Shear. Scrape.

"I cut off her ear and ate that. I thought it would be gross at first, but it wasn't. It was like marbling on a steak. Fatty and salty. Then I ate a finger. A toe. A part of her calf. I figured, why not? She's already dead."

Shear. Shear. Shear.

She stopped. "What did you just say?"

Her eyes seemed yellow to Coulter, the color of cream, like she hadn't been sleeping well. Coulter thought she might be sick; she had been drinking a lot of cough syrup lately, the stuff that made him so drowsy he'd pass out within fifteen minutes. He hated that stuff. Each time he drank it, he woke up with a terrible headache and couldn't remember a thing. She, however, was bigger than him—perhaps it didn't

232

have quite the same effect on her.

"Nothing," he said. "Just that I had fun today. Dianne's a really nice lady."

"Oh," she said. "I must be hearing things."

The children started arriving a few hours later. They were kids from school—Marcus and Anthony and Ryan and Kiley and Margot and Peyton and Matt and Andrea. His whole class had been invited. He had a few close friends, Ryan and Anthony mostly, who he'd spend the night with every once in a while. They had different interests, of course, neither one especially enjoyed science. They played basketball and video games and rode four-wheelers, and Coulter tagged along. He never felt he was invited out of pity or anything like that, but because he wasn't as good as them at these activities, he did feel marginalized, a bit out of place, weird even.

Dianne showed up, too, which surprised Coulter. He'd told her about the party earlier that morning, right after he'd taken a photograph of her, the tornado snaking away from them in the distance, and she'd said that it probably wouldn't be a good idea for her to go, but there she was, looking awkward as she held a present in her hands. She peered around until she found Dad, waved at him, and approached. He didn't look all that happy to see her. He scowled like when Coulter would use his power tools without asking, but she kept coming, threw her arms around his neck, pulled back to say something but didn't let go. Dad looked angry, said something, but Coulter couldn't make out exactly what he'd said. He'd tried to read his lips—*What are you thinking?* That's what it had looked like, but that didn't make any sense. She was, after all, just trying to be nice to Coulter.

As soon as all the kids got there, they started the events. They played Pin the Tail on the Donkey, each of them taking turns. Dad spun a kid around and around and around until she could hardly walk and then nudged her in the direction of the donkey, and the kids and parents tried to help her out. "Turn left!" they'd yell. "Turn right! Go, Go, GO!" The tail used Velcro instead of something sharp so the kids wouldn't accidentally stab themselves or someone else, which was probably a good thing as a few of them fell down. They broke the piñata next. Coulter went first, again being spun by his father before being handed an aluminum baseball bat—a bit paradoxical, Coulter thought, given that this really could hurt somebody—and Coulter was led to the piñata. Blindfolded, he couldn't see a thing, only had his father's voice to guide him. "It's right in front of you," he said. "Just swing as hard as you can." Coulter missed wildly, and the other children laughed. Although he knew they weren't mocking him, he was still embarrassed, his cheeks turning the color of ripe apples.

Mom didn't participate in any of the activities, instead opting to hang back in the periphery. She chain-smoked cigarettes out by the hedges and drank several Diet Cokes. Her mouth hung open, smoke trickling out between her lips. Occasionally someone, another mother, stopped by to speak to her. They kept their hands in their pockets and didn't stay very long, Coulter's mother not even taking the time to look in their direction. Soon the other women gave up and left Mom alone, smoking.

Once, about an hour into the party, Dianne went over there. She appeared timid when she approached, like she might be afraid of Mom. Dianne said something to her, her head bowed. Mom picked a stray piece of tobacco from her tongue, then ashed her cigarette toward Dianne's feet. Dianne nodded, cowered away as if in defeat.

Dad stopped Dianne on the other side of the lawn. Again Coulter tried to read his lips—*You need to leave.* He grabbed her by the shoulder, but she didn't budge. *You're making a scene*, she said. Mom lit another cigarette. Coulter climbed into the bouncy castle, tried not to be happy as he jumped around.

The gifts were eclectic and mostly didn't interest Coulter: Teenage

Mutant Ninja Turtle action figures, a baseball glove (it was spring, after all), a Frisbee, a video game from Anthony, one he probably had bought so he had something to play when he came over. None of these gifts Coulter actually wanted, or intended to play with, but he smiled and thanked the giver anyway; they were thoughtful if nothing else.

After presents it was time for cake, a German chocolate, Coulter's favorite. Everyone crowded around, even his mother, who lit the eleven candles. He'd thought long and hard about his wish for about a week now, flip-flopping between foregoing the ritual and keeping it. It was childish, after all, but a little piece of him, albeit a superstitious one, still clung to the idea of it having credence. Mind over matter. The power of positive thinking. There had been scientific studies giving them credibility. Besides, there stood Dianne, the object of his wish. She lingered near the back of the crowd, staring up at Coulter with a big smile on her face. She looked beautiful with an unbuttoned cardigan and white blouse. There was something about her that Coulter couldn't quite articulate. He'd never been very much interested in girls. They were simply people, just like him. He understood eventually that would change, that adult men and adult women were sexually attracted to each other, but it had always been an abstract idea to Coulter, like the "Allegory of the Cave" or rocket propulsion. Now, though, he started to feel something confusing within him. It was like going through turbulence on an airplane. His stomach dropped. His ears popped. He wanted her. He felt grown up. He had, and understood the object of, his first erection.

And that's what he wished for: Dianne.

He blew out the candles in one breath, and everyone clapped. He could've sworn Dianne winked at him—AT HIM!—but he couldn't be one hundred percent sure. For one, she was standing in his peripheral, and secondly, his father stood right behind him.

Mom moved in to cut the cake. She took the knife and scooted in next to Coulter and began to cut. When she brought the blade through, however, she caught her left hand by mistake. She held up the wound. It was deep, tissue glistening under the sunlight. Blood squirted onto the cake. The kids screamed, and the adults gasped. But Mom simply stood there, holding her hand up high. Coulter assumed she did so in order to keep the wound above her heart, slow the bleeding, but her expression didn't seem to support his theory. She looked proud—like she did the whole thing on purpose.

THE FUNERAL WAS HELD IN OKLAHOMA, BUT there was no body. It had remained in Massachusetts, evidence in the ongoing homicide investigation. I found the whole enterprise odd, burying a casket with no body, and had to fight the urge to point out the futility of it all when Gary and Marissa had first proposed the idea to me, but I didn't. They needed closure, and they needed it sooner rather than later. Who was I to take that away from them? I had already taken so much.

At this point, the police had not formally announced me as a suspect, but I knew they would. It was only a matter of time. I surmised that Sara's family had their suspicions. At the funeral, Sara's cousins cast sideways glances at me like they were plotting revenge, making plans to gut me, the bastard who had murdered their little cousin. I didn't blame them for this. They were angry and confused, and I would've been, too, if I didn't know the truth. Marissa was the worst, though. She could hardly speak. She could hardly breathe. She just wheezed. She wheezed and she gasped and she wailed. Gary tried to console her but nothing worked. He just held her as she shook in his arms.

Despite that, it was a nice fall day for a funeral. The grass had turned brown weeks before, the leaves already fallen, now brittle upon the ground. The mosquitoes were dead. Crows had flown further south. Amongst the tree line, white tails rubbed their antlers against the black-jack oaks, and above the canopy wisps of smoke rose from several chimneys in the adjacent neighborhood. The scene made me nostalgic in a way I hadn't felt in years, since Sara and I'd first moved to Boston. I remembered those first few weeks we'd talked about all the things we missed: Sonic cheeseburgers and fry bread and the rumble of a Ford F-150. Family and friends and Love's Country Stores. It was strange to feel that way again, especially at my wife's funeral. I'd expected to feel grief and sadness and regret and shame. But not nostalgia. A welcome, strange happenstance I suppose.

Sara's eulogy was done by committee. Her aunt and uncle talked about when she'd come visit in the summers and had to have pancakes every morning. They spoke about how she'd demanded to wear cowboy boots with these blue gym shorts and wouldn't leave the house without this stuffed animal buffalo she'd named Papsy. Friends talked about her teen days, how she'd sneak a little whiskey into her Oklahoma History class and mix it with Country Time Lemonade, about that one fourth of July she'd accidentally set a couch on fire with a Roman Candle, and how she used to draw cartoons of boys she thought were cute getting injured, victims of car accidents or a mugging. They always thought it was weird, but she just laughed, said it was easier than talking to them. Gary spoke about when Sara had been a little girl, how her laugh resembled the sound of a playful dolphin and how she led him on treasure hunts to the hall closet, ransacking it of old textbooks and photo albums. I couldn't help but note that all the stories recounted took place before I'd met Sara. I didn't know if this was on purpose, but I sort of reveled in this. It was as if they didn't know the woman who was my wife. That person was mine and mine alone. Selfish, I knew, but I couldn't help but feel somewhat special.

I considered giving my own little eulogy. Something short. Something personal. Something only I knew. There was one thing in particular I wanted to share, an event that had occurred about a year after we'd moved to Boston. We were broke at the time, as usual, and we hadn't really gone out since the move, so one night out of nowhere Sara asked if I wanted to go for a walk. A date night, she said, like we used to have. I agreed, and we headed over to Faneuil Hall. We didn't have anywhere to go in particular so we just walked and talked and window-shopped. That night there were a bunch of street performers out, entertaining tourists. There was a guy that set a wooden chair on fire and balanced it on his forehead. Another contorted his body until he could fit himself into a small, glass box. Another could recite your zip code by giving him your hometown's name. There were musicians and magicians and women acting like robots. It was all good and fun, and we watched a few perform. One particularly caught Sara's attention, a woman who breathed fire, swallowed swords, and performed acrobatic stunts on a low-strung tightrope. A large crowd had gathered to watch her perform, and she gave a little speech while riding atop a six-foot tall unicycle. She warned the children not to imitate her, or if they did, not to tell the authorities they got the act from her, and gave a little history about herself, how she'd traveled from Portland to Boulder to Nashville to Boston over the course of three years, making a living as a street performer, and she encouraged people to give according to how much they were entertained: a dollar for a "meh," a five spot for "that was kinda cool," a tenner for "wow," a twenty for "holy shit that was awesome," and a hundred dollar bill just for her to go away. The crowd laughed, and the woman began her routine, eating swords and juggling fire and riding her unicycle. When she was done, she dismounted and raised her arms like a gymnast sticking the landing, and the people clapped and cheered and whistled their approval. After taking her obligatory bows, she used a top hat to canvass the gathering for donations, and everyone chipped in what they could, a dollar here, some change there, a ten spot here. Soon the crowd dispersed, and the street performer began to assemble her belongings into a large trunk. I tried to walk away, but Sara grabbed my hand to keep me from leaving. She approached the woman and struck up a conversation. I stayed back and couldn't hear what they were saying, but she was smiling and Sara was smiling and it seemed like they were cordial with each other. But when the woman turned around, Sara bent down, grabbed a handful of cash from the top hat, and then stuffed the bills into her purse. When the lady turned around, Sara bid her goodbye, and we walked away, two hundred dollars, I later learned, richer. I didn't know why that was the particular story I wanted to recount. I guess I just wanted to let everyone know that she wasn't perfect. She wasn't always nice and thoughtful and empathetic. Sometimes she stole. Sometimes she just wasn't a very good person. I didn't, though. Staying quiet just seemed like the right thing to do.

Once everyone had spoken who wanted to, men who worked for the cemetery lowered the empty casket into the ground and then placed a shovel in front of the opening. One by one, family members shoveled a pile of dirt onto the grave. Some threw in mementos alongside it: a weathered note written years ago, a beaded plastic necklace, a photograph taken before she'd moved north with me. Afterward, a few friends came by to offer the family their condolences. When they shook my hand, they said they were sorry, casting awkward glances at their feet, but I could tell they said it more out of tradition than any sincere concern. I'd never really been close with any of them, Sara having mostly cut ties with them once we'd married, and I'd always secretly thought they'd advised Sara never to marry me, but when I asked Sara about it, she'd just shrug, say that everyone has their own opinions. Every once in a while one would come visit or we'd go visit them, but there'd always been this unspoken barrier between us, like a magnetic field created by like charges. I never really took the time to get to know them, and they never took the time to get to know me. We'd been comfortable in this arrangement. Everything was just easier if we remained strangers.

Afterward, most attendees lingered, stared at the ground or the sky or their hands. No one seemed to know what to do next, and instead they silently waited around for instructions. As I watched them, I couldn't help but think of them as subjects in a social science experiment. Funerals are supposed to offer some sort of closure. They are a dividing line. The loved one is gone, and then it's time to grieve until you can move on. Watching Sara's friends and family, though, I wasn't sure if they'd ever succeed. It was like they were waiting for some sort of cataclysmic event to mark the occasion: a thunderstorm, an earthquake, drought, tornado. They yearned for some sort of destruction, a physical manifestation of their inner turmoil, but Mother Nature did not comply. Instead, it was serene. Peaceful even. The result was that they just ended up looking lost.

$$\mathbb{X}$$

During my 10:00 am class, Quantum Physics 1, I lectured on electron-positron annihilation in quantum electrodynamics. This phenomenon occurs when an electron collides with a positron, its antiparticle, and creates particles like the Higgs Boson, otherwise known as the God Particle.

The process must satisfy a number of laws, and as such, there is only a very limited set of possibilities for the final state. While it is a dry lecture, the phenomenon is quite remarkable. Two antithetical subatomic particles collide, then create another subatomic particle through the collision's energy. Creation through antithesis.

"The subatomic world is quite strange," I said. "Intuitively, we have a hard time picturing the creation of matter through energy alone. Matter, biologically speaking, begets matter. Humans birth humans. Flowers produce flowers. Insects, insects. Energy of course is an abstraction. Ephemeral. An indirectly observed quality. Kinetic, potential, radiant, but not tangible or practical. We can't touch energy. We can't pick it up and throw it. But it is true. Energy can create matter, but it must destroy in order to do so. The colliding particles annihilate in order to create.

Destruction. Rebirth. It's almost a recurring cycle, isn't it?"

Students and guests packed the auditorium. As soon as my work had begun to garner attention, students who had previously dropped the class returned, students I'd never seen before showed up, even fellow graduate students attended my lectures, the attendance ballooning each class period on an exponential basis. They hung on my every word. They took notes feverishly. Some, I was convinced, weren't even students or affiliated with the university whatsoever. They didn't carry backpacks or bring notebooks or computers. They didn't take notes or record my lectures. They simply sat there, as if spectators at a sporting event. A few wore business suits. Others had gaudy jewelry dangling from their wrists and ears and necks. One especially looked familiar, a face I'd seen around the neighborhood, not around campus, but back in the Dot, a neighbor even. She seemed older than the rest of the students. Not old by any means, perhaps mid-to-late thirties, her features still had that fresh quality to it, her lips plump and full, her eyes bright white and wide, but she had that weathered look, chiseled and stern, having lived a longer life than her years would let on. She had a bruise on her cheekbone. It wasn't a fresh one, deep blue or purple, but a pea green color, like it was healing. At first, I tried to brush these thoughts away, thinking they stemmed from paranoia, the result of my recent interrogation by Detective Landsmen, but I couldn't quite shake them, racking my brain on how I knew this woman.

I continued my lecture. My next topic included the Higgs Boson. It's an elementary particle, I said, first theorized in 1964 and confirmed not too long ago by CERN. Its discovery was monumental as it explained why some fundamental particles have mass when they shouldn't and could give us greater understanding of the formation of the universe directly after the Big Bang. I scanned the audience as I spoke, and then my eyes rested upon the woman again. I lost my train of thought, and my tongue felt too large for my mouth and stuck to my teeth. I could not pinpoint the identity of the woman in the crowd, and it was driving me nuts, like the forgotten words of a cherished lyric, tickling the tip of the tongue.

Then it hit me: it was Becky, my next-door neighbor.

She noticed me staring at her. Her eyes narrowed a bit, and she smiled, raising her middle and pointer fingers in a subdued wave. I looked away, tried to forget she was in the audience, but I couldn't. My heart rate quickened, my mouth went dry—why would Becky come to one of my lectures? Strange theories soon distracted me: she knew I had murdered my pregnant wife, now planned to blackmail me into killing her husband lest she go to the police about my crime; she knew what I was capable of, now wanted me to euthanize her, alleviate her from the burden of her abusive husband; she wished to murder him herself and wanted to ask me, a practiced killer, how it felt to take someone's life, on and on and on, consuming my thoughts until I feared I might suffer from a panic attack.

"I'm sorry," I announced. "We'll pick up here next week."

Not wanting to walk past her, I left through an emergency exit near the front of the auditorium that led to a staircase. The auditorium was located on the third floor so I headed down toward the first. I tried to hurry, but my panic caused my air passageways to tighten, my blood vessels to constrict, so that my oxygen supply didn't traverse as quickly as it should. Consequently, my muscles shut down quicker, and I couldn't catch my breath. It felt like I was hyperventilating. I pushed through the door into the foyer, stumbled out into the open, and ran directly into Becky, causing both of us to fall to the ground. She grabbed her head with both her hands and began to laugh.

"You're running from me," she said. "Why?"

Students and faculty members stared as they walked by, seemingly confused as to whether they should intervene and help, at least ask if we were okay, or instead mind their own business.

"I wasn't," I said. "I'm sorry. I'm just not feeling well."

She sat upright and ran her hands down the front of her blouse, pulled her wool jacket so that it lay straight on her shoulders. "You hurt?"

I shook my head. "I'm fine. You?"

"You're shaking. Here." She grabbed my arm, helped me to my feet, and led me to a bench. She sat next to me and caressed a scar on the inside of her wrist. It was shaped like a peace sign with two prongs extending from a three-inch long base. Rubbing it appeared to be a nervous habit of hers, one she relied on to comfort her in awkward situations. "I'm sorry for surprising you like this," she said.

"It's okay," I said.

"I should've called first. Emailed or something."

"It's fine. Really."

"It would've been the right thing to do."

I didn't answer.

"Would you like to get a cup of coffee with me? Maybe some lunch?"

"I'd love to, but—"

"Please," she said. "I've been meaning to stop by ever since—well, ever since Sara disappeared, but I really don't care for your mother."

"She has that effect on people."

"So what do you say?"

"Sure," I said. "One cup."

She took me to a little coffee shop a mile or so away, Galileo's. It was a small place, housing only a dozen or so tables. I'd walked past it several times the previous three years, but I'd never stopped in. It was nice, quiet and relaxing. A couple of college kids read books over in the corner, and the room smelled of hazelnut and caramel. Classical music played softly over the speaker system. We ordered, a cup of honey and lemon tea for me, a mocha latte for Becky, and we took a seat near the window, overlooking the Charles. The water had frozen over for the winter, thick and blue. Wisps of snow snaked across the ice in the breeze. The rest of the winter would be much the same, everything dead and cold and grey. I'd always dreaded this time of year in Boston. I'd sleep in later and go to bed sooner. I'd have to reread passages several times over. I'd get lost in conversations, often daydreaming about being someplace else, even someone else.

"It's beautiful, isn't it?" Becky asked. "The river." Up close, her bruise looked even worse. It was the color of pea soup, with a bit of soggy eggplant floating just below the surface. The shape was rectangular, though not perfectly—it appeared as though the top portion, right below her left cheekbone, consisted of several successive arches, knuckle imprints.

"Yes," I said.

"You're not from Boston, are you?" Becky asked. "Don't tell me. Arkansas."

"No."

"Texas?"

"No."

"Not Alabama."

"Oklahoma."

"My next guess." She smiled. Her bottom teeth were a bit discolored, stained from drinking too much coffee. "I have some family down south. An aunt and a couple cousins. Haven't seen them since I was a kid."

I nodded.

"You don't speak much, do you?"

"I suppose not."

"Sara said as much," she said before covering her mouth. "I'm sorry. You probably don't want to talk about her."

"No," I said. "I like talking about her."

"I don't know if she told you or not, but we got close there for a little bit. Near the end."

"She didn't tell me. No."

"We were both home alone a lot, and she'd help me with the kids. She was a lifesaver, really. Helped me keep my sanity."

"I understand."

"Have they figured anything out?" she asked. "The police I mean. Any leads or whatever."

I shook my head, Detective Landsmen's words coming back to me: *she knew her attacker.* "They don't know anything," I said.

"So he's still out there then? Whoever did this to her? Whoever killed her?"

"Yeah," I said. "Somewhere."

Becky took a sip from her drink, whipped cream clinging to the top of her lip. I pointed to it, and she blushed. "It's not what you think," she said. "I fell in the bathtub. I'm so clumsy sometimes."

"No," I said. "You have some cream…" I pointed at my own lip.

"Oh," she said. She looked away and wiped her mouth. She stared out the window for a long time, a minute or so. I followed her gaze. Despite the weather, the city still bustled. Cars zipped past on Memorial Drive. Students walked to and fro, backpacks clinging to their shoulders. Policemen checked parking meters, and nicely-dressed women walked their dogs. It was so unlike Oklahoma—just a sprinkle of snow there and the whole city shut down.

"He doesn't hit me," she said, her tone becoming deeper, monotone. "He doesn't."

I nodded. "I know," I said.

She touched her face with her fingertips and glared at the tabletop. Her coffee was getting cold, the steam that had once risen above the rim now gone. She looked so sad sitting there, knowing fully well that I knew she was lying. Perhaps that was why she'd felt compelled to track me down—when Sara had died, she'd lost her only friend.

"That night. The night Sara disappeared," she said, "I heard you two fight."

I didn't say anything. My throat swelled. My mouth salivated.

"The walls," she continued. "They're so thin there. I didn't mean to listen, but I heard. I heard you guys. I'm sorry for that."

"What exactly did you hear?" I asked.

"Did you hurt her?"

"No."

"I heard a crash. It was loud. It was deafening."

"She threw a lamp. It got heated."

"You didn't hit her? You didn't do something worse?"

"No," I said. "I promise."

She looked at the table, out the window, at a barista brewing a cappuccino, anywhere but at me.

"You have to believe me. We fought. I said some things I regret. I'm ashamed of what I did, but I didn't hurt her."

She exhaled like she'd been holding her breath, took a sip of her coffee.

"Okay," she said. "I believe you."

"Thank you," I said. "It's just been so…I don't know."

"Lonely?"

"Yes."

"I'm always home," she said as she folded her napkin into a neat, equilateral triangle. "If you ever—you know. If you ever wanted to talk about it. I know what it's like to be lonely."

Our waiter returned and offered us refills. We both refused. She wouldn't look at me. I was too afraid to look away.

"Would you like to get out of here?" I asked.

She popped out of her trance and turned toward me. "I'm sorry?"

"Would you like to get out of here?" I asked again.

"And go where?"

I didn't really have any idea where. Where, it seemed, didn't really matter. "Let's go home."

When we arrived at our apartment building, she led me toward my door. "My husband will be home soon," she explained. The apartment was quiet, which was usual now that Sara was gone, and a mess. Dust lined the fan so thickly it looked like it was growing hair. Condensation rings stained the coffee table, vestiges of water glasses and Diet Dr. Pepper cans. An aroma of stale pizza and burnt toast clung to everything. Becky didn't seem to mind, though. She strolled in and slipped off her jacket, laying it across the couch armrest. This was the first time I'd seen her without a coat or sweater or some other draping garment on her. She had a nice physique. Her shoulders slumped a bit, but she had an endearing quality to her, an attractiveness, borne from perseverance and fortitude.

"I'm sorry for the mess," I said.

"No, please," she said. "It's fine."

She turned and straightened her posture, clasping her hands in front of her lap.

"It's a little strange having company over," I said in an attempt to break the silence, move the conversation along.

"No family came?" she asked. She took one step toward me, then stopped.

"My mother. Sara's folks stayed for a while. My father, too."

"That's good," she said. Another step. "I can imagine it's been very tough on you. On all of you."

I scooted toward the bar, propped my elbow up. "It hasn't been easy."

Another step. "I'm sure you've been lonely," she said. "I listen for you sometimes, when my husband's fallen asleep. I'll put my head up near the wall, trying to hear something, a television or feet sliding along the floor."

"I don't like to make a lot of noise."

"It sounds like you don't even move." Another step closer. She was now within arm's reach. "Are you alone now?" she asked.

"You're here."

She smiled, reached out for me. "No," she said. "I mean, are you expecting anyone?"

"My mother," I said. "She should be back sometime later."

"But not soon?"

I shook my head as she grabbed my fingertips, leaned in so close I could smell her—rubber and a harsh cleaner, like bleach. She tiptoed toward me, raised up for a kiss, but I leaned away.

"What's wrong?" she asked. "Isn't this what you wanted?"

"No," I said. "I don't know. Maybe."

I was confused. Why would Becky all of a sudden show an interest in me? We didn't know each other. Besides the one time she had locked herself out of her apartment, we'd spoken maybe twice, curt hellos as I returned home for lunch, as she left the apartment to go grocery shopping or perhaps to a job interview, hoping to save enough money to get out of the Dot, to get away from her abusive husband. Or maybe that was it—disillusioned in her marriage, she hoped to find some sort of connection with another lonely soul, a widow. I was, if honest with myself, interested. Since Sara's passing, I had been lonely. I missed her touch. I missed her lying next to me in bed. To feel that connection again, to be embraced by another woman, to feel wanted and needed—I yearned for that. But, then again, it didn't feel right. I was, unbeknownst to Becky, more like her husband than she ever would've realized.

"There's something you need to know," I said. She looked up at me. Her eyes were wide and moist. "I wasn't completely honest with you earlier."

"Oh?"

"I did hurt Sara. It was an accident. I didn't mean to hurt her. It all just happened so quickly."

"But you said—"

"I know what I said. I lied. I'm sorry. I'm so sorry."

She jerked her hands from mine and backed away. "I've got to go."

"Wait. Let me explain. Please—"

But she didn't. She didn't even look over her shoulder. She just ran, slamming the door behind her.

X

Sara stewed over in the corner, acting like she was perusing the Brinkman's family pictures when really, Coulter knew, she was finding an excuse to leave. She touched everything. She wiped her fingers across picture frames, the spines of physics volumes and scientific journals, over knick-knacks, a leather globe, a bust of Isaac Newton, and Coulter could not have been more embarrassed. The Brinkmans had gone out of their way to make her feel welcome here and yet Sara couldn't even summon the decency to formulate a sincere thank you. When they'd arrived an hour earlier, Sara didn't even shake their hands, opting instead to keep her arms wrapped around her pregnant belly, as if shielding herself. "Thanks for throwing a shower," she'd said. "This means a lot." Mrs. Brinkman smiled awkwardly at her, discomfited, afraid she may have overstepped her bounds. Coulter didn't know what to say, ashamed at his wife's audacity, at her complete disregard for even the slightest hint of social convention—she could, if she really wanted to, at least fake her appreciation. That would not be too much to ask.

Occasionally, another guest approached her. They told her she looked radiant from the soon-to-be-mother's glow and asked to touch her belly. "It's just a miracle," they said, and Sara grimaced at the touch of their fingers, how they seemed to think it was all right to grope her just because she was pregnant. Coulter didn't blame her for that feeling, but he didn't understand why she didn't just decline when they asked. It was almost as if she enjoyed getting angrier after each encounter, her blouse getting stained by potato chip grease, like she was a martyr, worthy of everyone's sympathy.

After cocktails, three scotches for Coulter and a Shirley Temple for Sara, Mrs. Brinkman announced that they were to play a little game and directed everyone into the den. The guests sat around the perimeter of the room, alternating men and women, in sofas and folding chairs and end tables, while Sara and Coulter took center stage in two brass-buckled, high-winged thrones. Mrs. Brinkman glided around the room handing out paper and pencils, explaining the rules of the game, "It's a bit like twenty questions," she said. "Each one of us will take turns asking the couple questions about the baby's name, if it was named after a family member, how many consonants does it contain, what is the country of origin, et cetera, and then once everyone has asked a question, write down your guess on your piece of paper." Sara shifted in her seat, the leather squeaking underneath her weight like the low rumble of a combustion engine, straining to catch fire. They hadn't told anyone the name yet, Isaac, not necessarily for any type of surprise factor, but instead because Sara still hoped, Coulter knew, to change his mind. Not able to come to consensus when they'd picked, they'd drawn the name out of a hat stuffed with their favorite choices. He'd only put the one in there whereas Sara had chosen five: Oscar, James, Finnigan, Milton, and Reese. "That's impossible," she'd said after he'd drawn Isaac. "You must have cheated."

Once everyone was settled with supplies, the game begun. The first questioner was Darrin, a fellow PhD candidate. He was an arrogant type, prone to long-winded monologues concerning dark matter and the cosmological constant—his dissertation set about to prove the existence of dark matter through observation of its effects on celestial bodies, much like how evidence began to accumulate regarding black holes. It was not a novel dissertation by any means, with groups across the globe already mired in similar research, but the way he talked about it, everyone would be led to believe that he alone had thought of the strategy and that he would, in just a matter of a few short years, win the Nobel. Coulter hated him and couldn't understand why he'd even bothered to show—he had never once, that Coulter could remember, said anything nice to him.

"What does the name rhyme with?" he asked.

Coulter had to think about this. Isaac. Lizek. Berserk. Fizac. He could not think of any words off the top of his head. It was an odd name in that consideration; it didn't sound like any other word Coulter could think of. This fact made him proud, as if his unborn son was unique in some way, extraordinary amidst legions of the ordinary.

"Gilligan," Sara said. "It rhymes with Gilligan."

Confused, Coulter peered at Sara. She seemed inordinately pleased with herself, like she had just extorted valuables from a sworn enemy, and then it dawned on Coulter: she was playing the game as if the name was actually Finnigan, not Isaac.

The next questioner readied her question. Coulter didn't know this guest, probably a date of one of the other attendees. She was middle-aged, her hair dyed an unnatural black, perhaps a faculty member's wife. "I don't know," she said. "There're just so many questions to ask."

"Anything," Mrs. Brinkman said. "Ask anything at all."

"Okay," the woman said, she tapped her paper with the pencil eraser. "Is the baby named after anyone in particular?"

"Yes," Coulter answered quickly. "After a scientist who taught at Cambridge."

The attendees each wrote down the answer, and Sara seemed unfazed, sitting upright and stately, as if accepting the challenge.

The next questioner was Dr. Brinkman. He seemed confused by the two answers thus far, puckering his lips in deep thought, attempting to catalogue all the famous professors he knew who had taught at Cambridge. "What field did this scientist specialize in?" he asked.

"Zoology," Sara answered. "He studied the masturbatory habits of primates."

"I see," Dr. Brinkman said, not writing down the answer.

Next was Dr. Cardoza, she holding back her desire to laugh at Sara's answer. "An interesting field," she said.

"He was very instrumental in Coulter's own habits," Sara said, and everyone did indeed laugh now.

"How many letters?" Dr. Cardoza asked.

"Five," Coulter answered.

"No," Sara said. "That's not right, sweetie." She patted Coulter's hand like he was a child. "There are eight letters."

"No there isn't," Coulter said.

"Of course there is."

"There are five letters."

"Eight."

"Five."

"Eight."

"Five!"

"Eight."

"Stop!" Coulter stood. The guests all looked awkward, fidgeting in their seats and avoiding eye contact. "You're insane," he said.

"You seem to be confused, sweetie," Sara said calmly. "Are you feeling all right?"

"Don't turn this around on me. You know damn well the name is Isaac and not Finnigan."

"Coulter," Dr. Brinkman said as he stood. "Maybe you should take a second."

"No," Coulter said. "This is crazy. She is lying to all of you."

"You are really starting to worry me, Coulter. Maybe you should slow down," Sara said, pointing to Coulter's drink.

"I am not drunk."

"Regardless."

"Stop treating me like I'm a child!"

Sara stood, her hands clasped in front of her, prim and proper. "I think we should probably go. Thank you for such a wonderful evening."

"Now you thank them?"

"I'm sorry?" Sara asked as she blinked at Coulter in mock confusion.

"You couldn't thank them before, but now that you're putting on this charade, you can thank them now?"

"Coulter," Dr. Brinkman said. He approached and laid his hand on Coulter's arm, either to calm him or perhaps ready to subdue him, if it came down to it.

The others didn't know what to do, whether to turn away or to continue watching—it was, after all, a guilty pleasure, being a spectator to the train wreck of a faltering relationship.

"I'll be waiting outside." Sara grabbed her purse, bowed her head, and headed for the door.

Coulter remained standing there, watching her leave. The guests all seemed to find something else to stare at now that Sara had left, ending the fight. Looking on as Coulter blew up was one thing, he knew, but now that his implosion had ceased and all that remained was him standing there, defeated and humiliated, a sort of empathy returned to them: they never, for the life of them, wanted to be in Coulter's position.

At home, Sara no longer played dumb. They were getting undressed and readying for bed, she trying to pull off pantyhose despite her swollen, pregnant belly, and he pulling off his tie, thankful to not be choked by it any longer.

"I've changed my mind," she said.

"You can't do that," Coulter said.

"Sure I can," she said. "He's growing inside of me. I get to choose his name."

"We're married. This is a partnership."

"You have watched too many romantic comedies," she said. "This is a dictatorship."

It was then, right after the word "dictatorship" slipped off her tongue, that he first wondered how it would feel to wrap his fingers around her throat. The thought came to him in an instant, unpremeditated, and seemed to belong to another consciousness, lodged within his own mind. It was almost a form of schizophrenia, he imagined, or Descartes' demons, like the daydreams he was apt to have. It wasn't him who imagined her eyes bulging from their sockets in concern, her mouth writhing in agony as she realized she could not, no matter how hard she tried, breathe. It was someone else thinking that horrible thought. Someone outside his responsibility.

"We agreed. We talked about it," he said. "We each got to write our favorite choices on a piece of paper, and then whichever one we chose, we would name our son."

"Like I said. I changed my mind. People do that, you know." Having gotten her pantyhose off, she now tried her dress, reaching back to try and snag the zipper, but her outstretched fingers couldn't quite reach. "A little help here," she demanded.

Without even thinking about it, he went to her and grabbed the zipper. Her flesh was cold to the touch, goosebumps forming around the hemline. If he wrapped his hands around her neck, he would be able to feel her skin warm. Her muscles may even relax at first, responding to his familiar touch. She wouldn't be any wiser, but then his grip would tighten, and she would grow tense. She would struggle for a bit, but she would be too weak to fight him off. Soon, she would convulse. She would collapse, and her tongue would hang limply out of her mouth. Spittle would form in a little pool underneath her chin, and she would be dead.

He unzipped her dress and returned to his side of the room, unbuttoning his shirt.

"Is this how it's going to be in the future?" he asked. "If you don't get what you want, then you'll demand that you get your way."

"Don't fool yourself," she said. "You won't even be consulted in the future."

I scoffed.

"I'm leaving you," she said. "I'm moving back to Oklahoma. I'm going to stay with my parents for a while, and you're going to stay here."

"I don't get a say in this?"

"My son's name will be Finnigan. He will be raised by me. We will live in Oklahoma, and you, if you can find the time, can visit him on the weekends."

"I know we've been unhappy," he said.

"This isn't a debate, Coulter. You'll receive divorce papers through the mail, sent by my attorney. You will sign them. We will not divvy up possessions. You can have all of it. I don't care. I just want out."

"This isn't how it was supposed to happen."

She stood and walked to the bathroom, only wearing her bra and panties now, her stretch marks snaking across her pregnant belly, and fiddled with her earrings. Her hair had been tied back into a ponytail, and Coulter could make out her pale, slim neck. Ever since she'd gotten pregnant, her skin seemed more sensitive than before. The slightest touch and her flesh would turn pink under the pressure. A bump against a corner of a table would lead to a weeklong bruise, purple and deep. If he were to grab her, he would leave a mark, a bad one, one that he wouldn't be able to explain.

"Lots of things don't work out as planned," she said, not even looking at him, her eyes locked on her reflection.

He approached her, his palms growing itchy.

"I thought you would know that by now," she continued. She turned her face to the left, admiring the right side of her face, then turned to the right to scan the other. "Just look at your failed dissertation."

He was only five feet away from her now. Four. Three. Two.

"You're going to end up some washed up high school teacher in the middle of nowhere. A nobody in nowhere. Fitting, I think."

Instead of the neck, he grabbed her head. His left hand covered her mouth, and the right lay where the spine and skull attached. She jerked under his touch. Her back went rigid, and she grabbed the bathroom counter. Now she looked at him, her eyes popped as wide as they could go. She didn't seem like Sara at that moment. When he looked at her reflection, she was not her confident, abrasive self. Instead, she appeared timid and submissive. She would do anything he wanted, anything he asked. All he had to do was form the words. This made it easier. She was a stranger, not his wife, not the soon-to-be mother of his child. She was an acquiescent stranger, pliant to his whim. So he threw her. He tossed her like a shot-putter, and her head smashed against the toilet bowl. Blood splattered like a water balloon bursting, and her skull bounced against the tile floor.

She didn't move.

He had expected her to. He'd expected her to gasp, to convulse, to writhe in pain and agony. Instead, though, her torso didn't even rise and fall with breath. Before he even went to her, he knew she was dead. It was a strange feeling. Oddly, relieving. The air even felt lighter, like a burden had been abolished from the earth.

※

After Becky had left, I waited for the police to arrive. I sat on the couch, the television on in the background, tuned to SportsCenter, Chris Berman's voice booming about the return of some heralded running back, and expected to hear sirens at any moment, the clog of police boots as they trampled up the stairs, the pound of a determined SWAT team member, his finger poised next to his gun's trigger, ready to take me down if necessary. It wouldn't be necessary, though. I was resigned to my fate, relieved somewhat that this ordeal would finally be over.

I did regret, however, not being able to travel to CERN to see my discovery proved. It was selfish, I admit, to want to be present when CERN proved the universe consisted of eleven dimensions. I wanted to feel the congratulatory handshakes, experience the approving look from Dr. Brinkman, embrace him as he hugged me, his prized pupil, destined to win the Nobel. I yearned to record the phone conversation when the academy called, informing me of my prize, and I desired more than anything to bask in the revelry as I accepted the award to the raucous applause of an idolizing crowd. This pride and ego made me feel ashamed, yes, but it did nothing to subdue my desire or purge my wish. It was, after all, undeniably human, to want to accomplish something great, to leave behind something lasting, a legacy. That, I don't think, is a crime.

It didn't take long for the knock to arrive. When it did, I first stared at the door, confused. The knock was not decisive, and it was not followed by the announcement that it was the police and that they had me surrounded. Instead, it sounded like any other knock, tempered, a bit melodic. At first, I thought maybe Becky had returned, and a jolt of excitement rushed through me: perhaps she didn't think I'd killed Sara. Perhaps she would hear me out, let me explain. Perhaps I could, after all, get a chance to see my dissertation proved.

I hurried to the door, but it wasn't Becky. Detective Landsmen stood in the hallway, hands clasped behind him like a man waiting for an elevator, alone. He looked much as he had before, clad in blue jeans and a plaid shirt, covered by a green down vest. Since the weather had turned colder, he'd grown a beard. It was neatly trimmed, short and meticulous.

"Mr. Zahn," he said. "Feeling better, I hope."

"I'm sorry?" I asked, confused at his question.

He blinked. "Losing your wife must have been hard on you."

"Of course. Sorry," I said. "I've just been scatterbrained lately."

"Aren't you going to invite me in?" he asked. I opened the door wider and stepped aside. He came in and studied the place. "How are things going?" he asked.

"As well as can be expected."

"I couldn't imagine what you must be going through. I'm married myself. Two children. If I lost any of them, I don't know if I'd be able to cope. Losing both a child and a spouse, it must be devastating."

"It has been tough."

He walked toward the wall where Sara had hung family pictures. Most were of us when we'd been dating, vacationing in Colorado, self-taken shots in front of shops in Estes Park, or us down on St. Thomas, lounging on the beach and drinking cocktails donning little, pink umbrellas. When she had been working, we were able to take little vacations like that. We could afford to travel, to shop, to eat out at restaurants when we wanted. As soon as she'd lost her job, though, our lives had changed. I suspect that's why there were no recent pictures hanging on the wall, with the exception of the 3D ultrasound of Isaac we'd taken earlier that year. As soon as we'd left the doctor's office, Sara made us go to a little arts and crafts store just outside the Dot to pick up a frame. "If we don't now," she'd said when I'd asked her why it was so important to do just then, "it'll never get done."

"You know," Detective Landsmen said, "there is a word for losing a spouse, widow, and a word for losing a parent, an orphan, but there is no word for losing a child in the English language. Don't you think that's odd?"

"It is," I said.

"Perhaps because it's the hardest to deal with we've refused to name it, opting to ignore it rather than to legitimize it with a moniker. A bit childish, don't you think? Ignoring the problem in hopes it will go away on its own."

"Maybe."

"Distractions help," he said as he moved further into the apartment. He now stood by the coffee table, continuing to study the room, peering into the kitchen and down the hallway towards the bedrooms. "In dealing with the grief, I mean. A lot of widows take up hobbies. Painting, writing, some sort of creative outlet. Others bury themselves in work. They keep busy. Which is a good thing. If they don't, all they do is dwell upon the past. What they could have done differently. Blaming themselves. Survivor guilt. That sort of thing."

"Is there news regarding the investigation?" I asked.

"Since our last talk, I've been asking around about you. Seems you're quite the big deal. People are likening you to Einstein. Some big discovery about the shape of the universe. You're soon to be quite famous. Once, I hear, you take a trip to Switzerland." He paused. "See, this confused me. I thought we'd recently discussed you staying here in Boston. Your wife has been murdered, Coulter, and by reason of deduction, you have now become the primary suspect." He picked at his fingernails, scraping a bit of dirt from underneath the cuticle, and then flicking it off to the side. "You're a smart guy. You do realize you're the only suspect, correct?"

I didn't answer.

"Let me tell you two scenarios, Coulter. In the first, you continue to lie to me. You tell me your wife went for a walk, was attacked, was brutally murdered. This will not bode well for you. I will have to tell the prosecutor and the judge that you were unwilling to cooperate with me. This will cause them to seek the maximum penalty possible. You'll serve the rest of your life in prison. You will not be eligible for parole. You will most certainly die in prison. You will be forgotten. You will not be as famous as Einstein. You will be just a number. A statistic of the Department of Corrections. You will be a $40,000 per year itemized expense in the state budget. Do you understand me?"

I nodded.

"Good." He sat down on the sofa and crossed his legs. "Or you could tell me what happened. You don't seem like a killer to me, Coulter.

You didn't plan for this to happen, did you? This was an accident. Maybe self defense. Who knows? Charges could be lowered from Murder One to Murder Two or manslaughter, even dropped. You didn't come forward because you panicked. That is understandable. The prosecutor will understand. I will understand. A judge and jury will understand. Do you see where I'm going with this? Don't you see that I am trying to help you?"

He reached out and laid a hand on my forearm. It was an intimate act. Practiced. Calculated. His whole speech was.

"Detective Landsmen," I said, "am I under arrest?"

"I'm sorry?"

"Am I under arrest? I believe you must tell me if I am."

"No. You are not."

"Do you have a search warrant?"

"Not yet."

"Then, by using *my* deductive reasoning, it appears you do not have much of a case, otherwise you would have obtained one."

He nodded as if considering my response.

"You, by your own admission," I continued, "do not appear to have attributed a motive to the murder. Most of your deductions are the result of circumstantial evidence. She didn't know many people. She must have known her attacker. The killer, therefore, must be her husband. Perhaps admissible in court, but not enough to overcome reasonable doubt. She lived here for several years. How could it be that she only knew me? It was dark, after midnight, when she was last seen. Could she not have been surprised by her attacker?"

"Valid arguments."

"Since I am not under arrest, Detective Landsmen, it would appear that I am free to go and to travel when and where I please."

I got up to leave, but stumbled. My foot had fallen asleep, and I had to grab the armchair to steady myself before I made my way, limping, toward the door. Detective Landsmen remained seated as I walked away.

"Coulter, this will be your last chance," he said as I opened the door for him. "Evidence will be found. Believe me. Evidence is always found. There will be DNA. A witness will come forward. They always do. It's only a matter of time."

I opened the door and stood as still as I could, too scared to look at him, too scared to look anywhere else.

Detective Landsmen sighed. "Fine," he said as he stood. He slapped his thighs like an impatient child, waiting for his mother to give the okay for him to be excused. "Have it your way." Once out in the hallway, he paused. "I recommend you confess, Coulter," he said. "I really do. It may not seem like it, but I am trying to help you."

Without answering, I shut the door, the latch clicking shut, but the detective didn't leave right away. I could see his shadow underneath the door. He was lurking there, as if listening for my movements, shifting his weight from left to right. Not knowing what else to do, I did the same. When he moved, I moved. He swayed left, I swayed left. He swayed right, I swayed right. He moved forward, I moved forward. He placed his ear against the door. I placed my ear against the door. We mirrored each other, like twins, separated by a few inches of solid wood.

✕

The pills Dr. White had given me, the ones that would quicken the frequency of my daydreams, tasted chalky, like an antacid tablet. They coated the inside of my mouth and my throat, numbing them. As soon as the chemicals began to seep into my system, my body felt like it vibrated. My hair rippled. Teeth chattered. Palms went dry, tingled. It was an odd experience, but it wasn't alarming. Instead, I felt euphoric, better than I had in years. I didn't understand why I hadn't started taking them sooner. My fears of losing touch with reality appeared unfounded, laughable even.

We were on our way to the airport, my mother and I, so that she could see me off to Switzerland. Since the interrogation by Detective Landsmen, my mother and I had hardly spoken to one another. Our plans for the future had been halted. We no longer discussed moving to sunny southern California nor what breed of dog we would adopt, workout regimens, apartment decorations. Instead, we largely remained silent. She'd flip through sitcoms, never staying on the same channel for longer than a scene, and I would work on my dissertation, revising and revising, sometimes working upon a single sentence for hours upon a time. When we did talk, we skirted the proverbial elephant in the room, opting for curt, one-sentence remarks: "How was your day?" she'd ask. "Good," I'd say. "Productive." I could tell she worried, though. Despite the television being on, she wouldn't even look at it, her eyes glazed over, lost in thought and chewing her hair. The object of her concern, however, eluded me. Did she worry she'd lose her son again after all these years of estrangement, or was she rather fraught by the notion that she may lose her own freedom, be punished for her role in Sara's death? It was hard to say. Despite living together for the past several months, I was still having a hard time reading her.

In the cab, however, I could tell she wanted to say something. She cleaned her fingernails and ran them through her hair. She held her breath and popped her wrists, clicking her hands inward toward her chest like she was having a seizure.

"I don't think you should come back," she said.

She looked afraid, like a child might, sleeping alone for the first time during a storm. It seemed odd to me that she was so afraid, empathy, somehow, beyond my faculties under this medication—I felt so good; how could anyone else feel any different?

"Why?" I asked. "There's no other choice but to come back."

Traffic was at a standstill. A Patriots football game was scheduled for later that day, and everyone was heading toward the stadium. In the car next to us, two grown men donned red and blue face paint and colored wigs. When they caught me staring at them, they blinked at me like I was the one who appeared out of the ordinary. Unsure what else to do, I waved. They, hesitantly, waved back.

Mom glanced toward the driver. He was Arabic, and every once in a while, he peered at us through the rearview mirror. His look wasn't sinister by any means, not distrusting, but almost quizzical, like he wanted to tell us something important but couldn't quite muster the courage to.

"You know why," she whispered so the cabbie couldn't hear. "That detective. He's been snooping around asking questions. I've seen him in the building."

"He's doing his job," I said. "I'd be more suspicious if we didn't see him around."

"He's going to find out what happened, Coulter. Aren't you worried about that?"

"Yes," I said. "I am."

"This will most likely be your only chance to get away."

"And what about you?" I asked. "What will you do?"

"I'm going to confess," she said. "I've lived a full life. You haven't because of me. Let me do this for you."

"You want to take the fall?"

"I want to give you a life."

"You, a martyr?"

"Hard to believe, isn't it?"

The cabbie cleared his throat, both my and my mother's attention turning to him. He peered at me through the rearview mirror, glanced back at the road to see if the traffic had moved at all—it had not. "You," he said. "I know your face."

"I'm sorry?"

"I've seen you before. Where do I know you from?"

"I think you may have me confused with—" I said.

"You're famous." He clicked his tongue as if he could propel the answer from his mouth. "You're a scientist. I read about you. String theory. Yes!"

"Yes," I said, admittedly proud to be recognized on the street. "That is me."

"Wow," he said. "Wow. Wow. Wow. In my cab, a celebrity."

"I don't know about celebrity," I said.

"Like Tom Cruise. Ha!"

"Yeah," I said. "I guess so."

Traffic began to move, and the cabbie returned his attention to the road, shaking his head as if in disbelief: in his cab, a famous scientist.

We arrived at the airport shortly after, and Mom helped me with my bags, pulling them out of the trunk instead of allowing the cabbie or I to do it. "I need the exercise," she said.

The cabbie returned to his driver's seat, and I waited on the sidewalk as Mom pulled the last bag out of the trunk. Once she struggled to get them up onto the curb, she stood in front of me like a mother dropping her child off at school for the very first time.

"I am so proud of you," she said.

The airport was busy, cars pulling in and out of the loading drive, the sound of plastic wheels scraping against pavement, the stench of car exhaust fumes billowing around like a chemical gas cloud.

"Thank you," I said, genuinely sincere. The medicine made me bounce.

"You'll call me when you land?" She picked lint off my sweater, flicked it onto the street. "I know it's irrational, but flying has always frightened me."

"You have a better chance of being killed by a terrorist. Or a tiger shark."

"You always were full of interesting facts like that."

"I read a lot."

"But you'll call."

I nodded. "You'll answer?"

"Yes," she said. "Of course."

Mom wrapped her arms around me and dug her face into my chest. She held me right above my elbows so that I couldn't lift my arms to hug her back. The pressure against my pectorals caused them to vibrate even more, like they were being pulsated by moderate voltage. The feeling sort of reminded me of my undergraduate days, popping Adderall in order to pull all-nighters. I felt nostalgic in a way I hadn't in years.

"So you'll let me do this for you?" she asked. "You'll stay there?"

The cabbie honked, rolled down the window. "You coming, ma'am?" he asked. "I'm blocking traffic here."

"One second," she said. She turned back to me. "Will you please let me do this for you?"

"Yes," I said, glad that I could give her what she wanted. "You can do this for me."

"Thank you." She pulled away and looked up at me. "Thank you." She patted me on the chest. "You should be going. You don't want to miss your flight." Before pulling away, she rubbed her thumb across my chin, then kissed me goodbye.

〤

At first it started out as itchy and red, a little spot on the inside of his elbow. He thought it might be eczema. He bought lotion. Jergens and Aveeno and Lubriderm. He tried Vaseline. Yet it still itched. It got bigger. It got redder. When he looked down, tiny spots of blood dotted his forearm. Not good. Not good at all. Sara asked about it, said he should probably go see a dermatologist. Coulter said he would if it got any worse. How much worse? It's like pornography, he said, I'll know it when I see it. They both laughed.

It got worse. It started to smell like copper. Coulter tried to convince himself that this was a good sign. Antibodies were in action. White blood cells. An immune system at work. Sara noticed this, too. Coulter could tell by the way she sniffed the air, trying to surmise the source. It didn't take long for her to locate it. This time, though, she didn't say anything.

A few more days passed. It got worse still. A small sore materialized. It looked bad. He could see the sinewy fibers inside his arm. Connective tissue. Capillaries with a slight tinge in there. Not long thereafter, pus oozed from it. It was a neon green color and had the consistency of infected mucous.

Okay, he told Sara. I'll go to the doctor.

He went to his general practitioner first. Nasty little bugger, he said. Bet that hurts something fierce, he said. Have you tried Neosporin? Yes. Have you tried other topical solutions? Not yet. Well, it's some sort of infection; that much is for sure. I'm going to get you set up with some antibiotics. That should fix you right up. By the way, how's your wife doing? Sally, right?

Good.

He took the antibiotics and a topical solution. He took these for several days. The pills were huge and got caught in his throat. It hurt to wipe on the cream, even when careful, hovering his fingertips just over the wound. He hoped this would cure the sore. He had faith in medical advancements; it was, after all, a simple infection. Yet it still grew. He applied more topical cream liberally. He doubled up on the antibiotics. It hurt worse. It smelled worse. He was scared.

The doctor appeared to be scared, too. Huh, he said. He refused to touch it; instead, his gloved fingers rested several inches down Coulter's forearm. What does that mean? That 'huh?' It doesn't look good. No shit, doc. Look at my arm, Coulter said. I can see the goddamn bone. I do, too. We need to run more tests. For fuck's sake, Doc. Ya think? The doctor sent him to the lab where they took blood samples. A technician named Ralph who had a daughter and an Afro swabbed his elbow with a Q-Tip and jarred the gooey substance for further evaluation.

It hurt so badly Coulter couldn't move his arm any longer. It was growing at such a pace that Coulter believed he could actually see the perimeter of the wound expand. He went to a dermatologist who kept him waiting in the lobby for two hours after he'd completed the paperwork, after he'd written down his general physician's name, his insurance company, his billing address, his permanent address, his emergency contact person, his occupation, his work address, all of his allergies, Benadryl yes and sulfa drugs sure, but he could take penicillin just fine, and he listed the entirety of his medical record, how he'd had measles years before, when he was like seven or eight or something like that, how he sometimes suffered from high blood pressure, more than likely the result of stress caused by a damn toddler that wouldn't stop crying and his damn dissertation defense that was coming up and all the revisions he wouldn't be able to get done in time, how he had TMJ and how his jaw clicked when he ate tough steak, and even how he'd gotten his wisdom teeth taken out when he was eighteen. Even that for Christ's sake. Written left-handed, the ink scribbled all over the paper like a child had filled out the form.

He kept his arm elevated, which alleviated the bleeding and the throbbing a little bit. Each morning, he and Sara had wrapped his wound in gauze several inches thick in order to keep the infection from spreading, and to prevent dirt or gravel from getting caught somewhere inside of him, gnawing raw his muscles like sandpaper. It didn't help. The tape would come loose, the adhesive worn thin by his sweat, and the pad kept moving on him, allowing particles of dust to seep in through the edges. He had also taken painkillers to ebb the pain, which didn't help either. Advil and Tylenol and Motrin and Ibuprofen and leftover Oxycodone from a surgery he'd had a couple years before on his foot, by themselves and in different mixtures, one or two or more taken together at different doses. Nothing helped. He couldn't sleep because of it. He couldn't drive. He couldn't work. He couldn't make love to his wife or hold his son or take a shower or eat or sit or watch television or water his plants or lecture or boil water or even open a bottle of beer. He couldn't do anything. Nothing. It'd been so long since he'd slept, he was afraid he was starting to hallucinate. Light refracted against his irises like it would a fractured prism, beams shooting through at awkward angles and glaring at impossible hues so that the world turned into a kaleidoscopic nightmare akin to a hall of mirrors. Everything was out of proportion. His son's head was larger than a basketball, his wife's eyes the color of a Dr. Pepper can. He was scared all the time. He scared his wife all the time. His son cried every time he saw him. Sara was at home with him now. She'd offered to come, find a babysitter, he needed her help after all. Coulter declined, though. He wanted to go at it alone.

A nurse called him back, finally. She took his blood pressure. It was high. She smiled reassuringly and called him sweetie and had hair pulled back so tightly that her forehead resembled a rubber band threatening to break. The doctor arrived a few moments later. He was older and smelled of hand sanitizer and alcohol-free mouthwash. How are you? he asked. I've been better. So what seems to be the problem? My arm. There's some kind of infection. The doctor carefully unwrapped the gauze. Pain rocketed through Coulter's nerve endings. His arm trembled. He bit his tongue. Jesus! the doctor said. Oh wow, oh my, oh goodness. How long has it been like this? A few days now. It's getting worse. In fact, it's grown since this morning. The edge of the wound was only a few inches from his wrist now. Each time he wiggled his fingers, he could see the bones and muscles move inside of his arm. It was like an anatomy exhibit, showing the inner workings of the human skeleton and muscular system. What do you think it is? Coulter said. What the hell is happening to me? It's hard to say. Until we run some more tests I won't know for sure, but it looks like necrotizing fasciitis. Necrotizing fasciitis? Flesh-eating bacteria.

GENEVA WAS BRILLIANTLY WHITE. ICE COV-
ered cars and hung from gutters. The Alps and the Jura were blanketed
in snow. The buildings were warmed with stove fires and overworked
heaters. The place smelled of electricity and coal and fish. The streets
were crowded, and the people were happy—teenagers teased one another in the streets, lovers crossed arms and strolled, looking through
hooded coats at merchandise hanging in shop windows—and so was I.
I was happy.

During the flight, I had dreamt mostly, though if I were actually
asleep or hallucinating, induced by the prescription, I wasn't quite sure.
It had been very vivid, the dream. I had been suffering from a wound on
my arm, a flesh-eating bacteria, and was about to be put under for surgery when I came to. When I did, I was still on the plane, my arm throbbing from pain. I reached down to the inside of my elbow, half-expecting
to find blood there, the cotton soaked with pus, or, worse yet, my arm
amputated, but it wasn't. It was still there, and dry, and for some reason
this disappointed me, like I wished my daydreams were somehow real.
This desire should have worried me, I knew, but the thought enthralled
me. I took another pill, ran my tongue against the roof of my mouth,
liking how it felt, and yearned for my dreams to manifest themselves in
reality.

In front of the hotel entrance, warming his hands by blowing into the palms, was Dr. Brinkman, waiting for me. "Come," he said. He grabbed my arm like a father would, and we pushed our way into the hotel. Inside the lobby, a welcoming committee greeted us. Busboys carried our luggage, and the concierge offered us cigarettes and a bottle of wine or champagne maybe and to take our coats and told us no need to check in, our hosts were already waiting for us in a conference room on the second floor, just get comfortable in our room and meet them when we were ready, and he handed us an itinerary filled with dinners and interviews and briefings and press conferences and closed-door meetings with top CERN scientists, Dr. Hutzinger and Dr. Widhouse and Cal Thomas, one of Dr. Brinkman's former students actually.

Upstairs we had a moment alone. We had a suite that overlooked the lake. It was frozen and glass-like. Not a perfect sheet by any means but like glass blown by an amateur, full of air bubbles and fissures. The room itself sprawled. It was spacious and luxurious and smelled of sandalwood and papaya. Dr. Brinkman searched for the mini bar, and I went to the window, touched the glass, smelled the curtains, rubbed my feet against the carpet, and then touched the silver fixtures on the windows. An electrical charge shocked me.

"You look good," he said. "You look happy."

Outside, across the lake, I could make out smoke billowing up into the sky. It came in puffs, like someone was using smoke signals to call for help.

"Dr. White has put me on a prescription," I said.

"It seems to be working."

"It is."

"I'm glad to hear that." I could hear ice clink against the bottom of a cocktail glass. "You want a drink?" he asked.

"I shouldn't."

"Just one. A celebration."

"But the medication."

"Did Dr. White say you couldn't drink on it?"

"No," I said.

"Then I'm sure it'll be fine."

A gaggle of geese stood on the side of the road, trying to cross despite the heavy traffic. It seemed bizarre geese would be around this time of year. Being migratory birds, I had expected them to have already flown south for the winter, but there they stood, tempting death.

"What's your poison?" Dr. Brinkman asked. "We have vodka, scotch, Irish whiskey, bourbon, gin. Good stuff, too. Top shelf."

"I'll have whatever you're having."

"Whiskey it is," he said. "Middleton Very Rare. Ever had it?"

"I'm not much of a drinker."

"Sheltered Coulter. Yes," he said. "I remember."

He handed me the drink and stood next to me at the window. "It's supposed to be served neat, but I prefer on the rocks. I hope you don't mind."

I didn't say anything. The medicine started to kick in again. I could feel my blood coursing through my veins, like it was filled with insects rather than liquid, their wings fluttering.

Dr. Brinkman took a sip of his whiskey, puckering his lips from the bitter taste. "We'll never forget this, you know."

"I know."

"Moments like these, they don't come around very often. Eddington when he proved Einstein's theory of relativity. Rutherford and the Higgs Boson. Batelaan and the double-slit experiment. This is going to be one of those moments, Coulter. You realize this, yes?"

"I do."

"And you're the one who cracked the code." He took another drink, sighed in satisfaction. "I have to admit, I'm a bit jealous of you."

"Really?"

"Yes," he said. "I am."

"You've won a Nobel."

"Yes," he said. "But it's not about the prize, Coulter. That's not what I'm jealous of."

"Oh?"

"Your manifold," he said, "is the greatest scientific discovery since relativity. You've determined the exact shape of the universe. The models we will be able to construct. Synthetic elements. Quantum computing. Conservation of energy. Deep space travel. The implications are mind-boggling. Infinite even."

"I hadn't really thought about it," I said.

"You will have forever changed the course of history, Coulter."

The geese, it appeared, had spotted the smoke across the lake. They convened on the edge of the highway, cars careening past, and squawked and fluttered their wings, almost as if pointing toward the fire. For some reason, they felt compelled to go there, and I silently encouraged them to brave the highway, step out in a uniform line, and be crushed by the oncoming traffic. I didn't know why I had such a desire, but I did—I wanted nothing more than to watch the geese die.

"Go," I whispered, encouraging them on.

"I'm sorry?" Dr. Brinkman asked.

I didn't say anything, remained staring out the window. Dr. Brinkman took another sip of his drink, smacking his lips in delight.

"I suppose I should be happy with my student doing so well," he continued. "Even though I did try to convince you to pursue a different avenue of research, I did, as your teacher, influence your findings, even if it was only in a small way. This doesn't really console me, though."

One of the geese pattered out onto the road, took a few awkward steps, but then jumped back onto the shoulder when a large truck zoomed past.

"Go," I whispered again. "Come on."

"It is a flaw, I admit, my ego. I've struggled with it ever since I was your age, finishing up my own doctoral research. I was working on the team that would eventually lead to my Nobel. We were constructing a history of what exactly had occurred directly after the Big Bang, to thousandths of seconds after the birth of our universe. It was a very exciting time."

The smoke grew thicker, darker, like a thunderstorm about to release torrential rains, lightning, and thunder.

"There was another doctoral student on the team, Carlos Alca. He was Peruvian, I think. Maybe Argentinian. I can't remember. Anyway, he was brilliant. Much smarter than I was. So much so, I felt threatened by him."

The same goose that had trotted out onto the highway before ventured out again, this time moving quicker, with more abandon. It made it past the first lane without any trouble, only five more to go, but in the middle of the second, a sedan careened down the road, heading straight for it.

"Please," I whispered. "Please. Please. Please."

"We had the same committee chair on our dissertations. He was studying the idea of a single, unified energy directly after the Big Bang, where gravity, the weak, strong, and electromagnetic forces were all rolled up into the same substance. About the same time, a group of German scientists was studying the same thing. I was aware of it. He was aware of it. Everyone was aware of it."

The goose didn't notice the car, waddled ahead without flinching, its fight-or-flight instinct inactivated.

"As you well know, we had to turn in pages of our dissertation at regular intervals, and our chair liked us to drop off our work all at the same time. I timed it so that I would come in after Carlos, armed with two dissertations: my set of pages, and then another, the exact paper the German scientists had published a few weeks before, with Carlos' name on the byline. I'm not proud of what I did, Coulter. I'm not."

The driver must have noticed the goose—he veered and hit the brakes, the car fishtailing, the tires squealing against the pavement. I stood on my tiptoes, my fingertips pressed against the window glass.

"He got kicked out of school a few weeks later. Academic dishonesty. Plagiarism. No one cared he said he didn't do it; there were his pages, with his name on it, another author's words. Proof beyond a reasonable doubt. He went home, a truant, and I went on to win the Nobel. I've never been more ashamed of anything in my life."

Right before the car slammed into the goose, it jumped into the air, spread its wings out wide, and let slip a shrill honk. The bird exploded against the hood of the car, the windshield splattered with blood. The car kept moving, the street wet with slush.

"Yes!" I yelled, raising my arms in triumph. "Yes! Yes! Yes!"

"Jesus," Dr. Brinkman said. "Oh my God."

The car kept sliding, it now moving sideways down the road, heading straight for a cement barricade.

"Please," Dr. Brinkman said.

"Please!" I said.

The driver flipped on the windshield wipers, but it just smeared the blood across the glass. I could make out his features, his face tinted red from the reflected blood. His expression was of pure panic, his eyes bulging, his mouth open in horror. He thought he was going to die. He did. I could tell by the sheer terror freezing him into place—he had the look of imminent death.

When the car slammed into the barricade, I could see his body lurch from the impact. Afterward, he didn't move, his shoulders and head slouched forward. "Oh my God," Dr. Brinkman said. "We should do something." Cars behind him slowed and stopped, and drivers exited their vehicles to see if they could help. The first one there knocked on the window once, twice, three times. After no response, he pulled the car door open. The driver didn't move. But then, there was a rustle. His head bobbed. His shoulders bounced. The rescuer bent down, trying, it appeared, to get the man's seatbelt off. Once they succeeded, the injured man emerged from his wrecked and bloodied car, and I couldn't have been more disappointed—everything was still the same. He was alive, his ordeal now over, the fire still raging in the distance.

Ж

It didn't take long for the blood test results. Coulter waited in the lobby—the doctor hadn't wanted him to go far. About an hour he waited. He tried to read *Popular Science*, some article about a scientist identifying evidence of dark matter, but he couldn't concentrate. The words melded into one another, snaking their way across the page. Pictures taken by the COBE satellite mapping out background microwave radiation from the Big Bang blurred together like television static just before a storm was about to hit.

The doctor called him back again. Coulter had to have help standing, wobbling for a few steps before a nurse grabbed a wheelchair. Instead of an examination room, they rolled him into the doctor's office. Pictures of blond children smiled back at him, one girl and one boy, the latter missing his two front teeth.

The doctor told him he'd have to go into surgery right away. If he didn't, the infection would eat away his arm. It would get into his bloodstream and ride his arteries back to his heart where it would attack his cardiovascular system and kill him. It wouldn't take long at all. A day or two, he said. If that. Maybe hours. I'm glad you came in. The doctor slapped him on the back. If you waited any longer, you'd be a dead man. He laughed. Ha! Ha Ha Ha.

Coulter didn't move or respond. His head still swam. He heard the doctor's words. He understood them: surgery, necrotizing fasciitis, amputation, dead man. The gravity of it all made him feel nauseated, but the pain and the vertigo kept him from showing fear. His organs all felt strained to the point of tearing. He wanted to ask if he would die. Was there a possibility he wouldn't wake up from this, to be put under, to slip away while unconscious, his last cognizant thought a trembling whimper of fear that no one beside himself could hear? But his tongue was too heavy to move.

The ambulance arrived only a few minutes later. An orderly wheeled him outside. He had earbuds in, and Coulter could faintly hear music. It was a pop song, something current, something Coulter vaguely remembered hearing before. He tried to think of the artist's name, the title of the track, but it wouldn't come to him. The orderly popped his chewing gum to the beat of the song, bobbed his head as they walked down the hallway. What song was it? This would bother him for the rest of the day, he was sure of it. He'd heard the song on multiple occasions, ubiquitously, on the radio, in cabs, on campus, a summertime anthem. Girls sang it incessantly, under their breath while waiting in line at the school cafeteria, bits of apple flying out their mouth as they made it through the chorus. Undergraduates would tap the rhythm on their desks during quizzes. Why couldn't he remember it? It was everywhere he went! Literally! It was even playing in the ambulance. The two drivers sang along to the words. It was driving Coulter crazy. His arm itched, but he couldn't scratch it. It was elevated and wrapped in gauze. The song blared through the speakers, taunting him. The singer was some young woman, perhaps a teenage star. Her voice sounded familiar. Sweet and melodic. Innocent and naïve. She sang of love and fairy tale endings. He hated the song. He hated the rhythm, the acoustic guitar, the simple bass beats, even the backup singers, singing OOooooOO AAA. The hospital wasn't far—close enough for the short pop song not to end. Another orderly greeted him out front in order to get him wheeled to the operating room. He looked much like the orderly at the small, specialist hospital Coulter had just arrived from. An uncanny resemblance, actually, now that

Coulter took a closer look. He had the same knotted, unkempt hair. The same two-day beard. The same glazed look in his eyes. The same mouth, chomping bubblegum. And the earbuds. He had in the *same* earbuds, and as Coulter climbed onto a gurney, he could hear the faint, melodic voice of that ubiquitous pop star.

Was he going insane? Was the infection from his arm already coursing through his bloodstream, poisoning his brain? It had to be. Calm down. Shock was playing tricks on his mind. He'd just received bad news, his arm to be amputated. He wasn't going insane. He was just in shock. But what if he was going crazy? What if he never returned to normal? These could be the last remaining, semi-lucid thoughts he might ever have. It finally sunk in. He might die. He might never see Sara or Isaac again, and it all came in an unexpected rush, like a large wave might, when you have your back to the water and you're gazing up at the shore, that he had to see them. He had to. At least one more time.

He grabbed the orderly by the shirt with his one good arm. "Is my family on their way?" he asked.

The orderly pulled out one earbud. Coulter could hear the pop song through the speaker. "I'm sorry?"

"My family. Did someone call my family?"

"I'm sorry, sir. I wouldn't know that."

The operating room smelled of zinc oxide. It was dim in there, which worried him at first—how would the doctor be able to see what he was doing?—but then he noticed the mobile lamp above the table, much like what he'd find above a dentist's chair. Surgical tools were laid out upon a table next to the bed. There was an electrical saw, the disc-shaped blade the size of a compact disc and serrated to slice through bone.

"Hi, Coulter," the doctor said. "How are you doing?"

"I need to speak with my wife," Coulter said.

"She will be contacted. I promise."

"I need to speak with her now."

"Unfortunately there isn't enough time. You'll be able to speak with her afterward."

Coulter didn't believe him. He had the urge to hug his son, to tell him this might be the last time they'll see each other, that what they had was special and more important than anything else in the world, but all he could do was nod and trust this stranger who was about to sever a part of him.

The surgeon leaned over Coulter. He smelled like doctors often do: clean, like laundry fresh out of the dryer. He placed a mask over Coulter's nose and mouth, the anesthesia.

"I want you to count backwards from a hundred for me, Coulter. When you wake up, everything will be as it should."

Coulter nodded and began to count.

100. 99. 98. 97. 96. 95. 94. 9—

※

"Coulter?" Dr. Brinkman placed his hand on my shoulder. "Coulter? Answer me. Are you feeling unwell?" he asked. "Maybe we should call for help," Dr. Brinkman said as he waved his hand in front of my face. We were in a ballroom, in the hotel I guessed, but I didn't remember leaving our suite. It was a large place, filled with white table-clothed tables, chrysanthemum centerpieces, and sparkling chandeliers. A grand piano was pushed into the corner, and in the center of the room was a scuffed dance floor. There were only three of us in there: Dr. Brinkman, a very large stranger, and me.

"Call for help?" I asked.

My mouth was dry, the roof rough, the texture of exposed brick. My throat felt swollen, making it difficult to speak. I tried to clear my throat, but I choked, and coughed into my sleeve.

"Thank goodness," Dr. Brinkman said. "You gave us quite a scare."

"I did?"

"Yes," the stranger said. "I've never seen anything quite like it."

"What happened?" I asked.

"You froze," the stranger said.

"Froze?"

"Yes. You simply stood there. You weren't speaking. You weren't moving. At first we thought you might be playing a joke on us, but then you stopped blinking. I even had to place my finger underneath your nostrils just to make sure you hadn't stopped breathing."

"And who are you?" I asked.

"Coulter," Dr. Brinkman said, "I'd like you to meet one of my former students, Cal Thomas. He works here at CERN."

Dr. Thomas was an intimidating figure, easily above 6'4", perhaps 235 or 250 pounds. He had the jaw of a linebacker and shoulders as thick as bowling balls. When he took my outstretched hand to introduce himself, his fingers wrapped completely around it so that his thumb and middle finger overlapped.

"I've been looking forward to meeting you for a good long while," he said, his voice not as deep as his build would indicate. "I'm a very big fan of your work."

"You're huge," I said.

He chuckled. "Yes," he said. "I get that a lot." He released my hand. I could tell a good five-degree difference from when he'd clutched it and afterward. "Though I've never rendered someone speechless like that before. I thought you may have fallen asleep standing with your eyes open."

"I apologize," I said. "I must be jet-lagged."

"It is a long flight," he said. "I never can quite get used to it."

"Dr. Thomas here was about to take us over to the lab," Dr. Brinkman said. "Give us the tour. Do you feel up to it?"

"Yes," I said. "I'd love to."

"Are you sure? We can postpone if you need to lie down or grab a bite to eat or something."

"How long was I out?" I asked.

"Three, maybe four minutes."

"And I didn't respond at all?"

"I even pinched you," Dr. Brinkman said. "Nothing."

"Strange," I said.

"But you seem better now," Dr. Thomas said as he slapped me on the shoulder, nearly causing me to lose my balance. "Sorry," he said. "Sometimes I don't know my own strength."

Dr. Brinkman and I followed Dr. Thomas out of the ballroom to a side street where a taxi waited for us. Before we got in the cab, however, Dr. Brinkman placed a hand on my elbow. "Are you sure you're feeling all right?" he asked. "Is the medication maybe getting to you?"

I no longer felt the effects of the medication, not like I had before, anyways. Gone was the sense of euphoria. Instead, I felt groggy, like I'd taken too much Benadryl. My muscles weighed more than normal; my eyes sunk into my head. My brain reacted as if it were underwater. If I lay my head down, I was certain I would fall asleep and never wake up.

"I don't know," I said. "Maybe."

)(

When he awoke, he could still feel his arm there. It hurt. It itched. It ached. It was unbearable because he could do nothing to stop it. Phantom limb syndrome. He'd read about it before the infection, an article about soldiers returning from war zones, amputees scratching thin air. Sometimes the pain would become so intense that it would be debilitating. Soldiers would scream from the pain. It would be sharp and blinding, like they were reliving the cause of the amputation over and over and over again. They wouldn't be able to walk or ask for help. They would be rendered incapacitated. That's how he felt. He lay on his back in a dark hospital room. He hurt so badly he couldn't move at all. Machines beeped in the corner. IV bags full of painkillers were stationed next to his bed. His arm pricked full of needles. At first, he didn't recognize where he was at, and he became afraid. The drugs, however, kept him from crying out. He was confused and couldn't organize his thoughts. Then it slowly came back to him. The flesh-eating bacteria. The doctor. The surgery.

He pressed the button to call the nurse. A few minutes later she arrived. She was short and squatty and smelled of hand sanitizer. "You're awake," she said. "How're you feeling?"

"Water," he said. "Please."

She filled a paper cup and raised the straw to his lips. "Is Sara here?" he asked.

"Who?"

"My wife."

She looked confused. "I don't believe so," she said. She picked up his chart. "It says here no immediate family was to be notified."

"There's some mistake."

"I am so sorry, sir," she said. "I'm sure she is worried sick. I will give her a call right away." She asked for the number, and he gave it to her. "I will be right back."

Alone again, he wondered what Sara must have been going through. She'd be at home at this hour, cuddled up in bed, her feet tucked underneath her. In her lap would be a book, some journalistic exposé over the 2007–2008 financial crisis, adjudicating the fraudulent packing of mortgage-backed securities in the court of public opinion, but she wouldn't be reading it. Her eyes would scan the same sentence over and over, the words forming in her consciousness, but understanding eluding her, formulating some plan of action if he didn't show up by morning, by midnight, within the hour. She'd be oscillating between genuine concern and outright rage. If something bad had happened, she'd be sure someone would have contacted her. No, she would instead think he had simply gone to the doctor, then headed to the lab right afterward, not even taking the time to let her know that everything was okay. Because of this, she would be devising some sort of revenge: Visine in his morning coffee, a hammer to his laptop, the accidental deletion of his dissertation. That was her way—always planning, always conniving.

Something, however, just didn't seem right. She'd known he'd gone to the dermatologist. She'd wanted to accompany him then, scared and worried, but he'd refused, playing the role of martyr, unwilling to be vulnerable. When he hadn't returned she would've called the doctor's office. They would've told her about the surgery. She would've contacted the hospital. She would've found out what room he was in. She would've been here. It just didn't make any sense. There must have been a mistake along the way. The receptionist at the dermatologist's office must have told Sara he'd never shown for the appointment or that he had been treated and left and nothing else.

Poor girl, he thought. She must be panicking.

The nurse returned. She looked confused. "I'm sorry, sir," she said. "But your wife is not at this number." She repeated the phone number back to him.

"No. That's it. That's her number."

"The woman said she's not married, sir."

"You spoke to Sara?"

"Yes. Her name was Sara, but she denied knowing you, sir. Is there someone else I can call?"

"There's some mistake."

"Maybe we can try again in the morning. The morphine and anesthesia together will make you groggy."

"Call her back," he pleaded. "Let me talk to her."

"It's late, sir." She patted him on the shin. He flinched at the contact. "We'll sort everything out in the morning."

"Please," he said. "I don't want to be alone."

"Here," she said. "Let me get you something to help you sleep." She fiddled with the IV, and the morphine dripped at an increasing rate. "There," she said. "This should do the trick."

He wanted to stop her, but he couldn't. He didn't have the energy. His eyelids drooped. He felt himself drifting off into sleep. "Please," he said. "Please. Please. Please." But she didn't listen. The nurse patted him on the forehead. There, she said. All better now.

Ж

The collider was impressive. It had 9,300 magnets, all pre-cooled to negative 193.2°C, making just one eighth of its cryogenic system the world's largest refrigerator. During the experiment, trillions of protons would lap the LHC 11,245 times per second, and approximately six hundred million collisions would occur every second. The beams flew through an ultra-high vacuum, the emptiest space in the solar system. The internal pressure measured 10 to 13 atm. When the two beams of ions collided, they generated temperatures 100,000 times hotter than the heart of the sun. It encompassed all the extremes of the universe.

Touring it before the experiment, however, I was distracted. Dr. Thomas led us through the tunnels, along the steel reinforced tubes that accelerated the particles and discussed the history of the project, the financial backing by various European countries, the thousands of independent contractors, engineering firms and university scientists and politicians and regulating bodies that had a hand in creating the largest experiment in the history of mankind, and I could not shake the feeling that I was walking underwater, doped by the medication prescribed to me by Dr. White. My brain felt heavy, my extremities weighty, my tongue non-responsive. I had to concentrate to walk in a straight line, and when asked a question I simply smiled, nodded, and gave clipped, curt answers. Are you enjoying your visit so far, Coulter? Yes. Would you like something to drink? No. Are you sure you're feeling all right? Yes.

Dozens of workers checked and rechecked the tube. If the integrity of one bracket were compromised, the result would be devastating. Even though the tunnels were so far underground, the resulting explosion would be catastrophic, many times the power of an atomic bomb, and I couldn't stop wondering what it would be like if such an event occurred. Earthquakes would devastate the area for many miles. Buildings would crumble, avalanches would pulverize highways, and monstrous waves would crash the beaches of the nearby lakes. Thousands of people would die instantly. Some would drown. Some would be crushed. Some would suffocate. Some would burn. Some would fall. Some would bleed out. Some may even kill each other, panicking and trying to evacuate. They would trample colleagues while trying to escape down a flight of stairs. Afraid of jagged mountain rocks, a driver would accelerate too quickly around a curve and hit a pedestrian, attempting to flee a smashed SUV. After being trapped in rubble for several days, one survivor might kill another so that he may eat and survive himself, extending even the slightest hope that he, miraculously, may one day be saved.

"We first fired it up September 2008," Dr. Thomas said as he patted the tube like it was his pet. "I bet you remember all the hullabaloo surrounding it."

"Yes," Dr. Brinkman said. "The protestors. They thought the collider would create a black hole that would swallow up the earth."

"It didn't matter that it was impossible."

"Some people refuse to listen to reason. They grasp onto the irrational and hold onto it."

Going out like that, in a devastating catastrophe, wouldn't be so bad. It may be painful. It may be unbearable. It may even be the worst moment of your life, but, in the end, it would occur in a moment encased in history. People would debate the causes, mourn the tragedy, and declare your death and the many hundreds of others that died alongside you as unnecessary. They would stir a movement, and create change. New safety measures would be taken, technologies built, research opportunities to be had. There would be cause and effect. Your death would be an indispensible link in the progress of mankind, and that's all that anybody ever wants—to have mattered.

"We should get back up to the lab," Dr. Thomas said. "We're about to get started."

※

He awoke the next morning feeling as if he'd gone on a drinking binge. He hurt everywhere. His teeth hurt. His toenails hurt. Even his hair hurt. At some point in the night, his catheter had malfunctioned, and urine soaked his bed sheets and gown. A rash burned his inner thighs. His ears seemed plugged, from an infection maybe, or a drop in barometric pressure. The blanket had wrapped around his feet, and blood caked the inside of his remaining elbow. What had happened *there*? he thought. And how did I keep from waking up?

He attempted to rise to a sitting position, but this feat proved too difficult. The panel to his bed came equipped with a button to call the nurse; however, he couldn't reach it. Every time he attempted to move his good arm, pain shot through his bones. It was paralysis without the paralysis, which, to Coulter, seemed even more infuriating. He knew to have full faculty of his limbs, the remaining ones anyway, but he could not control them due to the immense pain in trying.

Accepting his fate, he yelled. Or tried to. His throat was raspy and dry, and his attempts to shout for the nurse seemed more like a whimper than a plea for help. He coughed and choked on his own saliva, exacerbating his despair. He had no recourse for his predicament, instead imprisoned in a bed unable to move or speak.

The sun filtered in through sheer curtains, cheap things made of cotton. It was winter, but it felt as if the air conditioner was on, blasting cold air through the vents. Soon he started shivering. Mucous drained from his nostrils. He could feel it clog his throat. He choked on it. It obstructed his air passageways. He thought he was going to drown. Panic kicked in. His blood pressure rose, and he strained to pull up to a sitting position, but each time he moved, the pain drove him back down. He was going to die. He was going to drown in a pool of his own snot.

But then a nurse came in.

She opened the curtains and then picked up a remote. It had a cord running into the bed, and when she pressed the red button near the top, the bed raised to a sitting position. All of a sudden, Coulter could breathe again. He indicated he needed a drink of water, and the nurse obliged.

"How're we feeling this morning?" She wasn't the same nurse as from the night before. This one was younger, spunkier. She bobbed when she spoke, and she perpetually smiled. "On a scale of one to ten, could you rate your pain for me?"

"Ten."

"Is it sharp or dull? How would you describe it?"

"Unbearable."

"Do you need more pain meds? I could talk to the doctor, see if we could increase your dosage."

"I want to speak with my wife."

"I see," she said. "I'll see what I can do about that."

She averted her gaze when he asked, busied herself by checking his chart, scraping imaginary dust from the foot of his bed. She was hiding something.

"Please," he said. "I'm begging you."

She appeared to take pity on him. She licked her lips and looked away, as if trying to locate her resolve. Her lips were dry and chapped.

Bits of flesh flaked off of them like a dried and peeled sticker.

"Listen," she said. "The doctor had us order a psych eval. We checked public records. There's no indication that you were ever married."

The news settled in slowly. At first, what she'd said didn't quite register. It was too preposterous. He'd seen Sara right before going to the doctor the day before. She had tried to go with him but he refused. You have more important things to do, he'd said. When they had said goodbye, they hugged, and she grabbed his hand and said, "Be careful, Coulter. I can't raise Isaac alone."

"The doctor is actually on her way right now," the nurse said. "She should be able to help you."

As if on cue, a knock came at the door. In walked a short woman, a woman with disproportionate facial features, too large a nose, too large of ears, too large of eyes, a woman with a comforting and warming presence, a familiar woman.

"Hello, Coulter," Dr. White said. "Do you remember me?"

X

The lab consisted of several workstations in six rows, each having four computer monitors. There was a space for engineering, monitoring the integrity of the collider, one for modeling the movement and collision of the particles, one that tracked the temperature of the cryogenic system, another that monitored the magnets, and another the carbon beam dump. Engineers double and triple checked the integrity of the structure, the welding, the joints, the sensors and magnets, making absolutely, positively sure everything was up to specifications. The place crawled with people, IT gurus and quantum specialists and Big Bang experts and political benefactors and string theorist proponents, so that if I didn't focus my vision, the entire room appeared to move with their activity as if in waves, giving me vertigo. Like my students back in Boston, they even began to look alike, melding into a single person with the same pasty white complexion, the same stringy brown hair, the same cheerful eyes, everyone with the same wave and wink and voice and the same hopeful tone each time they bid me a good morning, good morning, isn't it such a Goddamn great morning?

Dr. Brinkman and I had a spot especially reserved for us near the back of the room, right in the middle with a great view of the monitors. The director sat near us, as did Dr. Thomas. A shared tension precluded us from having any meaningful conversation. We each had our own tics. The director cradled his cup of coffee in front of him, what could be seen as a posture of supplication or of prayer. Dr. Thomas chattered endlessly about banal topics, the harsh winters here in Switzerland, updates on the Patriots—there's just not enough NFL news here like back in the States—the average precipitation in Switzerland versus Massachusetts. Dr. Brinkman rubbed his chin raw so that pieces of dried skin flaked off his face. I gnawed my cuticles until they bled.

The room was abuzz with activity. Millions of working parts had to come together for a short amount of time for all this to work. There was zero room for error. Teams of three to five huddled over various monitors discussing the intricacies of what would transpire, how the mechanics should integrate, how much mass they anticipated should disappear. They had rehearsed this hundreds of times before. They moved with a synchronicity of an organism, almost without thought but in perfect harmony. It was breathtaking, really, a sight I was glad I got to see.

The experiment's project manager hushed the team and stood directly in front of us. He asked for a sound off, and each team gave their okay. Electrical. Go. Engineering. Go. Sensors. Go.

The countdown began. I stared at the display monitors up on the wall. One recorded X-rays. Another sonar. Others electromagnetic radiation, intrinsic brightness, gravity. That was the one I was glued to. If my dissertation were to be proven correct, then the LHC would show the dilution of gravity over small scales, proving my hypothesis of the universe being constructed of curled-up Calabi-Yau spatial dimensions.

The countdown reached zero. I had expected to hear churning, gears grinding, joints bending, something, but the tunnel sounded eerily quiet, and for a moment there I wondered if anything had actually happened. But then, without warning, the screens erupted into colorful, kaleidoscopic fountains. They resembled a Fourth of July fireworks celebration gone horribly wrong, all the rockets exploding at once in a magnanimous, catastrophic torrent, and the entire control room burst into cheers and congratulations and hugs and back pats and whistles because we did it, we DID it, WE did IT, and I couldn't help but wonder what next? What does it mean? Someone, please, just tell me what does it all mean?

$$)($$

Dr. White smiled warmly and sat in a recliner next to his bed. She leaned forward and crossed her legs and stared intently at him, as if he was the only important thing in her world.

"Tell me," she said, "about your wife."

"Sara?"

"Yes. Sara. Tell me about her."

"What would you like to know?"

"Everything."

He told her all that he could remember. She is audacious, he said. Some might call her cavalier. She introduces herself to strangers and collects business cards of men who she would never call. She lights matches and lets them burn until the flames reach her fingers. During holidays, she goes all out, decorating the entire house in reindeer and elves or little hearts for Valentine's Day or Leprechauns for St. Patty's Day. If she sees a homeless person, she will give him every last dime she has. She yells at mothers who spank their children in public. Take her to the *bathroom* and beat her ass, she says, like a normal person would do. She has to buy colorful toe socks every time she goes to Target. When bored, she plans elaborate pranks. One time, she convinced my doctor to fake a positive HIV test. She has that way with people—she can convince them to do anything. She worries constantly. If she doesn't know exactly where I'm at, she calls. Right after class, she'll call. Right after work. On the minute exactly. If work is over at 8:00 p.m., she calls at 8:01 p.m. It's annoying, but it's hard to get mad at someone over something like that, to love someone so much that she has to know where he is at all times. There's nothing wrong with that. There's nothing wrong with her.

I remember this one time, he continued. We were at a baseball game, watching the Redhawks, the minor league team in Oklahoma City, for like our second or third date. It was hot, really hot. We both poured sweat, and I couldn't help but become embarrassed. My t-shirt was soaked through so that you could see my torso, my nipples looking like two pepperonis, and I knew she noticed them—she kept peering over at me in disbelief, like she couldn't imagine a human being could sweat so much.

"I just think we're just not all that much alike," she said out of no-where, like we'd been holding a conversation even though we hadn't spoken to one another in three innings.

"I'm sorry?"

"I've had fun and all; don't get me wrong," she said as she took a sip of her beer. "You seem like a really nice guy."

"There's still a couple innings left in the game."

The visiting team was batting, and a couple of kids behind us heckled the third base coach. Mahoooooney! they yelled. You're full of baloooooney! The coach attempted to ignore them, but he was affected by the taunts. He kept peering up into the stands, an irritated look hidden by the shadow cast by his hat brim.

"Oh, I know," she said. "We can stay as long as you like. I still need a ride home."

"So you're breaking up with me?"

"I wouldn't say 'breaking up' exactly."

"But you no longer want to date me?"

"You're a science guy, right?"

I nodded.

"I'm ending the experiment. Let's say that."

"The experiment?"

"Sure. Why not?"

"Seems kind of belittling."

"I don't mean to offend."

MAHONEY! You big fat phony! the kids yelled. They smelled of cheap beer and cigarettes even though they looked like they couldn't have been out of high school. A former classmate now graduated had probably served them, or maybe they had fake IDs. Or perhaps the server didn't even care, too hot himself to card potential consumers, just wishing he could be back home, anywhere he could find A/C, some relief.

"You seem surprised," she continued. She pulled her hair back into a ponytail, popping it into place with a satisfying thump of a rubber band.

"I suppose I am a little bit."

"Really?"

"You did agree to come out with me."

"I did."

"You were just trying to be nice."

"No," she said. "I'm not good at nice. I was—well, like I said, experimenting."

"Did your hypothesis prove true?"

"It did."

"I see."

The teenagers continued to mock the third base coach. Mahoney!

they yelled. Mahoney! The pitcher delivered a fastball, and the batter dribbled a lazy grounder foul down the third base line. Mahoney bent down to field it, but the ball bounced off his hands and dribbled off to the side. Ha! the kids laughed. HA HA HA. Nice boot, cowboy! they yelled. You couldn't catch cold naked and wet in Canada!

"What a bunch of assholes," Sara said.

"And may I ask what it was?"

"I'm sorry?"

"Your hypothesis. What was it?"

"That I couldn't stand to be around a genius. That you would make me feel inferior and bad about myself."

"I'm not a genius."

"Close enough."

Oh my God, one of the kids behind us said. This dude's getting dumped right here. Ha, they cajoled. Ha ha ha. What a loser, they said. Right here in public. How goddamn humiliating is that?

"Why don't you kids shut up?" Sara said after turning and facing them.

I remained staring out at the ballfield. Mahoney stared back up at me from the coaching box, his expression having turned to one of pity— he knew what it was like to be the center of harsh ridicule. But then he turned his attention back to the game, perhaps relieved his time being mocked had come and gone, clapped his hands, and bellowed an encouraging cheer for the player at bat to pick a good one, the one in your sweet spot, only the one you want to swing at.

"What are you going to do about it?" one of the kids asked. "I ain't your old man." Something hit the back of my head. It was wet and cold, and I could feel remnants of it slide down my neck.

That was when she sprung from her seat. She jumped over the back of her chair, and all I could hear was a solid thump, followed by a single, solitary whimper. Turning around, I noticed one of the kids slouched over, holding the side of his face with his left hand. The other kids simply blinked up at Sara, who towered over them, hand cocked back to deliver another blow. Each appeared too afraid to move.

She turned back to me, grabbed my hand, and pulled me up to my feet. It was the first time she'd ever initiated contact between us. "One of these days," she said. "You'll have to learn how to take care of yourself."

Out in the parking lot, we kissed for the first time. It surprised me. She grabbed me by the collar, pulled me close, and pressed her mouth so hard against mine it hurt. When she was done, she told me not to worry, turned out her hypothesis had been false after all.

"For you to get better," Dr. White said, "you must accept that you will never see her again."

✕

After the experiment, I decided to forego the celebration and instead walked the town. It was, despite the cold, a nice city. The trees that lined the lake looked like frozen palms. There was a group of men unloading a truck, their breaths puffing out like exhaust fumes. An ice sculpting festival was going on, and I stopped to watch for a while. People sculpted angels and swans and motorcycles. They were quite remarkable. The artists chiseled them with chainsaws, and the precision needed to exact that kind of detail deserved awe. Tourists snapped photographs, and children galloped in the snow. Despite being below freezing, it wasn't that cold. There was no wind. With a warm coat on and some gloves, it could be called nice outside, a picturesque day. Families laughed and built snowmen and had a snow fight. Couples stuffed mittened hands into their spouse's back pockets. I felt comfortable there, at peace.

I contemplated what it would be like to live here, to never return as my mother had begged me to do. I could find a job, something low-key, an instructor at a local high school, teaching science to children.

I'd make friends with the faculty, and occasionally I'd go out to have drinks with a colleague. I'd have a few friends, two or three tops, who I spent most of my time with. We'd catch US blockbusters months after their release when the tickets had been discounted. We'd gripe about our students, how they year after year started to show even less interest in science, instead preoccupied with celebrity gossip, video games, and social networking. I would, after a while, evolve into a cheap cliché because I wouldn't be comfortable being anything else. Maybe, after a year or two, they'd set me up with a woman, a friend of theirs, an ex-pat like me. We'd take it slow at first. I wouldn't tell her much about myself, and she wouldn't tell me much about herself. She'd be embarrassed about something, her ears being of different sizes or maybe she'd have a cleft lip. Our conversations would be banal. We'd talk about the weather, how it's so much different than back home, her humid south Florida versus my wind-filled Oklahoma. Television shows we like. Music. We'd be attracted to each other, but we wouldn't act on it. I'd fantasize about brushing my fingertips along her neck, she tilting her head down as I did so, but we wouldn't touch, not even an accidental graze of our hands. Soon, though, we'd become impatient, and I'd kiss her for the first time outside a deli, someplace we could get cheap salami sandwiches. We'd fall in love and move in together and start a new life. We wouldn't ever marry, but we'd have kids. Three of them, named after our families.

I'd feel guilt at first. My mother would have taken the blame for my wife's murder, and she'd go to jail where she would likely die. I'd think of her often, daydreaming about how things could've worked out differently. I'd conjure fantasies of all four of us living together, my mother, Sara, the baby, and I, like we were some silly, archetypal sitcom. We'd suffer from trivial problems, ironic misunderstandings centered upon whether or not my relationship with a colleague was appropriate, or Isaac's disappointment at losing the spelling bee. My new family would become worried about me. I'd start to lose longer and longer blocks of time, these fantasies once again hindering my ability to live a fulfilling, functional life. They'd ask me to see a doctor, a psychiatrist, anybody, so that I could get some help, and I'd agree even though I knew it wouldn't. Only time would, bumbling slowly along until the daydreams ebbed away, like a throbbing ache after being sucker-punched.

I knew that to be impossible, though, living here. There was no way my mother could've acted alone. Physically, she was unable to transport the body. Her confession would sound false, and because of the experiment, the authorities would find me. Interpol would investigate where I'd escaped, they'd hunt me down, and they'd arrest me. I'd be extradited to the United States. I'd face life in prison. I'd die behind bars. Normalcy would be a daily routine of food, work, food, work, lights out, isolation, servitude. Although quantum mechanics doesn't bend toward certainties, reality often does. I hesitated to call it fate, but the notion of predetermination was there. Life, it seemed, boiled down to the elimination of alternatives until only a few remained. Each choice we make eliminates the ability to make countless others. After a while, we lose control completely.

Seeing no other option, I returned to my hotel room and sat there, alone, taking an occasional shot of whiskey from the mini bar. Dr. Brinkman returned late that evening, after midnight. He smelled of wine and was a little drunk, swaying back and forth like he danced to a tune only he could hear.

"We did it," he said. "We did it. We did it. We did it!" He grabbed me like he wanted to dance. He placed one arm around my waist and clasped my left hand with his and then twirled me. "The experiment worked beautifully. Elegantly. Mass was there, and then BANG, it wasn't. Ha HA! You were right, Coulter. You were *right*. I am so proud of you."

"That's great," I said. "Wonderful."

WHEN I ARRIVED BACK IN BOSTON, I EXPECT-
ed things to be different. I wasn't sure how exactly—if the city would
have somehow transformed, the way a movie can if shot through a lens
of a different hue and clarity, or maybe my disposition would be different in some way, my mood happier, my conscience clear of guilt. But
this wasn't the case. The city remained as cold as always, more so even,
my entire body aching as soon as I left the warmth of baggage claim and
stepped out into the frigid wind. My thoughts clogged with melancholy
and regret, tormented by how my wife and unborn son rotted, how my
mother sat in a county jail cell, how I'd never feel the weight of the Nobel
medal in my hands, my name now destined to be a mere footnote in the
annals of string theory, pushed aside due to my more than undignified
past. This last thought shamed me more than anything, the wallowing in
sanctimonious self-pity, pestering me like addiction does, that unrelent-
ing pull on a smoker's lung tissue, pleading to absorb just one more lung-
ful of smoke, begging to fulfill the incessant craving, failing, no matter
how hard I tried, to make it stop.

Outside the terminal, Dr. Brinkman's wife waited for him with their
car, she waving from the driver's seat at me, her face plastered with a
genuine, face-aching grin. She was happy for us, for me, altruistically
glad that all had gone as it should have.

"Your mother coming to pick you up?" Dr. Brinkman asked.

"No," I said.

"A friend? Anyone?"

"I think I'm going to just grab a cab."

"Nonsense," he said. "We'll take you home." He pointed to the car, idling in the fire lane.

"That's very nice of you, but I'm out of your way."

"No problem at all."

"I couldn't, really."

"We'd be glad to."

"I said no."

Dr. Brinkman flinched at my response, surprised at its abruptness. I hadn't meant for it to come out as such, and told him so, and he waved away my apology with a flick of his wrist.

"I understand," he said. "I do. Sometimes you just want to be alone."

"Thanks for understanding."

He reached out and hugged me. It was warm in there, surrounded by his big arms.

"I am so proud of you," he said. "I am. You hang in there, okay? I know it doesn't feel that way right now, but, in the end, everything will be okay."

"I know," I said.

He let go and picked up his luggage.

"I'll see you in the lab on Monday?"

"Yes," I said. "I'll be there."

"Good," he said. "I'll see you then."

Dr. Brinkman got in the car, and his wife leaned over and kissed him on the cheek. She seemed so glad to see him. Although we were only gone for three days, it seemed as if they hadn't seen each other in years. She held his face in her hands, staring into his eyes, her gaze seething with pride and love, and I couldn't help but wonder if Sara had ever looked at me like that. Perhaps in the beginning she did, when we had first been dating, still living in Oklahoma, when we'd been happier. She probably had, but I couldn't remember.

A bus stop wasn't far from the airport, around the terminal's egress end, so I pulled my coat tighter and walked. As always around airports, it was busy. Cars veered in and out of lanes, weaving through traffic. Every few minutes, a plane would take off, its engine rumbling. People shouted greetings and whined farewells. The scene reminded me of the double-slit light experiment in a way, a miasma of travelers as individual photons, racing through every conceivable path only to land in their most probable of destinations, imprinting against the Bostonian backdrop their own unique interference pattern. I found comfort in this thought, convinced I would land eventually where I was supposed to be.

A young woman and her child, perhaps two or three, waited at the bus stop. The little girl shivered from the cold despite being wrapped in a fluffy pink coat and wool toque. She had ahold of her mother's leg, no doubt obeying her mother's rule to always be within arm's reach when out in public, drilled into her ever since she had begun to understand English. When I approached, the little girl scooted closer to her mother, perhaps my presence initiating some innate desire to seek protection, security, warmth even. I understood the impulse, empathized with it. The search for sanctuary is, and always will be, an intrinsic human pursuit. Noticing her child digging into her leg, the mother turned to me and smiled. I, instinctively, returned it.

"I still can't get used to it," she said.

"I'm sorry?"

"The cold."

"Ah."

"We're from Florida." Her finger alternatively pointed between herself and her young daughter. "I'd never even seen snow until moving here."

"And now there's no hiding from it."

"I always heard it was beautiful," she said. "I don't see it. Everything gray and dead. It's never pristine like in movies, pure white. It's always tainted with dirt and grunge."

"I tend to agree with you."

"Marjorie," she said. "That's my name." She extended a hand to shake, and I took it. "Margie, actually. That's what I go by. And this little one is Samantha." The little girl hid her face behind her mother's leg, peering up at me with saucer eyes. "She's shy."

I told them my name.

"You from around here?"

"Not originally, no. Oklahoma."

"Tornado alley," she said. "Exciting."

"My dad chased them, actually."

"What?"

"Tornadoes."

"No!"

I nodded. "Took me out once, too."

"Oh my God," she said. "Really?"

"You've never seen one?"

"Never," she said. "Jesus, no. Weren't you just scared to death?"

"I was terrified. I was young, and we were out in the middle of no-where. Wheat fields lined the road so that I couldn't see the horizon in the distance. The clouds had turned green, the color of seaweed, and had become so thick and textured it looked almost lunar. You always hear that there's a quiet before the storm, but that's not always the case. Some-times there's a constant rumble, intensifying and weakening randomly. It makes you dizzy."

"The Doppler effect," Marjorie said.

"Yes. That's correct. How did you know that?"

She shrugged. "I don't remember."

"It started to rain and hail. Ice pounded the car. The wind blew us all over the road. I thought I was going to die. I really did. I remember thinking that my dad was crazy, that he had lost his mind driving us into something like that. He looked a little crazy, too. He had both hands on the wheel, and he leaned forward in his seat, his knees perched out so that he almost looked like he was riding a horse rather than driving a car. He kept bobbing his head like he could get a better angle to view the storm, and I was pleading silently for him just to keep his eyes on the road, but I was too scared to say a word, but that's when he pointed out the window and said a single, solitary word: 'there.'"

"Jesus," Marjorie said.

"At first, I couldn't see where he was pointing, but then we passed the wheat fields to open pasture. It looked like an entire cloud on the ground. The base, I learned later, was over two miles wide. The winds were clocked at over three hundred miles per hour. It was the largest tornado ever recorded. My dad slammed on the brakes, and we fishtailed to a stop in the middle of the highway. In front of us, this monster rampaged towards a farmhouse. 'Get the camera,' he told me. 'Get it, get it, get it!' I grabbed it from the floorboard and passed it up to his assistant, Dianne, and she snapped photographs of it as it took out barns and fences and people's homes. Every few seconds, an explosion burst out of the funnel when it hit light poles. This lasted for at least twenty minutes, and we just sat in stunned silence and watched as it sucked up everything in its path.

"Eventually, the tornado disappeared off into the distance. It hadn't dissipated, instead having grown stronger, and headed straight for the city. When we couldn't see it any longer, it was like a spell was lifted. Both my father and Dianne erupted in joy. 'Can you believe it?' they said. 'That was the biggest thing I've ever seen!' 'A once-in-a-lifetime storm!' They both jumped out of the car and into each other's arms, and it was there I first saw my father kiss Dianne. They had completely forgotten I was even there. That tornado killed sixty-seven people that day.

My birthday."

The bus arrived, air brakes screeching, and the driver pushed open the door. Samantha lunged for the steps, but Marjorie grabbed her by the hood of her coat, telling her to hold on for just a second. Marjorie turned to me. "You coming?" she asked. "I'd love to hear more."

"I'm afraid my bus is the next one."

She smiled.

"Funny, though," I continued. "I always remembered that story differently."

"What do you mean?" she asked.

"For some reason I always leave out the death."

She smiled a knowing smile. "Perhaps you can tell me that version another time."

"Maybe so."

"It was nice to meet you," she said.

"You too."

Marjorie released her daughter, and she climbed up the steps on all fours like a little dog, her mother following after her and dropping change into the bucket for their fare. Before the driver could shut the door behind her, though, she clamored back down to the curb. In her hand was a business card. "My personal cell is written on the back," she said. "Call me sometime. If you want."

I thanked her and told her I would before placing her card, folded, into a pocket of my suitcase, next to the pills prescribed to me by Dr. White. After the bus doors closed, I grabbed the prescription bottle and threw it into the trashcan.

Fifteen minutes later, my bus arrived to take me back to a home I didn't recognize. First, it was the smell—a chemical lemon scent greeted me. The entire apartment had been scrubbed and cleaned so that every surface shined. The glass coffee table perfectly reflected the now spotless ceiling fan; its blades no longer caked in dust. The carpets had been vacuumed, and the throw pillows fluffed. The sink no longer carried two or three stray dishes, bits of ketchup dried against its surface. My books had been neatly arranged on the bookshelf, alphabetized by author. Windows had been washed. Laundry had been folded and tucked into drawers, t-shirts and jeans hung on hangers instead of being strewn across the floor. The place had not looked this good since Sara and I had moved in years before.

A scrapbook I didn't recognize had been placed in the center of the newly oiled dining room table. It had a green cover and no label. Opening it up, I found newspaper and magazine clippings of my discovery, heralding me as a physicist to be watched, a doctoral student with a promising shot at the Nobel. There were pictures of the family, Sara, Dad, Mom, and I, on the first day of our reunion, eating at this Irish place outside Harvard Square. We didn't look happy in the photo, my father reaching out his phone to snap it while we all sat at the table. Because of the angle, our faces appeared distorted, like they were being sucked into a singularity centered behind us. Each of us smiled, but they weren't genuine. They were the plastered smiles of a coerced picture, the product of humanity's instinct to memorialize forever what we wished reality to be, not reality itself. I've seen pictures like that all my life, young parents and toddlers sitting Indian style, holding books and picnicking in a park, a couple holding hands and walking down a wooden bridge, extended family in woolen sweaters cuddling around a single leather chair. These family portraits are meant to look natural, but they're not, the viewer knowing fully well a photographer stands behind the camera directing his subjects into position, instructing them to smile, to look happy. They are artifice, full of pretense. We want to show the world that this is how we truly are, but, in the end, we deceive no one.

In the back of the album I found a folded piece of paper taped to the inside cover. It was a note from my mother. Coulter, it said, if you're reading this, I take it you didn't stay in Europe as I'd hoped. I don't know if this should surprise me or not. During my absence, I always clung to this idea of you, that you were still like the little boy I had raised, that I had imprinted upon you myself. This belief gave me comfort, that despite my abandoning you, you and I were somehow inextricably linked, that our physical distance didn't matter as much because you were still my son, and you were still like me. As I've gotten to know you over the past few months, I've been proven correct in some regards, wrong in others. You tend to dwell inside your own head, sometimes for hours on end, much like me. You oftentimes don't know how to act in certain situations. You don't face confrontation or doubt or the prospect of failure well. When faced with these, you retreat. You hide. You hope the problem will somehow solve itself. But, as you reading this note now proves, you're not a coward, unlike me. After you left for your experiment, I made preparations to turn myself in as I told you I would. I could've simply taken the cab to the police station, but I convinced myself I shouldn't allow you to come home to my belongings, that cleaning up after me would be unfair to you. So I returned to your home, packed up my things, and donated them. Upon returning, though, I told myself you deserved to come home to a clean home, that it was the least I could do, that somehow my final act would cleanse the past and let you start anew. Silly, I know. At first, I just tidied up a bit. I put away your laundry. I organized your books. I took out the trash. I put everything in its place. This, however, was still insufficient. I went out and purchased cleaning supplies. I lemon-oiled your furniture. I shampooed the carpets. I vacuumed. I dusted. I washed the windows. I scrubbed your grout. Every time I thought I was done, I found something new to clean, something else to fill my remaining time. I snaked your plumbing. I scrubbed your toilets. I replaced your light bulbs. I put in new air filters. I tightened every screw in the house. I re-caulked your windows. Eventually, I came to realize I was stalling. I was going to break my promise. I was going to run. Again. I blame myself for what happened. Wherever I go, I wreak havoc. I ruin lives. If I had not come here, I can't help but think that this tragedy never would've happened, that you would've lived a full and enviable life with your wife and son. I thought if I made myself into a martyr I could return to you some semblance of this life, but now I can't even do that. I'm sure this doesn't surprise you. Regardless, I'm sorry. I hope one day you'll be able to forgive me. I love you, Coulter. I know it doesn't seem like it, but I do. I promise—

The note ended there, the ink smudged to the right. There was no farewell, no final thought. It just ended, mid-apology. I felt as though her unfinished promise should gnaw at me, leave behind some unfulfilled hole like her initial abandonment had all those years before, but it didn't. It didn't affect me at all. I simply closed the album, locked up the apartment, and left the key at the super's door.

I then walked the few blocks to the police station.

⚡

There was no light. I could see no horizon. There was no sound or breeze or lingering smell. It was as if I was deaf, dumb, and blind. It was a strange feeling, but I wasn't afraid. I was surprisingly calm and content. I kept thinking about how my mother used to put me to bed when I'd been a kid. It was one of those memories where you see yourself as an observer would, like if you were experiencing your own life as an astral projection. I was lying in bed, and my mother sat on the edge. She had the expression of someone completing a chore as she said the Lord's Prayer. Her voice was monotone and brisk. I didn't look at her, and she wouldn't look at me. We both just wanted it to end. When she was done, she pecked me on the forehead, and then she clicked off the light.

When I opened my eyes next, I was walking into a hospital room. Sara sat in bed eating ice chips as a nurse checked her IV, pitocin, a drug to induce labor. She smiled when she saw me.

You made it, she said. I didn't think you would.

I didn't either, I said.

I've been worried about you.

I'm here now.

She patted the mattress, and I stood by her side.

Are you afraid? I asked.

Terrified, she said. Can you tell?

Everything will be okay.

It will?

I promise.

The pitocin kicked in quickly. Sara rocked back and forth from the pain. She grimaced and held my hand and squeezed. Every few seconds she moaned, a slight whimper escaping her lips, and then she pressed her lips together as if entrapping her pain. The nurse gave her the epidural. The needle wasn't as large or as frightening as I'd anticipated. Sara sat with her legs crossed underneath her and leaned forward. As the nurse plunged the needle into her lower back, Sara clenched in anticipation of pain, but then she relaxed.

Once the epidural took effect, she was smiling and telling us that she heard a cat mewing. Someone find the cat, she said. She leaned up in bed and made a telescope out of her hands and scanned the hospital room. It's just the machine in the corner, sweetie, the nurse said, laughing. There's no cat. But there is, Sara said. I can hear her mewing.

Not long after, she dilated far enough to push. The nurse sat on a swiveling stool, and she instructed me to pull back on Sara's legs when it was time. Every minute or two she told Sara to push, and I pulled back on her leg. She turned red, sweat poured from her brow, and her teeth ground together. It seemed like she made no progress whatsoever. After each push, she collapsed into the thin pillows propping up her head and back. She'd breathe short, curt breaths. Her skin was pale and resembled a wet paper cup. I don't think I can do this, she said. Sure you can, I told her. You're doing great.

We carried on like this for hours. Between pushes, Sara fought to keep her eyes open. I dabbed at her forehead with a cool, wet washcloth. I was glad she got to rest, even if it was only for short amounts of time. I fed her ice chips and massaged her forearms and hands. I asked the nurses questions, why is this taking so long, is there something wrong, what can I do to help, and the nurses nodded at me knowingly, the concerned but annoying father, always getting in the way. She's fine, they said. You just be there for her.

We're getting close, the nurse said. She crouched between Sara's legs, rubbing her fingers alongside the bottom of Sara's vagina, stretching the birthing canal. I could see the top of Isaac's head. His hair was matted against his skull. The pate was pointed and purple. It seemed so tight in there I worried he couldn't breathe, but then I remembered he received his oxygen through the umbilical cord.

The doctor arrived. She smiled and put on latex gloves and asked how we were doing. Good, Sara said. I'm ready to see my boy. As we all are, the doctor said. I'm sure.

There was more pushing, harder this time and in longer sequences. Sara screamed, the epidural either wearing off or the pain becoming more pronounced or perhaps both. I felt useless. I wanted to help in some way, to make this go by quicker, but there was nothing I could do but pull back on her legs and watch as our boy slid downward, his head protruding the birthing canal, and I'd get hopeful, here he is, finally, it's time, after so many months of waiting, we'd get to hold him, but then Sara would let up, and he'd slide back to where he'd started.

You're doing great, Mom, the doctor said.

Sara couldn't even acknowledge the doctor. She collapsed and said she couldn't do this anymore. Just cut me. Cut me open and take him out of me. Please, she begged. I just want this to be over with.

He's almost there, Sara. Just keep pushing.

I can't. I really can't.

She did anyway. I didn't know where she got the energy. It was like watching the law of conservation of energy being broken, a possibility only in the quantum realms. One moment she'd be laying back, staccato breaths her only sign of life, and the next she'd be leaning forward and pushing to the point her blood vessels threatened to burst through her skin. Then, with a cry that was half-groan, half-growl, Isaac slipped into the doctor's hands.

Nothing could've prepared me for this moment, seeing my boy born—such a tiny, helpless thing, wailing. It was like I had levitated. I felt buoyant. I felt as if I floated in a vacuum. I'd expected to feel something, perhaps the weight of new responsibility—this baby would now forever be in my care. He'd depend on me for his life. For his safety. For food. For shelter. For comfort. For everything. But that wasn't the case. I was freer than before somehow, as if the arrival of our son had relieved me of some great duty I was incapable of accomplishing.

The doctor brought our son up to Sara, and she held him close. His eyes were closed, and he was covered in afterbirth.

Oh, Sara said. Oh, sweetie, we did it. We did it. Look what we did.

Is he real? I asked. Is this real?

Of course, she said. Strange, isn't it? He's really here.

Acknowledgments

First and foremost, thank you to my wife, Allie, for your sacrifice while I was at school, or at the office, or in my study working on what would be this novel. Thank you for believing in me even when I did not. Without you, this book would not be possible, and for this I owe the deepest of debts.

Thank you also to my many friends and family members who read innumerable drafts of this work, both in full and in part: Roy Giles, Corey Mingura, Jake Foster, and especially my mother, René Milligan, who may be my most discerning reader. Thank you to my professors at the University of Central Oklahoma, Constance Squires, Steve Garrison, Kit Givan, and Rilla Askew, for setting such great examples. And thank you to my father, Carl Milligan, who didn't complain, at least out loud, when I told him I wanted to be a writer.

Finally, thank you to my publisher, Michelle Halket, for taking a chance on a little-known author from Oklahoma. I hope I don't let you down.

Noah Milligan splits his time between words and numbers and is a long-time student of physics, prompting him to write his debut novel, An Elegant Theory, which was shortlisted for the 2015 Horatio Nelson Fiction Prize. His short fiction has appeared in numerous literary magazines, including MAKE, Storyscape Literary Journal, Empty Sink Publishing, and Santa Clara Review. He is a graduate of the MFA program at the University of Central Oklahoma, and he lives in Edmond, OK, with his wife and two children.

noahmilligan.com